A SAVAGE
TRICK

DAMAGED HEROES· BOOK THREE

S A R A H
A N D R E

For information regarding subsidiary rights, please contact the Publisher:

BEACH READS
3250 Bonita Beach Road, 205-204
Bonita Springs, FL 34134

Edited by Anya Kagan, Touchstone Editing
Cover Design by Christa Holland, Paper and Sage

Manufactured in the United States of America
Beach Reads, First Edition, April, 2019

Print ISBN: 978-1-946310-01-9
Digital ISBN: 978-1-946310-02-6

To Mary Lynn,
For showing me the pathway to joy, gratitude and self-
love.

CHAPTER ONE

The ransacked living room spiked a fresh surge of panic. Trick Quinn paused in the threshold, forcing in a *pranayama* breath. Why the hell did this mayhem still catch him off guard? Sofa cushions and magazines were strewn across the carpet. Articles of clothing dangled from various chairs. Even the blinds hung at irregular angles... *Eve would have a heart attack if she walked in here.*

Trick shook his head. Who was he kidding? First, even without the restraining order, she wouldn't set foot in here. Second, it was way past time to stop seeing life through the lens of his wife's perceptions. This was Pete's house and Pete's mess. Trick's bedroom was spotless, as was his freshly ironed shirt with the CFD logo. That was good enough.

Trick crossed to the kitchen—another disaster zone. Today's *Chicago Tribune* lay among the debris littering the counter. From seven feet away, the photo of Trick's own face on the front page startled him a second time. *Firefighter Hero Accused of...*

"Damn it." He shut his eyes to the rest, a wave of

despair threatening to mow him down. All around the city, people—including his parents and brothers—were waking to new lies about Lieutenant Patrick Quinn's depravity. No amount of protesting his innocence, no stellar professional record, and definitely no cleansing yoga breath could combat the onslaught of accusations. "Damn it," he repeated, scrubbing his face.

He'd face the article soon enough—had to, so he'd know how to gear up for today's battle—but couldn't stomach it before coffee. He placed the CFD walkie-talkie on the counter beside the Keurig machine, which had a yellow sticky note taped to the handle. *Fed Blaze and put him out back. –6:30a. P.*

Trick crumpled the note, popped in a pod, then opened the back door and whistled. "Good boy," he called as his nine-year-old Irish setter loped happily across the fenced-in lawn. Trick smiled, embracing this one moment where his dog's joy superseded all the negativity in the wreckage of his life.

"Catch any squirrels, boy?" He scratched Blaze's head, then crouched down and accepted a couple of wet licks up his cheek. "You and me—we're gonna turn this crap around today, all right?"

The walkie-talkie toned out the alarm for Station 74. Not Trick's firehouse, and besides, his shift didn't begin for a couple hours, now that he was stuck on admin duties. "Engine Forty-Three, Ambulance Three," Dispatch began, "residential fire, two-twenty North Whipple Street..."

Trick's hand stalled in his dog's fur, a sense of déjà vu paralyzing him. That was his address... Eve and the girls! "Please, God," he whispered, bolting upright and snatching the radio. "Please be safe."

He sprinted out of the house and jumped into his pickup. His breath came in shallow gasps as he gunned the engine to life and slapped the portable strobe light on his dashboard. "Dear God, dear God, dear God," he chanted, but couldn't add to the prayer. Couldn't conceive of a life without Amy and Tina.

He flew down the residential streets, rolling through stop signs and roaring past slow drivers. "Come on, come on!" He should have been there to protect his babies... should have been a better dad...should have never let Eve push things this far in the first place.

Miles passed in agonizing slow motion until he finally squealed around the corner onto his street. His heart stalled. The entire house was engulfed. Flames leaped from the kitchen windows, and dark gray smoke billowed in viscous plumes from the back of the house, where their living room opened to a patch of backyard. The engine and truck were already curbside. The squad had charged the hoseline and stood poised for action behind the firefighter battering in the front door. Trick careened into the Farnsworth's driveway and scrambled out at a dead run.

"Trick," a high voice shouted, "Trick!" He craned his neck without slowing. Mrs. Collins stood near the engine, a garden spade in her right hand. "Your wife's inside!"

Next to her, the captain was waving him off. Trick wasn't on the crew. Wasn't in his turnout gear. Too emotionally attached for a rescue. Probably half a dozen other reasons. He didn't give a damn. "My kids," he yelled, racing up behind the men who'd breached the door.

The captain hollered his name as Trick grabbed the end of the hose.

"They went to practice," Mrs. Collins called. "Eve waved goodbye and went into the house."

Soccer. Jesus, it was Saturday. Trick nodded, his throat swelling with thanks for the grace of God. The scowling captain was striding up the path to stop him. Too bad. There was no way Eve would die by fire. The door gave way, and the men shuffled forward as the pressurized water strained to tear the hose up and out of their grips. Trick leaned into the powerful flow and nudged the man in front of him. "Haul some ass!"

"Goddam it, Quinn." The captain gripped the back of his shirt and dragged him out of the pitch-black inferno. "Are you out of your cotton-picking mind?" He thrust Trick several feet away.

"My wife's in there!"

"I was right beside your neighbor when she told you!" The captain waved irritably. "Go wait by the paramedics. Trust us to do our jobs, lieutenant. You know better than this. We'll get her out."

The paramedics stood beside their stretcher and gear, gaping at Trick. No doubt they'd seen his life free-fall these last couple of weeks. By their curious frowns, they probably figured he'd finally snapped. But who left their wife to die when they were trained to fight flames and rescue victims? He had the highest save record in the city, for cripes' sake, and here he stood, with his thumb up his ass!

Trick paced past EMS, too agitated to stand still. How on earth had it started? The flames predominantly centered in the living room. Had they found her yet? Visions of blackened corpses, curled in fetal positions, flooded his mind. A primal scream lodged in his throat.

"Heads up, lieutenant," one of the paramedics said, almost apologetically. He pointed over Trick's shoulder.

Trick glanced back, stifling a groan. Media vans were arriving. Lots of media vans, not just the three locals looking for an evening news snippet. Trick spun away, closing the distance to the front door again. Behind him, vehicle doors slammed and shouts of

"There he is," and "Lieutenant, did you set this fire?" rang out.

His new normal: life as a monster.

"Lieutenant! Are you trying to kill your wife and daughters?"

"Stay back," the captain thundered at them, waving his hands like an agitated referee. "Stay on the other side of the street!" The fire was mostly out, and light gray smoke poured from the windows. Inside the living room, the paneling would be charred, and rivulets of streaming water probably rained onto the matching armchairs Eve had recently recovered. Had the crew found her yet?

"Why aren't you in there helping?" a particularly aggressive man shouted, echoing Trick's thoughts. Trick gritted his teeth but didn't turn. "What are you trying to cover up, lieutenant?"

A firefighter burst from the house, a body in his arms. Trick raced forward, heart in his throat. He'd been with Eve when she'd bought that white-and-yellow striped shirt. "It's my wife," he rasped.

"Stay back, lieutenant," the captain warned again as the firefighter laid Eve on the stretcher, and the paramedics went to work. Trick stepped away and gulped the smoky air as her stats were shared. She was barely alive. One tech inserted a nasal cannula; the other prepped an IV epinephrine infusion.

Eve's entire right side up to her neck was blackened flesh, and burned fabric adhered in places to her skin. A swollen knot marred the left side of her forehead, which the paramedics made note of, too.

After carefully slicing open her t-shirt, the EMT stuck AED pads to her chest. The men worked quietly and efficiently as Trick paid humbled witness to their heroic attempts to save her life.

"Fire was deliberate," a firefighter muttered from

behind. Without taking his eyes from Eve, Trick strained to listen. "The sofa cushions were all piled together like a bonfire. The rest of the living room looked like it had been tossed beforehand."

"Yeah," another firefighter said. "Completely ransacked."

Chills coated Trick's arms at the word he'd used less than half an hour ago. *Ransacked* meant a prolonged visitor with time on his hands. A place got tossed when someone searched for something. *For what?* They had nothing of value. Had the perp already been inside while Eve waved goodbye to Amy and Tina, or had he slipped in later? Why try to kill her?

Her left index finger twitched. Trick inhaled sharply and stepped closer. "Eve?" he said softly, capturing the attention of the crew around him. Silence fell even from the media across the street. "Eve?"

Her left eye opened a slit, dull with pain, and focused on his face. Slowly, the corner of her mouth lifted. His heart stalled. In any other circumstances, he'd have interpreted it as an attempt to smile, sure it wasn't a grimace. But if he'd learned anything these last two weeks, it was to distrust his perception of reality. Especially with her orchestrating his reality. She hated him, and she was in horrific pain. There was no reason to smile. Unless... Unless *she* set the fire.

His mind recoiled immediately. He had to be wrong.

"Lieutenant," the paramedic said gently, "we need you to step back."

"Eve, did you..." The rest of the sentence died on Trick's lips. The question was too insane. He had to be misinterpreting. Look at the knot on her forehead! She wouldn't have knocked herself out.

She released a sigh, and her eye drifted shut. Her muscles slackened. "We need to transport now." This time the paramedic's directive was sterner, and Trick stumbled back. The stretcher rolled past, wheel indentations flattening the dewy grass. If she died... What? Opposing words and emotions swirled and clogged his stunned brain. *If she dies...what?*

"Lieutenant," that same aggressive reporter called, "who gets the millions if your wife dies?"

CHAPTER TWO

Two Weeks Earlier

"There's another lone wolf out there," one of the crew muttered as Engine 126 rocked to a halt at the curb. "Or else they arrested the wrong guy yesterday."

Trick secured his helmet, surveying the flames engulfing the west flank of a two-story warehouse. Pitch black smoke billowed from the structure, choking the Friday afternoon rush-hour traffic for miles. The darker the smoke, the more toxic the contents inside. Could be they'd luck out and this place stored ingredients for fertilizer. Or the other side of the coin: the dense smoke meant homemade explosives, like nitrourea.

Either way, this fire was too big for the first due. Truck 49 with Captain Lewis and the rest of the crew would arrive in minutes, and Cap would take scene command, but for now, Trick was the first-in officer. He'd better get his head in the game. "Lead with the deck gun," he hollered, climbing out behind his men. "Attack from the corner of D side. Backup can take A."

"Witness at two o'clock." Pete Dobson jogged toward

a heavyset man with a receding hairline who was waving his White Sox cap. A couple of cops ushered phone-wielding bystanders behind yellow barriers as sirens screamed in the distance.

Trick snatched the CFD walkie-talkie from his utility belt as he strode toward the inferno for a three-sixty take on the building. "On scene, Cap. This is a two-eleven. We'll need more apparatus, for sure a rescue truck. Fire's compromised D side, smoke is black and turbulent, marginal conditions at this point, could be too volatile for an offensive strategy."

"Copy. I'll call for a second alarm. Assess and report."

Trick hopped over the snaking hose and cut left to B side, his steps heavy and sluggish. Not from the jostling weight of his gear in the late May heat. Or even from nearing the end of a grueling seventy-two-hour shift instead of the usual twenty-four. It was because during this extended shift the only peep out of Eve had been a few cryptic posts to her social media pages.

When Trick did something wrong, he heard about it—loudly and in excruciating detail. The one time he'd forgotten their anniversary, she'd stopped speaking to him for a day. A *day*. Not three, like this time. Meaning he'd messed up huge. And every call he made that went unanswered ate up another chunk of his stomach lining.

"Witness said he heard an explosion," Pete said through the voice-activated telecommunication system, "followed by a male screaming inside the warehouse."

A victim in this inferno? "Copy." Trick buried his marital woes back into the compartmentalized vault. "Do we know what it housed?"

"He thinks it's imported artifacts."

"Roger." *Shit.* Yesterday, a bomb inside an artifact-filled warehouse had taken the lives of four FBI agents, including his brother Jace's best friend. But they'd caught that lone wolf, so who was behind this?

Cap barked in his ear, "On scene, over."

Trick bullet-pointed his assessment, confirming the change of attack to search-and-rescue, then headed around back. Heavy smoke spiraled out of an open steel door. "C-side entrance is open. Entering structure to search for the vic."

Cap acknowledged, followed by Pete: "Got your six, Lieu, over."

Trick adjusted his air pack just as Pete jogged up from behind and planted a palm on his shoulder.

They crouched and duckwalked into an inferno blasting heat upward of seven hundred degrees. Attacking a smoke-filled structure was as insulating as being blind. Trick paused and took stock, his breathing Darth Vader–loud above the snap, crackle, and roar around him. The firestorm was straight from the mouth of hell. Flames boiled up the drywall on the left and danced low across the ceiling. Embers of skeletal crates glowed in the blaze.

A thunderous pop sounded, like a blown transformer, and the men instinctively hunkered in place. A row of interior shelves collapsed, showering sparks and streams of fire with the precision of a flamethrower. Had they not ducked, they'd be dead. Divine intervention, instinct, luck—Trick never questioned it, but there was nothing like battling a fire to kick-start a screaming will to live. Pete's cursing through the comm came across loud and clear.

Adrenalized and determined, Trick rose, activating his thermal-imaging camera. He slowly scanned the blaze for the vic. "I feel him." One cosmic soul blindly reaching through the universe for another. *Where are you?* He stepped forward, Pete's gloved hand still clamped to his shoulder. Trick took in slow, deep breaths. The cool air from the SCBA and even the sci-fi sound effect steadied his nerves. He swept the TIC in another slow arc. Red, yellow, and orange hotspots lit the screen, but it was blowback from the pulsing heat; no shape of a body. They crept forward. The certainty that always preceded Trick finding a victim grew stronger. "He's close."

"You got this, bro," Pete muttered.

Trick ignored the reassurance. The second you started believing your own hype was the second you grew arrogant, careless—and ended up dead. Period. Fires were living beasts that commanded respect. A track record for prior lives saved was for shit when this blaze held a human hostage.

Another Darth Vader breath, a few more hunkered steps into the furnace. Trick strained to hear a cough or call for help, as remote as it might be over the roar. The infrared screen showed squat. A sonic boom reverberated, and they spun right like choreographed partners. An enormous crate at the back had exploded, raining flames and debris in all directions. The fire-ground conditions were declining rapidly, turning the operation into a defensive strategy. They'd have to pull out. *Just a few more seconds...* Trick stepped right, studying the TIC while projecting his *Ajna*, the sixth chakra or source of intuition, to turn him in the right direction. *Where are you?*

A deafening crack from somewhere close. "Eleven o'clock," Pete yelled, yanking Trick backward. A load-bearing beam mere feet away split, shooting flames to the ceiling. They were out of time. "Come on, Lieu. It's coming down."

The next instant, the twenty-foot beam pitched slowly, defying gravity and time as it groaned and timbered in a blazing fall. The ground shuddered on impact, and a surge of heat blasted them back a few steps. The impact broke the beam into three bouncing, rolling sections, and a trio of glowing readouts blitzed Trick's screen.

"The roof's gonna cave," Pete said. "Let's pull back."

"Not yet." Trick arced the TIC around the raging warehouse again. Nothing. They were out of time—the structural integrity was declining too fast. Chunks of roof began disintegrating feet away. Streams from firehoses were visible now, attacking from the left.

Trick gave his Ajna free rein. The vic was in here—a scream had been heard. *Go with your gut.* The TIC hovered as Trick concentrated on the man's spirit. Within seconds, Trick's hand jerked right, as inexplicably as a Ouija board. A distinct glow emanated on the screen where no flames were.

"There!" The body lay curled near where the beam had just stood. Trick sent up a quick prayer of thanks. Had that post not fallen, they'd have never found him. *Be alive.* He surged forward, clipping the TIC to his utility belt.

"The roof's going," Pete warned, his voice tinged with panic.

"We have time." Trick willed whatever universal power was out there to give him that time.

Pete reported the find into his headset as they serpentined through the bonfire. Trick crouched in front of the vic, gripping the unconscious man's upper torso and sitting him upright with bent knees. Pete folded the vic across Trick's shoulders, and helped him stand.

"Go, go, go!" Pete called as they navigated flames and falling rubble toward the back door, where blessed daylight shone like a dull beacon. "Thank you, hocus-pocus."

They charged out into the considerably cooler

temperature and jogged around front, where EMS stood locked and loaded on the sidewalk. As soon as Trick lowered the vic onto the stretcher, the techs slapped an oxygen mask over the man's gray face. Flecks of ash covered his forest-green jumpsuit, which was being sliced open. *Buddy* was stitched on a patch above the left front pocket. Aside from burns to the backs of his hands and singed hair, his body seemed unharmed. It was a freaking miracle.

Screaming sirens and the roar of three more engines, two trucks, and a rescue truck sounded down the block as the second due arrived. The sirens died as teams of fire-fighters jumped out and went into fluid action, tugging hose off truck beds and laying lines.

Trick yanked up his face shield, sweat streaming from his temple to his neck. His clothes were soaked under the heavy gear. His pulse thundered from the rescue, and adrenalin ignited every cell. The previous exhaustion was a memory.

Beyond the police barricades, two black Suburbans, dash lights flashing, screeched to a halt. Had to be FBI. *Please don't let it be Jace.*

"Pulse ninety, BP one-forty over ninety. Looks like he'll live," one of the techs called out.

"Let's get him into the ambulance."

Trick closed his eyes and lifted his face to the hot, smoky sky and the universe beyond. *Good going, Buddy.* Another life saved, another fire on its way to being extinguished. Trick allowed himself a small grin, his soul nourished and brimming with gratitude. Each time a victim made it out alive was proof that desire manifested reality. What a perfect life.

"Lieutenant," a reporter shouted from behind the barricade. "Hey, Lieutenant Quinn! Did you save another one?"

As busy as Cap was directing the second due, he paused to glare at Trick like that question was his fault.

Trick ignored the cameras. Someone on his crew had outed his sixteen-year save record a few months back, and now the local media hounded Engine 126 calls to see if the "Quinn Phenomenon" still stood.

"Lieutenant," another reporter called, "is this the work of terrorists?"

"Lieutenant, do you know where your wife is?"

Trick spun toward the last voice, frowning. A familiar woman with short black curls leaned over the barricade, microphone to her lips. Why would a reporter even know who his wife was? Why would she ask *where* Eve was? She was home, like always. Angry, sure, but home.

He swiped a gloved hand over his perspiring face and stepped off the curb. It was worth breaking from the action to get answers.

"Lieutenant," Cap shouted, beckoning him with an impatient wave. Trick huffed out a frustrated exhale and changed direction. He jogged by the vic being hoisted into the back of the ambulance. Buddy's face now had color under the oxygen mask.

"Good work in there," Cap said without taking his eyes off the full-scale battle. He paused and barked further orders into his headset, then turned the full weight of his attention on Trick. "I've told you before not to engage with the media. Especially not in the middle of an active structural fire."

"Sorry, Cap." *Do you know where your wife is?* What the fuck?

"Go help Danny. That probie's going to be the death of me."

"Yes, sir." Trick spun away, almost colliding with his older brother. *Crap.* "Jace."

"Trick." The tone was dismissive as Jace nodded to

Captain Lewis, flipped open his oversized wallet, and flashed his shiny gold badge. "Jason Quinn, FBI, sir. I understand there's a witness to the explosion?"

Cap glanced at Trick, who pointed out the White Sox man being interviewed by a cop. "Said he heard the explosion and a scream," Trick said. "We got the vic out." He jerked a thumb at the paramedics slamming the doors of the ambulance.

"Oh, good," Jace murmured, brushing by Trick. "You're still the angel of life, then?"

A firefighter from the 65th walked up, and although Cap turned to greet him, based on his tightening jaw, he'd caught Jace's remark. Captain Lewis despised strife—didn't matter if he witnessed it between blood relatives or among his crew; it triggered his rare temper. Problem was for the five Quinn brothers—especially the first four, each born a year apart—rivalry was a way of life. And as eldest, Jace had always elevated that fraternal competition to a blood sport.

Angel of life. Trick wiped his mouth, swallowing the half-dozen caustic replies. Jace was so not worth turning this grateful energy into something negative. A deep breath reconnected his chi to the high-frequency magic of the universe, where miracles like Buddy surviving the explosion happened. Where Trick manifested love for everyone, even Jace. He walked backward, calling out amiably, "Have a good one. See you at Mom's birthday party tomorrow."

Jace pivoted. "It's been canceled."

Trick paused, frowning. The backyard barbecue for fifty of their friends and family had been planned for months. He closed the distance so they weren't shouting. "Why? What happened?"

Jace's expression turned scornful. "The lone wolf bombings? Agents dying yesterday?"

"Thanks for the news flash. Most first responders have pulled back-to-backs helping the Bureau search the city."

"There's no way it's appropriate for Mom to hold this mega party." Jace shrugged. "I told her to reschedule it in a week or two."

"You *told* her?" Trick shook his head and gazed off in the distance. Why was this even remotely surprising? All the positive vibes morphed into exasperation. "What did Pop say?"

"He wasn't on the call. I'm sure he'd have agreed with me, though."

Trick tapped his helmet on his thigh. "Well, Jace, it's her sixtieth birthday tomorrow. There's no reason her *family* can't take her out to dinner or something. I'm sure the Bureau will let you off for a couple of hours."

"But I already canceled Sean."

As if canceling their youngest brother sealed the deal. Too fucking much. "So call him back. Make a restaurant reservation. Then call Mom and Pop."

The aggravated suggestions hit their mark, and Jace scowled. "How about you pull some of the load?"

"You made the mess, bro, you fix it. I'll bring Eve and the girls by Mom and Pop's tomorrow, and we'll drive them to the restaurant. Just tell me the time and place." Trick turned away before his brother could get in the last word and rejoined his crew, taking the mentoring time to call out instructions to Danny on the angle of attack or pointing out the smoke's changing color and viscosity.

Less than an hour later, the fire was out. Trick trudged toward the crew milling by the engine. "Job well done," he said. "The faster we pack up, the longer we'll have to stop for groceries before the AAR."

"And meditation," Danny said.

The guys snickered, and Russ muttered, "Yeah, fill up Danny's chi, Lieutenant Yogi."

Pete clapped Danny on the shoulder, which he shrugged off red-faced. Trick stifled his grin. As much as the guys pooh-poohed Trick's implementation of group meditation following an After Action Review—and still goofed on Danny for voicing his enjoyment—the entire squad secretly looked forward to calming the adrenalin and refocusing their mindfulness after an active fire.

"Yep," Trick said. "We'll kick ass with an epic meditation. Hop to it."

His team scrambled to their individual tasks, and Trick helped Danny haul and refold the supply line, immersing himself in the physicality and redundancy of the task. This two-alarmer clearly resembled the recent lone-wolf warehouse fire. Which meant that despite public reassurances and massive citywide searches, the FBI had not found and defused all the bombs. How many more hidden explosives were still out there? How many more innocent citizens would be injured or killed before this was all finally over?

He paused and looked around for Jace, but the SUVs were gone. Most of the media were too, although the dark-haired reporter still stared at him like she held the world's biggest secret. "Finish up here, Dan," Trick said impulsively. "I'll be right back."

He strode across the street, raking back his sweaty hair with a quick swipe. The closer he got, the more the reporter came to attention, nudging the cameraman, grabbing her mic off the floorboard of the open van, and facing Trick with professional poise. If it wasn't for what she could tell him, he'd never engage. He'd seen too many butcher jobs done on his fellow firefighters from media looking for a sound bite. He pasted on a congenial grin and greeted her with an easygoing "Hot day to stand this close to a fire."

She didn't bat an eye. "Traci Tedesco, Channel Thirty News. Is this the work of terrorists?"

He glanced back at the destruction. "Too soon to tell."

"Will the victim live?"

"The hospital can give you that information." He gently batted her microphone down and asked in a quiet voice, "Why did you ask about my wife?"

"Because you're a local celebrity. Why wouldn't Chicago want the scoop on why your wife was at court this morning?"

Trick frowned. *Court?* "It was nothing," he said quickly. "Paying a parking ticket."

Secret knowledge flared in Traci's eyes as she swung the microphone back to her mouth. "Why was your wife exiting the Cook County *Family* Court this morning, Lieutenant Quinn?" Her tone held a singsong, baiting quality.

Family court? His pulse spiked like when the beam had timbered. What the hell was going on?

"Lieu!" one of his men called.

"You're mistaken," Trick said affably into the mic, plastering on an easy grin. "No news here. If you'll excuse me, I need to return to my crew."

"Of course," she said sweetly, then glanced at her cameraman and drew a line across her throat. The second he lowered the camera, her smile slipped. "You realize, lieutenant, that court records are accessible to the public."

"There's no story here," Trick repeated. He strode back to his crew as if wading through hip-deep mud. His synapses were misfiring, his muscle coordination not assimilating with his goal of putting one foot in front of the other. *What the hell?* It had to be exhaustion from the multiple overtime, because the reporter's insinuations were laughable.

Sure, Eve got mad a lot, and yeah, their last interaction had been pretty brutal, which had to be why she'd been radio silent every time he'd called or texted. Overall, though, they were the perfect couple. Everyone said so. *She* said so. This was just a colossal misunderstanding.

CHAPTER THREE

The goodbyes on the other side of the two-way mirror were stoic and subdued. Not surprising, since the entire supervised hour had been steeped in misery. Zamira Bey slipped out of the observation room and met Mrs. Mulroney and her three kids as their playroom door opened.

"That went well," Zamira said, channeling genuine warmth and compassion into her smile. Only the youngest, seven-year-old Bobby, seemed receptive to the positive emotions and grinned back.

"When will we see you again?" the middle child, Heather, asked her mom. Guilt shadowed Mrs. Mulroney's face. Before she could hang herself with a caustic retort, Zamira sent out more vibes. *Let your love pour out. Show your kids how much you need them.*

"I don't know, dear." Mrs. Mulroney managed a thin smile. "As soon as possible."

The oldest, twelve-year-old Karen, rolled her eyes. "That's grownup talk for weeks." She marched down the hall without a backward glance.

Zamira grabbed Bobby's hand and motioned for the others to follow. At the juncture between the two designated exits, the group—minus Karen—clustered once more.

"I'll be in touch to schedule your next visit," Zamira said to the emaciated Mrs. Mulroney, whose flickering emotions hovered between resignation and irritability. "You did great today."

"Bye, Mama," Bobby said in an overly loud voice. His mother winced. The wince of a recovering addict barely hanging on. Again, Zamira mentally urged the woman to respond kindly. Two weeks ago, the initial supervised visit had to be discontinued due to anger and tears on both sides. No amount of positive energy from Zamira had diluted that outpouring of negativity.

"Bye, baby." Mrs. Mulroney's tone was filled with remorse, but love shone in her eyes as she kissed both children. "Give Karen a kiss for me."

Zamira led the two kids toward the south exit, where Karen stood with their father, who glared at his watch. They weren't late. Punctuality wasn't just a virtue for Zamira, it was a neurosis. Matter of fact, the session would conclude two minutes early, since the goodbyes hadn't required the factored-in time. She maintained her walking-with-children stride and streamed compassion toward Mr. Mulroney and his sullen daughter.

As they passed by her boss's open door, Andy called out, "Zamira, please see me when you're through."

She nodded and finished transferring the three kids back into their father's custodial care. Although Mr. Mulroney drilled her with questions and his suspicious nature never let up, she maintained a cheerful smile and answered with patience. Some custodial parents acquired the herculean compassion to support court orders that benefited their kids. Others, like Mr. Mulroney, found appointments at a supervision center a punishment and wanted any evidence it wasn't working so their lawyers could pull the plug.

Zamira waited on the top step of the parking lot until his Lexus departed. She inhaled the fresh spring air. Life was about perceiving and acknowledging *this* precious moment, *Insha'Allah*. In this instance, the beauty of her surroundings. The dappling play of sun and shadows across the windows of the postwar industrial building. How the three pink tulips blooming in the cracked flowerpot were an inch taller today. And how the gently swaying branches of the oak across the street looked like they were waving at her. Zamira would've waved back except for the cluster of kids playing basketball nearby. It was one thing to honor Allah by creating a life of joy and helping others, and another to come off as crazy.

She raised her face to bask in the warm sunshine and sighed her thanks for such a lovely afternoon. A minute later, she knocked on Andy's open door. He motioned to the chair across the desk. "I had a call from Nate Henderson's lawyer."

Zamira interlocked her fingers tightly in her lap. Mr. Henderson was another parent who couldn't see past his own pain to help his children through the familial crisis. She'd had to call security yesterday to escort him out his designated entrance instead of following her and his kids out the south exit, where his wife waited. The Henderson case was still relatively new; he just needed time to adjust. "Yes?"

Andy took off his glasses and immediately squinted. That wasn't a good sign. He only voluntarily blinded himself when he had bad news to impart. "He wants a different supervisor."

"I'm not surprised," Zamira said. "But I don't think

it's necessary. I followed company policy to the letter, and no one got hurt. Except perhaps his ego."

"It wasn't the escort back to his car he took issue with." His squint focused on her teal *hijab*, a soft, light-weight jersey cotton with beaded trim. It was new; the beauty of it had enhanced her inner joy all day. Wait, he was still looking at it... Had strands of hair escaped? She fingered her temple before the regret in his expression burrowed into her consciousness. *Oh.* Her heart sank.

He waved the hand that held his spectacles. "The whole bombing situation and those poor FBI men dying. And there was just a news alert about another warehouse explosion in South Shore. I know that terrorist has nothing to do with you, but...you know how some people are."

Making sure not one muscle on her face twitched, Zamira nodded. "Our community is expecting a back-lash, even though we're Sunnis from Egypt. Different country, different sect than the bomber. In Christian terms, it's about as crazy as American Mormons being blamed for Irish IRA bombings." She lowered her head at her sharp tone. Anger never solved anything. Henderson's Islamophobia wasn't Andy's fault, nor his problem. "I'm sorry it's interfering with my work." *And my social life. And my courage to walk anywhere alone anymore.*

She breathed in slowly. To stop this swelling frustration at Henderson's small-mindedness, she had to view it from another angle. Like pity for his small-mindedness? Compassion for his children's hard road toward healing? Relief she wouldn't have any more run-ins with such a mean spirit? Gratitude that her overburdened schedule had just lessened by one? *See? Many angles.* Anger at his bigotry was wasted energy, and this disclosure was not going to deplete hers. "A couple more Hendersons and I can cut out the overtime," she joked softly.

Andy's shoulders lowered. "Thank you for under-
standing. You're the most positive, forgiving person I've
ever met." He plucked a bright yellow file from his full
inbox. "But no, there's no rest for the weary. This just
came in. I was going to assign it to Ann, but I have a
feeling she'll be the one who gets Henderson."

Zamira reached for the folder. Before she could open
it, Andy continued, "Mother obtained court-ordered
supervision today on charges that the father is sexually
abusing the six- and eight-year-old daughters."

Zamira's heart clenched. "Andy—"

"I shield you as much as I can when it comes to
assigning these, Zamira, but everyone's overloaded.
You're losing Henderson, and this just came in."

The positivity she'd worked so hard to cocoon herself
in evaporated. On instinct, she sent up prayers,
beseeching Allah to intercede. Of all the horrific abuses
suffered by children, incest was the most heinous. She
despised these cases and loathed the offending parent.
After six years in this profession, it still took all her
training to supervise the predator, write unbiased observation reports, or testify without prejudice in court.

Zamira dug the nails of her free hand into her palm.
Losing Henderson was not the ray of sunshine she'd
believed. It was the gates of *Jahannam* cracking open.

Two QUESTIONS LEFT on the After Action Report
before Trick could wrap this up. The guys had to be
exhausted with the bomb-related back-to-backs, whereas
every cell in his body vibrated with impatience. His
thoughts scurried from the reporter's family court revelation to searching his memory for anything he could have
done to piss Eve off, to the two more calls that had landed

in Eve's voicemail. It wasn't like her to avoid confrontation. *Enough!* In Buddhism, this scattered inability to focus was called Monkey Mind, and boy, these monkeys were panicked. Fourteen more hours until his shift was over and he could go home and finally face this. Trick cleared his throat and summoned his laidback side. "Any thoughts on how communication went during the call?"

Danny raised his hand. "Yeah, uh, my headset didn't work properly. I couldn't hear Sam's directive."

"Maybe clean the wax out of your ears," Sam retorted, and the crew broke into jovial laughter, once again at Danny's expense.

Trick waved the clipboard. It was easy to get off task or keep things light, but AARs were designed to build trust, develop skills, and root out potentially critical issues like this—whether it was equipment failure or more headset-intercom training was required. "Sam, after meditation, switch headsets with Danny and verify any malfunction." Right on cue, Sam scowled, which Trick ignored. Their communication devices were four years old. To the taxpaying public, that probably sounded new, but not in terms of the beating these things took on scene, or compared to the newer technology that far surpassed these workhorses and would alleviate a lot of this engine company's headset/intercom complaints.

"Last item," Trick said. The crew straightened in their chairs, anxious to move on with their day. "What's one thing you learned today?"

"That Lieu is still one lucky sonuvabitch," Russ said. "Way to keep the record alive." Amid the laughter, he fist-bumped Santiago to his left.

"Yo." Trick tapped the clipboard on his thigh. "Looking for something deep so we can wrap this up."

The chuckling subsided, and the men glanced around at any inanimate object. Drawing out emotions from battle-worn firefighters was always a challenge, but the stats on substance abuse, mental burnout, and destroyed marriages significantly decreased when stations implemented this military exercise. Trick loved these men and this life; he'd do anything to protect both. Sure, talking about feelings made him a nerd, the Lieutenant Yogi, but so what? He was all over maintaining the healthiest brotherhood in Chicago. "Santiago?" Trick turned to the quietest member of the squad. "Any takeaways?"

The young man hunched his shoulders, his gaze fixed on the linoleum. After a silence that was fast becoming awkward, he said, "That we should relook at multiple back-to-backs like this. I'm so tired I'm a risk to my team, man." Others nodded solemnly. "I mean, I know these bombings were unprecedented, but maybe have the governor call in the National Guard or something. We're being spread too thin."

Mutters of agreement. Trick noted and starred the comment. "Thanks for the honest insight. Anyone else?" When no one responded, he shoved his chair back. "Okay. A quick meditation, 'cause I don't want any of you falling asleep"—someone coughed Santiago's name, and the group broke into laughter again—"and then chow."

He followed the men toward the rec room, where sofa and chair cushions would be used to pad the floor. Cap poked his head out of his office. "Lieutenant Quinn?"

Trick swiveled in surprise. Cap was rarely formal inside the house. Behind him stood a police officer with an official expression. Trick's adrenalin shot to red-alert range. Had something happened to Eve? "Yes, sir?" He gestured at Pete to start the session and headed toward the office.

As Captain Lewis stepped back to let him pass, the

officer held up an envelope. "Are you Patrick Oliver Quinn?"

What the hell? "Yes." It came out like a question.

The officer handed over the envelope. "Mr. Quinn, you've been served."

CHAPTER FOUR

W*hy would she do this?* The court papers trembled in Trick's hand. *How can this be real?* Spots floated in his vision, making it impossible to interpret the blurry legalese past the shock of the first paragraph. The roaring in his ears drowned out Captain Lewis' words, although he was probably asking about the contents. Trick swallowed past the rock lodged in his throat. "Eve's...um...Eve's filed for divorce." He managed a gravelly monotone instead of a welling sob. "She's seeking sole custody of Amy and Tina."

Saying it aloud had the impact of a one-two punch. His lungs screamed for oxygen. His brain kept chanting, *Why?* Sure, coming up on their seventeenth anniversary, the fiery passion was more of an ember glow. And most of their communication consisted of verbal shorthand or a facial expression because they knew each other so well. But seriously, how could he report for duty a happily married man Wednesday morning, and now—Friday afternoon—he was abruptly single? And losing *custody*?

Once again, Cap said something impossible to comprehend, and this time Trick didn't bother to answer.

His legs were as weak as a newborn foal's. The ink blurred again.

"Patrick!" Trick blinked at the drill sergeant–like yell. Cap was in his face, expression grim. He motioned to the chair a foot away. "Have a seat."

"I'd just as soon stand, sir."

Captain Lewis snorted. "You're about to drop. Sit. That's an order."

Trick obeyed, but it took all his remaining energy not to slump forward and rest his head in his hands. What was he going to do? Eve and the girls were his life. His stomach churned at this rollercoaster plunge into help-lessness. *Why would she do this?* Yes, his dangerous profession was hard to live with; yes, he screwed up from time to time as a husband; but he revolved around her love, broke his back to keep her happy.

Captain Lewis shifted in his seat, the ancient swivel chair squeaking in protest. He folded his hands between the neat stacks of admin paperwork on either side of his knuckles. His no-nonsense manner was so like that of Trick's father, Chicago's assistant deputy fire commis-sioner. Given that Cap and Pop had been best buds for decades, would Cap tell him before Trick had a chance? What would Trick even say to his parents? They adored Eve and their only grandchildren. This would kill them.

"Who's your lawyer, son?"

Trick blinked, mentally trying to shake his brain into focus. The shock on top of the extreme overtime made this so surreal. "I...don't have one."

"You wrote up wills when the girls were born."

"Yeah." Trick gestured weakly. "But he's an estate lawyer."

"Call him and get a referral." Cap motioned to the summons. "May I?"

Trick slid the papers over. As his mentor read them,

Trick's relationship flashed before his eyes. Eve in junior high, asking him to dance during the Sadie Hawkins number. Their first kiss under the bleachers. The going-steady ring she'd picked out, for which he'd gladly forked over all his saved allowance. The high school years when they'd even chosen electives together—then football for him, cheerleading for her—so very few hours separated them. Dates Friday and Saturday nights, hanging at the mall on Sundays. Hell, they'd earned that *Most Likely to Get Married* banner in the yearbook. They'd loved each other to the point of exhaustion.

Then his tour in Afghanistan, and the phantom ache that never left his heart at being apart from her. Choosing not to re-up and dropping to his knee in front of her on the O'Hare tarmac as troops swerved around them. The hasty wedding for no other reason than they couldn't bear not to be husband and wife one more second. Eve working retail while he enrolled in the Chicago Fire Department. The years of trying to conceive. *Years.* Finally, Eve's Christmas gift nine years ago: telling him she was pregnant with Amy. Coinciding with his news: a promotion to lieutenant. Winning the lottery two years ago. Could a man want for anything more? He had the perfect life. He lived in joy, literally thanked his lucky stars. What had gone so horribly wrong?

Cap tapped the papers. The concern on his face didn't need words. "Take the week off, Patrick," he said gently. "Call a lawyer and deal with this."

"It won't take a week. This is a misunderstanding." *It has to be.* Trick hadn't been paying her enough attention lately. And they'd fought over the lottery winnings again. More likely it was something he'd done. If only he could instinctively please her, but she kept moving the goalpost.

Cap held up the papers, the slow, two-blink stare sharing volumes of derision. "This is not a misunderstanding," he said. "She's been granted an emergency restraining order."

Trick froze. "*What?*"

"You can't get within a hundred yards of her. No communication whatsoever." He flipped to the second page, his eyes scanning left to right, left to right. "She's accused you of domestic abuse against her and sexually molesting the girls."

"Wha..." Trick slumped back, his breath streaming through a slack jaw. *Molesting?* The dull legalese his brain had refused to comprehend after the word *divorce* in the first paragraph. "I...didn't..."

"You're to file a response of declaration at Juvenile Justice on South Hamilton."

"Response of what?"

"I think it's where you answer the charges." Cap lowered the summons. "If you need to collect anything from your house, you're required to have a police escort and do it before four o'clock tomorrow."

On autopilot, Trick rose.

Cap held up a hand. "Not now. Since you can't go home, go catch some shuteye in the bunks, then call your lawyer. You're officially off the clock."

No way could Trick get some shuteye; the monkeys were in hysterics. "I have over thirteen hours left on shift, sir. The crew is just as exhausted."

"Patrick, rest. I insist. After you have your wits about you again, you can break this down into manageable parts."

Trick scraped a hand over his face. Manageable parts. Where to even begin the overwhelming legal process to fight the woman he loved? "Call a lawyer." He didn't realize he'd said it aloud until Cap nodded.

"A good one." Cap pushed the papers across the desk.

"I recognize hers. Cyprian Hunter took Ted Barnett to the cleaners last year."

Cyprian Hunter. The name reverberated like a gong of doom. Ted, the acting lieutenant over at Fourteen, had chanted his innocence on multiple infidelity charges, but after paying mediation, alimony, child support, and court fees, he'd pretty much ended up destitute. Had to go live in his parents' basement. Rumor was even though his engine company stood behind the AL, morale was still in the crapper.

Trick picked up the papers like they might bite. "Please don't say a word to my father."

"Naturally."

Trick looked him in the eye. "I didn't do any of this, Cap."

"You'll have a hard time proving it. Family courts generally err on the side of the petitioner, and Eve's hired a bull shark. The more you fight this, the bigger the bite he'll take of your lottery win."

Somewhere in the heartache, a defensive spark flickered to life. This wasn't about money. "It's in a trust fund for the girls. He can't touch it."

Cap nodded toward the closed door. "Go check on your bank accounts, son. I've heard too many stories of one spouse cleaning them out in the dead of night, and Eve's had a three-day head start."

"She wouldn't do that, sir."

Again the telling look. Trick's words echoed back on him, and he flushed at how duped he sounded. A legal ambush, false charges, hiring Cyprian Hunter, and yet Trick's go-to instinct was to defend Eve.

He headed out the door. The roaring in his ears made him want to bash his head against the wall. Thankfully, the locker room was empty. He absent-mindedly spun his combination lock half a dozen times. *I didn't do any of this.*

Wait a minute. When he'd said that to Cap, the response hadn't been an emphatic "I know." In fact, Cap had changed the subject to Cyprian and bank balances. Trick swore softly, raw fear knifing his chest. Cap believed him, right? Everyone who knew him would believe him. How could they not?

CHAPTER FIVE

Zamira murmured the final *rakat* of the *Maghrib* worship, her spirit cleansed, her fingers fatigued from rapidly signing the words along with the prayers. Most days their family performed *dua* at home instead of among the Mosque Mohammed community because here, the deviation of signing the prayers to include her eleven-year-old brother, Aakil, wouldn't draw curious stares or distract other worshipers. At least, that was her family's rationalization for the self-ostracism.

"*As-salāmu ʿalaykum,*" Babi said.

"*Wa ʿalaykumu as-salām,*" Zamira responded solemnly, along with the three other members of her family.

They all rose and rolled their prayer mats, which Zamira stored in the hall closet. She followed her mother and Jaddi into the kitchen to finish preparing the evening meal. Mami stirred the rice pilaf and kept a side-eye on Jaddi, who was too old and feeble to do more than shred lettuce or set the table these days.

As soon as Jaddi tottered into the dining room

clutching cutlery, Mami spun toward Zamira. "News from Shadi?" she asked in a low tone.

Zamira shook her head and calmly turned the *halal* beef-and-lamb meatballs in the cast-iron pan to soak up the rich curry sauce. Her older sister had, in fact, texted her new address and a picture of the cute Venice Beach bungalow along with a selfie of her and Martin on the beach at sunset. Shadi's lush hair flowed in the breeze behind them like a backdrop. Praying for her sister's soul, Zamira had quickly deleted that photo, although the image continued to haunt her. The elopement to a Jew from Brooklyn was too fresh a wound in the family, but Shadi not hijabing? It would kill her mom, the only other family member who dared whisper Shadi's name.

"I ran into Faisal Abdul at the mosque," Mami said briskly, motioning for the cardamom on Zamira's left.

Zamira managed an interested grunt as she handed over the spice, but already her skin crawled and a bitter taste coated her mouth. As second daughter, she now bore the brunt of her older sister's complete disregard for her Islamic upbringing. In January, when Shadi had absconded in the middle of the night with her secret lover, Zamira had mentally cheered her on. She'd chosen a side! Since birth, both sisters had oscillated between radically different cultures: obeying the strict Muslim traditions at home and the mosque, then morphing into contemporary women obsessed with fashion, rom-com movies, and hip-hop music.

But Zamira's envy of her sister's new life had quickly turned to horror. Faisal Abdul, the highly driven assistant to the *imam* at Mosque Mohammad had been Shadi's arranged betrothed, a huge match that the whole community had celebrated. Her secret elopement in January had therefore caused an enormous scandal until her parents began floating the idea of offering Zamira's hand instead.

If Faisal Abdul agreed, it would pluck her family from the barely concealed community shunning these last five months, and to move past that shame was a prayer Zamira repeated during every dua.

What turned her stomach, however, was Faisal Abdul. Aside from him being twelve years older and as attractive as a warthog, there was a look in his eyes...like he wasn't seeing *her* as much as gauging a breeder. Their two chaperoned outings had been dull, his conversational skills limited to touting his importance within Mosque Mohammad. Although his interest in her remained politely respectful, his word choices and underlying manner promised strict spousal dominance and an unwavering expectation of subjugation.

Each visit had ended with Zamira stricken with nausea at the impending decision she needed to make between this ultimate clash of her two cultures. Honoring her parents' choice of husband sat poorly with the feminist millennial whose day job was interceding in marriages gone horribly wrong due to one partner wielding all the power with unspeakable cruelty.

Surely Allah could see this was a horrible match. Surely He would find another way for her family to save face. Zamira sent up another quick prayer, gulped down her hysteria, and tuned back in to her mother's soft voice.

"...requested taking you to dinner next Saturday, thank Allah for this blessing." Mami's expression turned serene and hopeful. "Your father has agreed. Aunt Tafida will chaperone."

On cue, Zamira's stomach roiled violently. She had to speak up. It was past time to stop this speeding train. "Mami—"

Clanging silverware and a muffled cry interrupted her. Zamira dropped the spoon and dashed into the dining room. Jaddi swayed off balance as she reached for the forks she'd dropped.

"No, no, Jaddi, let me get them." Zamira stooped and gathered the cutlery. When she straightened, her grandmother grasped her forearm tightly.

"In the Kanzul ʿUmmal, the Messenger of Allah, peace be upon him, said: 'Who follows the orders of Allah with regards to obeying parents, shall have two doors of Paradise opened up for him.' You understand?"

So Jaddi, whom everyone discounted as cognitively declining, had picked up on Zamira's reluctance. Faced with her grandmother's clear and concerned eyes, Zamira's spark of bravery fizzled. She swallowed the threating tears. "Yes, Jaddi."

The lines carving her grandmother's face eased. "Blessings of Allah upon you, Zamira." She patted Zamira's hand. "You were always the good one."

Sixteen years ago

"THIS IS THE HOUSE," Eve exclaimed. "Oh, Trick, isn't it perfect?"

"We haven't even knocked on the door, hon."

She whirled into his arms, glossy ponytail flying. Her giddy excitement and contagious smile ignited his love for her all over again. "It's ours," she said. "I could tell the moment we drove by." They'd been on the way to her parents' for dinner when she'd spotted the "For Sale by Owner" sign.

The single-story gingerbread-style home had emerald-green siding with white trim. Jace would die laughing at the carved-out hearts in the shutters. Mom would love the yellow tulip beds lining the boxwoods. And the front lawn *was spacious—a perfect place to one day teach his sons the art of throwing a pigskin. God, sons! Trick sucked in a breath. A new wife and maybe a new house. Could any twenty-two-year-old be happier? Or more scared?*

He kissed Eve's forehead. "Let's look at the fact sheet." She grabbed the flyer from the round plastic holder under the mailbox and thrust it at him, clasping her hands in prayer as she spun back to view the house again.

His elation plunged. The price was fair for a two-bedroom starter built nine years ago, but even combining her retail sales salary and his cadet firefighter pay, this wasn't within their means. She radiated so much happiness, though, that he didn't have the heart to tell her. Maybe after they were long gone from here and she had a glass of wine in her. Or maybe he'd hand the flyer over to her pragmatic dad, who never minced words. The blow would be blunt and quick.

"Let's go in," she urged, tugging his hand up the walkway. Trick went willingly, even though it was a waste of time. Within minutes, the old man of the house, Henry Barnard, toured them through.

Aside from a musty mothball smell, the home was in decent shape. The kitchen and bathrooms would need remodeling, and if they took down the walled partition separating the living and dining rooms, a spacious great room would make the ground floor look twice the size. Wait. Why was he thinking like this?

The more Eve gushed about each room and flirted shamelessly with the old man, the tighter the noose squeezed Trick's neck. It wasn't just the price. There were closing costs, taxes, upkeep... Renovating would be far down the line.

Fifteen minutes later, they were back on the front walk, Eve kissing Mr. Barnard's cheek and making him promise to hold off on any offers for a day. It was now or never. "We can't afford this yet," Trick said as they walked to his pickup.

"We'll find a way," she said airily.

He reached for her hand. "Maybe we should keep the apartment another year and bank our salaries."

She yanked out of his grasp as if he'd burned her. "No," she said in a frosty voice. "We'll get help from my dad. And yours."

Trick opened her door for her, only now seeing Mr. Barnard still on his doorstep watching them. "Eve, we're not asking our parents for money."

Instead of getting in, she folded her arms. "We can't let this beautiful home go to someone else."

"Be reasonable—"

"You be reasonable." Her voice rose. "You're the one who stopped. You're the one who wanted to go through it. If you didn't want it, you shouldn't have gotten my hopes up!"

He'd only done those things because she'd wanted to. He jerked his head toward Mr. Barnard, who was frowning. "Shh. I think he can hear us."

"I don't care. This is your fault." The one thing about Eve: she was adorable until she got angry, and then her argument style went straight into the blame game with a side of crazy.

"Just get in," he said between his teeth.

"Why not get another job?" At least she got in the truck.

"On top of my night courses?" He shut the door on any response, mustered a smile, and waved at Mr. Barnard, whose only response was a speculative gaze. They'd probably blown it with the bickering. Eve would blame Trick for that, too.

He walked to his side of the truck in an unhurried lope. There was no chance she would calm down in the *extra few seconds he allowed himself, but he needed the space. If only he could give her what she wanted. If only he could swing a second job on top of his degree and the strenuous boot-camp–type candidate training to become a firefighter. His steps slowed further. Wait. Training was seven to three, and class didn't start until seven at night. What if he could convince Mark's dad to hire him part-time for that new construction project on North Wabash? A few hours on weekdays and all weekends?*

He opened his door, grinning. "I think I've found a way."

In an instant, Eve went from scowling to her sweet, sunny self. "Oh, I knew you come through for me."

He climbed in, relieved to note that Mr. Barnard was catching the ecstatic way Eve embraced him, and then they were on their way to dinner, his wife chattering happily, their marriage a picture of bliss.

Gut churning, Trick gripped the wheel. He'd spoken impulsively without factoring in the latest interest rate hike and dire warnings of a mini recession in the near future. He'd need all the luck in the world to get on that construction crew.

Given *the severity of the plaintiff's accusations, the defendant is hereby ordered supervised custodial visits only, effective immediately.* The legalese still looped like a despised song through Trick's head. At least he'd found a lawyer, Gina Koneman, who could help him with the response of declaration. She'd even managed to get his hearing scheduled for Monday, a miracle owing to the scheduling clerk recognizing Trick's name and hero status. Guess there was one advantage to the media's cloying obsession.

Trick turned into Pete's driveway and parked behind his best friend's Ram. "Move," he muttered, but the insulating cocoon of the cab kept him immobile, rubbing a thumb across the faded photo on his keychain. Eve as a bride, glowing with happiness. "Why?" he muttered to her smiling face, undoing the clasp. He slipped off the silver key to the gingerbread house he'd held two jobs to afford, and dropped it in the cup holder.

"Yo," Pete called from the porch, holding up two beers and nodding to the open front door.

With an inward groan, Trick grabbed his duffel bag and climbed out of the pickup. He trudged up the driveway like his body fought a swift current. Took the porch steps like he wore cement boots. "Thanks for letting me bunk here."

"Anytime." Pete thrust a beer at him. "Thought you might need this."

Trick shook his head. "If I start, I'll never stop." He'd heard too many tales of troubled firefighters drinking themselves into rehab, eroding the trust and brotherhood in those companies. Trick wasn't about to let his men down like that. He was no one without them.

Pete nodded. "What's the update?"

"Eve's got temporary custody of the kids, the dog—whom she barely tolerates..." Trick exhaled and leaned his weight against a railing post. "The house. She's cleaned eight grand out of our checking and savings, but I was able to pull the direct deposits and save next week's paychecks. Until then, I'm living on the cash I've got inside my wallet." Forty-three dollars.

"You know I'm good for a loan, pal."

Trick shook his head, belatedly forcing a smile. It'd be a cold day in hell before his dignity nosedived to that level of desperation. Gina had kindly accepted a handful of dollars as a retainer, and if he preplanned the rest of the week carefully, he'd get to payday.

Pete nodded to the two suitcases still in Trick's truck bed. "Need help with those?"

"I'll get 'em, thanks. I need to keep moving."

"Okay." Pete squinted. "Stay as long as you want. I mean that."

Muttering his thanks, Trick headed down the shotgun hallway. The avalanche of clothes, newspapers, scraps of food, and empty bottles was right out of a reality show. He buried the reflex to dump his duffel and begin panic-cleaning before Eve saw the mess. She wouldn't be visiting.

"Come out to the patio if you feel like it," Pete called, and a moment later, a screen door slammed.

Trick tossed his duffel onto the navy bedspread, rejecting his body's urge to follow it. Since getting the summons, he'd been unable to do more than doze fitfully at the station, even though sleep would've given him a clearer perspective. This was also the perfect time for reconnecting with his soul, but his mind balked at meditating. The monkeys were still too jacked up on grief and confusion. There was only one thing to do: solve some of these catastrophes. He dug out his cellphone and tapped the Notes app. The to-do list blinked on screen. 1: *TELL MOM AND POP.*

The instinct to skip to the next item struck like an arrow. He'd spent a lifetime clamoring over four brothers to be the perfect child, and this was as imperfect as a son got.

But what if Mom and Pop accidentally found out another way? No, this definitely was a top priority. Jace had scheduled Mom's birthday dinner for tomorrow night—might as well tell the whole family at once. Maybe he'd have more answers then anyway.

2: *Tell the crew.* What if they didn't believe in his innocence? Because jeez—who got slapped with physical and sexual abuse charges unless there was some element of truth to them?

"Me. That's who."

This was like those times Eve hurled accusations until he doubted his sanity, because she wouldn't be that unhappy unless he *had* done what she was accusing him of. So with these abuse charges... Sure he was innocent, but clearly he'd done *something*.

"Fuck it." He exited the app and pressed Eve's number.

It rang once. "Talk to my lawyer," she snapped.

"How about we not fork over our life savings to them?" Trick adjusted the impulse to be sarcastic and softened his tone. *Priorities. Damage control. Keep to the high road.* "I love you, Eve. We can figure this out on our own. I want to see the girls. And Blaze. I want to come *home*."

"Get within an inch of this house and I'll have you arrested."

He chuckled without humor, the higher road be damned. "See, you don't sound like a woman who needs a restraining order. How did anyone fall for your lies? We both know I didn't do any of that stuff."

"You know damn well what you did."

"I swear I don't, Eve." Heart in his throat, he frowned at the navy carpet. "Just tell me what I did, and I'll make it right."

"The fact that you don't even know has become a major problem in our marriage."

He knuckled his tense gut. She was his soul mate—he *should* know. There were so many ways he didn't measure up. He didn't work nine-to-five. He'd held down a second job for most of their marriage, so yeah, a lot of times he wasn't there for her and the girls, especially when things around the house broke. She went ballistic when she thought women were coming on to him—which they weren't—and often accused him of flirting when, hand to God, he was only being polite. Then there was the most recent fight, *again* over transferring the lottery money into a trust for the girls, which had been a no-brainer decision to him. "Is this about the money?"

She snorted, and he visualized the eye roll usually paired with the sound. "How dare you think I care about that? *You're* the one who's stuck on everything being about money. *You* ruined our family."

"*How?*"

"Because you don't trust me. And here's another perfect example: *you* figured I couldn't do the right thing with the money. Of *course* I would've put it in a trust for the girls, but you went right over my head, didn't even bother asking for my opinion. What kind of marriage is that?"

He had asked her opinion—he'd listened to her opinion for hours—and this was not remotely the position she'd taken. But it wasn't worth getting her angrier. "So," he said cautiously, "if we both agree the winnings should be in the trust, then aren't our end results the same?"

She sputtered an obscenity. "And once again you completely miss the point, Trick. It's always been like this!"

"But to level abuse charges...the molestation, it—"

"I'm just getting started. *Namaste*, babe."

CHAPTER SIX

Sunday shifts at the Chicago Abuse Hotline were notoriously hectic, since they followed the drunken, violent Saturdays when cops and hospitals were busiest. Today's quiet was therefore a rare reprieve that was perfectly timed, thank *Allah*, given the outrageous incidents from last week that Gretch Allen was recounting.

Zamira gaped at her friend in the adjoining cubicle. If it hadn't been for the new inner strength, sorrow, and joy radiating from Gretch's beautiful face, Zamira would've discounted half of these adventures. Gretch's ability to twist mundane events like an El ride to work into larger-than-life drama was legendary.

Oh, to experience that spirited independence and confidence. Just for a day to act impulsively and willfully, without the filter of strict family expectations and life-long teachings...

That was a pipe dream. It was comforting to follow the rules, honor her parents, and live according to Allah's teachings. Look how much pain Shadi had caused with her recklessness.

"You have no idea how great that felt," Gretch said,

eyes glinting, "seeing that shithead laid out flat. Because of *me*. What's the sign for *ass kicking*?"

Zamira spread her arms and demonstrated the ASL sign in two sharp gestures. "I'm so proud of you, Gretch. Think of all the confidence you'll have with your next caller."

"Right? Which reminds me"—Gretch slipped the headset around her neck and reached for her cellphone —"I need to call the South Shore shelter and check on Eve."

"Oh, that's what I forgot to ask you." Zamira twisted in her seat, reaching for her purse. "What's her last name?"

Gretch paused in scrolling through her directory and shrugged. "Isn't that funny? It was such a frantic week, I never found that out."

"I think I've been assigned her case." Zamira pulled out the yellow file, unclipped Eve's photo, and passed it over. "Is this her?"

It was a breach of her company's confidentiality policy, but this was Gretch, a champion of battered women. She'd spoken to Eve on this very hotline so many times over the last couple of months that Gretch had become the catalyst for Eve and her two daughters to finally seek shelter last week.

Gretch nodded. "Isn't she pretty?"

"Eve Quinn," Zamira read, "age thirty-eight."

Gretch's smile froze. "*Quinn?* What's the husband's name?"

A warning flutter in Zamira's belly caused her to hesitate. But then again, this was Gretch, her crisis center bestie. "Patrick. Also thirty-eight."

Gretch gasped, hand flying to her mouth. "It can't be."

The flutter in Zamira's stomach seized into a cramp. "You know the abuser?"

"I—I met him Thursday." Gretch's wide brown eyes stared at Eve's picture. "He's like this Zen firefighter. So calm and dependable and...and *kind*."

"You of all people know how an abuser can be a model citizen outside the home and manipulate opinions effortlessly. That's what makes them so dangerous." Zamira retrieved the photo and thrust it back in the file.

"Yes, but..." Gretch frowned into space. Her cellphone lay forgotten in her palm. "There truly has to be some mistake. He's Sean's older brother."

Zamira's heart spiked. Sean. The geeky hero Gretch had been cooing over the entire shift. Of all the small worlds! Of course Gretch would know the abuser. Of *course* the breach of ethics would explode in Zamira's face. She lied or broke rules so rarely that she could count the times on one hand. They were etched so starkly in her memory because each time she'd gotten caught and punished. Severely.

She inhaled a deep breath. Negative thoughts invited negative feelings, which opened the door for more negative events. Everything would be all right, and this slip-up would not get back to Andy, Insha'Allah.

She tucked the folder back in her purse as Gretch whispered, "Seriously. I can't believe this."

"You've worked here two and a half years, Gretch. You know the dark world we deal with—"

"I mean besides that. This abuser must be another Patrick Quinn, and I'll tell you why." Gretch's usual authoritative tone returned. She straightened her shoulders. "A photo of Sean was plastered all over TV on Thursday night when I was with Eve. She didn't react. Not even a muscle twitch. No way could she have pulled that off. She'd have been frantic about her brother-in-law, no matter what she's going through with Trick."

Trick? She knew Mr. Quinn well enough to be on a nickname basis? It was time to shut down this conversation. "Well, both the abuser and your firefighter friend share the same name and occupation, so odds are they're one and the same." Zamira snapped her purse shut. "I shouldn't have shared this much. This is extremely confidential—"

Gretch held up a hand. "Wait! Tell me what happens next."

"I can't."

"Not with this case, in general. What happens? What do you do Monday through Friday? I mean—" Gretch huffed a laugh, "—I know what you do. But what exactly *is* a court-ordered supervisor?"

Zamira sighed. What would it hurt if she shared information Gretch could easily look up online? "I'm actually called a provider, not a supervisor."

"But you'll supervise Trick with his daughters?"

Why did Gretch keep calling him that silly name? "Yes. Whenever there's a question over a child's safety, Child Protective Services is called. No doubt the shelter's director did that as soon as Eve and her daughters checked in last week. If CPS finds reason to believe a child will not be safe in their home environment, an emergency court hearing is scheduled, a guardian ad litem is assigned to advocate for the child, and the judge rules on supervised visitation for the parent in question. My company is one of the contract companies assigned to supervise those visitations."

"So, you go to his house and just sit there?" The appalled expression on Gretch's face would be amusing if this man wasn't someone she knew, someone she was clearly conflicted about now.

"No," Zamira said gently. "Patrick will have to schedule his visitation times in advance, and unless there's extenuating circumstances, during regular work-week hours. He'll have to come to our center downtown; the two girls will be shown into a room, where Patrick will be waiting. There are toys and games and puzzles..." She shrugged. "And I sit in an adjoining room that has a two-way mirror. I make sure the kids are safe in all inter-actions with their father. I take notes after they leave. I testify in court if there is a need."

A long minute followed as Gretch absorbed the infor-mation, her face an ever-changing kaleidoscope of emotions. Then she slumped in her chair with a sigh and slipped her headset back on, adjusting the mouthpiece. "It's so hard to reconcile Eve's horrific stories with that serene man. I mean...love and tranquility just seep from his pores."

Zamira glanced impatiently at her phone console. If the conversation kept going, she might say something she couldn't take back. Gretch knew better than this! It was normal for an untrained person to doubt the revolting acts that went on behind closed doors. And yes, the reality behind each case was never totally black and white. But after reading the file's intake sheets, including copies of Eve's prior ER visits combined with photos of horrific bruises, Zamira had no doubt Eve was a victim of physical abuse, and her daughters of sexual abuse. When it came to choosing sides, that was all Zamira needed to know.

Gretch clasped her hands together. "Keep me posted?"

"I can't." Zamira walked the censuring tone back. "I should never have shared this much. I could get fired." *Allah, I beseech you to make this conversation stop.*

A phone line lit up. In her awe over this blessing,

Zamira didn't reach for the console fast enough. Gretch swiveled forward and punched the blinking line. "Thank you for having the courage to call—" She paused as her spiel was clearly interrupted. "Eve? I was just about to call you!"

Ugh. Zamira bolted to Gretch's side and hovered a finger over the hold button. At her friend's startled glance, Zamira murmured, "Let me take the call."

Gretch frowned. "Eve, hold on two secs, okay?" She pressed the red button, gazing up at Zamira with grave concern. It was extraordinary to interrupt a crisis call or put a caller on hold. Another rule broken. The room felt stifling.

Zamira dabbed her moist upper lip with the hem of her hijab. "I don't recommend you continue a relationship with her. You're compromised."

"*Compromised?* This is a crisis center."

"You know both parties. You like them both. You can no longer support Eve like you did these last two months."

Gretch, the least naïve of all her acquaintances, looked like she'd been slapped. "How can you say that?"

"An hour ago, you told me you offered to testify in court on her behalf. Now that you know her husband is Patrick Quinn, the 'Zen firefighter,' are you still prepared to go through with it? Your testimony may well ruin his life." *Which I'd be perfectly fine with.*

Gretch's elegant sophistication crumbled. "They're both such lovely people," she whispered. "There has to be some explanation."

There was: Patrick was a sociopath who'd fooled everyone but his wife and kids. "Let me take the call, Gretch."

"I want to know why she didn't recognize Sean on TV."

"You can't quiz her on that. This is her call, her agenda, and you can't slip up and accidentally use her last name, or her husband's name, or reveal that you're dating her brother-in-law."

Gretch pursed her lips, then nodded in resignation. Zamira slid back in her seat and groped for her headset. Her limbs trembled at the idiotic risk she'd taken. She *never* gossiped about a case. Even taking this call skirted a fine line. Technically, as the newly assigned visitation provider, Zamira should excuse herself from associating on any level with a Quinn parent other than greeting them at the drop-off and pick-up areas. But she was a better choice to speak to Eve right now than Gretch with her impulsive nature.

Zamira pressed the button. "Eve, this is Zamira Bey," she said into her headset. "Gretch is regrettably indisposed. How may I help you today?"

After a pregnant pause, Eve softly said, "I—I can call back."

"That's not necessary. I'm up to speed on your courageous choice to seek shelter."

"Oh."

"How is everything going?"

"Um. Fine. I had a court hearing. I just wanted to update Gretch."

"I'd be happy to deliver the message."

"The judge granted my emergency restraining order," Eve said. "And Tri—I mean, my husband can only see the kids with supervision."

"And how do you feel?"

A soft sigh. "Vindicated. Hopeful. Afraid."

"Why are you afraid?"

"He'll be mad, you know?" Eve sighed. "And he's got as many friends in the police department as he does in the fire department. I don't think CPD will be in a big hurry to uphold my restraining order if he decides to show up."

Zamira grimaced at the exaggeration but didn't pooh-pooh Eve's belief of the tight bond between first responders. Beside her, Gretch fidgeted with her pen, her mouth pulled into a pissed-off pout. "And what steps are you taking at the shelter to create a life for yourself, Eve?"

"Well, the judge is allowing me to have the house, so I'll be returning shortly."

Zamira paused. "Not just you and the kids alone, though, right?"

"I guess I can ask my parents to come stay with me."

"Do that." Based on Eve's age, her parents would probably be in their sixties. Certainly young enough to deal with an emergency, but Patrick was probably a fit and fearless firefighter. Even with an order of protection, Eve would need to take other precautions. "There are also personal safety devices that you can wear like jewelry. Have you heard of them?"

Gretch's pen froze as she glanced up. Considering her adventures last week, she'd have benefitted from wearing one too.

"Jewelry?" Eve said. "No."

Zamira listed some well-known websites and added, "They're also known as panic jewelry or smart jewelry. They look like regular accessories, but if you find yourself in need of help, you press them, and a pre-typed message and your GPS coordinates are sent to whomever you program it to alert. I urge you to buy one."

"Wow, I appreciate the advice." Eve's voice warmed from the tentative, shy one.

"And you'll call a locksmith to change the locks on every entrance?"

"Already done yesterday."

The tension coiling Zamira's muscles eased. Eve

seemed prepared, Gretch hadn't had a chance to spill any confidential case details, and Zamira's lapse in judgment wouldn't be discovered. She exhaled a silent sigh. "Excellent. You've climbed giant rungs up the ladder this week, Eve. Stay strong and positive. As always, please call our hotline if we can help you in any way."

Once the call ended, Zamira updated Gretch, who drummed her shapely acrylics on the desk, lips thinned into a grimace. "None of this adds up," she muttered. "I almost want to stop by the fire station and confront him."

"Enough," Zamira snapped, as her heart zinged back into medical emergency range. "I told you I'll get fired if you leak one detail of this."

"Yes, yes. Of course. I promise not to say a word."

Right! "You want to stop by the station. You're dating his brother." *You have a big mouth!*

Gretch slowly signed as she said, "I promise to stay quiet." Then she held out her pinkie finger. "Pinkie swear. Just promise to keep me updated."

Arguing with Gretch was like banging one's head against the wall. The only recourse around her brash need to get her own way was through trickery. The English language was chock-full of ambiguous words; that was the type of update she'd would get from here on out.

Zamira nodded, despite the warning bells. "I swear."

CHAPTER SEVEN

Half blinded by the sunset, Trick squinted out the windshield at the quiet neighborhood he'd grown up in. The Johnsons were mulching a bed of daffodils. Old Man Dudley shuffled down the opposite sidewalk with his ancient Dachshund, Bugle Boy. It looked like the Mortons had a new SUV; that must be big news around here. The comfortable sameness of it all was now a colossal problem. These families were his extended family. Everyone doted on Eve, Amy, and Tina. Each of them would notice his family wasn't in the pickup cab with him. Each would eventually hear the news. His only defense? *I didn't do it.*

In today's #MeToo accountability movement, he was going to get slaughtered. The irony was he was all for his gender being held responsible for their unacceptable behavior—he'd even marched with Eve and her friends last year. But now his feeble, clichéd assertion sounded exactly like every other accused abuser.

Trick knuckled his gut where helplessness and apprehension lodged like twin ulcers. Baby steps. Getting his own family to believe he was telling the truth came first.

Two blocks away, Sean rounded the corner holding a small box wrapped in bright paper. Though he was dressed in his usual jeans and a navy windbreaker and waved halfheartedly at neighbors in that almost grudging manner, there was a distinct new confidence in how he carried himself. Maybe it was last week's heroic adventures or his budding relationship with Gretch. What a riot that the youngest brother's life was soaring just as Trick's sailed off a cliff.

When Sean reached the crosswalk a block away, Jace whipped around the corner in his black SUV, honking as he roared past. Sean jumped and scowled, and Trick rolled his eyes at the needless fuckery. Jace careened into their parents' driveway and braked hard beside Trick, who instinctively plastered his cellphone to his ear. On Trick's best day, Jace's need for alpha dominance was hard to tolerate. No way could Trick deal with him one on one, even for the few seconds it would take Sean to reach them.

Jace got out, holding a bouquet of flowers, and frowned in the window, eyes scanning the empty cab. Trick pointed at his cell, nodding and throwing in a couple of "yeahs" and "okays." The farce worked, and Jace spun around to wait for Sean instead, then both entered the house.

Trick climbed out of the pickup slowly. He still had no game plan. Maybe march in there and impart the news like ripping off a bandage? *Eve and the girls aren't here because I'm up on bogus abuse and molestation charges. Why? I don't know. What will happen? I don't know. Will any of us see the girls again without a stranger supervising? I don't know. Can any lawyer fight Cyprian Hunter? I'm hoping to God Gina can.*

As he headed inside, the aroma of pot roast, cheesy potatoes, and something fudgy wafted through the screen door. His stomach instantly went from churning to growling; he was saving money by barely eating. Inside, the Sox game blared from the living room, forcing Pop and Jace to raise their voices as they discussed Rodriguez's RBI.

"And we're so proud of you," Mom was saying in the kitchen, her back turned as she poured brownie batter into a pan.

Sean grunted an acknowledgement, reaching for something in the fridge. Rex, the ancient tabby curled on Mom's chair, deigned to open one milky eye before resuming his disinterest in Trick's arrival. Sean shut the refrigerator door, a bottle of water in his fist. "Hey, Trick."

Mom glanced around brightly. Her eyes widened. "Honey!"

Here we go. "Happy birthday, Mom."

"My goodness, you look awful. What's the matter?"

Now... Trick opened his mouth. His courage faltered. "Nothing. I...uh... It's been a long week." *Crap.* "Who makes their own birthday dinner?" he quickly asked, and kissed her cheek. Eve usually bought the presents, but Trick hadn't found anything when he'd packed his bags, so he handed over the lame box of chocolates he'd picked up on the way here. Twenty bucks out of his forty-three. He'd make this up to Mom the second he fixed his financial disaster. "Why didn't you want to go out tonight?"

"Oh, who needs to go to all that expense?" She looked past him. "Where are the girls?"

Now! "They, um... Amy's got a temp." *Jeez.* "And Tina looked a little flushed this afternoon." Flu season was long over. Mom wasn't stupid. "Could be, uh, chickenpox. School's like a petri dish. They all say happy birthday..."

Mom's shoulders fell. She'd never hidden her disappointment in her other four sons for not marrying and producing children by now, nor did she hide the fact that a Sunday dinner with her granddaughters was the high-light of her week. "I'll send you home with leftovers," she murmured dispiritedly. She put down the mixer and wiped her hands, glancing at the old-timey wall-mounted phone. "Let me call Eve and see if there's anything I can do."

"Don't!" Trick sucked in a breath. He had to act normal. Mom could sense panic the way a cadaver dog detected a buried body. "I mean, that's not necessary, Mom." He pulled off the casual tone. "You know how kids bounce back. Grab me a pop, Sean." As his brother dipped back into the refrigerator, Trick reached over Mom's shoulder and helped himself to one of the batter-coated beaters.

"You'll ruin your dinner," she said. Her fretful-indulgent lament was as familiar as any childhood memory, and for a split-second routine ruled and everything realigned in Trick's world. When the nanosecond ended, the crushing weight of his situation almost brought him to his knees. Would unguarded moments like licking batter and being scolded by Mom ever happen again? He barely managed to nod his thanks to Sean as he traded the second beater for the Coke.

Mom turned back to the cake pan. "How was Eve's PTA meeting Thursday?"

Trick froze. How would he know? She was probably a no-show. Sweat popped out above his lip. Diversion time. He turned to Sean. "Why didn't you invite Gretch tonight?"

Sean's cheeks flamed. He ducked his head, his gaze darting to Mom, who was placing the pan in the oven. "She wanted to chill out," he mumbled. "She volunteered all afternoon at an abuse hotline." Shoot. Her presence could've really helped run interference. "Matter of fact—"

"She's living with you now, right?"

"What?" Mom shut the oven door hard and rounded on Sean with *that* expression.

"Her place is a crime scene..." Sean sputtered.

Trick eased away, sending his brother an apologetic salute. "Think I'll go check on the game."

He called a greeting to Pop over the crack of the bat and roar of the crowd, ignored Jace at one end of the ancient brown sofa, and slumped on the other side, stretching out his legs. They all watched Callaghan round second—a few more seconds of normal. How had Trick not appreciated the ordinariness? The aging comfort of this small house, the delicious smells emanating from the kitchen, the lack of drama in every part of a Sunday evening at the Quinn home. All that was missing was—

"Where are my girls?" Pop asked, without diverting his attention.

"Sick."

Pop grunted and shoveled roasted peanuts in his mouth. The game went to commercial.

"One of the agents saw a news segment of Eve coming out of a courthouse Friday morning," Jace said, his tone implying the question.

Here was the perfect opportunity—a dress rehearsal with Pop and Jace before taking on Mom. *Something horrific happened...* He faced his brother's raised brow. Pop's chewing slowed as he looked over.

"She went to pay a ticket." *Shit.* Why couldn't he just say it?

"Is that the right court?"

"You know Eve. Probably multitasking a hundred things and ended up at the wrong one."

"But she was with someone who looked like a lawyer."

"I'm not her prison guard, Jace." Trick focused on the Geico commercial like his life depended on it. This was why he couldn't break the news. Fucking Jace would probably jump up and Riverdance around the room.

"Have either of you found the origin in the latest warehouse fire?" Pop asked.

Family dynamics kept Trick silent. Jace believed he had the superior job, even though at the moment he was a low-level FBI agent associate. He also believed he was the superior kid, given he was the eldest. Ergo, Jace would interrupt anything Trick volunteered.

"Fire was electrical in nature," Jace said, his voice edging toward arrogant authority, which was rich, given Pop was the assistant deputy fire commissioner. "The Bureau is looking into anything suspicious about the wiring."

"But there was no evidence of bomb remnants?"

"Doesn't appear to be a similar event."

"Did your task force find any other bombs planted around the city?"

Jace hesitated. It was so easy to figure him out. On the one hand, he really wanted to toss the classified-top-secret card down, but it warred with his pride at enlightening his dad, one of the most decorated, badass firefighters in Chicago. "We've discovered five," he said. "Suspect claims we've found them all, but we have an extended task force still searching. Hundreds of man hours."

The game came on and Pop nodded, his attention riveting to the TV. A few minutes later, Mom called dinner. Trick collected their bottles for the recycle bin and washed his hands in the kitchen sink. His insides were as frayed as the warehouse wires Jace hadn't explained well. There was no way Trick could tell his family about the charges tonight. It would be suicidal until he had more answers himself. He set his shoulders as he entered the dining room and took a seat next to Sean.

Pop said grace, mentioning the middle sons, Cage and Kevin, overseas and asking God to bless Eve, Amy, and Tina and keep them well. Platters were passed. Trick devoured two delicious mouthfuls before Sean turned to him. "Why did Eve file a restraining order against you?"

Mom's fork clattered onto her plate. Pop frowned. Jace perked up.

Trick swallowed his bite with care, given his throat had just squeezed shut. Amid the thick silence and stunned gazes, it suddenly seemed imperative to clear up the prior misunderstanding. He turned to Pop. "There was degradation in the warehouse's electrical circuit," he said, "and it failed closed. The combustible gas-to-air ratio needs further investigation before they can rule whether it was natural or incendiary."

"Honey," Mom said. "What's going on?"

"Yeah." Jace forked a potato. "Whadya do?"

"I didn't *do* anything." Trick exhaled loudly, his face growing fever-hot. "I've never laid a hand on her. Not ever. All of you know this."

More silence. Sean divided his food groups without expression. The other three gazed steadily at Trick; no doubt they were recalling each time a laughing Eve had arrived at a family function limping or sporting a fresh bruise. They all knew her! Her clumsiness used to be the family joke. She was insanely energetic and distracted. Her various injuries, even back in high school, weren't because she was accident-prone as much as hurried paired with preoccupied. That ditzy charm was what had captured his adoration and innate protectiveness.

"Then why would she seek a protective order?" The dread-inducing tone of a father of five overactive sons whose conduct frequently required judging and sentencing. No way would Trick pony up the other, *much* worse charge.

"I'm still trying to figure that out, Pop. The whole thing has been an ambush."

Jace snorted.

"Hush, Jace." Mom's tone held a mama bear's fierceness, unquestioningly choosing Trick's side. That she believed him left him weak-limbed. Christ, he was about to tear up!

He rounded on Sean, who'd begun mowing through his plate without a care. "How do you even know about this?"

Sean put down his fork, but no one around the table was fooled. Nothing preempted his excruciatingly long chewing process, and by his serene expression, he was unconcerned with the agonizing tension as his family fidgeted and waited. He finally swallowed. "Gretch? Abuse hotline?"

Trick frowned. Gretch was in the middle of this? She'd lain on that cot in the station only days ago, clutching Trick's hand and baring her soul as they'd awaited Sean's arrival. Trick might be a lot of things—evidently, a bad husband was one—but he knew how to read people. Gretch had shown no sign she was involved in or aware of Eve's accusations. Although if she'd spoken to Eve on the hotline, maybe she knew what was behind the insanity. "What did she tell you?"

"That's it." Sean shrugged. "Seemed in a hurry to shut down the conversation, so I'm pretty sure she slipped up mentioning it."

"Ya think?" Trick gripped his fork so the trembling wouldn't show. Who else knew? Eve's parents, who were like second parents to him? His heart thudded off beat. They'd believe her lies—look how Mom had unconditionally backed him. Did Eve's two besties know? Sondra was still single, and Marisol recently divorced. Had they lured her to the grass-is-always-greener side?

"Seriously, son. What's this about?"

"I don't know, Pop."

"Eve didn't come up with this off the top of her head." Pop studied him from under knitted brows. "Finer firefighters than you have brought their frustrations home."

Trick winced. That stung on all sorts of levels. He was a triple recipient of the Medal of Valor, soon to receive the highest decoration a firefighter could achieve: the Medal of Honor. His crew had informally awarded him MVP four years in a row. When would he be the *finer firefighter* Pop kept measuring him against? "Pop, I'll swear on a stack of Bibles I never laid a finger on her. I was served papers Friday out of the blue. She's seeking a divorce and has falsely accused me for some reason."

"Well, where are you staying?" Mom asked.

"Pete Dobson's."

Her brows furrowed. "How are you going to see the girls?"

"We're still figuring it out." That wasn't a lie. "It's all been a shock."

"I don't know why," Jace said with breezy sarcasm. "It's pretty typical for a happily married wife to wake up one morning and seek a restraining order."

Had he not been on the other side of the table, Trick would've happily engaged in a beatdown. He clenched his fists on his lap. "I can work this out. I just need to talk to her face to face."

Mom dabbed her mouth and set her napkin on her plate—meaning she was through with her birthday dinner three minutes after they'd sat down. "I'm going with you."

"Mom, I'm thirty-eight years old. I don't need you going anywhere with me."

"You're not going anywhere either." Pop hadn't used that tone since Trick was a testosterone-driven teen. "No communication with Eve or you'll make things worse. Who's your lawyer?"

"Gina Koneman. I'm going to appeal the restraining order tomorrow. It's temporary anyway," he added, as if that made it less horrifying. More silence. The rigid set of his shoulders was beginning to trigger spams, but he remained hunkered in place like a trapped animal.

Pop cleared his throat, his face still carefully neutral, meaning he wasn't buying any of Trick's explanations. "Who's representing Eve?"

"Cyprian Hunter."

"Shit," Jace muttered. "Even I've heard of him. Say goodbye to your lottery winnings."

"Eve can't get to the trust without my co-signature."

Sean shrugged in that loose-limbed way. "Unless the court finds you unfit in some way."

Trick gaped at his younger brother as tumblers clicked into place. Were Eve's sexual abuse accusations simply to guarantee she became the sole trustee? The destruction of a sixteen-year marriage, the obliteration of Trick's honorable name, and the girls growing up without a father mere collateral damage?

The ring of truth almost knocked him off his chair. Eve had fought against the trust like he'd suggested piling the four million in the backyard and setting it on fire. He rarely got his way. He should have known the fight wasn't over.

He pushed back from the table. "I have to go."

Pop jabbed a finger at him. "Don't you go anywhere near her."

"I wouldn't dream of violating the order," Trick said through gritted teeth. The judge had stipulated a hundred-yard barrier. Time to find the industrial-length measuring tape in the tool kit of his truck bed.

CHAPTER EIGHT

H is girls were up there. A tightness spread across Trick's chest at the soft light streaming from the upstairs window across the street. They'd probably had their baths by now and were arguing over what book Eve should read for bedtime. Which was his job when he wasn't working, thank you very much. Just one more thing to resent about this bullshit. He redirected the hurt to cleansing thoughts and surrendering his problems to the universe in return for the miracle of seeing his girls without getting caught. Sure, his belief system was peculiar to his family and friends, but it made his life so lucky, so why change?

"This is taking too long," he said, resuming his pacing.

"Maybe." Pete stripped off more duct tape. "But violating a restraining order could mean jail time, so you're welcome for all the extra precaution." He slapped the strip across the sidewalk then backed away to survey his handiwork.

"Come on, man," Trick said quietly.

Pete grunted his approval. "Okay. Pay attention." He

gestured to his left. "This is where you stand if she stays in the doorway. Here if she walks out on the porch. But go over there if she comes down the steps. All are exactly a hundred yards." He pointed to his far right. "Now, if she exits the garage—"

"Got it," Trick bit out. "Go ring the bell."

"Hope you know what you're doin'." Pete handed over the roll and measuring tape. "Don't seem worth it to me."

I need to see my girls. I need to talk some sense into Eve.

Pete sauntered across the street, humming a country done-me-wrong song off-key.

"Hold up," someone called from down the block. *Jace.*

Trick spat on the neighbor's grass. He should have known—leaving his parents' house an hour ago had gone just a little too smoothly. No one entrenched himself in someone's business as aggressively as his older brother. Sean loped a few feet behind.

Jace whistled a low tone and crooked two fingers at Pete. "Come on back."

"What are you doing?" Trick snapped.

"Saving you from making a serious mistake."

Yeah, like a perpetual bachelor knew anything about marital warfare or losing custody. Knew anything about loving another human *period*. "I don't need your help."

Pete crossed back. "Hey, guy." He fist-bumped Jace. "Heard you were back in town. Congrats on the FBI, man. Hey, Sean."

"Thanks," Jace said at the same time Sean muttered a greeting and shoved his hands in his pockets. What was *he* even doing here? Sean lived life in a drama-free bubble.

Jace scuffed a toe at a strip of tape. "What's this? Demented hopscotch?"

Pete grinned, letting the sarcasm roll off him. Even as a kid, he'd hero-worshiped Jace. Trick said nothing, folding his arms and waiting for big brother's inevitable advice or opinion.

"It's the wrong strategy," Jace said, right on cue. "You need to come at this in a position of power."

"I have no power," Trick said. "That's why I'm here and the front door is way over there."

"Give me a day or two. Let me see what I can dig up, call in some favors, maybe find out what brought this on."

"I think Sean nailed it. It's the trust fund."

"You don't know that for certain, doofus."

Trick paused, skepticism twisting his lips. Jace wasn't normally one to call in favors for family. On the other hand, he went at a problem with a relentlessness that wore others down. After the shock of the court papers, Trick couldn't solve his way out of a paper bag; he could use any and all help. Especially seeing Amy and Tina. He gestured to the upstairs window. "I'd like to say goodnight to my girls, but I can't get any closer. I figured I'd sneak closer and toss pebbles at their window."

His pitiful tone solidified Jace's determined expression. He turned to Sean. "Go get Mom's brownies. You run interference with Eve."

"Me?" Sean blinked like he'd just woken up. Jace must be giving him a ride home, or he wouldn't even be there. "I don't know how to run interference."

Jace gestured impatiently. "We engage her in small talk, then I say I want to say goodnight to Amy and Tina. I go upstairs and bring the girls to the window. You keep Eve talking downstairs."

The apprehension on Sean's face would have amused

Trick in any other situation. "Please, Sean. I'll owe you big time."

Sean turned to the SUV without another word, his shoulders hitched, a sure sign he wanted no part of this. Their brother Cage used to call it his trapped-rat look.

Jace motioned to the great elm on the Farnsworth's property. "Both of you go stand behind there until I give the all-clear."

Trick followed Pete wordlessly. His blood whooshed in his ears, and his breath grew shallow as his brothers met up on the porch. It was unusual for them to stop by to see Eve, and she was not a stupid woman. On the other hand, there had never been a Sunday Quinn dinner without Eve and the girls, so maybe delivering Mom's dessert wouldn't arouse any suspicion.

Jace clapped Sean twice on the back and pressed the doorbell. A full minute passed before the porch light came on, more seconds until the door cracked open. *Cracked* open. Even that wasn't like Eve. She adored his brothers. Now she peeked through the inch-wide opening like they were evangelists with pamphlets.

Jace spoke, his body language loose and relaxed, an ex-SEAL in his element—anything for the mission. He commandeered the plate of brownies from Sean and thrust them toward Eve. After a hesitation, she opened the door wider. With a cautious look up and down the street, she grasped the plate, stepped back, and gestured for them to come in. Her expression was tired and guarded—this woman who never stopped laughing and joking with a Quinn brother.

Once his brothers were inside, Sean holding himself as rigid as a beam, Eve quickly shut the door. The faint sound of a lock turning carried across the quiet neighborhood.

"Sheesh," Pete muttered. "What the hell did you do, man?"

Trick shrugged. He was sick of hearing himself say, "I don't know." He stepped out from behind the tree and focused on the glowing light upstairs, waiting for two precious faces to appear. After an extraordinarily long time, the lacy curtain parted and there they were, peering out with wide, excited eyes. Trick's chest constricted further under the crushing grief.

Jace knelt between the girls, said something, and gingerly lifted the pane. He put a finger to his lips as he gazed solemnly between them. They nodded impatiently and scanned the darkness. Trick crossed the street on unsteady legs, trying to swallow past the thickness in his throat. Tina spotted him first and opened her mouth, no doubt to squeal or something, which Jace immediately shut down with a palm across her lips. More instruction from him, a cautious nod from her, and he released his grip.

Trick stood on the sidewalk, partially lit by a street-light. Breeching the restraining order to step on the front lawn seemed far too reckless. He waved both arms and blew kisses. "Hi, girls," he gruffly stage-whispered. "I miss you!"

Tina, his little drama queen at six years old, pressed her lips together to remind herself not to speak, then beckoned him up. When he shook his head, she clasped her hands in a pleading gesture. The swelling in Trick's throat intensified, trapping the oxygen in his lungs. He managed to shake his head again, but whispering any other words was impossible. How would he live without them?

Jace flapped his hands in a clown wave, his face animated and silly. The girls immediately mimicked his actions, and Tina erupted in giggles. Amy leaned further out the window, hands cupped on either side of her mouth. "Don't forget the dance, Daddy!" she said much too loudly.

Jace yanked her back, shushing her, then stiffened and cocked his head. The girls turned so only their profiles were visible. Amy called out something toward the closed door.

Trick rapidly backtracked across the street, unable to turn away from these last moments with his girls. Still focused on the bedroom door, Jace eased the window down, and in seconds, the lacey curtains obscured the pane.

"That went well," Pete said.

"I forgot about the dance." Trick scraped a palm across his mouth. The elementary school's father-daughter dance was Friday, and Amy had totally turned the event into a mini prom. Last week, back when they were the perfect family, Eve had taken her dress shopping and even promised a little bit of Mommy makeup. Ordering a corsage was still on his cellphone's to-do list. He couldn't miss this, couldn't bear another night of not sleeping in his house with the three loves of his life.

Well, two now.

A horn blared one street over, followed by a sharp whine from the right side of the house... Or inside the garage. Trick pivoted, frowning. "Did you hear that?"

Pete nodded. "Yeah. Is Blaze outside? He'd have come running."

A sick dread descended. The Irish setter hadn't been bounding around Jace and Sean in the foyer. Why hadn't the lack of happy barking not immediately registered? "Let's go."

"You can't get that close, man. I'll go."

Trick ignored him and jogged to the closed garage. "Blaze? Here, boy..."

A sharper whine. Definitely from inside the garage. Without another thought, Trick sprinted to his pickup and pressed the garage opener. As expected, Eve hadn't gotten around to changing the code. The single garage door squeaked as it lumbered upward. The inner light blinked on. Somewhere beyond the storage boxes and Eve's Kia, Blaze began frantically barking. There was no way Eve didn't hear all this.

Trick ducked under the half-open door. "Blaze?"

He stopped cold.

His beautiful boy was choke-chained to the handle of the outer side door. Had Trick pulled open that door, he'd have seriously injured his dog. "Blaze!"

"That's messed up," Pete muttered from behind.

As they hurried over, Blaze whined pitifully, standing in a puddle of urine. His breathing was shallow, his eyes wet and reproachful. "Wait a minute." Trick used his calmest voice as he held the dog still and wrenched the chain off the door handle. As soon as he yanked the links off Blaze's neck, the dog began panting. Behind them, the door that led to the kitchen opened.

"I knew it!" Eve's shrill voice echoed across the garage.

"Trick, what the fuck," Jace said, equally as pissed, but Trick, shaking with fury, couldn't bring himself to turn around. He wrapped his boy in a bear hug. Perhaps it was his imagination, but his pup seemed thinner, more fragile. Blaze's matching bowls of food and water weren't nearby. Probably still in the pantry, where they should be. How long had he been tortured like this?

Trick winced. He hadn't even looked for his pup when he'd packed his bags yesterday—just assumed Eve had taken anything he loved away until after the four o'clock deadline. That Blaze had probably been in here, suffering the whole time...

He straightened and turned slowly. Eve stood scowling in the threshold. The thin flush, high on her cheekbones, was a sure sign she was seriously pissed. *Pissed.* At what? Being caught?

Jace's expression was thunderous. Sean looked on cautiously.

"How long has he been chained here?" Trick asked.

Pete walked down the driveway and whistled softly. After a moment's reluctance, the pup dashed out after him, veering to the nearest bush to relieve himself.

Eve lifted her chin. "This is a hundred percent your fault. He peed in the house for the last time. You know what I think about that. You should've taken him with you."

"Did he pee because you didn't walk him while I was at the station for three days in a row?" It was rhetorical. They'd quarreled about Blaze's care a million times. Eve had begged him to buy the pup at the insane AKC-certified breeder price after the last in-vitro round had failed. They'd long since run out of money for another procedure, and if they couldn't have kids, Eve insisted on the twelve-week-old purebred. She needed to love on something, she'd said, especially with Trick busy with two jobs and spending any downtime studying for the lieutenant's exam.

When Trick had acquiesced and forked over what amounted to a ransom, it was Eve who'd named the dog Blaze. Good luck, she'd said in her blissful outpouring of love, for Trick's future promotion to lieutenant. To this day, Eve took credit for manifesting the chain of events, because the next day word came down: CFD Lieutenant Patrick Oliver Quinn.

Just weeks into babying and spoiling the puppy, she became pregnant with Amy. Blaze turned into an instant source of irritability. Another chore Eve had to deal with on top of her violent morning sickness. Trick had shifted as many responsibilities as he could off his plate to spend time with his boy, and here they were nine years later. Only now Blaze was a pawn in this sick game of hers.

Trick swallowed his guilt. How could he have known leaving Blaze here would lead to this? And yet, on some level he was fast becoming conscious of, he had known. Eve could be merciless when angered.

But *this*?

"You realize I could call the cops right now," Eve snapped, her flush growing darker.

"Do it." Trick gestured to the darkness beyond. "I'd be happy to tell them and the neighbors how you, the martyr in all of this craziness you've dreamed up, have been torturing the family pet."

Her eyes glowed with malice. Her scowl etched such deep lines on her face that she became unrecognizable. This was not the woman he'd married. She didn't resemble or act like the love of his life. Their fights used to be normal disagreements, where he admitted he was wrong even when they both knew he wasn't. But an apology meant great make-up sex, while standing firm meant sleeping on the sofa—it was a no-brainer lesson he'd learned early in their marriage. No longer.

Trick dropped the chain in a pile at his feet. The resulting *chink* echoed in the stillness. "You should've called me."

She shrugged. "It's so like you to forget all of us the second you leave." She pushed her way past Jace and Sean. "Fuck all of you," she said without turning around. "Get off my property." She slammed the door.

"What the hell?" Sean murmured, frowning at the door.

Jace exhaled heavily, shaking his head. "Wow, has *she* changed."

"You're telling me." Trick walked out into the night where Blaze and Pete waited beside the pickup. A braver man would turn around and ring the doorbell for the leash and dog food. It wasn't worth the risk—she was claiming physical abuse, and he was shaking with rage. Nor would he subject his brothers or Pete to that kind of animosity again. There was still a twenty and some singles in his wallet. "Mind stopping at Jewel on the way home?"

"Sure." Pete helped Blaze into the truck, ruffling the dog's fur. "This should help your case tomorrow," he said without turning around.

"You'd think." But even if the judge was a dog-loving, PETA-supporting, compassionate ally of all living things, Eve still held the trump card: Cyprian Hunter.

CHAPTER NINE

Nine years ago

Trick pinned next week's schedule to the break room bulletin board. He'd done his best to give the married men Thanksgiving off, except Sam, who was recently separated and living in a barely furnished apartment. It'd be best for him to be around his brothers in the company.

Cap had privately disclosed that he'd suggested Sam take advantage of the counseling available from the employee assistance program. As lieutenant, it was perfectly within Trick's job description to check if Sam had followed up on that, but Trick's promotion was only a month old. Not only had Sam been his fiercest competition in cadet class way back when, but Sam, Pete, and Trick had all been in the running for this promotion. It didn't seem appropriate yet to push his authority in either of his friends' faces.

"Holiday schedule's up, men. And Cheryl." Trick cringed at singling her out again to correct his gender-biased term. Cheryl Jankowski was their first female firefighter and, after only a few months on the job, seemed more dedicated than most of the men in the unit.

Based on the breath streaming onto his neck, many of the crew already stood behind him. A few erupted in soft "yeahs!" One groaned. Sam swore. Trick swung around. "You had plans?"

Sam shook his head, scowling. "Doesn't mean I appreciate you lumping me in with these young guys." He turned away along with the crew who'd already checked their schedules, and more surged forward. The scenario repeated itself: "yeahs" or groans.

Trick followed Sam out, grabbing his elbow. "Wait a minute."

Sam glanced at the physical connection, his jaw tightening.

Trick hastily removed his hand. "Look, I didn't want you staring at four walls all day."

"You think I'd rather be sent out on burned turkey calls?"

"I thought I was doing you a favor."

"Yeah? Well, the sign of a good lieutenant is to communicate. If you'd'a asked me, I could've told you I prefer to be alone for the holidays instead of the only married man stuck with rookies."

Trick raised a placating hand. "I'll make sure you get Christmas—"

Dispatch toned an alarm, and both men paused, then relaxed. Not their station's.

"—off," Trick finished over dispatch droning the assignment.

"Engine Forty-three, Ambulance Three. Residential fire, Two-twenty North Whipple Street..."

Trick stared at Sam, his jaw dropping. Had he misheard?

"Isn't that your address?" Sam asked, all annoyance gone.

"Shit!" Trick spun around, sprinting for the parking lot. Eve! Jesus, after nine years of trying, she was twenty weeks pregnant. Panic shut down everything but his laser focus to get home. He leaned on his horn and blew through every red light, screeching to a halt in front of his neighbor's house. The crew of 43 was scrambling with the lines.

Trick's heart spiked as he raced for the front door. Black smoke poured from the open kitchen window. Open? On this bitter, windy day?

He burst into the house. "Eve!" Smoke and heat engulfed him. The kitchen directly to his right was an inferno. Boot steps stomped up the porch behind him. Without turning around, he screamed Eve's name again, climbing the stairs two at a time.

"Quinn!" someone shouted. "Quinn, she's okay. She's out here."

Trick pivoted and hurled back down the stairs. A vaguely familiar firefighter was in the doorway, thumbing behind him. As Trick plunged past, his breath hitched. Eve stood on the sidewalk across the street, practically buried under Mrs. Nusbaum's enormous arm. The new puppy, Blaze sat at Eve's feet, looking delighted at all the activity.

"Thank God, thank God..." Trick hurried over on unsteady legs, questions swirling. Mrs. Nusbaum was almost legally blind, but hadn't Eve seen him race into the burning house? Why hadn't she called out to him?

It didn't matter. She was okay.

"Eve." He embraced her with all the love inside him. Pulling away, he cupped her baby bump, gazing into her teary eyes. "What happened?"

"I was making breakfast," she said. "The pan just ignited!" She threw herself at him, sobbing hysterically, and he kissed the top of her head. Across the street, the firefighters were trooping out, heroically at ease. The lieutenant removed his helmet and gestured to Trick.

"I'll be right back, hon." Trick eased Eve into Mrs. Nusbaum's arms and headed over.

"Kitchen's totaled," the lieutenant said. "Some water damage in the foyer. If you've got a good contractor, you should be all set."

Trick nodded and went to survey the damage. A niggling voice in his head regurgitated the argument with Eve last week. Now that a baby was on the way, she desperately wanted a bigger house. For several years, they'd poured all their savings into in-vitro procedures. On the specialist's advice, Eve had quit the stress of retail and lain low, so acquiring a more expensive home had never been on the table. Until Trick got the promotion and new pay grade last month.

Just as he'd dug them out of enough debt to contemplate quitting the extra shifts with Mark's construction crew, Eve had begun her campaign. A relentless nagging that led to slamming doors and frequent hysterics. Trick had written it off as hormones, but what if...? And the open kitchen window in the middle of November?

What was wrong with him? He shook off the suspicion and gauged the damage. The lieutenant was right. With Trick's building experience and Mark's contacts, renovating would be a piece of cake. Sure, it would cost time and money, but fiscally it was still the better option.

At the sound of quiet sobbing, he turned. Eve and Mrs. Nusbaum stood in the doorway. "What a mess," Eve cried.

Trick enfolded her in his arms. No. She wouldn't have deliberately started the fire. She wouldn't have risked her and the baby's lives. "It's okay, hon. I'll rebuild."

"ALL RIGHT, ALL RIGHT!" Trick tried wrenching out of the steel grips of the court security officers. Everyone came to a standstill as his raised voice echoed around the staid hallway. Standing stiffly near the three grappling men, Gina Koneman clutched her briefcase, eyes wide with shock.

"Let him go, officers," came a voice from behind. "I'll vouch for him."

"We're escorting him all the way out of the court-house, Mr. McNally," said the African-American officer, who probably did this on the side when he wasn't line-backing for the Bears.

"Aw, come on, guys. He won't cause any more trouble."

After a slight hesitation, the CSOs loosened their grips, and Trick swung round to his rescuer. The tall, lean man holding a briefcase in one hand and a to-go coffee in the other was a complete stranger. Trick kept his mouth shut.

After a last warning look, the guards turned on their heels and slipped back into court.

"Gina." The lawyer put down his briefcase and shook her hand, then turned to Trick. "Morgan McNally. That was quite a display in there."

Trick shook the offered hand without commenting. Everything, including his tongue, seemed uncoordinated after his breakdown in court, a scene any man would be ashamed of. But hand to God, he'd had the perfect marriage... It wasn't right that an old man in a black robe could gavel so much damage in so little time.

The door behind both lawyers remained closed. Surely Eve and her counsel would be leaving right about now, too? Maybe he could get a word in, make her see some sense...

Morgan gestured over his shoulder. "They went out

the back way. Under the circumstances, I'm sure that was for the best." His smile was lizard-like. Even though the suit was high quality and his shoes were shined, there was something rough and streetwise about the lawyer. Like the outer sophistication was a thin veneer for something darker underneath.

Gina cleared her throat and stepped forward. "I'll be in touch, Mr. Quinn," she said in a disapproving tone, and he managed to murmur something banal and shake her hand. She'd been about as good in there as a mouse attacking a lion. Was there a way to search track records for divorce lawyers? Had *anyone* gone up against Cyprian Hunter and won?

"A minute?" McNally asked when Trick began to head in the other direction.

"No disrespect, Mr. McNally—"

"Call me Morgan."

"—but it's been a long couple of days."

"Nice gal," McNally said, nodding to Gina's retreating figure and flashing that lizard smile again, "but you need to fire her and hire me."

Great. An ambulance chaser. Trick opened his mouth, but the lawyer held up a palm.

"Hear me out."

Stifling a weary sigh, Trick nodded. His suit was airless and unfamiliar, his mental and physical fatigue at an all-time high. He needed this lawyer's pitch like he needed a hole in the head. "Go ahead."

McNally stuck his index finger in the air. "Restraining orders have been weaponized."

Trick blinked to attention, which the canny lawyer seemed to catch. His smile was more genuine this time, and his stance relaxed. "There's a statistic floating around that ninety percent of restraining orders issued during divorce proceedings are unnecessary. There's generally no substantial evidence of abuse, but the courts err on the side of the alleged victim, and it's an easy and temporary order to grant. A just-in-case factor, if you will. Meanwhile"—McNally waved his hand like Vanna White —"your spouse just drew first blood." He waited a beat, then jerked his head at the courtroom door. "Had you been my client, I'd have gotten that charge dismissed."

"Huh."

"Secondly, you have a stellar reputation in this city. Three-time Medal of Valor recipient, am I correct? Up for the prestigious Medal of Honor in a few weeks? Are you *kidding* me?" McNally shook his head. "You need a lawyer who's going to take all your courageous deeds as a firefighter, and all the ways you've given back to the community during your downtime, and wield it like Thor's hammer."

Hope trickled through Trick's veins. "You think that would help? No one believes the guy in domestic cases."

McNally arched a brow. "That's because most men don't walk in here with this much prestige. Your risk-taking and bravery have made you a local celebrity. The public can't get enough of your looks, luck, and charm, and that includes judges. Sure, they're formidable, but they're as susceptible as the rest of us in the presence of a bona fide hero. I'm betting you haven't done half the things your wife is accusing you of—"

"None."

"—so if I were your lawyer, I'd be singing your reputation like a commercial jingle and demanding burden of proof. You get that she has to come up with a preponderance of the evidence, right?"

Trick nodded. He kind of knew. "Gina recommended not fighting the restraining order. Something about if I argued it and they didn't believe me, it could significantly harm being awarded custody of the girls."

"A classic conservative approach." McNally strolled to a nearby bin and tossed out the coffee, then switched his briefcase to his other hand. "Should you hire me, I'll have a ten-point plan on how to fight her allegations, and how you should be conducting yourself in the interim."

Trick nodded, halting the urge to blurt out, "You're hired," by clamping his lips together. This spiel was almost too good to be true, and con men existed around the courts. Trick needed time to think clearly. And certainly to thank Gina for standing up for him during that debacle in there.

Once again, as if reading Trick's mind, McNally produced his business card. "It would be an honor defending you, sir, and it'd be a damned shame if a man of your stature took the fall your wife has planned for you."

Trick fingered the card, a flush spreading up his neck. "I don't have a lot of money right now—"

"Not a problem. Representing you will give me a massive amount of free promotion."

"My first priority is getting to visit with my girls as soon as possible—"

"Say no more." The lizard smile was back. "How does this afternoon sound?"

Trick shifted his weight, his muscles tightening at the rollercoaster plunge of hope. The guy was a shyster after all. "To be perfectly honest, it sounds too good to be true, Mr. McNally."

McNally waved a hand. "Call me Morgan. The faster you fire Gina and hire me, the faster I can begin working on getting your wife's cooperation to bring your daughters to their first supervised visit."

CHAPTER TEN

Zamira paused before turning the corner into the visitation center's waiting area. This Patrick Quinn had some kind of pull for Andy to suddenly request she work overtime. Clearly the hero firefighter was used to his whims being obeyed and had impulsively decided he wanted to see his kids. The second she introduced herself, he'd probably greet her with the false gratitude of the entitled and imitate a mild-mannered, victimized father, not realizing how many Sundays she'd sat beside Gretch listening to Eve's horrific life.

Zamira exhaled sharply. What was wrong with her? Wallowing in negative thoughts and getting herself all antagonized before she even met a new client wasn't remotely like her. She had to stop compounding her unprofessional conduct with this particular case. Her job was not to choose sides; it was protecting the best interests of the daughters.

She drew a deep breath and marched around the corner. A well-built man in a navy CFD t-shirt and jeans was slumped in one of the blue plastic chairs, staring at the recycled rubber flooring. His muscled arms were crossed, his expression morose. Patrick Quinn. A stunningly handsome man, not a compliment as much as another mark against him. To have been blessed with the human equivalent of a god's perfection and harbor such evil inside...

He glanced up, his brooding gaze holding a slightly threatening quality when directed at her. Goosebumps bristled along her arms. "Mr. Quinn?" At his nod, she forced her feet forward. *Positive thoughts create positive outcomes.* "I'm Zamira Bey, your court-ordered provider."

Mr. Quinn hauled himself to his feet like he was hoisting four times his bodyweight. He murmured a greeting, which she completely missed because of the emotion in his dark blue eyes. Stark anguish. Unconcealed grief. Abusers who'd finally been caught generally harbored guilt, defiance, or barely checked rage. This shell-shocked look was original and cunning; he was quite the adept actor. He held out a hand, another clash of her cultures. Zamira demurred by keeping her palm glued to her torso, until he awkwardly lowered his.

"I appreciate you seeing me at the last minute like this," he said. "I really miss my girls."

She managed not to roll her eyes. *Phony? Check.* "Of course."

He held out the clipboard of paperwork, and she leafed through the pages with minimal attention. His handwriting was neat and masculine, his signature a bold, indecipherable scrawl.

He shifted restlessly beside her, studying the happy family posters lining the wall. She came to his Marvel Comics hero's square jaw, which was covered in late-afternoon bristle. His t-shirt was deeply wrinkled, his dark hair a tangled mess. She breathed in a clean bay soap scent, though. Like he'd gotten out of a shower, dressed in whatever clothes were on the floor, and ignored the comb on his way out. That was another tell. Some men barely knew how to exist once the worker bee in the marriage left.

"If you'll come with me," she said, in a clipped tone. "Your daughters will be here in a few minutes, and a volunteer will escort them to the assigned playroom."

His handsome features morphed into dread. "They're outdoorsy. Can I take them to a playground or something?"

"I'm sorry, no. Not during this initial evaluation."

"What are you *evaluating*?" His question came out harsh.

Their level of fear around you, you bastard. She clenched her teeth, partly to keep the sentence unsaid, partly to hide her horror at this *haram* word. *Forgive me, Allah.* That the obscenity jumped so viciously to mind was appalling. She never swore, even in her private life. Where was her inherent optimism? And how would she maintain it around someone like him? *How, Allah?*

She pasted on a sympathetic smile. "The evaluation is a standard family court document centering on your interactions with your children. I encourage you to ignore the institutionalism of the next hour and try to enjoy their company."

A muscle along his jaw tightened, then—just like that —his expression cleared. He definitely carried an aura about him, though. Gretch had called it a Zen-like calm. She was wrong. There was too much power swirling in his energy field. That calm was for show; something much darker lay beneath.

"Okay," he said tightly. "Let's do this."

A FAINT FLORAL scent trailed in the wake of the supervisor's rapid steps, and her pale pink headscarf fluttered as she walked. Trick followed at a respectful distance. The hallway was as sterile as a hospital's, despite the attempt to mask it with kiddie art and posters of baby animals.

He'd forgotten the supervisor's name—something with a Z—in his haze of pain. His whole body ached with the effort to appear like this was a normal Monday afternoon, when what he really needed was a savage physical release, like a cage fight, where primal rage meant survival. Where pounding another man to smithereens was encouraged. Or fighting a four-alarm high rise, the more challenging the fire ground, the better. As soon as this visit with the girls was over, he'd go straight to the station and beg Cap for some shifts. He didn't need a week off to get his life in order. He'd begun the legal process and vacated the house. Sure, he still couldn't sleep or meditate or realign his chakras, but time off work wasn't going to change that.

"Here we are." The woman pushed open a door and waved him into another bright room. A painted rainbow stretched the length of one wall, another had balloons in flight, and a third looked like effervescent pink bubbles. The west end held a long kiddie table and chairs, while on the east end, a cluster of neon beanbags littered the multicolored area rug. She pointed to her right. "Puzzles and games are on this shelf, coloring books over there. DVDs under the TV are alphabetized by title, and the toy chests along this wall have just about every toy you can imagine. All donated, of course."

Her smile was fleeting, and her gaze slid away—like the sight of him repulsed her. He swallowed the urge to defend himself. She was a means to an end: custody of his girls. *This is a complete waste of your time, lady. Once Jace uncovers proof, Eve can't get away with this much longer.*

"We do ask that you and your daughters put back anything you've played with before the end of your session. Any questions?"

"Yes." He took a deep breath. "There's a father-daughter dance at the elementary school this Friday that I'd like to attend. With Amy, the eight-year-old."

She blinked at him like he'd grown another head.

"My wife bought her a dress and everything," he went on rapidly. "Amy's talked of nothing else for a month. We're very close."

A flash of distaste was quickly covered by bland professionalism. "It's way too early to discuss that, Mr. Quinn."

Too early? It's already Monday. Trick hesitated. The way she grasped that yellow file humbled him. She held his fate within those pages.

"I meant," she said, in that patient way impatient people tried to fake, "do you have any questions about this evaluation?"

He shook his head. "No, ma'am."

For a moment, her professional mask slipped, and humor shone in her brown eyes. "There's no need to age me unnecessarily, Mr. Quinn. You may call me Zamira."

"Zamira." Her name rolled off his tongue in a pleasant, foreign way. Like other uncommon words he came across, or words spoken in accents, he instinctively repeated it in a quieter tone.

She blushed the shade of her scarf.

He quickly gestured to the fourth wall, entirely mirrored, which reflected their awkward body language together. "I presume you'll be in there watching?"

"Yes," she said. "And taping. You authorized that with your signature." She held up the clipboard.

"Of course." Was now the time to blurt out his innocence? In the last few days, it had become a chronic urge.

"Thank you for spending your afternoon with us, Zamira."

A spark of surprise was followed by a genuine smile that transformed her face into serene beauty. "And thank you for thanking me," she said. "Your daughters will be here shortly."

This glimpse of her inner self touched something parched inside him. He recognized the old soul within her warm eyes, the way her spirit in this life reached out to those who were struggling. She had to be made of strong stuff to choose this career. And unlike a firefighter, she probably wasn't thanked very often. But her tranquil demeanor had the same effect as his yoga instructor's, and a peace he hadn't felt in days suffused him.

As she closed the door, he inhaled a prana breath, shook off his musing, then slowly circled the room, glancing at all the activities. The girls would freaking hate this. They were tomboys. DVDs were for when they were sick or a babysitter came over. Puzzles? As far as he remembered, they'd never done one. He paused by a thick-plated window and tested the latch. It had been painted shut. A huge fire hazard. He took out his keys and chipped at the paint, torqueing the latch until it gave way. With a quick, violent heave, the windowsill groaned upward, and warm air caressed his arms. City noises seeped in—two horns battling each other, the roar of a garbage truck down the block, fire engine sirens in the distance. Probably Firehouse 51 over on South Blue Island Avenue.

He glanced at his watch. Ten minutes late. Any other ten minutes he'd barely pay attention, but this was his sole hour with Tina and Amy in six long days. He shoved his hands in his pockets and strolled. At the end of the bubbles wall, he pivoted and circled the room the other way. For some reason, he couldn't bear pacing near the mirrored wall. He halted at one of the toy chests and lifted the lid. Multi-ethnic dollies, tea sets, tiaras, and costumes were tossed in haphazardly. Jeez, Eve would've had a grand mal seizure at this mess.

The next one held Lego blocks, soldiers, and toy vehicles. "Now we're cookin'." He left the lid up—the girls would gravitate right over. Most of the board games were ones he'd played with his four brothers, and unexpected memories of epic arguments and blistering accusations of cheating made him chuckle. Too late, he glimpsed himself in the damn mirror. He'd forgotten where he was for a moment and had turned to the very wall he was trying to avoid. He swiveled around as nonchalantly as possible and counted the balloons along the opposite wall. Twenty-seven.

Another glance at his watch. Quarter after. Maybe they were caught in rush-hour traffic. Maybe it had something to do with those sirens. An accident causing traffic on the Chicago Skyway? He slipped the cellphone out of his front pocket. He'd have heard the chirp and felt the vibration of a text, but maybe Eve had emailed...

Nope. Nothing. There was no way she'd blow off a meeting that could get back to the judge. No way this was some weird payback for him gaining the upper hand last night. She didn't even want Blaze. She was just running behind.

He ran a thumb down the tight muscle at the back of his neck. Either the *splenius capitus* or *upper trapezius*. He massaged surrounding muscles and labeled them too. Yeah, he was definitely going to the firehouse after this and demanding his shifts back. A man in crisis belonged with his buddies, not sliding into madness recalling anatomy class notes.

He switched to counting the effervescent bubbles on the south wall. Had to start over when he spaced whether he'd counted one already. Fifty-seven. Dug out all the trucks for Amy and lined them up by category. Long-haul, construction, snow removal... Tina would like the Legos. He spread them out on one of the desks and grouped each pile by size. Although color was a better grouping for her. He started over, becoming increasingly obsessive and concise in his piles. He gave up with a frown. Wow, under enormous stress, he gravitated right to adopting Eve's nitty-gritty methods of maintaining control. That was weird.

He dusted off his hands, arranged the two kiddie chairs, and hauled a beanbag over for himself. Four thirty. Hopefully Zamira had a magazine or novel back there. Hopefully she wasn't watching him standing here with his thumb up his ass. She wouldn't record him without the kids, right? He probably should've read the fine print on the clipboard, but not much was getting through lately.

He wandered over to the open window and watched the pedestrians. Counted cars.

Forty after. *Fucking Eve.* He dug out his phone again and pressed her number. Voicemail. He hung up. Paced. Twenty minutes to kill, 'cause clearly he was being stood up.

Was this part of her game? Chop him out of the family picture altogether? More importantly, was he just going to stand here like a chump or fight the sexual abuse charges and her demand for sole custody?

And if she'd hurt Blaze to get to him, would she be sick enough to hurt their daughters, too?

CHAPTER ELEVEN

"You realize," Mr. Quinn said in a seething tone, "that painting the windows shut is illegal and a fire hazard, right? Your organization could be fined or shut down."

Had Zamira known him better or liked him the slightest bit, she'd have addressed the gargantuan elephant in the room, or rather hallway, given he'd stepped out at her soft knock. His inner pain was palpable. "I'll notify our director immediately," she said lightly. "We pride ourselves on our city and state compliance." It wasn't worth telling him the center had recently been repainted by well-meaning volunteers from the congregational church down the block. His mind was far from the latch he'd attacked with such ferocity.

Zamira motioned him toward the designated exit and fell into step beside him. "I've already left a message with your children's mother to reschedule the evaluation."

"Good luck with that." His chuckle held no mirth. They passed a boy wailing and clinging to his mother's leg. Mrs. Henderson and Kenny. Zamira nodded at her former client as their new supervisor, Ann, hurried around the corner after them. Mr. Quinn glanced away as if unable to bear the boy's pain. "That doesn't usually happen," Zamira said quickly.

A muscle fluttered along his jaw. "Why do you work here?"

There were many ways to interpret the abrupt question. Given the quiet curiosity, she chose to believe it was admiration. "I've always gravitated toward advocating for children," she replied. "Before this, I was a teacher for the deaf."

"Do you have kids of your own?"

She shook her head, warmth infusing her cheeks. In her world, this was an incredibly personal question for a man to ask, but he wasn't worth the few words it would take for the teaching moment. "You left your available dates off the paperwork, Mr. Quinn—"

"Call me Trick."

Nope. "I'd like to set a standard day and time going forward."

Twenty feet ahead, Mr. Henderson stalked through the heavy outer door, which clanged shut from the force with which he'd flung it open. His focus landed on Zamira, and her breath stilled at his scowl. Perhaps he didn't know his provider had been reassigned. *Poor Ann.* Zamira forced a smile and gave him a slight nod. His ruddy complexion turned pure crimson.

"...depends on my shifts," Mr. Quinn ended.

"Okay," Zamira mumbled, unable to tear her gaze from Mr. Henderson as their distance closed. It even looked like he was purposely heading straight for her. Heartbeat accelerating, Zamira edged right, even though it brought her shockingly close to bumping into her new client.

Mr. Henderson adjusted left. They'd collide in mere feet. Gasping, she plowed into Mr. Quinn.

"Excuse me," he murmured in an unexpectedly polite tone.

"Go back to your own country," Mr. Henderson hissed, wrenching off her hijab. Hairpins ripped out along with strands of her hair, and she howled, clasping her stinging scalp.

In a blur, Mr. Quinn tackled Mr. Henderson up against the wall, the thunderous impact rattling a lamp on a nearby table. Mr. Henderson's breath whooshed out.

"Show some goddamn respect," Mr. Quinn growled, inches from the other man's face. He snatched the hijab and thrust it at her without breaking his gaze from his livid captive.

"So, you're just going to let people like her bomb our city? You bleeding-heart liberal."

Still shaking at the unprovoked attack, Zamira clumsily rewrapped the silk. They'd seen her hair! Her humiliation would've been no less acute had her clothes suddenly fallen off. Tears welled in her throat. Insha'Allah that she could get to her office before she lost it.

"Apologize to the lady," Mr. Quinn said through gritted teeth.

"Get off me!"

Mr. Quinn hoisted Mr. Henderson onto his tiptoes. "Apologize."

This was too much. Mr. Quinn was obviously redirecting his anger at Eve, and while a part of Zamira cheered the retaliation on behalf of all maligned Muslims, Mr. Henderson didn't deserve that level of wrath.

Even though she avoided physical contact with men who were not her family, she instinctively laid a palm on Mr. Quinn's bicep. The foreign solidness and steely strength sent her stomach tumbling. She instantly let go and clenched her fingers. "Mr. Quinn," she said softly, her gaze darting to the security cameras. Surely a guard would be sprinting around the corner. Oh no... Her uncovered head was on the security footage too! She shuddered out a breath. "Please, let him go."

A long moment passed. The men stared at each other, lips stretched, teeth clenched like rabid wolves. Hasty footsteps sounded down the hall.

"Mr. Quinn. Security is coming."

Mr. Quinn slowly eased the other man down. The instant Mr. Henderson's feet found purchase, he pulled out of the fisted grasp, yanked his shirt into place, and wiped the spittle from his mouth. "You call yourself an American?" Without another glance at either of them, he stormed down the hall, encountering Fred, the security officer. Zamira waved at Fred to show she was all right and turned back to Mr. Quinn.

He tracked Mr. Henderson's retreat, animosity pouring off him. Clearly, he wanted to take off after the man. "He isn't worth your trouble," Zamira said, her frayed nerves causing her voice to tremble. She was as American as both men, but also a Muslim in a post-nine-eleven city that had just been bombed. Overt prejudice was nothing new but still cut deep. The horror of strangers' hate. The unfairness of blanket bias. How, just once, she wanted to fight violence with something other than bleak acceptance.

No. Negativity begat negativity. Anger would get her nowhere. *Forgive me, Allah.* She exhaled and forced her shoulders to relax, tried to visualize calm flowing through her. "Mr. Quinn?"

He finally redirected his attention, his storm-blue eyes snapping with life, his focus so intense it was like he peered into her soul. She couldn't look away from the brute force of him. More haram behavior. So was her pounding heart. And noticing how his long lashes swept his cheeks when he blinked... What was happening to her? He was an *abuser*.

"You shouldn't have to stand for that." He glanced down her body then centered on her hijab, which had to be a mess. "Did he hurt you?"

"No." It was a squeak. Where was the disgust she'd fought in the waiting room? He may have protected her from assault, but he was a despicable man in his own right. *Pull yourself together.* She inhaled sharply, her oxygen fragranced with his clean soap scent. Her knees began to shake, obviously a latent reaction to the assault. "Thank you," she said stiffly. "For your help."

He leaned closer. Every molecule in her body froze. His fingers brushed her hijab, and she jerked like she'd been struck by a cattle prod. "Sorry." He withdrew his hand, his grimace sheepish and charming. "Your scarf," he murmured. "It's, er, very crooked."

She pressed the silk protectively to her ears. Yes, many strands of hair still escaped. "I'll...I'll fix it."

Although he eased back, he still seemed too close, that energetic aura encircling her, as tangible as conducted electricity. "I'll...um...follow up with a new evaluation date, Mr. Quinn."

He nodded, and his expression shuttered back to the role of stoic dad still waiting to see his daughters. "Will you be all right? With him in the building?"

"I— Yes. I have paperwork to finish. I'll be in my office until long after he leaves." Why couldn't she stop stammering?

"Okay. Keep your door locked." He headed to the exit.

She followed. What on earth...? What was she doing now? *Turn around before he sees you!*

Too late.

As he pressed down on the thick metal bar, he noticed her and hesitated, morphing split-second surprise into a courteous mask. "Zamira?"

Those same traitorous molecules that had sucked up his energy now blistered with heat, as if she stood in the middle of the asphalt parking lot in August. Perspiration dampened her upper lip. "I...I just wanted to thank you again."

He cocked his head and smiled. "You're welcome." His gaze roamed to her hijab again. He opened his mouth and hesitated.

I know it's a mess!

"You're...very beautiful," he said softly, instantly grimacing again. "I'm sorry. That just popped out. Please forgive me."

Her lips refused to shape a reply. Her brain demanded a retreat. She remained frozen in place.

"Be safe." Mr. Quinn braced a shoulder on the door, and as it opened, sunlight streamed onto him, highlighting those angular cheekbones and that broad smile. Such white, even teeth. "I'll call you with my schedule."

Zamira trembled the entire way back to the observation room, which was thankfully empty. *You're very beautiful.* Besides her father, no man had spoken those words in her entire twenty-seven years. Mr. Quinn was a stranger. Who'd seen her hair! Going without a hijab was only allowed in the exclusive presence of close family members.

With stilted movements, Zamira gathered the Quinn folder and pushed the camcorder's eject button. A thoroughly wasted hour of recording if viewed as an official court exhibit, but for curiosity's sake, she was keeping the memory card. Mr. Quinn was not as he seemed. Once she got home, she'd review the care he took clustering the Legos, study his spontaneous laugh at perusing the board games. Assess the annoyed set of his jaw as he chipped away at the paint on the latch. And if she hit the pause button at the exact frame his arm and shoulder muscles bunched to wrench open the window, it would be... because her tea needed refreshing.

Before the smile fully developed, Zamira hesitated, holding the memory card like it was a motion-activated explosive. It was against company policy to take this off premises. Worse, Mr. Quinn was a...a pedophile! What was she doing? *Forgive me, Allah, for all of this.* Especially the giddiness that still pumped through her for a man who would harm his wife and daughters. Why was she fixated on him?

The answer struck like a lightning bolt: because something wasn't right. A niggle of doubt now warred with the documented evidence of spousal abuse. Was this like the irreconcilable confusion Gretch had expressed yesterday after she'd learned of the accusations against her Zen firefighter friend? The uncomfortable feeling had only one solution.

Zamira snatched her cellphone and called her lovely, crazy friend. "Gretch? Can you get together for dinner? I need you to tell me everything you know about Patrick Quinn."

CHAPTER TWELVE

"Put me back on the schedule," Trick said tightly. "Please."

Across the desk from him, Captain Lewis sat back and folded his arms.

"Come on, Cap. I hate feeling useless."

"It's only been a few days. This isn't a job for the distracted."

"I need *this* distraction. I need the crew. Just a couple of shifts."

Cap pursed his lips. "Dinner's in a few. You may as well stay. I'll give you my decision afterward, but don't get your hopes up."

Trick stood, his muscles as stiff as if he'd been curled in a ball all day. He hadn't run, done yoga, meditated... Nothing since Friday's warehouse fire. He needed a release. His soul longed for a cosmic reconnection, but it was still impossible. "Thanks, Cap." His cellphone buzzed a text, and he stopped at the threshold to check. *Jace: Have some info. Where ru?*

Trick typed *Station* and turned back to the captain. "Anything new from the FBI?"

A weary look passed over his boss's face. "The Feds are still conducting searches. Tonight's Cubs game was delayed half an hour because of tightened security."

"Are we still helping the search?"

"No. Just their team in the field. And the cops are grinding through their overtime budgets now, because the anti-Muslim blowback is intimidating the Islamic community."

Trick nodded and left with a halfhearted salute. He'd seen that for himself at the center today. He squeezed his fists, wanting to engage that bastard all over again. The fear and vulnerability in Zamira's eyes at the unprovoked attack had stuck with him. So had the striking peripheral view of her cascading hair before she'd retied her headscarf.

Before that moment, she'd just been a court-ordered supervisor—a means to an end—but her mask had slipped in the mayhem, and those images of her femininity replayed with distracting frequency. He'd always preferred lingerie magazines over nudie ones because the *hint*, the hope of a reveal was so much sexier. Who knew the attraction also encompassed the mystery of a woman's hair underneath Muslim headscarves?

He did a search on his phone, and *hijab* popped up. "Hijab," he muttered as he crossed the firehouse. "Hijab." Jeez, why was he focused on this? With his life in the crapper, he didn't need the distraction of a stranger's hair and what covered it. He needed to stay busy working. The construction company Mark had inherited from his dad was in a slump. If Cap didn't authorize shifts, then Trick would have to swallow his pride and ask Jace for some hours helping the FBI search.

Trick followed the sound of *SportsCenter* and slipped into the break room, stiff and self-conscious like his first day as a probie. He hadn't seen his mates since he'd gotten the summons, but hiding secrets around here was as rare as hiding chocolate chip cookies, and Pete gossiped like a fishwife.

Cheryl spotted him first and jumped to her feet. Rounding the red vinyl sofa, she approached with her hands in her pockets. "Your life went in the shithole fast."

That was what he liked about her. She didn't bother with empty niceties like "are you okay?" or "anything I can do?"

Trick searched her face. No censure there, but no sympathy either. "I didn't abuse my girls," he said abruptly.

"I know." She motioned behind her. "We all know. We've got your back, Lieu."

Sam saw him next and didn't disguise the smug look for long seconds. Danny did a double take and turned down the volume. One by one the guys glanced over their shoulders and fell silent. Expressions sobered. Several looked downright worried. Understandable. Firefighters were a superstitious lot, and Trick brought his lifetime of shiny good fortune to every shift. It was like an energy field that covered anyone in the vicinity. Victims never died on his watch, and firefighters working the scene remained miraculously unscathed. Engine Company 126 had become a coveted station to join, and despite Cap or Trick's continuous warnings to cease the daredevil risks, the crew believed Trick's supernatural luck rubbed off on them, too. Now Trick stood before them with just about the worst luck imaginable to a husband and father. What did that mean for them?

"Hey, man," Danny said, his big puppy eyes sorrowful, his knee pumping rapidly from all that youthful probie energy. "Anything we can do?"

Cheryl rolled her eyes. "You can get up and let your lieutenant have a seat," she snapped.

Trick held up a palm. "I'm good, thanks."

"Seriously, Lieu," Hank said, "how can we help?"

"I'm still trying to help myself." Trick forced a grin. "If anyone knows why a wife goes from loving and supportive to wanting my nut sac, I'd appreciate some infor—"

The earsplitting tones of their station drowned out Trick's words. Adrenalin and anticipation knifed through him as the crew rose. Dispatch droned the assignment. Two-thirty-four Holmes Street, residential structure. Engine and ambulance only. Five of the guys headed out, and Cheryl patted Trick's arm as she passed. "Take care, Lieu."

As the remaining crew members sat back down, the visceral pull to suit up and grab a seat in the engine forced Trick's feet into the garage. He'd give his left arm to go on this call. Fight the flames, immerse in the almost choreographed teamwork that came with every life-or-death battle. The apparatus roared to life, and the flash of swirling red lights lit the garage.

Wait a minute—what was to stop him from tagging along? Sure, he wasn't on the schedule and wasn't wearing his gear, but he could go as a bystander. Supervise Danny, still an impulsive trainee...

Trick bounded toward the engine. Sam frowned behind the wheel and mouthed, "What the fuck?"

Across the garage, Captain Lewis barked Trick's name. *Damn it.* Trick exhaled harshly and waved the crew off, watching as the engine screamed down the street. He spun around and met his captain's steely displeasure. Totally reminiscent of Pop when he used to catch Trick being a numskull. He flushed under the glare, which didn't make him feel any more mature. "Thought I'd supervise Danny, sir."

"If you're gonna stick around, make yourself useful." Cap jerked his head. "Potatoes need peeling."

KP duty. Still better than pacing Pete's house. Trick thanked him tonelessly and headed in.

Russ had his back turned, mixing something in a large stainless-steel bowl. When Trick washed his hands, Russ started. "Didn't expect you here. You doin' all right, man?" The pity in his eyes shredded the remnants of Trick's dignity.

"Hangin' in, thanks."

"If there's anything I can do..."

The offer was genuine but already exhausting to hear. Trick grabbed the ten-pound bag of potatoes. Unless Russ or the crew had a magic wand, no one could do anything to get him out of this nightmare. "Appreciate it."

Russ cleared his throat. "You know, my brother had an issue with anger." He continued mashing the ground beef in the bowl. "He got help at a center on West Van Buren. I can get you the contact information if you want."

Trick stared at the sack in his hands, numbness tingling through him. He inhaled slowly, pushing through the hurt and outrage. Russ was only trying to help. And realistically, there would be many people in the future who would believe the charges too, unless Eve took out a full-page *Tribune* ad admitting to her lies. "Not necessary, but thanks."

Trick ripped open the sack so forcefully that potatoes bounced out and rolled in all directions. "I got it," he said, as Russ stooped to pick one up off the floor. "Seriously. I got it."

"Okay, Lieu." The response was light, easygoing, like the way they were trained to talk someone down from a ledge. It wasn't worth addressing, since, for all intents and purposes, Trick *was* on a figurative ledge, but another layer of frustration built in his gut.

Clustering the potatoes back on the counter, Trick directed his attention to the bantering analysts on the small TV. It took heartbeats too long for Russ to follow his lead. Luckily, the show replayed Gomez hitting a triple, so the two of them chatted about yesterday's game as it went to commercial.

Trick was peeling the last potato when Jace sauntered in, wearing the standard FBI black suit/white shirt/holier-than-thou expression. If not for his earlier text, this would've been a completely unwelcome visit. Based on his smirk, Trick was in for more big-brother gloating, but it was worth it if Jace had uncovered any clues behind Eve's attack.

"Got a minute?" Jace jingled the keys in his pocket.

"Go on, Lieu," Russ said. "I got this."

They headed out into the still-warm evening, the sun low on the horizon. The roar and exhaust of rush hour on the Kennedy Expressway filled the air.

Jace nodded toward his SUV, gleaming next to Trick's ancient gray Ford F-150. "Let's take a ride."

Trick frowned. "Way to sound like a mobster."

"Trust me. You won't want your crew catching your reaction to this. We'll grab a to-go dinner and talk in my car." Jace's grave tone was identical to the one he'd used last Thursday when he'd shown up here looking for Sean. But Trick wasn't near as naïve as his youngest brother, and he didn't need the fraternal concern.

"Thanks, but I'd prefer to have dinner with my crew. Just give me what you got."

Jace jingled the keys again, his expression harsh and tired. "Suit yourself. Let me get the file." They walked to the SUV. "Why didn't you tell us you were having marital problems?"

"Because I wasn't having problems," Trick replied carefully. "This is some sort of crazy impulse on her part."

"No, it isn't." Jace popped the lock, opened the door, and retrieved a file. "She contacted her lawyer over a month ago."

Trick opened his mouth, but his brain refused to supply words. A month ago, he'd surprised Eve with a trip to Telluride. His in-laws, who'd been in on the secret, had taken the girls. It had been a great weekend, the days so crisp and warm they'd skied without jackets, even ended up with sunburned noses. They'd rekindled the kind of romance from their earlier years: gobs of leisure time for each other, lots of laughter. They'd drunk wine with six-course dinners and cordials after, then made love slowly. Trick had spent a bundle of their savings, made sure no expense was spared. No way Eve could have been going through the motions. Inconceivable that she'd been planning this kind of warfare.

Trick braced himself against the passenger side of his pickup, away from anyone peering out of the station. "Thanks," he said, accepting the file and flipping it open.

The first pages were copies of ER admissions to Chicago Methodist. Six visits in total. Jace had arranged all the facts on a spreadsheet stapled to the back of the file. Date, the doc who'd seen her, presenting complaint, and which tests were done. "How did you get this?"

"Called in a favor from a nurse I've been seeing on and off."

The roaring was back in Trick's ears. Eve's ER visits began *three months* ago. How could he not have known? He wasn't some dipshit, clueless husband... "How is this possible? How did I not get any of these bills?"

"She didn't use your insurance."

"Abrasion to the left orbital lobe? Contusion to the

trachea..." Trick slapped the page with the back of his hand. "That's strangling!"

"Did you ever see her bruised? Injured? Wrapped in bandages?"

"Yes to bruised—you know how clumsy she is." Trick frowned. "Back in March, she said she tripped on the treadmill at the gym. Her left thigh was a purple welt; her knee required four stitches." He scanned the page for March visits. "Here it is. She even lists the treadmill as a reason." He glanced up. "What am I missing?"

"You're missing the classic victim syndrome. They'll tell admissions personnel they tripped, fell, walked into a door, etcetera. Maybe one or two times it's legitimate, but six times sends up a flag."

"You think she didn't fall off the treadmill?"

"I can try to use my badge to influence her gym to release any security tapes, but I'll bet it's an unverifiable injury, which means a judge or jury is left to *wonder* if she actually tripped on a treadmill like she told the ER staff. You get what I'm saying?"

"This is insane. She tripped on a treadmill, she reported tripping on a treadmill, and, through inference, I get blamed for abuse? How am I ever going to prove my innocence?"

"Start with any evidence of where you were during those dates."

Trick took out his cellphone and tapped the calendar app. His shifts were highlighted in red. He correlated the date of her treadmill ER visit. "She went the evening I reported for my twenty-four and told them it happened the day before when I was home. It didn't happen the day I was home. I'd have taken her to the ER."

"Flawless," Jace said. "The injury happens the *night before*"—he used air quotes—"you leave for an extended period. You aren't around to refute it."

Trick tapped a sticky note that had an address listed. "What's this?"

"The women's shelter she checked into last Wednesday. And guess who helped get her there? Gretch... Sean's Gretch. She'd been mentoring Eve to escape the abuse for months."

Trick rubbed a palm across his mouth. This was too much. All the plans that had gone on right under his nose. For *months*. And all these *accidents* or— "I remember seeing bruises around Eve's mouth," he said. "I think...six weeks ago? She said she'd done those filler injections for wrinkles. I joked with her not to go outside because people would think I hit her. We *laughed*." He stared at Jace, icy dread leaving him chilled. In a hundred years he would never have described his wife as diabolical.

"Anything else? Limping? Welts? Burns?"

Trick racked his brain. "Yeah, limping, now that you mention it. A few weeks ago... Here." He tapped the sixth row on the spreadsheet. "Same reason she gave me: tripping over one of Tina's toys and spraining her ankle. I iced it and asked if she wanted to go to a walk-in clinic before I went on shift. She said she was fine."

"All minor mishaps that her lawyer will use to imply something much more brutal. She's brilliant, I'll give her that. Manipulative. I've thought so since junior high. Never figured she was this twisted, though."

"Manipulative?" The word somehow flipped on a light switch. Like how she always waited until they were in front of an audience to announce a "mutual decision" when they were far from agreeing on the point. Like pronouncing they were holding Tina back a year in front of his in-laws. Or telling the fertility specialist she was forgoing any employment to reduce stress, despite their mountain of debt. Naturally, after the outside parties expressed approval, Trick would surrender his opinion. Why bother making his stance known since hers was right?

Or there was how she'd privately react in fury over something he did, but compliment him for the same behavior in public—like his overdeveloped work ethic or his devotion to living mindfully. The vignettes all ended with the same result: him walking on eggshells, never knowing what would please or anger her, constantly trying to be good enough and yet so often failing.

How had he never figured this out before?

Trick closed the file, his heart clamped in a vise. Manipulated and used. What a freaking waste of the twenty-four years since he'd given her that going-steady ring. His throat clogged painfully. Christ, if he teared up, his brother would never let him forget it. He coughed roughly. "Thanks for this. I'll take it from here."

"Oh, yeah?" Jace cocked his head. "What's your plan?"

Trick shrugged. The shock of seeing his wife in this new light had emptied his mind. "Speak to Gretch?" He hadn't meant it to come out as a question, but the idea was solid. When he'd first met her last Thursday, she hadn't reacted like she knew Eve or the bullshit abuse allegations.

Jace nodded and pursed his lips. "Put her on speaker phone. I know her better than you."

A lifetime of despising his brother's interference warred with Trick's utter inability to cope with any of this. "I can manage. I just need to quiet my soul and manifest—"

"That peace and love bullshit isn't going to help you now. It's time for offensive strategizing." The sharply critical tone cut through Trick's numbness. Jace, the brother who never risked more than one or two dates, thought it was easy to chuck a sixteen-year marriage and all these emotions?

Trick slapped a palm against his passenger door. "I'm dealing with a wife I suddenly don't know," he snarled. "She's got six ER visits, a three-day stay at a shelter, and a pit bull divorce lawyer. I'm fucked. Forgive me for needing time to process this."

"Process this, idiot: she's going to take your house, your money, and your kids. Start. Fighting."

Trick tried to swallow the hard lump still choking him. This was the time to tell Jace the rest of the story. The sexual abuse accusations that carried potential sentencing of four years to life. Registering as a sex offender for the rest of his life for something he didn't do. Losing custody... Trick's chest ached at the bleak future of rare days with his girls that could end up like today, canceled on a whim by a wife who inexplicably hated him. A devious woman who held all the cards and had planned a detailed strategy for this marital ambush months ago.

His life of joy and gratitude was over. What else was there to process? He nodded grimly. "Yeah, you're right."

"It's taken way too many years for you to realize that, sport."

Trick texted Sean. *Need to talk to Gretch. What's her #?*

A few seconds later, his phone dinged. "Sean's meeting her at Windy City Thai on Van Buren," he read off, texting back: *Will drop by.*

Jace pulled out the keys he'd been incessantly jingling. "I'd go, but I used up my dinner hour stopping by."

Trick grimaced at how rudely he'd turned down the invitation to grab food. Besides being blown away by the revelations about Eve, he'd just seen a side of Jace he'd also never known existed. A brother who helped instead of tore down. "Thanks. I owe you for the intel."

"*De nada*. You'll get through this. As the SEALs say: embrace the pain."

As Jace drove off, Trick gazed at the cloudless blue sky, envisioning the stars and planets and vast silence beyond. *Help*, he beseeched the heavens. *Send me a sign that I'll make it through this.*

CHAPTER THIRTEEN

"This is going to sound crazy"—Zamira leaned forward, lowering her voice in the noisy restaurant —"but what if Eve Quinn is setting up her husband?"

Gretch's eyes widened. "It would mean I have no business working with abused women anymore. Every word she's uttered has been authentic; the woman's been abused, Zamira. And her trauma over her daughters being sexually assaulted... You can't fake that. Besides, you're the one who told me the perpetrator—"

"Lives a double life," Zamira interjected. "Yes. I've told myself that for hours, but something's not adding up. I need to know more about Patrick Quinn without him finding out."

Gretch leaned diagonally in the booth and peered at the entrance. "Sean should be here any minute. He'll clear things up. My only interaction with Trick was at the firehouse last Thursday."

"When your perception of him was as a serene firefighter sheltering you from danger. And today he protected me from that senseless attack." She'd detailed every minute of Mr. Henderson's aggression the moment she'd sat down. "What if our initial instinct is wrong? What if he really is just heroic Patrick Quinn?"

Gretch shook her head. "We've had two encounters with him and months of Eve's horror stories—"

"I know," Zamira said, raising her palm. "And the ER evidence. It's the consistency of her character I'm beginning to question. Like why she didn't recognize the photo of Sean on TV last week, and why she'd blow off a court-ordered supervisory visit she agreed to hours earlier. When I called her after the appointment, she said she'd forgotten about it. Sounded very blasé. Not at all the timid woman we've spoken to on the hotline. Nor the slightest bit frightened her husband might be livid. And you *know* that's not a normal reaction for an abused wife who just escaped."

Gretch nodded. She had to be feeling the same unease. In between taking heartbreaking calls, they'd passionately supported the #MeToo and #TimesUp movements, marched in five women's protests this year alone, and expressed fury over congressional skepticism of victims' accounts and Hollywood's blackballing of brave women who shared their encounters with predators.

To even question Eve Quinn's interpretation of her troubled marriage was not only disloyal to her but a betrayal to all victimized women. On the other hand, falsely accusing a well-known hero was not only despicable but could detonate the forward progress for so many other courageous souls. The cynics were just waiting for an example to hold up as evidence that none of the women should be believed.

Gretch tapped her acrylic nails on the martini glass, glancing impatiently at the front entrance again. "Does Eve know you're the Zamira she spoke to at the hotline?"

"I'm not sure she caught my name yesterday, and I

didn't make the connection for her today because the personality over the phone this afternoon bore no resemblance to hotline Eve."

"I'm glad you called me, then."

Zamira nodded and smoothed the napkin in her lap. *Good.* Gretch was on board. It meant this wasn't an asinine idea. Both women were dumbfounded. What was *really* going on in the Quinn marriage? And what kind of a small world was it for Gretch, who'd convinced Eve to move to a shelter, to have randomly started dating Eve's brother-in-law the same week? "Did you tell Sean about your connection to Eve?" *I'll bet yes.*

Gretch winced. "I accidentally mentioned she'd called the hotline and had gotten a restraining order. Sorry."

Rather than waste energy getting annoyed at her friend or fearing for her job, Zamira sent gratitude to Allah. Because of Gretch's slip, Sean could shed much-needed insight on Eve's personality. "What was his reaction?"

More tapping on the martini glass. "He's good at hiding his feelings—exceptionally good—but this shocked him so much that I don't think he has a clue his sister-in-law was in that shelter. Or that his brother's facing worse charges."

"I can't imagine being part of a family where that much drama stays secret," Zamira murmured. The entire Muslim community knew of the Bey family's humiliation.

Gretch shrugged. "Sean's not that close to his family."

"If this situation gets any messier, it'll make the papers. Patrick Quinn is a highly decorated firefighter."

Gretch lifted her glass, her gaze shrewd. "Google much?"

"It was on my intake sheet." Zamira flushed hotly. "Honestly, Gretch—"

"Oh, I get the attraction, believe me—"

"I'm not attracted—"

"—if Sean weren't so— Oh, here he is." Gretch waved at a tall, thin man slipping through the door. Except for height, he looked nothing like Patrick. "Pay no attention to his odd eating pattern. He's a doll once you get to know him."

Zamira's stomach suddenly churned with anxiety. She was really doing this. "Remember," she whispered, "how I'm connected to his brother is confidential."

"Of course, of course." Gretch sipped her drink and lowered it as Sean stopped at the booth. "Hi, sweetie!"

"Sweetie?" A faint grin tugged the corners of his mouth. "How many martinis have you had?"

Gretch patted the area beside her, and when he slipped in the booth, she planted a loud, smacking kiss on his cheek. He ducked his head shyly, and Zamira swallowed her laugh. Such opposites! After quick introductions, she couldn't help but tease, "So you landed the most chased-after woman in Chicago. What's your secret?"

The grin spread, morphing his features to just shy of handsome. "She landed me," he said emphatically. "And who says no to Gretch?"

Gretch shrugged, entwining her fingers in his. "When have I ever been subtle about what I want?"

"When have you ever been subtle, period?" He kissed the back of her hand, and Gretch beamed like he'd paid her a tremendous compliment. Happiness seemed to shimmer off her as she waved the waitress over and ordered another martini. Sean ordered bottled water. After the waitress left, Sean glanced between the two women. "Am I interrupting something?"

"Zamira and I volunteer together at the abuse hotline. She's spoken to Eve too."

"Oh." Sean immediately cut eye contact and began lining up his cutlery.

Zamira shifted uncomfortably. "What do you think of Eve?"

"She's always been a fantastic sister-in-law and mother."

"So who do you believe?" Gretch asked.

"Neither." Sean finished with his place setting and stuck his hands in his lap. "I thought about it last night, and it's probably something benign. My brother wouldn't hurt a flea, but Eve isn't a shrinking violet about stuff that annoys her. This would be classic payback."

Zamira exchanged a questioning glance with Gretch. The Eve who'd called the hotline all those Sundays for months *was* a shrinking violet. Again curiosity surged, and Zamira leaned forward. "What do you mean, classic payback?"

"Eve's like...moody on steroids. Lots of love bombing when she's happy, lots of punishing drama when she's not. If Trick didn't back down from a huge argument, I could see Eve throwing down a gauntlet like a temporary restraining order."

"That seems pretty extreme," Zamira said cautiously. "Has she sought a restraining order before?"

"Not that I know of. But at one of his medal ceremonies, she didn't like the way he was laughing with another couple and marched over—completely sober, by the way—and accused him of having an affair with that woman right in front of her husband."

Gretch and Zamira traded another glance. "Were they having an affair?" Zamira asked.

Sean half laughed, half snorted. "My brother's so in love with Eve we call him the Big Sap. He's a doormat."

"What about Eve?" Gretch said. "Has she had an affair?"

"I doubt it. This is just the way they roll. Honeymoon-happy until he screws up."

Sean's expression remained stoic. He didn't seem to question this bizarre behavior, but the more he spoke, the more questions formed. Who else could shed light on this weird marriage? "Does Eve work?" Zamira asked.

He shook his head. "Not for a long time. I think she's busy being a homeroom mother and in charge of the peewee soccer booster club. Oh, and a Brownie den mother, or whatever they're called. Everyone calls her Supermom. I never see her relaxed or goofing off. She's the champion multitasker, a real ball buster, always giving orders. It's actually exhausting being around her."

Gretch quirked a brow at Zamira. Again, Sean's description was not the same woman who'd called the hotline.

"How would you describe Trick?" Gretch asked.

Sean shrugged. "The only brother who's got it together. Married, kids, great career. He's following right in my dad's footsteps."

"Does Trick have a temper?"

Zamira flushed at Gretch's blatant nosiness, but then, that was why they'd set up this dinner. Amusement lit Sean's face again, which instantly softened the intensity on Gretch's.

"Naw. He's the epitome of calm and collected. The only times he loses his temper are when Jace is around. The two are like oil and water."

"But surely firefighters are under a lot of pressure." No way could he battle fires calm and collected. At the supervisory center, a lot of domestic cases were due to continuous work-related stress brought home.

"Maybe on the job," Sean said, "but any other time,

he's totally into connecting with the universe, woo-woo stuff. His perfect vacation's a silent Buddhist retreat."

Gretch blinked in disbelief. "Eve agreed to that?"

"Hell no. And she wears the pants."

"This is really getting strange," Gretch muttered, studying her almost empty glass.

A shadow fell over the table. "Hey, kids."

At the deep, smooth voice, Zamira glanced over her left shoulder. Right into Patrick Quinn's astonished face. "Oh my gosh." Of all the people in Chicago she did not want to run into. Of course Allah was teaching her a lesson!

"Hello," he said in a confused tone, his expression instantly guarded. His gaze swept around the table. "How— Do you all know each other?"

Zamira fumbled with her purse clasp, ensuring it was closed as Gretch countered archly, "What are you doing here?"

"Sean said you two were eating together, so I thought I'd stop by and—say hello."

Even with her head lowered, Zamira felt his glance during the pause in his sentence. Her heart pounded painfully against her ribs. Was he picking up on her overwhelming anxiety? His file and the memory card were right *here* in her purse. What if something happened and the contents accidentally spilled?

She had to get out of here; that was all there was to it. She'd come to find out about the Quinn marriage, but certainly not in *front* of him. Besides, no way could she even attempt to swallow a morsel of food now. The giddiness that had overtaken her after he'd saved her from Mr. Henderson was back with a vengeance. There was something magnetic about him that threw off her equilibrium, and she wanted no part of this weird feeling. "I, um, should go," she stammered, clutching her purse. "My parents are expecting me."

"What?" Gretch laughed. "You asked me to dinner. Don't be silly. This'll be fun!" She threw Zamira a wide-eyed look like *this is our chance* and gestured for Patrick to sit next to Zamira. For professional and religious reasons, that was *not* going to happen.

Cheeks inflamed, Zamira waved a hand. "Actually, Gretch, um, how about you sit with me." She darted a glance around the restaurant. This cozy foursome looked like a double date, with neither man of her faith, which would be a huge scandal if it got back to her family or the community. It would not surprise her if an esteemed member of Mosque Mohammed was witnessing this entire interaction. Taking notes, maybe a discreet cellphone photograph of a non-chaperoned, non-Muslim man joining their party. Then word would get back to the imam and Faisal Abdul. The engagement would be a non-starter. Her family would literally have to move out of Chicago after the second scandal. The Bey daughters and their disgraceful behavior...

Finally, Gretch clued in and nodded. Even Mr. Quinn seemed relieved as the others shifted around, switching up seats. Still, goosebumps covered Zamira's flesh as she frantically eyed the patrons again.

"We're glad you stopped by," Gretch said, "because we've been discussing Eve."

Zamira sucked in a hollow breath, her attention jolting back to the horror at this table. There went her job. Mr. Quinn would lodge an ethics complaint, and who could blame him? He probably thought she'd been sitting here telling them all about his charges, maybe how Eve had stood him up today. *Enough.* She had to fix this. "I...I haven't been discussing you, Mr. Quinn."

"I told you earlier to call me Trick."

There it was again, the gentle tone, the considerate suggestion completely at odds with his situation. As if he, too, didn't dwell on the negative in life. She'd noticed it after today's assault, when he'd instantly overlooked her role as a legal roadblock to aid and comfort her. And now, in the face of the three of them admitting to gossiping about Eve, he didn't bluster or accuse; he offered this symbolic truce to call him Trick.

But no. That also wasn't going to happen. "The informality would make me very uncomfortable."

"Patrick?" He gestured to his brother. "Are you calling him Sean?"

She flushed and nodded stiffly. He propped his forearm casually on the table. His watch was old, its face slightly cloudy, the leather worn in places. His arm was tan, muscled, and scattered with black hair. "What have you been discussing, then?"

He'd been here only a few minutes, but each time he moved, his warm bay scent curled soft tentacles around her. She inhaled shallowly. "If Eve had an occupation."

"That's not in your file?"

Sean frowned. "I missed how you two know each other."

"It's not important." Patrick's curt answer was like a bucket of ice water dumped on her dreamy thoughts of truces and concern. Seeing his kids had sure seemed important this afternoon. Had he gotten her voicemail about the rearranged evaluation Eve had agreed to tomorrow?

Zamira glanced between the two brothers as awkward silence blanketed the table. Clearly Patrick wanted to keep the sexual abuse charge and supervisory visits to himself, but how could he keep such difficulties from family? Who else was there to support him?

The waitress sidled up to the table with their drinks,

zeroing in on Patrick's handsome face while she passed the glasses around the table. "Can I get you anything?"

"The largest size of whatever beer you have on tap. Thank you."

Once she left, Sean said, "I can't remember the last time I saw you drink beer."

Patrick slouched against the back cushion. "I've had a few shocks this afternoon. I need to numb down a bit." His gaze swept the three of them. "You never answered— how do *you* all know each other?"

"Zamira and I volunteer together on Sundays," Gretch said. "At a hotline for victims of abuse."

Patrick shook his head, as if he'd misheard. "This is a real small world." His expression grew guarded again.

Gretch sipped her fresh martini. "I helped her move into a women's shelter last Wednesday."

"What?" Sean's brows shot sky high. "She was there?"

"Yes," Patrick said, a muscle tightening along his jaw. "Jace just told me." He regarded the women across from him. "Whatever she said to you is a lie, I swear, but I can't figure out how to prove it. I'd appreciate any information, so I know the extent of what I'm fighting here."

Zamira stiffened. It was one thing to find out more about Eve from her brother-in-law. It was another for a client to overtly ask her to side with him. "I really must leave. My job is to remain impartial."

"What job?" Sean asked.

Patrick waved him off, his handsome face carved in raw tension. "If you'd listen to me for a moment, Zamira..."

His blue eyes were vulnerable and beseeching. Who could possibly look away? This man who'd seen her hair. Saved her from Mr. Henderson. Called her beautiful.

This pedophile. This married man. This Catholic.

The conflict churned her stomach.

She was in way over her head, in so many more ways than disobeying supervisory regulations. "I really must leave," she repeated, despite the perplexing reluctance that welled inside. It was the right thing. Patrick's cellphone dinged an incoming text, as Zamira nudged Gretch to let her out of the booth.

TRICK EXHALED IN RELIEF. Cap's text—*Report back for the Wed shift*—was the second sign that his luck had returned. Now he just had to get Zamira to stay. Some blessed part of the universe had put her *here*. If he could convince her of Eve's deception, it would go a long way in court. Amid the clatter of plates being stacked into a rubber bin in the booth behind them, he said, "Please don't leave on my account. I'm the one who interrupted your dinners."

She shook her head. "I wasn't going to order anything."

"Liar," Gretch scoffed. "You insisted we get together to talk about"—she gestured toward Trick—"this."

He didn't need any further sign. "I want my girls back, Zamira." Not bothering to hide the despair, he said, "I don't know how to fight the allegations. Please tell me what to do."

Her soulful eyes softened. "I'm in no position to hand out advice, Mr.... I mean, Patrick." His name died into a whisper, inexplicably erotic, and tingles scurried beneath his skin. *What the hell?*

She blushed fiercely, gazing at her lap. Something about her guileless virtue was soothing to his spirit. There was no battle in her. No anger. No blame, which was like a healing balm in this train wreck of his new life. But why was his body responding like it was turned on? He barely knew her. He was still married! All he should be concentrating on was getting her to suspect Eve, too.

"Please stay," he urged, his confusion adding a curtness to his words. "Five more minutes." His thumping heartbeat ticked away each agonizing second as her lashes stayed lowered, hiding whatever answer lay in her eyes.

Finally, her tight clasp on her purse loosened, as did the rigid set of his shoulders. "Just five," she said softly. Her gaze darted around the restaurant, something she'd repeatedly done since he'd sat down. Was she here to meet someone else?

The waitress brought his beer in a frosted mug, and they asked for a few more minutes to look at the menu. After she left, he downed half the beer before coming up for air, then caught Zamira's wide-eyed stare, like he was some primitive animal. Was this going in her file? *Possible drinking problem.* He put down the mug and wiped his mouth. "Eve set me up. I have a file in my car that shows her ER visits for injuries that occurred *after* I left for my shifts."

"How can you prove they occurred after you left?" Sean asked. "I'd think a victim of abuse would stoically suffer out of fear of more reprisals, and then visit the ER after the abuser left the premises."

Well, shit, he had a point. Hope sputtered like a dying flame. "You know I didn't do this, Sean."

"I'm not your problem." Sean gestured to the women across from them. "She's convinced these two. Start by finding out who else thinks she's a timid victim."

"Timid? *Eve?*"

"She was a mouse to both of us," Gretch said. "What struck me as suspicious is she didn't acknowledge Sean as her brother-in-law when she saw him on TV last week."

"Gretch—" Zamira began.

"I'm sorry," Gretch said, sounding anything but. "His life was in jeopardy, and there wasn't even a trace of recognition. I can't get past that." She turned back to Trick. "It was just before I arrived at your station."

"Other people must have bought this act," Sean continued. "Her friends at PTA meetings? Her hairdresser? A babysitter? I'm willing to bet someone out there besides Eve knows her motivation or future plans. Like, maybe she's having an affair."

Trick's heart stalled at the thought. "No. No way."

"Wake the hell up, Trick. Maybe this is all for a new guy. Or as I said before, control of the lottery money—"

"Lottery?" Gretch and Zamira echoed together.

Not the damn money story again. "I won four million dollars two years ago," Trick said grudgingly.

Gretch pointed to Sean. "We need to discuss your abject failure at gossiping."

"There's nothing to say," he protested. "He's never spent a penny."

"That must have been exciting," Zamira said shyly. "For both you and your wife." It was an invitation to dig deeper, which was a dual-edged sword. He hated talking about the win because it seemed like bragging. On the other hand, her interest was exactly what he was hoping for—it was closing in on five minutes, and she was planted in her seat.

"I won while I was at work." He folded his forearms on the table, reluctantly settling in for the long version. "Surrounded by my crew." He'd bought the ticket that morning on a whim. He rarely wasted money on gambling, certainly not on long shots. But an inner voice had urged him while he'd been paying for gas, and most of his luck was just him listening to his Ajna intuition. "By the time four of my eight numbers matched, it's like I stopped hearing, you know? I had some weird case of hysterical deafness. I *knew* the outcome. Does that sound crazy?"

A faint smile crossed Zamira's face, revealing the serenity she held below the surface. Someone should tell her how beautiful she was. Oh yeah, he'd already done that this afternoon. A catastrophic breach of respecting a Muslim woman's modesty.

"Go on," she said, thankfully unaware of his thoughts. "This is fascinating."

Where was he? "In those next few moments, two visions appeared to me, clear as day. In one I was in a Ferrari F430. I mean, I was literally *there*, like some kind of time warp to another dimension." He reached up, pantomiming one hand on a wheel, one hand scissoring near his mouth. "I had a cigar hanging out of my mouth. I was driving up to a large brick house with a white picket fence." He dropped his hands around his icy mug. "That's it. This split-second vision. But it was clear I wasn't a firefighter anymore."

"And the other?" Zamira asked in a breathless voice.

"I was hauling an unconscious woman from a patio home that was engulfed in flames. She wore a purple velour jumpsuit and had orange hair, and I mean neon-pumpkin orange. I didn't see my crew, but I knew they were there behind me." The vision had been so tangible he'd assumed it was a cosmic prophecy, a glimpse into the future. He still expected that rescue to occur.

"And then you won," Zamira said.

"Yes." Goosebumps coated his arms each time he recalled that moment. "In an instant, I knew I didn't want anything to change. I mean, who doesn't want a Ferrari, but not if it meant I'd stop being a firefighter. Not if it meant one iota of my world would transform. I was happy exactly the way everything was, only now I was rich."

"Did you scream and yell?" Gretch asked. Zamira was wide-eyed. Sean held himself even stiffer than usual, his only animation an engrossed expression. Come to think of it, his little brother had never heard the details before.

"No," Trick said. "Which is one of the hardest things I've ever done." He waved a hand. "Actually, not picking up the phone and calling Eve was harder. But I know her; she'd have pre-spent the money before I got off shift. She wanted our lives to change. Desperately. I needed to strategize how to tell her. I checked the state rules—I had sixty days to claim it. So when my shift ended, I opened a personal savings account. I figured if I used a bunch of hypotheticals, I could get her around to my way of thinking. *Then* I'd tell her."

Only that had blown up in his face. The hypotheticals had reminded her of all she did not have, and the sixty-day deadline came in a flash. Illinois didn't keep winners' names anonymous, so when he'd gone to claim the jackpot, his semi-famous "lucky firefighter" status had fed the flames of this ultimate-luck news like a blowtorch. Trick grimaced. "She found out before I manned up and told her. I'll admit, it looked like I was trying to hide the winnings, which I swear I wasn't."

Man, the accusations... Besides being incensed that he'd concealed the news, Eve had immediately demanded luxuries they didn't need, just as he'd predicted. New cars, a bigger house, quitting his job and getting a risk-free, nine-to-five replacement. *Everything* in that other vision he'd viscerally rejected. He'd never put his foot down before, but this time the idea of him surrendering to her whims had been a nonstarter.

"She grew suspicious I'd take off with the funds. Me."

He shook his head. "Leave the only woman I've ever loved."

His gaze drifted back to his mug. A new and vicious Eve had emerged. She loathed not being in charge. Despised being thwarted. Refused to listen to reason. Yet at the same time, she'd clung to him in paranoia. He'd gone up to the attic to get the Christmas decorations and all the suitcases were gone. Another time, when they were out of shampoo, he'd crossed to the girls' bathroom and found Eve scrolling through the texts on his cellphone. "It was a confusing time."

"Did you take it out of the savings account and share?" Gretch asked.

He pried his attention from the beer and glanced at all three of them. "No," he said quietly, owning his share of the demise of their marriage. "It became the principle of the thing." Their fights grew in pettiness. Savagery. How many nights had he spent on the sofa wishing he'd never won the damn money? Wishing he'd signed the whole check over to charity the day he'd claimed it.

"Hindsight, huh?" he said, hoisting his mug. "People say money doesn't buy happiness, and I'm a walking poster boy. All it does is harden you, you know? We took stands, dug ditches, and brought on a war." But he sure hadn't seen this coming.

"Why don't you just give her the money, then?" Sean asked. "If you don't want it."

"I wanted it for my daughters." Trick folded his arms. "Three months ago, Eve finally agreed we should set up a trust for them, and things between us immediately stabilized. What I didn't know until today is that's when these bogus ER visits began. Like you said, maybe she's trying to get at the money without needing my signature."

Sean turned to Zamira. "Are you with his lawyer?"

Trick's heart seized. "No," he answered shortly,

before she could open her mouth. "Aw, hell." Why keep it from Sean, from anyone in his family anymore? "Zamira is my court-ordered supervisor. It's the only way I can see my kids. Eve's also accused me of sexually abusing them."

The baldness of the remark shut something down in Zamira. Or reminded her of her role in his girls' lives. She shifted in the booth and clasped her purse again.

Sean nodded, seemingly unsurprised. God knew what he was thinking about all this. The guy might be short on expressing himself, but, like an iceberg, a whole lot of deep shit went on below the surface. "I'd be happy to help anyway I can."

"Me too," Gretch said solemnly.

Against all probability, Trick waited for Zamira to chime in her support. She adopted a page from Sean's playbook and fiddled with her utensils.

"And you should probably have your lawyer schedule a doctor to examine the girls as soon as possible," Gretch said.

Trick went rigid. "This sickness is between my wife and me. I'll never put my girls through needless trauma just to prove my innocence."

Zamira's fidgeting stopped so suddenly that his attention swung to her. "It's part of the court proceedings," she said softly. "I'm sorry, I thought you knew. You, Eve, and your lawyers no longer have power or say over the process."

"*What* process?"

"The law requires a mandatory in-depth physical examination any time there's a sexual abuse charge on a minor."

Trick stared at her sympathetic expression, the whooshing heartbeat in his ears drowning out all sound. Somewhere inside, a dam broke, releasing a repressed fury that flooded every cell. In Eve's greed to control the lottery money, she'd torched bridges and laid waste to all aspects of their marriage, but this went too goddamn far. Trick stood abruptly, unable to utter a sound, and stalked out of the restaurant. Fuck the restraining order.

CHAPTER FOURTEEN

Eve ushered the bickering girls inside and dumped the heavy nylon grocery sacks on the kitchen counter. "Go upstairs and get in the bath," she said wearily. "Grandma and Grandpa will be here in a few minutes."

"I call the back of the tub," Amy shouted, racing to the stairs.

"Mo–om," Tina whined above the thundering footsteps.

"Bath, Tina."

"But she *always* gets the—"

"Tina! I just took you out for pizza, and this is how you repay me?"

"It's not fair!" Tina's little fists clenched. "Just because she's older, she gets *everything*." She stomped up the stairs sobbing.

"It's the back of the fucking *tub*," Eve whispered fiercely, sagging against the counter. This was all Trick's fault. All she'd ever asked for was a husband who pulled his weight, and now her burden was worse. "Fuckity fuck, fuck." These last five days at the shelter had been an eye-opening experience. Trick had spent most of their marriage working, but at least he'd spelled her with these hooligans. Seriously, how did single mothers do it? Was she crazy to take this on?

The ancient pipes knocked overhead as the water went on, and shrill voices still argued, but at least the girls were on task. Eve sighed and grabbed the closest grocery bag.

"I could kill you."

She gasped, whirling around. Trick stood in the dark threshold of the laundry room, arms crossed, torso rigid with fury. "Your bogus charges mean Tina and Amy have to go through mandatory vaginal exams," he growled. "So you can be proven *wrong*. You get that, right? The needless violation you're putting them through?"

Her heart pounded. How had he gotten in? The locks had been changed yesterday. "I'm not responsible for that, Trick. This is all on you." She pointed to the door. "You have two seconds to leave." Damning her breathy voice, she cleared her throat roughly. "I swear to God I'll call the cops."

They both glanced at the far counter where she'd dropped her purse. Where the top of her cellphone poked from the outer pocket. He'd reach it long before she would. She bristled. "Who cares? Mom and Dad will be here any minute. You are so fucked."

"Why are you doing this?" he asked in a deadly soft voice. "Is the money so important you'd ruin the girls' lives?"

Her lip curled. "Yeah, that's it." She turned her back and reached for the bag. "Gimme the millions, and I'll go quietly." She slapped the box of cereal onto the counter, then the animal crackers, keeping track of his reflection in the window. He shifted his weight, which brought his face out of the shadows. Anger and exhaustion etched deep lines. He looked even worse than this morning, when he'd flipped out in court. Well, too damn bad. Everything was one hundred percent his fault. Including *her* anger and exhaustion. "Just go, Trick." She tossed the variety pack of chips on the counter. "We have nothing left to say to each other."

"How can we possibly have nothing left to say," he said, striding over, "when we haven't said anything?"

She spun around, summoning her chilliest voice. "Stay away from me."

He didn't speak. Didn't even meet her gaze. Instead, he scooped up the cookies and chips and transferred them to the pantry. Came back for the cereal and put it in the cupboard. The stoic martyr. Still voted "least likely to lose his cool" at high school reunions. God, how like him!

She unloaded the second bag even more violently.

"Why'd you blow off the visitation today? Because I took Blaze?"

She headed for the refrigerator before her face gave her away. "Try: because I forgot?" She yanked open the door. His broad palm shut it with the same force. Chills raced down her spine. She'd forgotten how silently he moved. How fast. His closeness, his body heat were right *there*, pricking her.

He effortlessly whirled her around. "Bullshit, you forgot." His eyes spat fire, his mouth pressed into a sullen line. How she used to love getting him riled up to see this look. To see how she could affect him.

She was so over his face. So ready to start a new life!

"You owe me an explanation, Eve."

She shrugged. She owed him nothing. Let him stand there and talk. Mom and Dad would witness him violating the restraining order, and he'd be locked up. She glanced at the hand gripping her shoulder and arched a brow. He let go like he'd been burned. Fast learner—she'd give him that. "That supervisor rescheduled for tomorrow at three," she said. "Okay?"

"*Okay?* Nothing's okay," he spat. "Accusing me of sexual abuse? Are you *insane?*"

"Sucks to lose power, huh?"

"Pow—" He exhaled harshly. "Look if you wanted a divorce, why didn't you just ask for one?"

"All right." She flipped a hand in the air. "I want a divorce. And alimony. Full custody. Child support. *You* not coming anywhere near me. And..." She paused as other ruthless strategies Cyprian had laid out bubbled to the surface. No need to tip their hand yet. "Other stuff."

He looked at her like she had two heads. His prolonged pause meant the wheels were spinning, though. He was trying to gain the upper hand.

"There's a sequence to this, Eve. We've never even gone to marriage counseling. How about we talk this out in front of a professional and save ourselves the lawyer fees?"

And there it was: quintessential Trick. The instant focus on saving money. The belittling tone like she was unintelligent. Things always had to be his way. And his way meant after one marriage counseling visit, he'd convince her they didn't need to pay someone to *communicate*, and life would go right back to *normal*. Her being the perfect mother, the adoring wife, and living a shell of a life. Forget about *her* wants and needs.

"Why pay for counseling when I only have one line to utter: you're a failure as a husband." She flicked a finger between them. "We're done here."

He slammed a palm against the refrigerator, tipping it. Eve swallowed dust as it banged back into place. He was as close to the edge as she'd ever pushed, and that was saying something. Where were her parents?

Trick's powerful shoulders sagged. "I didn't want the lottery to change us, Eve. Is that so bad?"

Like they hadn't fought about this enough. "What sanctimonious bullshit." She pushed him, and he staggered back. "The fact is, Trick, you're a cheapskate who hates *any* change." She waved an arm wildly about her. "Look at our lives. This shitty old starter home. The ancient appliances. Hell, we still drive our high school cars!"

He clawed a hand through his hair. "There's nothing wrong with the house," he yelled. "And the cars and appliances all work. And when they break"—his voice grew thunderous—"I fix them! What's so wrong with being grateful for what you have?"

"Daddy!" came dual squeals from upstairs, followed by water splashing, scrambling feet, and more squabbling.

"We're millionaires, Trick, living like blue-collar nobodies. For no reason!"

"You'd never fit in with the North Shore set, honey—"

"Don't you honey me. It's my money too."

"It's the girls' money."

Footsteps thundered down the stairs, and Trick held up his palm. Of course! God forbid they argue in front of the girls. Within seconds, Amy and Tina sped around the corner, damp bodies in saggy towels. They leaped, squealing, into his widespread arms.

"Hello, Tiger! Hello, Munchkin!" He swung them off their feet in a bear hug. "Daddy missed you so much."

"We went to a hotel that looked like a house," Tina said in her outdoor voice. "Only for mommies and kids. Mommy let us take off school and everything."

Amy placed both hands on his cheeks and twisted his face her way. "I can't wait for the dance! Did you ask for the day off like you promised?"

The euphoria in his deep blue eyes crystalized to ice as he met Eve's gaze. She smothered a smile. The dance was against the new court order. *I have all the control, you bastard.*

"I'll give you anything you want," he said between still-smooshed lips. The girls giggled. "Anything," he repeated. "Just stop the visitation ruse."

Power swelled in her chest. The tables had finally turned. "My attorney assures me I'll end up with everything, Trick, so negotiating isn't on the table. Guess your luck finally ran out."

"I'm not negotiating. Listen to my words. You don't need a lawyer. I'll give you *everything* for the girls."

"Really? Two minutes ago, it was me you were trying to keep."

He removed Amy's fingers. "If it's an either–or option," he said, enunciating each word, "I'll take the girls."

"Yay, we're going with Daddy," Tina shouted, raising her arms in victory.

Eve's vision narrowed, the edges tinted red. How dare he... And her girls, looking this delighted to stay with him?

She ground her teeth. It wasn't enough that her parents would be here any minute to catch him. There he stood, so self-assured that he'd *still* walk away with his life unscathed. That he could charm his way into getting everything he wanted. "Lucky Trick," who'd never experienced anything rotten in life. She'd had a hand in enabling that expectation. He'd never appreciated how much she did to make his life so easy. Keeping a perfect house on a tight budget, raising these hellacious daughters, knocking herself out volunteering at school events, flirting with any CFD superior who might have a hand in promoting Trick... And year after year, he just assumed his life was *lucky*. God, how she despised that word. "Put the girls down and get out."

Tina dropped her arms, confused and watchful. Trick's lips parted in a tense smile, his mounting fury obvious as he kissed each girl. "Make me," he said in a false friendly voice. "Make me stop hugging my two best girls in the whole world."

Eve scrambled to her purse and whipped out her cellphone. A few taps gave her a live video feed. She pointed the camera at him. "Get your hands off them and get out."

"Mommy's so silly." He blew a raspberry on Tina's bare shoulder, then cocked his head at Eve, the smile slipping. "That's not a weapon, hon."

"Isn't it? We're live on Facebook. Hello, everybody, meet my husband, Lieutenant Trick Quinn of Chicago Fire Station One-twenty-six, who has a restraining order to stay away. Yes, folks, this is my kitchen. He's also sexually assaulted his daughters and isn't allowed near them without court-ordered supervision. And yet look...at...this." She focused on her half-naked girls with their sagging towels draped over Trick's arms. Tina waved uncertainly.

"You're filming our daughters half-nude."

"I'm showing the world that my soon-to-be-ex *still* won't keep his hands off them."

He was so royally screwed. His darkening expression meant he realized just how much.

A frozen second passed. She could almost see the wheels spinning again as he tried to figure a way out of this. His gaze dropped in defeat. Wordlessly, he set the girls down, their loose towels showing partially bare butts. *Perfect!*

"Will you read us a bedtime story and do the kissie

monster, Daddy?" Tina asked. The lens caught his wince. Eve smirked in triumph.

"I gotta go, Munchkin."

Eve held the phone steady as he kissed the tops of the girls' heads and straightened. His posture was rigid, his face menacingly flushed now. Without a glance her way, he turned toward the door.

"Stay the hell away from us," she called to his retreating back. "Contact my lawyer if you have anything else to say." Once the door shut, she stopped the video feed, her breathing fast and uneven. Adrenalin pumped so forcefully that she trembled; the parting shot was probably blurry.

Damn. She should have preplanned an injury to show her live feed. The phone chirped and buzzed like it was alive. Dozens of likes and shares as it went viral! If only she'd known he was in the house. If only she'd started filming the second she saw him, had caught the way he almost pushed the refrigerator through the drywall.

Were live feeds admissible in court?

"Why did you make Daddy leave?" Tina wailed.

Eve palmed the vibrating device. "Get back upstairs and finish your bath." She used *that* tone and gave them her harshest glare. They wordlessly obeyed her for once. A grin spread. This was what total control felt like.

Headlights arced around the walls as a car drove up the short driveway. She parted the lace curtain. Her parents were climbing out of their Lexus. *Finally.* If only they'd been here a few moments ago... *Wait. What if...*

Eve whirled around and scurried to the pantry. She'd seen something once, in a movie. Never thought she'd have the guts to do it, but it'd get her skeptical parents behind her once and for all.

CHAPTER FIFTEEN

"That's an extraordinary request, Zamira," Andy said with a frown.

She clasped her slick palms in front of her. "Yes, but under the circumstances, I think it would show the father in a more natural setting. And he did pay for a wasted hour yesterday." Her stomach churned. Once again, she was hugely overstepping boundaries, but on the other hand, Patrick had come to her aid yesterday with Mr. Henderson. The least she could do was go to bat for him in this instance.

"Isn't this the firefighter who's plastered all over the *Tribune* this morning?"

Zamira nodded reluctantly. At *Suhoor*, the pre-fast meal before dawn, she'd glimpsed Patrick's sooty face on the front page of Babi's paper and almost choked on her tea. The handsome, smiling image of him was the setup: a trustworthy firefighter and loving family man with reams of accomplishments and medals listed in the caption. The dichotomy of the lengthy article listing the abuse allegations was ghastly. The newspaper's invitation to view Eve's Facebook video linked to their website was nails in a coffin. Once Zamira had reached work she'd watched the video. Several times.

Evidently, after leaving them so abruptly, Patrick must've gone straight there, but what idiot up on abuse charges forced his way back into his house? On the other hand, Eve had never sounded frightened or timid on the feed, nor had the daughters appeared uncomfortable. After all her years at the center, Zamira knew the body language to look for in sexually abused children. The dead eyes, stiff demeanor, overall reluctance to be held in the offender's arms, the pleading looks at their mother to save them... No. These boisterous, joyful girls had acted just the opposite. But without her trained perspective, how many thousands of viewers this morning had judged him guilty?

Though she hadn't totally made up her mind on the allegations, the injustice of a one-sided slant had lit a fire under Zamira. If his kids were outdoorsy, like Patrick had said, then conducting today's evaluation in the park leveled the playing field. Either the hour-long video in a natural setting would help solidify his innocence, or—if the kids did display fear—she'd capture documented proof.

"Well." Andy scanned the room absently. "It's highly unorthodox..."

"You know I am all about following procedures," Zamira said emphatically. "And I've never asked for leeway before."

He conceded her points with a nod. "All right. Just this once, though."

"Of course. Thank you so much, Andy." The response was too enthusiastic—Andy's brows furrowed again. Zamira excused herself and hurried back to her office.

Her first client would be here momentarily, and she

had a crushingly full Tuesday ahead. She grabbed the phone. In front of her, Patrick Quinn's file lay open to the page where he'd handwritten his cell number. She dialed with trembling fingers. It took all her courage not to hang up on the first ring. For goodness's sake, she was his court provider, not some giggly teenager. But try as she might, she hadn't gotten him out of her head since the restaurant last night. He'd made her *feel*. From the giddy horror of staring up at his face and hair-raising thrill of calling him Patrick, to the shock of his abrupt departure.

Second ring. How had he not known about the gynecological exam? The look on his face, like his world was coming to an end... Even that could be interpreted both ways: devastation over the experience his daughters would go through, or because the exam would provide damning evidence against him. But the daughters' joy in their father's arms...

Third ring. She traced his signature. Who to believe in this murky marriage? He had to be partially guilty at least, because even with four million dollars at stake, what woman would do such a thing to her own daughters?

But *how* was he guilty?

Patrick picked up on the fourth ring, his voice groggy and deep. Zamira's heart stalled as she glanced at the time on her computer screen. Eight twenty. A blush rose to her hairline.

"Hello?" he repeated, even gruffer.

Her heart pulsed to a start so abruptly that it hurt her chest. "Patrick? This is Zamira Bey. I'm sorry, did I wake you?"

"Huh." The sound of movement and a guttural grunt. "I must have finally fallen asleep. I know I was awake to greet the dawn."

The rasp of a palm scratching whiskers. She

squirmed in her chair, picturing him seated at the edge of the bed, those broad shoulders hunched, his thick hair a mess. Was he wearing pajamas or... Last night's dreams of him roared back in vivid detail. When she cupped a palm around her hot cheek, the cool silk of her hijab was like a bucket of ice water. Enough with the haram thinking! She had a job to do.

"Yes, well, I didn't know if you'd received my voicemail yesterday and didn't want to discuss it in front of Gretch and your brother. Your children's mother agreed to reschedule her day so you could see your daughters at three o'clock. If you're available."

The pause took so long that she repeated his name. Maybe he'd fallen back to sleep.

"Sorry," he said. The word came out stiff and formal. "Yes, I got the voicemail. That was considerate of her. Three o'clock is fine."

She smoothed the page in front of her, then repositioned the vase of daisies she'd brought in this morning. "I spoke to my boss about how you weren't evaluated with your daughters yesterday, and he's agreed to allow today's session to be conducted outside if you'd prefer. There's a park three blocks down, and you'd mentioned your girls like being outdoors." Was she blathering? Her sentences sounded long and breathless. She plunged on. "Once in a while, we make an exception and schedule a supervisory visit there, never an evaluation, but, well, we'd like to offer it to you. If you want to meet us there, I'll text you the address."

Another long pause. No way could he have fallen asleep to this asinine blurt-fest. "Patrick?"

He cleared his throat. "You'd film me interacting with my kids in *public*?"

"We can make it look like any family who videos their kids at play."

More silence. She tuned in to his breath, strong and even over the line. Goosebumps scattered along her arms. Finally, he said, "I guess that'll work."

Zamira slumped weakly in her chair. "I'll have your girls go through our sporting equipment and bring whatever appeals to them."

"Thank you for going the extra mile, Zamira." His voice was warm now and, well, like those intimate moments in romance movies.

"It's no problem," she said, retracing his signature. The second her brain registered the movement, she slapped the file shut, sending up a prayer for forgiveness. "See you this afternoon."

"I knew it was a lucky sign running into you at that restaurant."

She shook her head at her moony reflection in the computer screen. This was a hundred percent her fault. Because she was conflicted, she was sending him inconsistent messages. Why couldn't she follow rules around this case? Time to start acting professional. "Last night was a fluke," she said crisply. "And today's meeting in the park is a courtesy. I am not your advocate, Patrick, and I cannot be your friend."

"I UNDERSTAND," Trick said, and he did. He'd pushed every boundary Zamira had last night. "See you this afternoon." He hung up and rubbed his gritty eyes, groaning at the jackhammering inside his skull. *Note to self: alcohol is not your coping skill.*

Thank God the vibrating phone had woken him. He had too much to do to sleep off a hangover. He turned the ringer back on. The missed calls icon registered over two dozen messages. The only ones he recognized were Pop,

Jace, and his new lawyer, Morgan McNally, who'd also texted: *CALL ME ASAP!* Trick's queasy gut flip-flopped as he called. *Please, God, don't let this be about the restraining order.* Eve had him over a barrel with that live feed.

McNally answered on the first ring. "What were you thinking?"

Great. Trick closed his eyes, which set off a bout of dizziness. *Enough with the self-pity.* He rose from the bed. "I wasn't thinking, Morgan. I found out the girls will have to go to a gynecologist, and I lost it."

"I just got off the phone with Cyprian. Eve told him to pursue contempt of court charges for breaching the protection order."

No surprise there. Trick swallowed sour saliva. "What am I looking at?"

"Depends on Judge Price. It's a misdemeanor, so you could face a slap on the wrist, a fine, or jail time. You shouldn't have gone over there, Trick."

"I know. But I've gotta prevent that doctor's appointment." Trick scraped a palm along his whiskers. "Maybe Pop has connections with Judge Price."

"You sound like you just woke up."

"Yeah. I barely sleep anymore."

An exasperated sigh. "Last night's incident and your charges are plastered on the front page of the *Tribune*. It's an ugly article, Trick. Your time to call in favors has passed."

"Shit." That explained Pop's early morning call. Because of Trick's cowardice, his parents had found out in the worst way possible. He sank back onto the bed. And now that the press knew, this nightmare life was going to remain in the glaring spotlight, to be picked apart until the bitter end. Everyone would believe Eve. His only defense was chanting, "I never beat her, I never molested them." And no one, himself included, ever believed the big, burly guy on TV calling his bitty wife a liar. His gut churned.

"I'll get to work cleaning up the mess from this end," Morgan said, "but you have to lie low. Go to work, go back to your friend's place, eat, sleep. Do not go anywhere else. Do not engage with the media, no matter what. Got it?"

"Yep. Thanks." Trick hung up and scrubbed his face, groaning. He should call his parents next, but not without a clearer head. He staggered to the bathroom, then followed the tempting aroma to the kitchen, wincing at the brilliant shaft of sunlight streaming through the patio door. Blaze chased two black squirrels up an elm, barking in frustration. He seemed no worse for wear after the choke-chain incident.

Pete sat with his bare feet resting on the round table, reading the *Tribune*. Slightly odorous dishes were piled on counters and sinks, and the garbage can overflowed onto the linoleum. Everything about this scene would have sent Eve into a screaming fit. "How has Blaze not caught fleas from this pigsty?" Trick asked mildly.

Pete glanced up. "Wow. You look like shit."

"Shots at O'Malley's till they closed."

An expression flickered across his friend's face. "You're not a drinker, Quinn."

Not since way before Amy was born. Trick had given it up year one into trying to conceive. Embraced yoga and meditation instead for a pleasurable altered mental status. These last few days, though, the monkeys racing around his head at all hours made meditation a nonstarter. At least alcohol had given him an hour of oblivion.

"Brace yourself." Pete refolded the paper and tossed it onto the placemat. A black-and-white photo of a younger Trick, sooty and wearing a shit-eating grin, took up a giant section of the front page. The bold headline was a guaranteed eye-catcher: *CFD Hero Accused of Pedophilia.*

Trick scraped his whiskers again. "How bad is it?"

"They list the charges, mention your breakdown in court, and describe Eve's live feed. Apparently, it went viral, which is how they picked up the story. Cap and your dad had no comment."

Pop. Trick sighed raggedly. The one man he'd tried to emulate since he was old enough to sit up. "I can't cope with this fallout."

"That's because you keep trying to absorb the chaos like a tranquil yogi. Get angry. Take action." Pete's advice was almost identical to Jace's last night. What was with that? Look where it had gotten him? Contempt of court charges and a *Tribune* article. Besides, the emotion was a waste of time and not healthy for one's soul.

Trick headed for his clean mug in the dish drainer. "There has to be another way. Anger only reinforces Eve's charges." He popped in a coffee pod as Sean's advice popped into his head. "I'm gonna talk to some of Eve's friends this morning. See if anyone can pony up info on her."

Pete peered at him skeptically. No one ever had anything negative to say about Eve. She was sunny, sassy, and popular, had been since grade school. No one saw the nasty side, the countless times she'd reinforced Trick's belief that he fell way short as a husband. "You think I'm a lunatic to go looking for dirt on someone so perfect."

"Nope. Wondering if you want company."

Gratefulness clogged Trick's throat. Pete coveted his days off. But maybe he could get answers from some of Eve's besties, who'd no doubt react to Trick with pitchfork hostility. "Thanks, Pete. I'll owe you."

Pete's chair thudded on all four legs, and he sauntered out. Trick sipped coffee and scrolled to his parents'
number on his cellphone. It wasn't just Trick's reputation
that was being hauled through the mud. Pop's thirty-six-
year career, Jace's struggle to make special agent, and
maybe something in Sean's life at the restoration firm
were all going to take a beating as a result of the article.
At least Cage and Kevin were overseas, neck-deep in
fighting worthier battles.

Pop also answered on the first ring. "I assume you've
read the paper," Trick said. "I'm sorry I didn't have the
guts to tell you about the rest of Eve's charges."

A momentary silence. "It's time you told us the truth,
Patrick."

"I am, Pop. I swear to God. The charges are all lies."

A long silence. "Jeb paid us a visit last night. Long
after we were in bed. Scared your mother half to death."

Trick's queasy gut tightened. What was his father-in-
law doing at his parents' home? The four were more like
holiday acquaintances, their granddaughters being the
only thing they had in common. Worse, his father-in-law
was a shoot-now-ask-questions-later kind of guy. If he was
feeding into Eve's accusations, a huge element of danger
had just entered the arena. "What would he want with
you and Mom?" Trick asked in a cautious voice.

"You. He thought you were staying with us. He's so
hellbent on finding you that it took a while to convince
him we didn't know where you were."

"If he ever comes by again, tell him I'm at Pete's. I'm
not afraid of him, and I don't want you or Mom involved
any further."

"Why don't you stay with us for a while," Pop said
gravely, "until some of this blows over. You'll have a full
alibi each evening."

The idea was abhorrent, and not just because he'd be

a thirty-eight-year-old running home to Mommy and Daddy. *You'll have a full alibi.* Like he needed one? Or like they wanted to keep an eye on him? Trick tightened the grip on his mug. "I'll, uh, I'll think about it."

"At least come by for dinner tonight and explain yourself. You owe your mother that much."

Trick's face heated. This week was showing him all sorts of gutless facets he had hidden within. "I will. I gotta run."

"Be safe, Trick. Don't do anything stupid." Those were phrases Pop reserved for Jace, the hotheaded son. Trick's defensiveness prickled, but then again, everything he'd done recently had been the epitome of idiocy.

"Sure thing, Pop."

After Trick hung up, he plopped into the chair Pete had vacated and dropped his head in his hands. It was one thing to be in a sudden and vicious war with the only woman he'd ever loved. It was another when her lies began eating away at the love and support of his family. And now her family was positioning to declare war with his.

Someone was going to get hurt.

CHAPTER SIXTEEN

"Just tell me if Eve said anything," Trick said. "Any complaints about her marriage? Or me?"

Her personal trainer shook his head, shifting uncomfortably behind the gym's reception desk. "We don't discuss that kind of stuff during sessions. It's more like what Amy and Tina are doing, how they like school..." Drew was a reserved, silent type, like Sean. Surely he'd picked up something in the three years they'd worked together.

"Did she tell you I hurt her?" Trick asked.

Another shrug.

Trick gazed helplessly around the reception area. Beyond the glass partition, several dozen adults were single-mindedly pushing through their workouts. The clang of weights being racked and effortful grunts were backup vocals to the streaming hip-hop overhead.

"She's showed me bruises." Drew's tone was cautiously neutral. "That she didn't get from working out here."

Eve bruised if she leaned on a counter. Drew, as her trainer, had to know that. "Bruises? Where?"

"Her inner thighs, a couple on her upper arm... She had some around her mouth one time. Said it was Botox."

"Because it *was*." Trick wiped a palm across his mouth as he fought for patience. "She went to the ER on March third saying she'd fallen off a treadmill. Did you see the accident?"

"No. I was off that week."

"Is there security camera footage?"

"That's not something I can show you. Besides, I'm pretty sure March has been erased by now."

Still. It was worth mentioning to Morgan—maybe he could get a subpoena to view that day. "In the last month or so, has she changed in any way? Gotten quieter or complained more, maybe? Was something pissing her off?"

Drew nodded to a client heading out the door and then knocked softly on the counter, a gesture he'd done more and more frequently as the questions had become more intimate. "Hmm. Not really quiet or angry. If anything, she's been working out harder recently and seemed in happier spirits."

Trick absorbed the internal punch in the gut. That made sense if she'd been planning this all along and was expecting to get millions.

The phone rang, and Drew all but leaped for it, the relief painfully obvious on his face. "Excuse me."

Trick wandered to where the carpeted entrance met the interlocking black rubber tiles of the workout area, where a dozen or so men in sweaty tank tops were working the free weights. The ambiance was all wrong. The patrons ignored each other, even in passing. Give him outdoor air and a brutal workout with his crew. Or long stretches of blacktop with Blaze by his side.

A couple of the guys glanced at him curiously in the wall-length mirrors, and Trick eyed each one steadily in return. Was Sean right? Was there a guy on the side? Maybe one of these guys? Most were younger than him and Eve by a decade, but that didn't mean anything. The acronym MILF came from places like this, and Trick would have been the first to describe Eve as drop-dead gorgeous.

Drew hung up, and Trick returned, pasting on an easy-come-easy-go smile. Would the trainer rat out another client? He nodded to the workout area. "Should I talk to any of these guys?"

Drew shook his head. "Naw, they work out at the same time of day. I don't think they even know Eve. Guess you could come back tomorrow morning, see the crowd that works out during her time for yourself. Her training session is at ten."

Yeah, except for the small detail of staying a hundred yards away. "Can't. I'll be at the station then," Trick said. "How about the name of a gym member that's here around that time, though?"

Drew knocked on the counter, shrugged, and privacy-policy hedged. Eventually, Trick thanked him and stepped out into the sunny afternoon of a hellishly wasted day. Hopefully Pete was getting somewhere, though he'd have called or texted if he'd uncovered something.

Trick took out his phone just as it buzzed with an unrecognizable number. He let it go to voicemail and climbed in his pickup. The countless messages from unknown numbers had all been local and national press. National! He slammed the door and started the engine. Eve's video and the sensational story of a deco- rated firefighter living a secret life as a domestic monster were burning up the media. No doubt the morning news and women's talk shows were scrambling to get her to be a guest. The wall of public opinion and shaming was growing, and he had no clue how to battle the tsunami.

Trick grimaced and checked the time. *Finally!* He grunted with relief and scrolled through his texts until he reached Zamira's directions to the park. For the next hour at least, he could just be a dad.

If he ignored the video camera.

ZAMIRA GRABBED the folded tripod base for the video camera, and hurried to the entrance where Eve Quinn would pull up. She inhaled the fresh air, her heart filled with joy as she descended into an exquisite afternoon. The temperature was perfect, and the sky stretched a cloudless pastel blue. The rarity of a park visitation was like playing hooky from work, and she'd been on pins and needles since this morning's call, knowing she'd see Patrick again. Snippets of his fleeting grin, his dark blue eyes, and the way he'd called her beautiful had kept her giddy and distracted. Prayers for forgiveness and requests for common sense went unanswered; she was stuck with this haram obsession.

A Kia turned into the wide parking lot right on time, and Zamira waved. She had yet to meet Eve Quinn, with whom Gretch had established such a close relationship these last few months. Zamira grinned at the two young girls in the back seat as the car pulled alongside. "Hello," she said enthusiastically through the partially open windows. "Welcome. We have a fun hour planned."

Zamira opened the passenger door, and the older girl released her seatbelt and slid out of the car. "I'm Amy," she said, shaking hands solemnly. "Where's my dad?"

Zamira gestured toward the glass door where the beach bag and tripod were. "I'll take you right to him."

On the other side, Eve leaned in and unbuckled the other girl, named Tina, according to the paperwork. A doll on the video feed. "I'll be right here when you're through, honey," Eve said in a reassuring voice, and took off her sunglasses as she straightened. Zamira stifled a gasp. Eve's right eye was purple-blue and swollen shut. The restraining order had been issued on Friday. This wound was not four days old.

He did this. Horror flashed through Zamira, followed by nausea so overwhelming that she almost doubled over. It must have happened after he'd pretended to leave on Eve's video feed. To have harbored dreamy feelings for such a monster. To have continually ignored her upbringing and coveted a married man, an abuser, a demon. And then to have bent over backward for this evaluation... Zamira's stomach flip-flopped again at his cunning ability to trick people. Probably the reason for the dumb nickname.

Eve walked up with a pleasant smile, as if half her face wasn't painfully disfigured. "Hello. I'm Eve Quinn. I'm *so* sorry about yesterday's mix-up." She patted her daughter's shoulder. "This is Tina."

"How can you even drive like that?" Zamira blurted shrilly.

"Carefully." Eve emitted a self-conscious laugh. "But I know how important it is to the court that the girls interact with their dad. Amy, tie your shoe."

Zamira stared at Eve's beautiful, stoic face, at her toned, petite body. To her horror, tears welled for the woman. "You're really so brave," she whispered. "I—I'm a friend of Gretch's. I spoke with you on Sunday when she was unavailable."

"Oh. Yes." A guarded look came over Eve. "I should have made a connection at your pretty name."

"I only tell you because I know how hard and how long you've worked for your freedom."

Eve swallowed hard. "Please don't." She gestured at Zamira's eyes. "That's totally contagious for me, and if I start, I'll never stop."

"But...if there's anything I can do." Her abuse hotline persona jumped to the fore. "You need to change your locks *again*. You need to report this violation to the—"

Again the petite woman flipped a dismissive wrist. "I did both. You learn as you go, I guess. Like not forgetting to change the code for the garage door. Not asking one of your husband's buds to come change the locks in the first place. Who knew?" Again the stilted laugh. "My problem is I don't have any friends of my own anymore. And my husband is a hero in the community..." She trailed off, and her smile slipped as she stared at the passing traffic. "No one believes he's capable of the abuse I've suffered all these years."

Zamira nodded, still sick at Patrick Quinn's deception and her stupidity at crushing on someone so unworthy. At questioning a victim's account.

"The girls and I take it one day at a time. Right, sweetie?" Eve kissed the top of Tina's head.

"Right, Mommy," Tina parroted. At least the little girl seemed oblivious to her mom's injury and the conversation of abuse. Eve waved at Amy, who'd wandered over to the stairs and stood impatiently. "Look after your sister, honey," she called. "I'll meet you both right back here. Have fun with your father. Stay safe."

"Don't worry," Zamira assured her with steely determination. "They'll be perfectly safe with me."

———

As HIS GIRLS appeared a block away, regret surged

through Trick like a tidal wave. What was that phrase— you never knew what you had until it was gone? Day after day, he'd taken his perfect life for granted.

Thankfully, both girls looked unaffected by the parental tug of war. Amy gripped a soccer ball, her bouncing walk and slanting, overly large Cubs cap making him chuckle. Beside her, Tina chattered as she skipped, her hand in Zamira's.

Oddly, Zamira looked way different from the wide-eyed woman at the Thai restaurant last night. Or the slightly naughty image behind the warm voice that had woken him this morning. While his daughters hadn't spotted him yet, Zamira had and held steady eye contact, eyebrows knotted and lips...stern. Angry? His smile faltered. *Shit.* Of course she'd have read the paper and seen the social media feed.

Trick crossed his arms, grimly reaffirming to ace this visit, charm her with his fatherly skills, and press her to approve the father-daughter dance this Friday. Professionally, her opinion was too critical to his future. And in the twenty-four hours he'd known her, Zamira possessed an aura of empathic compassion that was off the charts. He'd looked forward to seeing her and the girls all day. There was no room for Eve and her stupid video in this hour.

He forced the grin and waved at the trio. The girls saw him, dashing away from Zamira. "C'mere, Tiger," he called. "Run faster, Munchkin!"

He caught them both in a bear hug, swinging them in a circle and smelling their kiddie shampoo and sweat from a day of running and playing. These hugs would be few and far between now, and probably only under the watchful eyes of the court. A wave of grief made him squeeze them harder than usual. How would he bear it? What could he do?

"Ow, Dad," Amy said, wriggling. "You're hurting us."

Whoops. That sure wouldn't look good in front of Zamira, who'd quickened her steps the second the girls had sped away from her. "Sorry, Ames." He released them and straightened. "Good to see you again, Zamira," he said. "I really appreciate this." It took a second to register the tripod and beach bag. "Here. Let me help."

"No need, Mr. Quinn." She breezed by him. "I'll set up over here."

Mr. Quinn? He frowned. She stopped twenty feet away at a park bench and set the equipment down with care.

"Daddy." Amy yanked his arm, and he cut his gaze back to his eldest daughter. "Why did my teacher tell me you weren't going to the dance?"

"When did she say that?"

"Today. At school. And the other kids whispered about me."

His breath shuddered out. "Whispered like how?"

"They say you aren't coming home."

"*What?*" Tina's lip quivered.

"I am, girls," he said hurriedly, crouching to their level. He gripped each girl's hand. "It's going to take a few days, you know, like sometimes when Daddy's busy at work? But I'm coming home, and"—he lowered his voice—"for *sure* I'm taking you to that dance, Amy, okay?" The girls nodded. "All right then, hugs all around, and let's get this soccer game going." Another bear hug, and Trick stood. Zamira was bent over the tripod, her body language still way too stiff.

"Come on, Dad," Amy shouted, kicking the soccer ball. "Tina, you be goalie."

"Wait." Trick faced the girls and shook off the weird feeling. "Tina's too little. We'll just kick the ball back and forth, okay?"

"That's boring." But Amy kicked it to him, and he gently tapped it toward Tina. The ball sailed past her and both girls chased it. He swung around. Zamira yanked one of the tripod legs, her mouth a firm line.

"Can I help?" he called. When she glanced up, the big brown eyes that had held so much compassion yesterday looked snappish. An impatient twitch in her shoulders sent him closer.

"There seems to be a screw missing. The video camera won't stay attached." She eased her hand away an inch, and the camera immediately flopped at a dangerous angle. She grabbed it again, huffing a breath.

Trick glanced around the park. His toolbox was in the pickup, but he'd parked at the other end, and he wasn't missing out on one minute of his precious hour. And the only other people in sight were an old man nodding off on a bench thirty yards away and a woman walking two Schnauzers even farther off. Some two hundred yards away, on the other side of the wrought-iron fence enclosing the park, a group of people were forming, posters and signs by their sides. Trick squinted but couldn't read the messages. He hadn't heard of a planned protest, but then again, he hadn't been on duty for days.

"Whatcha doin'?" Tina called as the girls came running up.

Trick turned from the milling crowd and ruffled her hair. "Camera trouble."

"Why are we on camera?"

How could he explain? "People want to see us play together." He eyed his older daughter, who'd definitely want more information, especially after the school whispers, and added hastily, "We're trying to find something we can wrap around the camera to keep it on this stand."

Amy plucked at his t-shirt. "Use this."

"Absolutely not." Zamira straightened like someone had rammed a pole down her spine. "I can just hold it."

"You can have my shirt, Daddy." Tina whipped her little t-shirt over her head. Trick would've burst out laughing at Zamira's scandalized expression of a six-year-old's bare chest if the weight of his court charges hadn't crushed the humor right out of him. "Put your shirt back on, honey," he said tonelessly, avoiding looking down at his daughter's nakedness. "We'll figure something else out."

Amy toed a tuft of grass. "Why can't Zamira use her scarf? That's the smartest choice, if you ask me."

"Never mind, everybody," Trick said hastily, avoiding whatever Zamira's reaction was to that suggestion. God, this was going to hell in a handbasket. He gestured to the bench beside them. "You're right, Zamira, sit right here and hold the camera. We'll stay well within your lens range, okay? Okay, girls?"

Everyone nodded, and Trick planted the girls in the right spots, then resumed the game.

Within minutes, Amy complained of boredom and Tina accused her older sister of not kicking the ball to her. "Girls," he called irritably. This wasn't just a fun game of soccer. This was a court-ordered evaluation of his parenting skills. A chance to show he could *never* sexually abuse his daughters. A video that would hopefully lead to an endorsement for partial custody. This soccer game was life or death.

"Amy, kick the ball to your sister, please." He folded his arms and waited. After screwing up her face and snorting in disgust, his eldest daughter complied.

He glanced at Zamira, who stared down at the camera. The sullen look on her face filled him with unease. It had to be last night's video feed, but damn, that she of all people couldn't see through Eve's lies.

Tina kicked him the ball, and he sideswiped it over to Amy. "Do it again. To Tina, honey."

Amy grumbled a few words under her breath and kicked hard. It went sailing past Tina, who scurried after it, calling, "I'll get it," in her high, eager voice. Trick's smile was half formed when he again caught sight of the crowd on the other side of the park, throngs of people now, with someone squawking, "Drive them out!" into a bullhorn. Huge anti-Sharia posters mingled with *Muslims Go Home* banners and American flags.

Shit. Trick pivoted back to Zamira, who'd been facing the rally all this time. By her worried expression, she'd caught on well before he had. "Do you want to leave?" he called.

She firmed her mouth and shook her head. "Just ignore them," she called back, but cast another wary glance over his shoulder.

"Damn it," he muttered, turning to his girls as Tina raced back. "Let's reposition, team," he said. "Let me stand over here." At least he could keep an eye on the demonstrators. The protest was growing, but only two cop cars were parked at a respectful distance, lights flashing.

"Here, Daddy." A breathless Tina kicked him the ball, which he tapped to Amy.

"Back to your sister, Ames."

"Come *on*, Daddy!"

"We don't have much time left."

Amy fisted her hands and screwed her mouth into a scowl, but at least adjusted her stance to send the ball to Tina. She reared her foot back and kicked so hard that her breath left her with an *oof*.

The ball sailed straight at Tina's face. "Ohhh" he breathed—*smack!*—"shit."

Trick raced over, almost beating his youngest's high-pitched howl after her momentary shock. He carried Tina to the bench as Amy dragged herself behind them, loudly and repeatedly reassuring everyone that she didn't mean to do it. Zamira slid to the far end, and he sat down, holding his baby tight.

"I know, Munchkin, I know. Lemme see," he said until Tina finally quieted and unclamped her hands. A bright red spot tattooed her cheek. He held her pointy chin and twisted her face left and right. "Hmmm. Doesn't look like we'll need to operate." He tilted his head. "Can you do this?" He exaggerated a silly smile, and she copied. "How about this?" He did the same with a frown. By the time he crossed his eyes and stuck out his tongue, both girls were giggling. The love and innocence surrounding him warmed his heart, such a contrast with the "Muslims go home!" chant from the crowd across the way. So far, his girls had paid no attention to the rally.

"Sorry, Tina," Amy said. "I'll stand right here, and you can kick the ball at me as hard as you want."

"Okay," his youngest piped up, fully mended and looking forward to the payback.

"Uh—no." Trick grinned at them, then over at Zamira, who was still bowed over the camera but barely seemed to be breathing. He glanced at the camera lens sparkling in the sunlight, recording all of this for court officials. *See this excellent job of parenting, folks?*

"Think of it this way," Amy said, helping Tina off his lap. "Now you look like Mom."

Trick's smile faltered. *"What?"*

"She got a black eye, Daddy, and now I do too!"

Comprehension dawned, and he slowly faced Zamira. This time when she raised her head, the accusation in her eyes was as damning as the judge's impending gavel strike. Dread coiled through him. "I didn't do it," he rasped.

"There are only forty minutes left, Mr. Quinn."

PATRICK LOOKED STUNNED, like she'd struck him. "You believe me, don't you?"

Zamira tightened her hold on the camera and nodded to his daughters a few feet away. "Please continue. Pretend I'm not here."

"I don't want to pretend that. I'm tired of pretending." He clawed a hand through his hair. "None of this is normal, and I want to know what happened to my wife!"

Everything about his words and actions seemed at odds with his circumstance. Unless, of course, he had a split personality and didn't know what his other half had done. Despite herself, Zamira rested the camera on her lap and met his stare. The only sounds were whistles, cowbells, and a mass of people yelling, "America first! Muslims go home!" *Ignore it.* They were far enough away, and she had a job to do.

"Girls," she said, maintaining eye contact with Patrick so he couldn't sway them with a look. "What happened to your mom's eye?"

"We don't know," Amy said, and little Tina nodded in agreement. "We were upstairs."

"But your daddy *did* come over last night."

He flushed as the girls confirmed it. When he *was* guilty, it was obvious. So how else could Eve have gotten that horrible injury? "Did you hear your mom talk to anyone else?" Zamira asked.

"Grammy and Grampy came over, and Mommy was crying." Tina pointed to her cheek. "And looked like me."

"Aw, honey." Patrick swept the little girl onto his lap again and smothered her pink cheek with kisses. Just as abruptly, he stopped and flushed again. "Sit right here,

Munchkin," he said in a stiff voice, easing her onto the bench beside him. These spontaneous gestures of affection that ended so abruptly and awkwardly didn't seem to faze Tina either way. In fact, she studied the video camera with interest.

"Can I hold it, Zamie?"

Zamira smiled at the nickname until she looked down and realized she'd been filming Patrick's crotch the last few minutes. Good gracious, how was she going to explain *this*? She jerked the camera into position as Patrick finished correcting his daughter.

"It's okay," Zamira said, cloaking herself in her professional demeanor once more. "It's an unusual name for American children."

Tina tilted her head. "Aren't you American?"

Zamira's gaze flicked to the protesters. The bullhorn chanting seemed to have grown louder, closer. Had they seen her? The only person in the surrounding park wearing a hijab? Her heart tripped wildly, like she'd just finished a sprint. She wiped her free palm, slick with perspiration, on her kaftan. "Yes," she said in a slightly breathless voice, "I'm American. I was born here, but my parents weren't."

"Muslims go home!"

It was definitely louder. *Insh'Allah. Please keep us safe.*

"Why are those people so angry, Daddy?" Amy asked, trying to bounce the ball on her right foot.

Patrick seemed at a loss for words. His stunned reaction at hearing of his wife's injury had yet to let up.

Zamira glanced from the protestors to the girls. "There were some bombs that went off around the city a few days ago, and these people are very angry."

"I'm angry too," Tina said, her darling blue eyes

widening. "Everyone knows you shouldn't hurt other people, right, Daddy?"

Patrick had turned to study the rally, large enough now that demonstrators spilled into the park in droves. Zamira glanced at her watch. Thirty-five more minutes.

"Watch this," Amy said, kicking the ball up in the air and trying to catch it on her foot. "Wait, let me try it again."

"Please." Zamira motioned to Patrick, trying to get his attention. "You're wasting your hour. The girls want to play."

He blinked, and with reflexes so quick the movement blurred, he snatched the wayward ball as it sailed toward them. "That's going to end up in someone's face again, Tiger." He rested the ball on his knee and turned back to Zamira. "We should go. This isn't safe for you."

"*Muslims go home!*"

"Why not, Daddy?"

He ignored Tina and motioned to the camera. "Turn that off. Let's get you back to the center."

Appreciation welled in Zamira's chest. She exhaled shakily and nodded. Patrick helped her gather the equipment, and they each took the hand of a girl. He set a brisk pace, and both girls jogged to keep up.

When they were out of the park and the noise was slightly less threatening, he slowed and turned to Zamira. "That man yesterday"—he jerked his head toward the crowd—"and those people. How do you deal with this?"

He'd seen how she'd behaved when Mr. Henderson had assaulted her, basically stood there helplessly, so she answered as if the *you* in question was her community. "Our imam publicly condemned the bombings immediately after they happened, and our mosque has raised thousands of dollars for the victims' families so far, but our efforts never get picked up by the media. The hardest part of this aftermath is the public perception that we're doing nothing. That we're condoning it." She paused then glanced back at the crowd. Her skin prickled at the hate on their faces, the fervor in the collective chant. "I can't blame their perception when they're only getting one-sided information."

They all crossed the street in silence. Even the girls were subdued. There was half an evaluation to go; her best intentions for a natural setting had gone to waste. There had to be some way to turn this visit around. Change the negative by looking at the positive... The easy interaction between father and daughters had been recorded, and the affection between all three was genuine and unforced. She'd uncovered more puzzle pieces in this enigmatic family by personally witnessing Eve's gruesome injury, her stoic response, and Patrick's profound shock. Zamira didn't know what it all meant yet, but it was valuable information. This was not a wasted eval.

Her stomach rumbled, giving her the perfect idea for the three of them. "You know what?" she said brightly. "There's an ice cream shop a couple of blocks up, if you'd like to finish the hour there."

"Yippee," Tina squealed, skipping by Zamira's side.

At the hesitation on Patrick's face, Amy yanked on his hand and whined, "Please, Daddy?"

"I don't know." He eyed the crowd over his shoulder, then scanned both sides of the street.

"You can't hide from it," Zamira said. "Or live your life avoiding public places out of fear."

"I'm not afraid for me," he replied, his gaze landing on her. His concern touched a place in her heart, as it had when he'd suggested they cut the evaluation short, and when he'd taken on Mr. Henderson. Patrick faced soul-crushing problems of his own, but his protective

instinct kept bounding to the forefront in their inter-
actions.

"Me neither." Zamira smiled her thanks. "I vote you
guys enjoy ice cream." Only a handful more hours until
she could break her fast at sundown.

He nodded once. "Ice cream it is," he said in his jovial
father's voice, and the girls erupted in gleeful cheers.
They continued past the center, their steps lighter, the
sisters chattering about what flavors they'd order. Using
their animated voices as cover, Patrick asked quietly,
"Would you be willing to ask my wife what happened to
her eye?"

Zamira inhaled sharply. "Absolutely not."

"Why not?"

"It's against company policy to get involved."

"Then why were you at the restaurant asking about
me and Eve?

Her face boiled with the heat of her blush. She had
zero response.

Patrick studied her in silence for an excruciatingly
long minute. "This is my life, Zamira," he finally said in
softly enunciated words. "She's taking everything I have.
I can't ask my family or friends to help, because she'll
never give them a truthful answer."

Zamira looked away before he could pick up on the
guilt that had grown too overwhelming to hide. *Insha'Allah!* She was the worst of hypocrites. Repeatedly
watching the video of him in the playroom, dreaming of
his embrace. The giddiness and care in choosing her
clothes this morning, specifically for this evaluation.
Then when he overstepped these ambiguous bounds, she
had the nerve to quote company policy to him.

She had once again wedged herself smack in the
middle of this very sick marriage the second she'd asked
the girls about Eve's black eye. And this time in Patrick's

presence had only ramped up her uncertainty. On the one hand, given his shock at Eve's injury, it seemed inconceivable that he was responsible. And his interactions with his daughters were darling, straightforward, and paternal. The girls displayed no fear in his presence, didn't freeze up when he touched them. But *someone* had given Eve that black eye. And Eve *had* escaped the house last week to get away from his abuse, after months of Gretch's intervention and encouragement.

The mystery of this particular family feud had already captured Zamira's curiosity to the point of career sabotage. No point denying that as soon as she returned to her office, she'd be calling Gretch to share all these details. It'd be beneficial to also have Eve's response to the black eye.

Zamira lifted her chin and turned back to Patrick. "Yes," she said, meeting his eyes boldly. "I'll ask her."

CHAPTER SEVENTEEN

Trick hugged and kissed the girls once more. "See you on Friday, Daddy," Amy said, as if the father-daughter dance was a given.

"You bet," he said, ignoring Zamira's startled frown. One battle at a time. And this one wouldn't be in front of Amy.

After a pregnant pause, Zamira motioned to her office. "Please wait in there. I'll be right back."

Trick watched the girls turn the corner, then walked in and dropped into the chair across from Zamira's neat desk. She had a picture frame of her family next to a thin vase with three daisies. Easy to pick out the parents, grandmother, and Zamira, who was next to her mother. In the center, with an arm wrapped around a young boy, a beautiful young woman stood, her lips parted mid-laugh—Zamira's sister? The woman's vivid spirit came across loud and clear. This was the sibling who lived large, excelled easily, and had loads of friends. Until this week, Trick would have bet money that was him in his family.

He replaced the frame and powered on his phone.

Seventy-four more missed calls. If the media ever found out he was bunking with Pete, he was fucked. He tapped the text icon.

One from Pete:

FYI: Stopped by the station and your father-in-law showed up looking for you. Cap took him in the office for 10 min, seemed to defuse the sitch. Didn't ask for details.

Trick swore softly, texting back a thumbs-up icon. Jeb wasn't physically intimidating, but he was as relentless as a junkyard dog, especially when it came to his daughter's happiness. Or, in this case, her black eye. Trick scrolled to his lawyer's number. No, he didn't need Morgan involved yet. He hit Jace's number instead.

"You should have told us about the sexual charges," Jace barked in lieu of a greeting. "Mom and Pop are beside themselves."

"I need your help."

Silence.

Trick glanced at his phone. The seconds were still tallying onscreen. "Jace?"

"Sorry," his brother said gruffly. "Still picking myself up off the floor."

"Great. My life's going down the toilet and you're making jokes."

There was a muffled sound like a half groan, half sigh. "Anything to help me stay awake. I can't remember the last time I slept in my own bed."

"The bombings?"

"The public doesn't believe our assurances that we found all the bombs, and the anti-Muslim vigilante incidents keep growing. It's a powder keg of hostility out there."

"I know." Trick slumped in the chair, propping his ankle on his knee. "I just left the park because of hundreds of protesters." *Why are they so angry, Daddy?*

Yeah, there were many people out there who'd lost someone in last week's terror attacks, people in a lot more anguish than he was. "Do you want me to call back?"

"No, I know why you called," Jace said in a sympathetic tone. "I don't know how anyone can help you, though. Going home was legal suicide. Good luck getting a fair trial."

Trick brushed a hand across his mouth. Who knew there were so many armchair lawyers out there? "It's gotten a whole lot worse. Eve has a black eye, which she *didn't* have when I left her at seven twenty last night." He filled in the details he'd gleaned from the girls, as well as the reason he'd gone home to confront Eve in the first place. "Her lies have gone too far. I need ideas on how to stop her, because I'm going to protect my girls, no matter what."

"Forget my advice from yesterday and stay out of it," Jace said briskly. "You'll just make matters worse. I'll pay her a visit after I get off work."

"No," Trick blurted. "It'll look like the Quinn family is harassing her. Besides, Jeb's on a tear—he showed up at Pop's last night and the station this afternoon."

"I hope he's there to take note that I'm *not* harassing Eve. I'm FBI, asking questions. I'll make it seem like the full weight of the Bureau is involved, especially if he keeps gunning for revenge."

Trick paused to consider it. Maybe that would work. Jeb definitely respected the alphabet soup agencies. That still left the problem of Eve getting injured and blaming Trick. Who was really hurting her, and why was she covering for the actual abuser? "I know Illinois isn't a one-party consent state, but federally, could the FBI record her without her knowledge?"

"Not without court approval. But I'll think of something. I doubt I'll get to this today, but the second this city is secure, it'll be my top priority."

It was strange, being the underdog. Stranger still going to Jace, of all people, for help. Strangest of all: Jace volunteering, what with his plate so full of terrorist activity. "Guess it's my turn to fall on the floor."

"I know you, Trick. There are two huge reasons these charges can't be true."

Trick straightened in the chair. Meaning he could've been giving these reasons out to people the last few days instead of the lame *I didn't do it*? "Two?"

"First, ever since eighth grade, you've been so gaga over her it's made me nauseous. The constant touching, the baby talk, the happily ever after..."

Shoulda known not to set him up. Trick jiggled his knee impatiently. "You can get to the point anytime."

"You love her *too* much," Jace said. "That's not an act. And second, you're incapable of hurting her. You may be this city's firefighter calendar boy, but inside, you're a weeny pacifist. So even though the woman in question happens to be half your size, nobody fucks with my kid brother."

Trick inwardly sighed. Jace's help always came with a supersized side of attitude. "I'm ten months younger than you."

"Yeah, but maturity- and experience-wise, I'd gauge it more like ten years."

"Fuck off."

Jace chuckled. "Calling it like I see it. We may goof on Sean for being a nerd, but that guy excelled at the school of hard knocks and knows how to *cope*. Your lifetime of luck means you never learned that skill—"

Zamira walked in, and Trick abruptly signed off, his temper barely in check. The phone immediately vibrated, caller ID: CNN. He shut the damn thing off again. Under the circumstances, he was coping just fine.

She rounded the desk and sat. The hour outside had given her face a healthy glow, and the lavender hijab softly framed her flawless complexion. She wasn't an extrovert like her sister, though. Zamira's soul was quieter, deeper. The good girl, he'd bet. The sensitive one, who absorbed other people's feelings. What must it be like for someone so empathetic to deal with the growing blowback right now? Probably, on some level, all the hatred was comparable to the ugly attention he was receiving even though he was innocent.

He jerked a thumb in the direction of the park. "You okay?"

"It's always hard being blamed for something you didn't do," she said. "The lone wolf was a nationalist making a political point. His bombs had nothing to do with his Islamic faith."

"But what about that guy yesterday? The one who ripped your hijab off."

The color on her cheeks deepened. "I'd been his provider, but he took offense to me having perceived control over when he could see his kids. Even though he'd been reassigned, he still felt the need to humiliate me."

"He attacked you, Zamira. Why are you humiliated and not furious?"

"It's easier to internalize it." Her fingers fluttered to the silk covering her torso. "But both are negative emotions, and I try not to stay in such an unhappy space."

He started at the familiar sentiment. But this was her job. "Has a client ever done that to you before?"

She shrugged. "I've been reassigned because of preju-diced beliefs, but no, not physically attacked. I find most people who dislike Muslims only have the bravery to say so when they're in large groups or anonymous on social media."

That seemed accurate. Whenever Trick encountered stories about Islamophobia, there was not only a mob mentality behind it, but a desire to judge by a label. Everyone was a label these days. Republican, Democrat, gay, liberal, neo-Nazi... "May I ask you something personal?"

After a hesitation, she nodded, blushing.

"This is highly ignorant, okay? But I've always wondered." He inhaled deeply, trying to figure out an intelligent way to phrase the question. "Why are Muslim women so strict about wearing hijabs? Wouldn't your life be so much safer, like in the park just now, if you just blended in? Wait. Jeez"—he'd known it would come out boneheaded—"I mean... Can't you believe in your faith without displaying such an overt symbol of it?"

Her smile was patient, like she'd been asked this a million times before. "Before I answer, may I ask *you* a personal question?"

He nodded, shrugging.

"Are you religious?"

Trick shook his head. "I'm more of a holistic spiritualist; yoga, meditation, the study of chakras, Buddhism... I mean, I go to church on Christmas and Easter, but you wouldn't be wrong to call me a lapsed Catholic."

She pointed to his torso. "And yet you still wear that."

His fingers fumbled with the cool, hard metal before his brain registered the miniature cross Mom had given him after his first communion. He slipped it underneath the fabric where it belonged. "It's not the same."

Again that smile. "Oh, but it is, Patrick. It's an item you're not ashamed to wear, and it clearly delineates your faith from any others." She touched her hijab. "I'm proud of my beliefs and honor the Quran's instructions for modesty."

He nodded cautiously. "But in our culture..." He paused, because this definitely wasn't going to come out right either. "Guys focus on a woman's face. On her sexy lips"—he studiously avoided her plump ones opening in surprise—"or expressive eyes more than her hair, you know? If you're going for modesty, you're covering up the wrong part."

"Which is why some Muslimas wear *niqabs*, where only the eyes are visible, or *burqas*, where all is veiled. Only their family gets to see the real them." She flicked a hand past her face. "There's a lot of control in choosing fully veiled. Think how they aren't wolf-whistled or sexually harassed. They can wander anywhere without makeup and not care about blemishes. Make ugly faces at people they don't like..." She laughed, proving his point again about the Quran not covering up the most beautiful parts of her. "If it wasn't so hot inside there, I may have chosen the niqab life, too."

He let a pause go by. "That would be a great injustice for the rest of us."

Her long eyelashes descended again. He'd botched that, too. What he'd meant was without the normal distraction of hair color and style, her hijab became a spotlight that actually made him focus on the beauty of her face. Her smooth complexion and the remarkable almond shape of her eyes. And those lips, jeez...

It took a moment too long for her closed expression and the way she fidgeted with some files to register. *Oh, crap.* She must think he was coming onto her. His gut tightened. "I apologize—"

"If we could discuss your schedule."

It was like a two-by-four to the head. How had Eve

escaped his sole focus for even an instant? "What did my wife say?"

"She didn't answer me directly." Zamira's tone was bemused as she continued to rearrange files distractedly. "I said, 'Who did this to you?' And she said, 'It's being taken care of.'"

"Why didn't you press her?"

Zamira's gaze flew to his. "Because"—she gave an exasperated half laugh—"I shouldn't be in the middle of this."

The reality of her words struck him right in the solar plexus. Neither should Jace. Or Pop. Or Pete. On any normal day, their involvement would shame Trick. He never looked to others for help. Mostly because nothing in his life ever went wrong.

"She's definitely been battered, Patrick."

He caught the name change, and somehow, in all the shit that had rained down on him these past few days, this simple informality meant the world. His shoulders relaxed a fraction. "I was wrong to get you involved, Zamira. I don't know where else to turn."

She waved away the apology with a flip of her wrist and a tremulous smile. "That remark Sean made last night about gaining control of the trust. Why don't you just give it to her? She won't leave your girls penniless."

He bobbed his knee up and down. "That's the reason I broke the restraining order last night. If the money will get her to drop the lies so the girls don't have to be examined...if it gets me my girls back...then hell yes, she can have control over the trust and spend every last cent."

"You're saying she didn't accept it?"

He shook his head. Even with all the drinking and this morning's hangover, he'd had time to parse Eve's surprising disinterest. "Think about how it would look. She throws down a bunch of accusations, gets the courts involved, and then suddenly withdraws her complaints when she gets the trust turned over to her name? How would that look to her family and friends?"

"But why wouldn't she accept your offer if that's what she's been planning for months?"

"Maybe once you get courts and lawyers involved, once you're invited on news and talk shows, you're stuck playing your hand. Nobody's going to sympathize with a wife and mother who's doing this for four million dollars. So last night when I called her bluff, she doubled down." He spread his hands. "She got someone to punch her in the eye."

The mother of his girls, the woman he'd married, the girl he'd fallen in love with. Her sparkling laughter, so clear and effortless. The cute way her nose wrinkled when she was deep in thought. The perfect way she snuggled in his arms. When she loved, she loved so hard. He leaned his elbows on the desk. "All I care about is gone," he said in a hollow voice. "That stupid money."

Zamira's hands slid across the desk, stopping a millimeter from his arms. She eased back, blushing furiously. Her eyes had dilated to smooth black onyx, and he was helpless to look away. She did, fiddling with the vase of daisies until her professional expression returned. "I'm sorry you're going through this, Patrick."

Still he couldn't look away. He wanted to bask in the serenity emanating from her. Stare at each part of her to figure out what made her so beautiful. Though he couldn't detect any makeup, her cheekbones were high enough to cast a faint contrasting shadow of color beneath. Her mouth was tinted a natural rose, the full upper lip shaped in a distinctive Cupid's bow. Intelligence and humor shone in her eyes. It was a damn shame they could never just hang out as friends. "Thank you for all you did for us today, Zamira." *Damn.* He sat back in his chair to distance himself from the overly warm voice that had emerged.

Emotions raced across her face. "You're welcome," she stammered. "Let me know your available days, and I'll set up the next visit."

"There's the father-daughter dance on Friday."

"Yes." The word was said gravely, like she meant the opposite.

"The event is in a public place"—Zamira began shaking her head, but Trick pressed on—"in front of many witnesses."

"I'm sorry, Patrick. Today was a huge exception. The dance is way beyond the scope of our visitation agreement."

"Why?"

"Your case is brand new—"

"You saw how the three of us clicked out there today. Give me the benefit of the doubt."

"First of all, it would require scheduling another supervisor, because Friday night is the holy holiday celebrating the end of Ramadan. I won't be available." An expression flickered before smoothing into professional blankness. Almost like she didn't want to go to her celebration.

"Second," she continued, "it isn't just my evaluation that goes into the decision. There's the GAL, the guardian ad litem, who's got the most pull, and I'm not sure who's assigned to your case. And the child psychologist." As she flipped through the file, she asked absently, "Have the girls seen the psychologist?"

"I...I don't know. Eve would."

"Your GAL is Renata Jackson." The grimace that crossed Zamira's face wasn't a positive sign. "Plus, proper supervision would be too difficult in a crowded setting. Anything could happen."

"Anything like what?"

She shrugged. "You could abscond..."

He bowed his head so she wouldn't catch the impatience he could no longer hide. This was *Amy*. And a freaking elementary school dance. He blew out a breath and folded his hands in prayer. "Please, Zamira," he said with all the desperation in his soul. "I promised my daughter. We've looked forward to this for months. I have no intention of 'absconding' with her."

"I'd be happy to present your request to my supervisor and Renata, but don't get your hopes up. This would be unprecedented."

Trick clenched his jaw. This was what having no power felt like. No luck. Even if he could get Zamira to sign off on Friday, there were still the higher-ups. Even if the three she'd just listed agreed, they'd still need Eve's cooperation.

Which meant he wasn't going to that dance. Rage for Amy's disappointment coursed through him, lethal and all-consuming.

"Is your lawyer attempting to add your parents or brothers onto the supervisory list?"

"Wait, what?" Trick frowned. "People I know can become supervisors?"

"Well, it's more complicated than that. Your lawyer would submit a list of approved people to Eve's lawyer, and ultimately she has to agree the children will be safe in their company. Then the list gets submitted to court for approval. In this case, I doubt it can get done by Friday, but if Eve agreed to include family and friends and the court approves, then yes, supervision doesn't necessarily have to be in centers like this."

Trick squinted at her. Morgan's strategy was to get the supervision dismissed altogether—a noble goal, sure, but it would've been great to know that in the meantime, family and friends could supervise, and in their own homes. Maybe Morgan had already floated the idea by Cyprian and been shot down, so he hadn't mentioned it, given he was so focused on showing Trick his capabilities. It was worth a call. "Thanks for the intel," Trick murmured.

"So." Zamira reached for a pen. "Besides that evening, please name a backup day so I can arrange it with your children's mother."

"Any date I pick only gives her ammunition to blow off the appointment or show up with a black eye. Let *her* tell you the date. I'll rearrange heaven and earth to be here."

"Fine." Zamira jotted a note.

"But you'll still ask your supervisor, psychiatrist, and guardian about the dance?"

"As soon as you leave."

He spread his hands. "I have nowhere to be..."

She smiled. "I have another appointment, Patrick. I'll call you the second I get an answer."

"Of course." He stood up, holding out his hand. "I appreciate you going to bat for me."

She stood as well, eyeing his hand like it was a coiled snake.

"Oh," he said awkwardly. "Are you not allowed to shake hands?" Had he shaken her hand when they'd first met yesterday? That whole introduction was a bit of a blur.

"No." She pressed her right hand over her heart, like she was about to recite the Pledge of Allegiance. That's right, she'd done that when he'd handed over the paperwork.

"Then thank you again," he said sincerely.

She folded the palm to her belly. "I'll do my very best, Patrick."

"If I can ever buy you a cup of coffee or something, for all your help..." He let the sentence die at the look on her face.

"I'm sorry. For personal and professional reasons, I can never do that. Last night at the restaurant, in my culture, was, um—" She waved away the explanation. "Going out for coffee can't happen."

It's just drinking liquids together. Talking more about the subjects we discussed here. He nodded affably to defuse the awkwardness. She was right to shut him down. His life was in too much turmoil to explore an attraction, but clearly she'd picked up on his fascination with her when he should only consider her Zamira-the-supervisor. "I apologize if I overstepped some boundaries."

"I think we're both guilty of that, Patrick."

Yep, she'd caught on. He stuck his hands in his pockets. "Okay. Well, I'll, uh, wait on your call about Friday."

He made his way to the parking lot, turning on his cellphone. Another thirteen messages popped up with anonymous or media caller IDs. He deleted the voicemails and started the pickup. Kind of like how Zamira chose not to dwell in the negativity of prejudice, he had no intention of getting frustrated at the media harassment. His sole focus had to stay in two areas: stopping the gynecologist appointment, and going to that dance. Both were ditches he was willing to die in.

CHAPTER EIGHTEEN

H ow stupid and careless! Zamira stared out the passenger window, her face hot with humiliation. "I'm behind at work. That evaluation was due today." So her life had come to this: lying to her father. *Forgive me, Allah. Forgive me, Babi.*

Silence descended, dragging out the already slow rush-hour drive to Mosque Mohammed. Did he believe her? She gripped the still-warm pan of *umm Ali*, her family's offering for *Iftar*, the breaking of this evening's fast, even though they weren't attending. Her mind was weak from twelve hours without food and water, her heart heavy with the falsehood.

But there was no way she could confess the awful truth. Something about Patrick Quinn obsessed her enough that she'd scrutinized Monday's playroom video for hours last night, finally freezing the recording at the exact nanosecond he'd glanced at the two-way mirror. His gaze was so intense, the clarity of the footage on her laptop so lifelike, it was as if he were feet away, watching her boldly undress for bed.

Because of this wicked thrill, she'd tossed and turned

most of the night. Allah saw all. Even the erotic dreams of Patrick rescuing her in a myriad of settings where she wasn't quite hurt, but he still felt compelled to carry her close to his chest. Dreams where she freely called a married man, who may or may not have shamed his family name, *Trick*.

How unfortunate that this morning, when she'd returned upstairs from *Fajr* prayers, her exhaustion and the shock over the *Tribune* article made her forget the dark screen on her desk. His enlarged expression was right there, just waiting to be jostled to life, which her mother had discovered with the corner of the laundry basket.

"You told us you're forbidden to take case information like that out of the office," Babi finally said, glancing over.

"We're all so behind keeping up with our paperwork that the center takes a blind eye to bringing files home." That, at least, was the truth. Memory cards were another matter. "It won't happen again."

"Your mother was startled, to say the least."

"A thousand apologies to Allah and to you and Mami."

Her gaze strayed back out the window as she effortlessly conjured up the image that would have greeted her mother. Patrick's piercing blue eyes. The knotted brows and slight frown. Those dark whiskers covering his hard jaw like a savagely handsome Disney pirate.

"She said he looks dangerous and homeless," Babi said.

Yes, he did. "He's not." Zamira kept her tone light, like this whole conversation was no big deal. "When you called Fajr at dawn, I must have paused it at an awkward frame."

"You're being careful around such men?" The worry

in his tone fed her shame but also awoke the feminist outrage she tried so hard to hide from her family. At home she was sheltered and guarded, as if the world held only evil and treachery. In reality, especially at the center, she was fully capable of managing daily drama and highly trained to defuse heated situations. She could take care of herself. *Well...* Her fingers brushed her hijab as she recalled yesterday's unexpected attack. How the security guard had shown up way too late. Babi could never know that.

"Of course I'm careful," she said stubbornly. "This is a clinical setting, and these parents aren't violent as much as desperate to visit their children."

"Perhaps I should speak to your boss again," Babi said, taking the last left onto Wabash.

Zamira clenched the pan harder. No one else's father talked to Andy. "I am a trained social worker in a busy building that has alarms, lockdown doors, and security guards."

"And you wonder why we worry. Why couldn't you choose to be a secretary or teacher?"

"Babi, most offices and schools around the nation have taken such precautions, too. I have to live my life outside of your protection."

"But these protests around the city are only growing—"

"I'm nowhere near them." She closed her eyes in prayer as the second lie registered. These untruths were spilling out effortlessly now. What was wrong with her? "I mean, I know how to take care of myself."

"Perhaps I should speak to your boss," Babi repeated after a long moment.

Zamira bit her lip. This overprotectiveness had mushroomed out of control since Shadi's elopement.

Half a block from the mosque, the traffic slowed to a

crawl. Even from the cocoon of Babi's luxury car, the reason became ominously clear. A writhing mass of raised fists and anti-Muslim posters spilled into the street. Words shouted with palpable hatred into a bullhorn were drawing responding chants. Stoic cops in riot gear faced the fury on one side of metal barriers, but there were so many more demonstrators than cops. So much rage and hostility. The scene was a tinderbox. "This is what I'm trying to protect you from." Babi was barely audible over the din.

The same terror from the park returned, tightening Zamira's throat until it felt like someone was choking her. Her grip on the pan grew slippery. She *didn't* know how to take care of herself in the face of this much hate, her third lie of the evening. *Forgive me again, Allah.* If her father ever knew she was this fearful he'd never let her out of the house.

"Duck down," Babi ordered. "I don't want anyone making eye contact with you."

She complied, resting almost on top of the plastic wrap. Time slowed as the car crept forward. Goosebumps pebbled her skin as the ugly chants grew louder, now directly out her window. At any time one of those haters could spot mild-mannered Babi with his *taqiyah* on the crown of his head. Would they surge forward? Break the windows? Riot? Her pulse pattered like a rabbit's, her breath came in shallow gasps.

Finally, Babi turned left. The mosque parking lot. "Look at all the guards," Babi muttered, and Zamira slowly straightened. They passed dozens of uniformed security guards, several of whom carefully peered in the windows before waving them on. The parking lot, this close to Maghrib prayer, was filled like a stadium on game day. The gold-domed temple loomed before them, beauti- fully lit to welcome the dusk on this twenty-seventh day of Ramadan. Despite the terror of the last few minutes, Zamira cheered up immediately. Since childhood, this holy place had grounded her in serenity and acceptance. Ironic, since the community within was chillingly unreceptive to the Beys at the moment, and the protesters outside the mosque walls reviled the worshipers.

It took several minutes for Babi to find a parking spot, and more for them to walk past the rows of cars. Although the bullhorn and chants were less distinct this far from Wabash, Zamira hurried after her father's rapid pace. "We meet here in fifteen minutes," he said as he opened the door, then kissed her cheek.

Zamira nodded and stepped through the entrance for women and children, slipping off her sandals at the rack. The foyer glittered with twinkle lights for the month of this High Holiday. At the far end, women gathered around long tables covered in bright fabrics. They chatted quietly as they placed Ramadan treat boxes for the children in neat rows and covered other tables with platters of food, since it was almost sundown. Zamira waved to a few of the volunteers. One smiled uncertainly; another outright turned her back. The Beys' disgrace was also regarded with collective shame because most Muslims centered their lives around their mosque, so it became more like a small town where everyone knew each other, and got in each other's business. Shadi had always been the epitome of a devout Muslima, and hugely popular so her defection from here and elopement to a non-Muslim were viewed as personally injurious to each of these women who'd adored her. And although Zamira had grown accustomed to their collective rejection of the Beys, the individual condemnation and scorched-earth wrath still hurried her footsteps as she passed by the banquet tables.

Inside the enormous kitchen, the festive atmosphere

was tinged with underlying frenzy. Dozens of women bustled about, some wearing bright kaftan *abayas* with coordinating hijabs, others modestly covered in niqabs. Amid the laughter and calls of greetings, a steady stream of English melded comfortably with Arabic terms, the chatter ceaseless over the banging pots and chinks of dishes being stacked. Younger women plated delicious smelling stews and casseroles under older women's directions or mild scolding. Others spirited the platters out to the foyer.

Zamira blended into the familiar chaos, unwrapping the pan of umm Ali as she glanced about for an unused platter. Several of the elders noticed her and quieted or turned away, speaking under their breaths. Perspiration broke out on her brow. The Bey family had accepted the outrage for months, but it was time to ease back into their community. Babi was consulting with the imam now on how to successfully reenter the mosque activities. On whether the time was right to openly offer Zamira as a respectable marriage alternative to Faisal Abdul. Mami had made this sweet dessert for Iftar celebration. The Beys were trying, and yet Zamira stood, stiff and awkward, scanning the kitchen for one friendly face.

There. Gufran Menjarra, her mother's closest friend stood near the industrial sinks, a flurry of shimmering turquoise silks and jangling bangles. Zamira sent up a prayer of thanks. "*Khalti*," she called out, even though the older woman was not her aunt, and bravely scooted through the commotion. Seconds later, the dessert pan was whisked from her grip, and she was pulled into a jasmine-scented embrace.

"As-salāmuʿalaykum, my dear," Gufran said, and kissed both Zamira's cheeks.

"Waʿalaykumu as-salām." Zamira gestured to the pan. "Mother made this for Iftar."

"A thousand blessings upon her soul. Come, let's put it with the desserts over here." Gufran snatched a spatula from a drawer and nodded to a clean aluminum platter near Zamira. "Grab that," she said, then, in a louder voice, "and ignore these busybodies. May Allah, who knows best, forever freeze the expressions on their faces."

Zamira blushed at the gasps close by, her gaze trained steadfastly on the dessert. "I don't mind—"

"You must tell me everything. How is your job? Your mother talks of the homeless man on your computer."

"He's a firefighter, Khalti."

Gufran paused, blinked once, then raised the spatula dramatically. "Ah ha! The one they call lucky? I read the paper."

A canary-yellow niqab swirled into Zamira's personal space. "As-salāmuʿalaykum. Is your mother here too?" Above the face veil, Zeba Nahem's critical coal-black eyes regarded Zamira. Zeba was her mother's nemesis and hands down the likeliest purveyor of most of the hateful gossip that had reached the Bey family.

"Waʿalaykumu as-salām," Zamira responded with stilted deference. "No, only Babi is here. Probably waiting for me in the foyer... I should go."

"Your father should be ashamed to show his face in such a holy—"

Gufran reared back, screeching, "Stop!" which effectively halted all conversation in the great kitchen. She grabbed Zamira's arm and wrenched her bodily behind her. "It is you who should be ashamed, Zeba Nahem. 'They ask ye about *wine* and gambling. Say, "In them is great sin and yet, some benefit for people. But their *sin is greater* than their benefit..."'" Quran two–two-nineteen."

Zeba's face veil trembled as her breath huffed out. "I know not of what you speak, Gufran, and you would be wise not to spout accusations you cannot know."

"Oh, I know, my friend, as does our all-seeing Allah. One more word about Shadi, or any of the Beys, and I will climb our tallest minaret and broadcast my proof of your drinking to the far corners of this mosque."

Zeba spun away, muttering darkly as she stalked from the kitchen. All around them, mouths gaped, and Zamira absorbed the horror of the heavy silence with stinging eyes and a burning face. A few of the women shrank back as Gufran waved her hand in the air. "The food, ladies, the food!"

She clutched Zamira's wrist and led her back to the foyer. "Here we can talk quietly. It's too much, those silly cows." She smoothed a thumb along Zamira's cheekbone and fluffed her hijab. "So beautiful. Allah willing, you will be a welcome bride for Faisal Abdul. He will be your family's redeemer, and soon your father will once again take his seat at council."

The crippling burden that had first descended onto Zamira's shoulders when Babi read Shadi's goodbye note to the family grew even heavier. If only she could tell someone of her fears, ask what would happen if she, also, were to reject the marriage arrangement and wait for love.

She swallowed hard and opened her mouth. *No.* This entire visit was her answer. Her community would never accept the Beys back into their fold. Besides, it was too haram to say something so rebellious aloud, even to someone as dear as Khalti. "And if Allah isn't willing?" she asked softly. "Or Faisal isn't forgiving? If the marriage does not come about, what becomes of our family?"

"That is not what you fear," Gufran said with a knowing smile as she squeezed Zamira's hand. "You are more nervous it *will* come about. All of us had qualms in our own marriage arrangements, but your parents know best. Let Allah guide the way. You are the good daughter; you will follow your parents' wishes."

After more kisses, hugs, and *salams* for the family, Gufran returned to the kitchen, head high, back straight. Oh, to have her confidence. Or a speck of Shadi's daredevil determination to live life on her own terms. Compared to her, Zamira had been born a spineless wimp. She helped disadvantaged women and children attain their dreams of independence while ignoring her own.

She sighed, glancing about the noisy foyer, but her father was not among the growing groups circling the food-laden tables and counting the last minutes to Iftar. For the first time in her life, she passed the stunning *Qibla* wall with its gold-and-azure geometric motif without pausing in awe. She glided through the crowd like a ghost, heart still beating rapidly from the encounter in the kitchen and the off chance of running across Faisal Abdul out here. The need to reach her entrance became an overwhelming panic. No sign of him, but men were now pouring in from their side of the prayer room.

Zamira slipped on her shoes without making further eye contact with anyone, which shamed her. Shadi would have stood boldly in the center of the crowd, initiating conversations that were so friendly the community snubbing could never have lasted.

Zamira hurried out into the dusk, where Babi waited, his back to her as he studied the protesters. "Babi?"

He turned, his face cheerful despite the ugly chants. "We'll go out the back way," he said. "The imam is making everyone do this tonight."

Once the car was clear of the city, he reached over and squeezed her hand. "Allah be praised," he said joyfully. "The imam has insisted our family attend Eid-al-Fitr Friday evening. He is ready to formally approve joining you with Faisal Abdul. We shall say extra prayers during *Isha* for Allah's blessing on your engagement."

"Yes, Babi." She managed a smile. "Allah be praised." Zamira gulped back rising tears. Eid-al-Fitr was the huge celebration at the end of the holy month of Ramadan, three days away. The imam's personal invitation was a great honor. She bowed her head over her clasped hands. The engagement was for the best. Her family's name and dignity would be restored. Her father would be back on the head council. And her ambiguous identities as a Muslima and a modern American woman would finally be resolved. Yes, it was for the best.

So why did one side of her mentally bring forth Patrick's forceful expression on her computer as a reminder of all the passion she'd give up by remaining the good daughter? Accuse her of a cowardice that stung like a thousand bees?

Tears welled beneath her eyelids. What should she do? Save the family honor, or save herself from the revulsion of tying herself to this man?

CHAPTER NINETEEN

"Your mother and I brought you up better than this."
Pop rested his forearms on either side of his
untouched bowl of pasta. "A wife and children are God's
gift to protect and cherish. I thought you of all my sons
were mature enough to handle the heavy responsibility."

Trick clapped a hand on his chest. "I am—"

"But why hide the charges from us?" Mom
interrupted.

"I was afraid you'd believe Eve's accusations. Besides,
it was your birthday dinner, Mom. I'm still pissed Sean
blabbed about the restraining order." He turned back to
Pop. "I *am* sorry you both discovered it through the
newspaper."

Pop acknowledged the apology with a short nod, but
his gaze drilled into Trick like he was combing for lies.
Despite a pulse of heat that left a prickling film of sweat,
Trick maintained the eye contact. This was *Pop*, his hero,
whom he'd emulated since his earliest memories. Trick
searched in vain for a flicker of compassion. How could
Pop, of all people, believe Eve's word over his?

"I get the feeling you aren't convinced." Trick meant

for his voice to come out assertive, but it was a pathetic croak. Pop's mouth firmed into a bloodless line, his shoulders taut like a bull staring down a red flag. The fact that he didn't answer spoke volumes.

"Why would she accuse you?" Mom asked worriedly. "You two are perfect for each other."

"Were." Trick forked his pasta. "I've run myself ragged wondering what changed. It has to be the money. But why put the girls through a gynecological exam that's going to come back clean? Why harm *them*? Why stop feeding Blaze?" Why, after four days, didn't he have the answers?

Pop scowled. As much horror as he'd seen in his career, nothing got under his skin more than when children and animals were harmed. The question remained: did he think the culprit was Eve or Trick? "Maybe you should look into some counseling, Patrick," he said.

Question answered. "I didn't do anything." The repetition was killing him. He shoveled in the pasta to clog any further words.

"Maybe if you said sorry," Mom suggested gently.

The food turned into a lump that took two swallows to clear. There it was again, this disconnect. Like after explaining the whole story, his parents still weren't grasping the depths of Eve's scheming. Yes, the revelation must be a shock to them and he should be patient. He, too, was just waking up from the massive manipulation he'd fallen for all these years. Her insisting he'd misheard, he was confused, he was lying, and that *she* was the one wronged had scrambled his inner compass, made him think not only was he always wrong but that he was losing his mind. His role as the spouse who screwed up, the well-meaning goof who once again owed Eve an apology, was well known in both families. How could he get them to recognize her lies and manipulation too?

"I'm not sorry, Mom," he said, his light tone at odds with his screamingly tense muscles. "Because I didn't do anything."

"But Eve is so good to you and the girls—"

"I thought so too," he interrupted. "But I'm beginning to think happily married was an act for her."

Pop scoffed. "You mean her steadfast support behind everything you've accomplished?" That particular sarcastic tone was usually reserved for Cage, the numskull son.

"Pop—"

Pop threw his napkin on the table. "She didn't just wake up one day and randomly decide to accuse you of—"

"Connor," Mom said. "Let's listen with an open mind. This is Trick."

"Yes," Pop burst out, "that's what's so infuriating." He jabbed his finger at Trick. "You're receiving the Medal of Honor in two weeks, and yet you're mired in accusations that shame your unit, your profession, and your family. This is a disgrace."

Trick clenched the napkin in his lap. "I. Am. Innocent."

Mom patted Trick's free hand, her expression begging for patience. "When can *we* see the girls?"

Trick collected his breath and his temper. "I imagine any time. In fact, as soon as possible. I'm worried about their welfare."

Again, Pop shook his head, and silence descended except for the ancient cuckoo clock on the living room mantel and a trio of kids out front playing a loud game of tag. The prickling sweat was itchy, but Trick kept still, his posture military-erect. Life as he knew it had changed here too.

Being born ten months after hotheaded Jace meant

Trick's easygoing nature had garnered Pop's positive attention and the coveted label "the good one." No more. Probably not ever again. Trick bowed his head, shame washing through him. If he'd have been a better husband, a better son—a better human—the outcome would have been different. Now everyone would suffer. And the worst part? Trick hadn't figured out a damn thing he could *do* about it. He was figuratively castrated.

"What about work?" Pop asked without looking at him.

"Technically, I report back tomorrow on admin duties."

"Technically?" The tone was sharp, like Trick was using semantics to trick them.

Another deep breath. "I violated the restraining order, which is a misdemeanor charge. Morgan is scheduling a meeting with Judge Price." Morgan had also nixed listing family as additional supervisors until this matter was sorted out. It wasn't even worth bringing up, he'd said, since the other side was too antagonized to discuss the arrangement. Trick scrubbed a hand over his face.

Pop stared at his pasta, his jaw set. The clock ticked. Outside, a horn beeped at the shrieking children. "I'll see if I have any pull with the judge," Pop finally said.

Mom audibly exhaled, and for the first time in what felt like days, Trick sent gratitude to the universe. "I appreciate it, Pop. Anything you can do to get me out of admin duty too?" he added in a joking voice.

"I think it's wise that you stay behind the scenes awhile."

I don't. He could fight fire in his sleep. Read the color, volume, and viscosity of smoke like a psychic. He needed the distraction, the adrenalin, the camaraderie of the fire ground. "If I could just explain—"

"So help me God, Patrick, you've done enough

explaining, and still, the Quinn name is being dragged through the mud."

His father's flushed, tight face was only marginally harder to stomach than his mother's pleading one. Her eyes were still damp from the tears she'd shed when Trick had first arrived. "I'm sorry to put you both through this," he said, heartsick for their pain and embarrassment. And that Pop didn't think better of him. When would he ever measure up? "I ought to go."

"Yes," Pop said dismissively as he picked up his fork. "Perhaps you should."

"Connor!"

"The boy said it himself." He pierced Trick with a vicious look as he stabbed his pasta. "Come back when you have this resolved, and not a moment before."

CHAPTER TWENTY

Trick rolled into the parking lot of Station 126 an hour before his shift, ready to take on the day. Enough with the kicked-dog mentality. By God, today his misfortunes would turn around. The positive vibes coming from the cosmos hummed through his blood.

He breathed in giddy joy as he killed the engine. His luck was back. It viscerally embraced him as he stepped from the vehicle, cloaked him like a cape as he headed up the short driveway.

He whistled as he stuffed his backpack into his locker. There was something to be said about having a purpose. After days of being off routine, the ordinariness of this morning was a godsend. The five a.m. jog with Blaze down empty streets where the world felt like his, a bracing shower, and now grabbing breakfast with the gang about to clock out—Pete's suggestion.

"Lieu," Joey said from behind. "I hear you're on admin."

"Yeah." Trick turned with a grin. At least he was here. "It'll give me a chance to catch up on some paper-work." He clapped Joey's shoulder. "How's it going?"

"This place is fucked. Ramirez called in. Marie went into labor three weeks early."

Trick instantly sobered. Given the city budget cuts last year, they were already operating with a skeletal staff. Pete had even come in yesterday afternoon to help out. "Jim still on grand jury duty?"

"Yup."

Trick ran potential subs through his mind as he followed Joey into the large kitchen, where the team was raucously laughing around the long table. The laughter halted in degrees, first the row facing the doorway, then the ones turning in their seats. Except for Danny, this crew hadn't been here for Trick's brief explanation Monday night, so anything they'd have heard would've come from the perpetually overblown station gossip, the *Tribune*, and last night's national evening news broadcasts, all of which had shown at least part of Eve's video. Morgan had warned that today she'd be featured on several talk shows and the world would see her black eye. This would be an uphill climb, but the positive possibilities were limitless as long as he stayed calm and centered.

"Morning," he said, as if it were any other day, and strode to the coffee pot near where Pete stood flipping pancakes. "You got this, bro."

Trick nodded, filled his mug, and took a seat beside Collin at the uncomfortably quiet table. Several of the crew didn't meet his gaze; a few did, then distracted themselves moving their own mugs or fiddling with silverware. A sudden queasiness entered Trick's gut. What if his squad reacted like Pop? What if the trust and respect had already imploded before he'd even opened his mouth? He tightened his grip on the piping-hot ceramic. *No.* Today was the day he regained control of his life. He waited for the fidgeting to die down.

"Here's the skinny," he said, eyeing each member. He

recapped the basics of Eve's machinations, ending, "But I swear on all that is holy that I've never hurt my family." He held up the mug like he was toasting something. "Any questions?"

"Yeah," Danny said, "can I have Saturday off? I've got—"

"Oh, for fuck's sake, Danny," Joey snarled. "We all know the Whole Foods produce manager asked you out." He turned to Trick. "What can we do to help you through this, man?"

Immediately murmurs went around the table, everyone echoing support. As they ate, Trick fielded questions, though most he couldn't answer because the crew was focused on motive, and he was one big question mark there himself. Danny squirmed in his seat more than usual, a sure sign he was still focused on getting Saturday off. It was time to deal with the massive staff shortage.

Trick held up a hand, and the crew quieted. "Ramirez is on baby watch, so can anyone pull a double?"

As one, the crew hesitated. Who could blame them? They'd done triples and quadruples just last week. "No pressure," he said amiably. Today was his lucky day. *Release your intentions to the universe and miracles will manifest.* He'd find someone. "Danny, give me an hour to clear you for Saturday." He rose and headed to his office to call Monday's personnel, still on their forty-eight off. Cheryl never said no to anything Trick asked of her. Hank was always amenable for extra hours. So was Sam, but why ruin a good day?

When the station's tones sounded ten minutes later, Trick hadn't found anyone. He rose, grunting in exasperation at the timing. This team had less than half an hour to go before clock-out, and the new shift hadn't arrived. He headed into the garage where the men were donning their gear. Talk about budget cuts... That was a whole lot of overtime about to ride out the door. Trick nodded to Pete, the acting lieutenant assigned for this shift. "I got this."

His friend quirked a brow. "Cap said you—"

"I know, but it's his day off, and we're way over on OT thanks to last week. Go on home. I'll take the assignment."

Pete waved him off. "Your kit is in your locker." True, but they were the same height and near the same weight. Pete's turnout gear, laid out in front of the shotgun seat, would fit.

Following his line of sight, Pete murmured, "That's *real* bad luck."

And hugely against regs.

Collin climbed in and started the engine. Amid the vibration of the rumble, the stink of exhaust, and the red swirling lights, a reckless desire inside Trick roared to life. He was going on this call. "It's me and you. What can be unlucky about wearing your kit?"

"You're the boss." Pete handed over the station's radio, the official signal for command change. Trick hastily pulled on his friend's gear and hopped aboard the engine, smiling broadly. The apparatus coasted down the short driveway and hung a left, sirens shrieking toward the residential fire.

The usual adrenalin rush pulsing through Trick mingled with the euphoria of working a call with his crew. It was a godsend how not one of them had questioned his innocence. The universe was already providing miracles.

They pulled up to 1205 South Sixty-fifth Street, a one-story patio home where an elderly woman in a house robe stood on the front stoop, waving frantically. Thick gray smoke roiled from the back of the home. "C side,"

Trick called. "Short hose. Joey takes Grams." They jumped down and went into their well-practiced routine. Joey jogged over to the old lady to gather facts, and Trick headed around back. The smoke was too dense to see in the windows, but by the smell of burning bacon, he'd reached the kitchen.

"Yo," Joey said over the comm. "Mrs. Greenspan says her husband was cooking breakfast. Fire ignited in the fry pan and he keeled over. Still inside. Over."

"Roger. Going in."

"Got your six, Lieu," Joey said. "Be right there."

Mask in place, Trick tried the back door. Locked. He spent a few precious seconds grabbing air instead of the ax on his utility belt. *Oh right.* Everything was opposite because Pete was a leftie. Trick snatched the ax, awkwardly transferred hands, and swung. The flimsy door gave way, and smoke streamed out, stealing his vision. He kicked the panel inward, crouched into a crab walk, and swept his arm in an arc on the ground before him. Arc right, step, arc left. A breeze streaming in partially cleared the dense smoke, revealing the scene. Nobody in the vicinity. The stove was blackened, the pan half melted on an active burner. The fire had raced up curtains that now hung in half-disintegrated black tatters. Flames danced along the top of the window frame. He turned off the burner just as a hand clamped on to his shoulder. Joey.

A stream of water blasted past Trick's shoulder, toward the top of the sill. Within thirty seconds, the fire was contained and the visual began rapidly clearing. Trick entered the hallway. "Vic sighted," he called.

The old man lay in a fetal position, situated as if he'd collapsed on the way to the front door. It would've been seven feet to the back door, yet the vic had chosen the long way out. No accounting for panic. May have been trying to reach the missus.

Trick hooked his arms under the old man and carried him around front, where firefighters scattered to provide a pathway.

Chad and Marie, the squad's paramedic and EMT, had their equipment open and readied. The instant the vic was laid on the grass, Chad took his pulse and Marie readied an IV and epinephrine bolus. Trick and Joey tore off their masks and knelt to assist.

"V-fib," Chad stated, flipping switches on the defibrillator. "Lieu, start chest compressions." Trick ripped open the buttons of the vic's pajama top, leaned forward, and began CPR. Joey grabbed the respirator mask from the EMS paraphernalia stacked neatly nearby; Marie inserted the needle; Chad scrambled to apply the cardiac leads attached to the defibrillator; Joey covered the vic's nostrils and mouth with the high-flow O2 mask; Trick continued rhythmic chest compressions. The four worked like a well-oiled machine as the defib charged.

"Clear!"

They paused and leaned back as the shock was transmitted. The vic bounced loose-limbed on the ground. Trick and Joey waited, panting and wiping sweat from their faces as Chad registered the vitals. He shook his head. "Going again. Four hundred watts. Marie, up the CCs."

As the four worked, Trick recited his usual mantra. The man would be all right. Without the slightest doubt he would recover. Trick waited calmly as the paddles were applied again. *Come on back from the light, mister. This isn't your time.* The body bounced in violent electroshock.

Chad read the vic's vitals and swore under his breath. All three glanced at Trick with frowns. "It'll work out," he panted. He'd had some close ones before. It wasn't worth the resignation he saw in the others' eyes. The vics always came back. "Charge 'em up again." Trick leaned forward to resume applying CPR.

"It's no use, LT," Chad said. "He's flatlined."

Mrs. Greenspan was being held back by Danny, but her cries of "George, don't go!" reached an ear-piercing shrill. Trick stared at the old man, picking up on the mantra. *George, don't go.* All his life, Trick had relied on his luck. The foul ball he'd caught in his lace while doing a spontaneous backflip over the boundary wall to win state. The IED that his tank ran over that ended up being a dud. The unlikely promotion to lieutenant over Sam nine years ago. The lottery. And not a single casualty on the job.

This was old George's lucky day; he wasn't going anywhere. Chest compressions might still work, but Trick was too winded. "Joey," he gasped, "take over for me."

All three remained motionless, shoulders slumped.

"The rhythm is a-systolic. Discontinue CPR." Chad glanced at his watch. "I'm calling it at eight-oh-two." Marie began withdrawing the needle from the old man's veins.

But what if CPR could still work? Trick stared at the vic's gray face, the reddened chest, the barrel of ribs he'd compressed so hard he'd probably broken some. *George, don't go. Come on, universe, give him back!*

Joey laid a firm hand on his arm, like he could read Trick's scrambling thoughts. "It's over, Lieu. Your streak finally ran out."

Trick shuddered an exhale and slowly took in the scene around him. Chad and Marie gathering equipment. Joey still watching him, his face troubled. Mrs. Greenspan standing feet away, sobbing in Danny's arms.

Behind her, the engine lights swirled and the crew mingled, helmets off in respect. The shell-shocked looks on their faces held a tinge of accusation. Like Trick had come back to work too soon. Like all this evil mojo Eve had doused him in had poisoned everything he touched, too.

All the times he'd avoided change so this lifelong streak would hold. As inexplicable as an athlete wearing the exact same thing and eating the identical food, to ensure the same miraculous win. It was a fragile superstition, one Trick had instinctively followed since he was a kid, with perfect results. Only now, life *had* changed, drastically, through no fault of his own, and the mystical part of him he'd cherished but never understood had disappeared. Just like he'd always feared.

Trick took off his coat and gently placed it over the body, the irrefutable proof. *George, don't go,* echoed in his head as he stood on trembling legs. Mrs. Greenspan wept louder. He stopped beside Danny and squeezed the old woman's hand. "I'm sorry," he mumbled, suddenly as weary as the seventy-two-hour shift last week. He'd never had to face a grieving spouse. He had no idea what to say. How to get past this. "I'm sorry," he repeated faintly.

Trick turned and trudged toward the engine. Blinding camera lights flashed amid the whir of clicks, freezing his steps. How had he missed the massive sight and sound of all this media?

"Lieutenant! Did you sexually abuse your children?"

"Lieutenant! Why did you give your wife that black eye?"

"Do you deserve the Medal of Honor next week, lieutenant?"

"Lieutenant! Have you registered as a sex offender?"

"Hey, lieutenant! Did that man just *die*?"

CHAPTER TWENTY-ONE

E ve tore through the toys, throw pillows, and sofa cushions, looking for the ringing cellphone. There! She tapped the green button a nanosecond before it went to voicemail. "Hello?"

"It's Gretch. Got a moment?"

Eve grimaced. The living room was a mess. The overflowing clothes hamper of whites waited on the bottom stair. The house smelled of Amy's hamster; God knew how long it'd been since the newspapers and straw had been cleaned. So no, she didn't have a moment, but Gretch was an important witness. "Yes." Eve plopped onto the disarrayed cushions with an exhausted sigh. "Of course."

"Did you get my voicemails? I've been so worried."

Good. Eve channeled her victim persona with a higher, softer tone. "I did. I'm sorry I haven't called back. All my energy is going toward the mountain of legal problems and helping my daughters return to normal lives."

"But what about you? I saw you on the talk show. Your eye!"

Eve let silence fill the line. "I'll be okay," she said at

last, mastering the tone of the meek martyr, but already her patience was thinning. "You said in the messages that you had a question for me?"

"Yeah. Last week when you were in the shelter, we watched updates on the news about Amy's little buds being taken hostage. Why didn't you tell me you knew one of them?"

Eve swept the hair off her forehead, frowning. "Because I didn't. I think Amy told us she knew them."

"But they showed a picture of Sean. He's your brother-in-law, right?"

Eve froze. Had Gretch just asked why she'd shoplifted the Reckless Red lipstick in her purse, she could not have been more dumbfounded. "How did *you* know?"

"Because when I'm not at the abuse hotline, I work with him. Your last name was in the papers, and I made the connection."

The fear slashing through Eve almost made her drop the phone. Who could possibly have factored in this bizarre coincidence? "Wow," she said lightly, "small world." Her synapses fired a mile a minute. What was behind this call? How much did Gretch know about the rest of Sean's family? About Trick?

"My question is," Gretch said, "why didn't you react when Sean's photo was on the TV screen?"

Eve gave a small laugh, which came out hollow because her jaw seemed locked. The urge to hang up gripped her so strongly that her finger hovered over the red *End* before she regained control. That would make matters so much worse. "I, um, honestly don't recall paying very much attention that night," she said. "I was still so traumatized by my escape. By your rescuing me the day before, remember?"

"I do." The voice on the other end was chilly-polite.

"And the picture was a really bad rendition of your cute brother-in-law, but still, they mentioned him by name, and that he was in danger. You had *zero* reaction."

The room suddenly seemed sweltering. Eve swiped her forehead. "As I told you, I may have physically been in front of the television, but I don't recall any part of that news segment." A phone rang on the other end. "Do you need to get that?" she asked hopefully.

"It'll go to the office voicemail."

Eve bit her fingernail. She had bigger worries than Gretch and this silly question, but Gretch was paramount in the long-term scheme of things. All the phone calls between them at the abuse hotline, the gut-wrenching confessions and tears in the women's shelter... Those divulged details had to come out in court. Eve couldn't afford to screw up this friendship now. "I'm really embarrassed," she said in a timid voice, "at how much of that stay was a blur. Except for your comfort and understanding, and how much of yourself you shared. I think about our talks a lot."

Someone must have come into Gretch's office, because a male spoke in the background. It sounded an awful lot like Sean, come to think of it, and Gretch muttered, "In a minute." What were the fucking odds they worked together? Eve mentally screeched obscenities.

"Eve, I have to go. I'll talk to you later."

"I'm here and cherishing every day thanks to you." Yikes. Did that sound sarcastic? Eve hung up and threw the phone into the laundry basket. "Fuckity fuck, fuck!"

To have her whole future blow up because of her dweeb brother-in-law? No. Freaking. Way! Eve pounded her thighs with trembling fists then blew out a ragged breath. She'd have to tread carefully with Gretch. The woman had been around the block. If Eve screwed up again, like not reacting to dumbass Sean, who'd always taken good care of himself anyway—damn, she should have said that—she'd lose a valuable witness.

She swiped her damp forehead again and checked her watch. The girls would be home in an hour. There was time to throw in the wash and straighten this pigsty. What the hell was wrong with her, anyway?

Somehow in all the gains she'd made to crush Trick's life, her own was sliding downhill. Where was the multi-tasker who could effortlessly keep every part of her and her family's lives organized? It was like her high stamina had ended the moment she'd entered that shelter last week. Like she suddenly *was* a ditsy victim instead of it being an act.

And now Gretch was sniffing around where she didn't belong...

Eve shook her head. "Get it the fuck together," she muttered, picking up the laundry basket. The first thing she'd do when the money freed up was hire a house-keeper. Maybe a personal chef. Definitely a nanny.

Bending over, she tossed the wet darks in the dryer. Large hands gripped her hips. *Trick!* She stifled a scream.

"Just the way I like ya, bitch." The voice was deep and rough with lust.

Her body instantly drained of tension. "Fuck, don't scare me like that."

"Had to have some of this." He cupped her through her yoga pants, rubbing and squeezing, igniting a torrent of anticipation.

Eve threw back her head, grasping the machine for purchase. "You shouldn't be here," she breathed, wrig-gling against his groin. "You'll ruin everything."

Wordlessly he tugged down her pants, pressed a palm between her shoulder blades, and flattened her over the dryer. So predictable and exactly what she craved.

In one thrust, he plowed into her, deep and forceful, and she accepted his girth, the crude and dismissive violence of the act. She embraced the sides of the machine and moaned out encouragement, almost coming when he muttered dirty words in response. God, how she wanted him, wanted *this*. The lewdness, the lust, the lack of intimacy...

For the last two years, she'd craved this kind of sex with almost any man she came in contact with. Making love wouldn't do. Kissing made her want to throw up. She just wanted to be fucked in a base and primal way, preferably from behind. Her raging hormones demanded it. Already the tingling was pushing her close to orgasm. He grabbed her ponytail and yanked her head back. "You like it like this?"

Flesh slapped and her thighs banged the front of the dryer, the unforgiving metal bruising her pelvic bone.

"Yes," she said. "Harder."

He thrust faster, his breath becoming a labored growl. She tightened her muscles, slitting her eyes as her climax rushed like a freight train. Almost there... "Uh...harder... God, yes," she gasped, grinding beneath him. He cranked the dryer dial and punched Start. Immediately the vibrations rocked through her, the shock of the added sensation pushing her over the edge. She shrieked in pleasure and agony, twisting beneath his powerful thrusts, squeezing her pelvic muscles with all her might. His groans were bestial. His forceful thrusts banged the dryer into the wall. Plaster dust from the ceiling rained on her cheek. Within seconds, he was spent, his pace slowing. She brushed the debris from her cheek, coughing.

Even before he withdrew, the animal in her wanted it again, even lewder. She'd never been that interested in sex until recently. It had to be because of him. "Flip me over and eat me," she begged.

He spanked her, one full-palmed, stinging slap on her right cheek. "Hungry bitch. Just the way I like 'em."

"I need it again, baby, please."

"I'm late. I didn't intend on doin' this." Clothes rustled, sliding over his skin. "Came to bring you a burner phone and there you were, all laid out for me." He caressed her ass in small circles, soothing the burning sensation.

She wriggled instinctively. Just a few inches over and down and he'd be at the sweet spot. It would only take seconds; she wanted him that badly. Her need to come again made her almost delirious, but he hated pleading. This was all she'd get. She bit her lip until she tasted blood.

He moved away, and the sudden coolness gave her the shivers. "When are you and your lawyer getting my money?" He zipped his pants.

"Soon, baby. Real soon." She scooted off the dryer, turned, and rubbed her hands down the fabric covering his chest. "It'll all work out and we can be together"—she cupped him gently—"and do this anytime we want."

He grabbed her chin, his green eyes dilated, cruel lust still sparking as he peered at her eye in disgust. "I saw that on TV. You look like shit. How'd you get it?"

"An accident."

His fingers tightened. "*How?*"

She loved the challenge of taming him. There would come a day when he wouldn't get what he wanted, but she'd kept the secret long enough. Someone had to appreciate her brilliance. "I stuck a soup can on the top pantry shelf and knocked it onto my face."

He burst out laughing, and she warmed like she was drinking hot chocolate on a snowy afternoon. Marriage to *him* would make her this happy every day.

"You're a piece of work. Take it from me—your husband's not doing well without you."

That pleased her more than the orgasm. "I got everything under control, baby. I just need a bit more time."

Without warning, he gripped the sides of her mouth again, so tightly that she fought the urge to scream. He didn't like that either. "After you get the money, it's all about us," he growled. "I don't want the children hanging around. You remember our agreement."

She nodded. When she had control over the money, no one was telling her what to do. "I remember." The words were garbled, the pain excruciating. Tears stung her eyes. His grip would leave clear bruises bracketing her mouth. Her hemoglobin had always been low—it took nothing for her to turn black and blue.

Trick would be blamed. She almost smiled, despite the agony, and whispered, "Harder."

NOT ONE MEMBER of the crew coughed or shifted in his seat. As minutes passed, the stillness took on a life of its own. The air conditioner rattled on, and a second later, cool air streamed onto them. Out front, the steady whoosh of cars passing the station lent a lulling sound. The solemn faces around the circle all avoided Trick's eyes. Maybe he was projecting, but a heavy depression blanketed the room.

The cohesive unit they'd been at the beginning of the shift was broken, fragmented into jagged pieces that would require expert leadership to mend. On any normal day, this would have stimulated his love of mentoring. But he was the direct cause of this quagmire, and overwhelming guilt rendered him useless. He clicked the pen a couple of times and studied the sample AAR questions, not from the standard list but the ones under the heading "catastrophic calls."

Preoccupations with failure?

Reluctance to simplify?

How about death resulting from pressing your luck? The very issue he'd lectured them on so many times.

"I can't lead this," he confessed in a gravelly voice.

After a second's hesitation, Joey reached across the circle and gently tugged the clipboard and pen from Trick's grasp. "No one's denying you had a tough day, Lieu, so why don't you begin?" He smiled encouragingly then read, "What worked the way we wanted it to?" He was reading from the usual list. The easy questions. What *had* worked?

"Collin did an exceptional job as driver," Danny said. "Way to get past the construction on South Yates."

Collin nodded. Joey wrote it down, and when no one else spoke, he said, "We had the water on and the fire knocked out in seconds."

They all nodded and lapsed into silence again. Joey glanced around the circle, then at the page. "What could we have done differently?"

Silence and furtive looks at Trick. Exhaling audibly, he sat forward, forearms on his knees. All his points had been well rehearsed during the long ride back to the House. All were due to his hubris, relying on his luck. "I broke Cap's directive to remain on admin tasks only," he started, holding up an index finger. Then the next digit. "We all know it's against regs and bad superstition to wear someone else's gear, but I made the call to use Pete's versus losing seconds going to my locker. Therefore, I lost precious seconds on scene being discombobulated with where he keeps tools on his belt..."

"I was there." Joey flicked the pen on the paper. "It was a clean rescue, Lieu."

"It couldn't have been."

"So your run of luck is over," Collin said. "Death happens. On your days off, *we've* dealt with clean rescues where the vic still dies." He paused as a few men muttered in agreement. "You do the best you can during a rescue and respect the times when God calls someone home."

It was humbling taking advice from men with less experience. Trick acknowledged the point with a nod.

Still, luck and his no-deaths record aside, firefighting was the only area of his life where he'd excelled. Did these men think less of him now? The support of his firefighter family was his last saving grace. He couldn't lose it.

Trick took his time eyeing everyone around the circle. "Who here," he finally said, "feels confident to climb in the apparatus with me should we get a call right now?"

Everyone's hands rose, but the troubled expressions and shifting gazes told a different story. The tight connection with his team—the lifeblood in this career—was gone.

CHAPTER TWENTY-TWO

"Brace yourself," Gretch said over the line. "Eve is having an affair."

Zamira's hand stilled on the prayer mat she'd been about to roll out on her office floor. Leaning it against her desk, she sank abruptly into her chair. "How could you possibly know that?"

Gretch filled her in on the conversation with Eve. "She was very squirrely and couldn't get me off the phone fast enough." The censure in Gretch's voice was obvious, the murky mystery of which Quinn to believe clearly solved for her. "Eve thought she'd hung up. I heard her throw the phone somewhere and swear, then minutes later I heard a man's voice and the obvious noises. Right there, like the phone was next to them. Thank God it was over fast, but it was hardcore raunchy, if you want to know."

"I don't," Zamira said emphatically. Her skin bloomed in a hot flush at Gretch's nonchalance. Who eavesdropped on such an intimate act? "Surely you hung up as soon as you knew what was going on?"

"I did not. What if she called out his name? What if he said something that gave us a clue who he was?"

That was actually brilliant. Dread at delving any further into this conversation warred with Zamira's ever-present curiosity at the Quinn warfare. "And?" she squeaked.

"No such luck, but *he* knows Trick. He said Trick wasn't doing well without her. I also overheard how she got the black eye."

Zamira gasped, her hold on the phone receiver tightening as Gretch described the sordid details. "How sick!" Zamira exclaimed. "Who would do that to themselves?"

"Someone who wants all the money and the new guy. And *he* doesn't want the kids, so I'm not sure what her long game is with the sexual abuse charges and seeking full custody."

The unequivocal evidence of Patrick's innocence and the implication of how one woman's lies might harm the thousands who sought help from abuse was chilling. "We have to tell Patrick."

"We have to *help* him," Gretch said. "You and I aided Eve in her sick game. The only way to assuage our guilt is finding evidence that clears Trick of all charges."

"How are we going to do that?"

"Sean's calling his brother, Jace, who works for the FBI. Maybe we can get her phone tapped or the house wired. I called to see if you wanted to join us at Seafood Harbor tonight at six."

Zamira bit her lip. "Will Patrick be there?" She couldn't seem to catch her breath. It had to be all these revelations.

"He's at work until tomorrow morning, but Sean updated him, and Trick knows we're behind him and brainstorming how we can help."

"Count me in." They coordinated a time to meet and

hung up. Zamira stared off into space. From her end, she could push harder for Patrick to get approved for that father-daughter dance. She'd started the ball rolling yesterday but hadn't heard back from Andy.

When her final appointment of the day was through, Zamira knocked on her boss's door, the Quinn file clutched in her hand.

"I was wondering if you'd made your decision," she said, taking a seat.

Andy peered at the name on the label "Ah, the manipulator for special treatment."

Zamira bit her tongue. Yesterday, when she'd been so confused over Eve's black eye, she'd have agreed. What a difference a phone call made. The horrific self-harming lengths Eve was instigating to make sure Patrick was blamed was more diabolical than anything Zamira could have ever imagined. There was no way to tell Andy this, though. If he knew the half a dozen rules she'd violated lodging herself in the middle of this brutal tug of war, she'd be written up. Or worse.

"I've witnessed the daughter remind her father about this dance twice," she said instead. "Her level of excitement is such that if we deny the father's attendance, I think it would be a serious setback to this family's healing."

Andy took off his eyeglasses and squinted. "You've spoken to Renata and Kayla?"

"Yes." She'd spent almost an hour with the GAL and psychiatrist at Child Protective Services this morning. "Renata completed a home visit yesterday afternoon and said there are family photos of him everywhere, which she thought was a bit surprising." Renata's reaction to Eve's black eye had been similar to Zamira's, the human urge to help Eve at all costs warring with the lack of standard signs of abuse. Therefore, the report she was finishing was written with reluctance. "She didn't pick up any fear or aversion toward the father during her sessions with the girls. Her clinical opinion is that the daughters are well adjusted and happy. Neither show any indication of knowing why the father was not living at home. I think his twenty-four-hour shifts and their stay at the shelter, which they thought was a vacation, have a lot do to with that. Kayla's psychiatric evaluation is scheduled for tomorrow afternoon."

Andy picked at his scraggly eyebrows, a habit of his when he was deep in thought. "What's Renata's thought about the dance?"

"She approves, *if* I attend. Which I can't." Zamira grimaced. She would potentially be getting engaged then. "I'm wondering if I can swap hours with someone—they take my client's dance this Friday evening, and I'll supervise the next off-hour request they get."

Andy grunted noncommittally and riffled through the file, stopping at the copy of the restraining order. "And getting the daughter there?" The order could prevent Eve from dropping Amy off into the direct safety of her father.

Zamira splayed her hands. "That's the family's problem."

"This is unprecedented."

"I told the father that." This wasn't looking good. Andy was a fair but cautious man. The entire center's reputation would be at stake if the visitation were allowed and something went wrong. But how to tell him nothing would go wrong, that the father was being maligned in the most horrific way? "I get a weird vibe from this family," she ventured. "I don't think the father sexually molested the daughters. This seems like a ploy in a very sick divorce."

Andy let the paper slip back in the file. "Rule number

one is don't choose sides. It's not our jobs to figure out who's right and who's wrong."

She nodded. Tattoo that on her arm, make her recite it like a prayer, and she'd still fight the compulsion. Defending an underdog was what got her up in the morning. The charges Patrick faced were bogus, and his family life and reputation were being methodically destroyed. He could use a little help. "In the interest of compassion, I'd like to see this father-daughter dance happen...if any of the staff can swing the hours."

Andy nodded and put his glasses back on. "I'll discuss it with the director. Don't get your hopes up."

Zamira thanked him and stood. Patrick catching a break was essential. She'd had an unwitting hand helping Eve's duplicity, so it wasn't Andy's warning of getting her hopes up that gnawed at her. It was living with herself if she, as the voice of the center, had to tell Patrick his special evening with Amy wouldn't happen.

"Thanks to Gretch, we know Eve's having an affair," Jace Quinn said, eyeing everyone at the table with an intensity that pebbled goosebumps down Zamira's arms. "And the guy is a close enough friend to Trick to know he's not handling the divorce well. I told Trick to email me a list of names—guys who flirted with her in the past, maybe something that didn't look suspicious then but, given this new detail... Not now," he barked at the waitress who sidled up, pad in hand.

She glided right past for a second time. Without missing a beat, Jace leaned in as if he didn't already have their undivided attention. "Trick and Pete interviewed some of Eve's friends yesterday and came up with squat. But I'd be willing to bet she's told one of her friends about the guy. We find that friend, extract the information, and track down whoever the lover is. Then we out Eve for the lying bitch she is."

Zamira shivered at the violence in his tone, considering him through lowered lashes. He had none of Patrick's calmness. Although they shared a fraternal resemblance in their ruggedly handsome looks, Jace's build and facial expressions held an extreme-alpha edginess. Just like Monday night, the four sat in a booth, Gretch next to her while Sean and Jace squeezed together on the other side. What a different dynamic, though. Patrick had blended in with the personalities around him; Jace hijacked the agenda, dominated the conversation, and hadn't displayed patience with their questions. That forceful and dynamic personality would have affronted her in any other instance, but maybe this kind of unapologetic arrogance could stop the avalanche Eve had set upon Patrick. It was highly doubtful that Jace accepted defeat in any part of his life.

"Trick said he spoke to the three people closest to her," Sean said with a wary tone that also hadn't surfaced around Patrick. "If they don't know or won't tell, it's highly doubtful we'll get such a huge secret out of anyone."

"Trick was an idiot to think he could get them to open up," Jace growled. "Sometimes his belief in everyone's decency astounds me." He dug out his wallet. "Here's what we're going to do." He pointed at his brother. "You take the trainer. Here's his address." Jace scattered bits of paper around. "Gretch and Zamira talk to her best friends, Marisol and Sondra." He smiled grimly. "I take Eve."

Gretch scoffed. "Now who's the idiot? Like Eve is going to confess." Zamira shrank into herself at the challenge that charged the air between them. Oddly, Sean seemed to perk up, as if wondering who'd win this test of wills. Jace blinked first.

"I'm going for psychological intimidation," he said in a quieter tone. "She thinks she's gotten away with this, and I have quite a different message." He met each gaze around the table with that elevated intensity before adding, "We meet back here tomorrow, same time, for a sitrep, clear?"

Was that even English? Was anyone else completely out of their league? Zamira looked to Sean, whose gaze was already on her, warm eyes squinting with humor. "Situation report," he said. "You'll pick up the lingo if you hang around him long enough."

Gretch noted the addresses. A determined smile lit her face. "Oh, I have a great idea how to get Marisol Cruz to open up."

CHAPTER TWENTY-THREE

At seven o'clock Thursday morning, the shift from hell finally ended. Trick slunk into the thankfully empty locker room. Bone-deep exhaustion made his limbs feel like the Earth's gravitational pull had doubled, but once again, sleep had been out of the question. He stared listlessly at the contents in his locker—the smiling pictures of Eve and the girls, the colors and mantras of the seven chakras, the little jade Buddha on the shelf. He donned his Cubs cap, grabbed his wallet, and shut the door.

The back-to-back emails from Jace and Sean about how Eve got her black eye and her having sex had demolished his already flagging spirit. Initial disbelief at her alien behaviors eventually morphed into a paranoid guessing game. *The man knows you,* Jace had written. *Well.*

Except for Cheryl, that left the rest of the unit here and several guys on Mark's construction crew. Eve flirted with everyone—always had. There'd never been a reason to be jealous because that was the essence of Eve: she craved reactions and reassurance that she was attractive, perfect, and well loved. She seemed genuinely happiest when the spotlight was focused solely on her. Birthdays, their wedding, even last month when she was awarded the coveted MVP—most valuable parent—status at the end of a peewee soccer retreat. She shone so brightly during those times, and he'd bask in her subsequent love bombing for hours or days afterward.

Trick absently rubbed his bristled jaw. Who had taken his place?

In the break room next door, Russ told a joke, followed by the distinct laughter of Jose and Sam. That horrible paranoia leached through Trick's brain again, dragging these longtime friends through a mental kangaroo court. Russ and Jose were happily married, and Sam wouldn't poach another guy's wife. Sure, in their long career together their chronic rivalry had blistered their friendship, but for the most part, he and Sam were copacetic. Other bachelors? Danny had barely reached puberty. Chad was divorced, but way too uptight for Eve to ever consider him attractive. Hank—chronic halitosis. And Pete—well, it definitely wasn't Pete.

Trick scrubbed his eyes. He was trying too hard. Maybe if he didn't concentrate, someone obvious would come to mind.

He sighed and dug out his cellphone as he walked through the station. Except for meeting Morgan about the contempt of court charge at three, the day stretched endlessly before him. If he didn't fill every second, he'd go crazy. Maybe interview more of Eve's friends? Had Zamira given permission for the dance tomorrow? How had the dinner at Seafood Harbor gone last night? He paused and checked texts, voicemails, and emails—including roughly four hundred and thirty-eight requests for interviews from international news media and gossip magazines, which he collectively deleted with grim satisfaction. A sparse game plan from Jace. Radio silence from Pop. Zip from Zamira. He checked the time. She wouldn't be in yet. He sent her an email inquiry, his previous confidence in things going his way irretrievably shaken these last twenty-four hours. His certainty in the universe's all-encompassing love shattered. He got why people laughed at "Lieutenant Yogi" now.

"Lieutenant?" Captain Lewis called as Trick walked by the office. Trick spun back, masking his dread with a quizzical tilt of his head. Cap motioned to the chair across from him. "Got a minute?"

Heart dropping to his gut, Trick closed the door behind him and slid into the chair as if he were back in grade school, handing Pop his report card.

"You look like hell," Cap remarked, his tone more critical than sympathetic.

"Shuteye was impossible." Even if Trick had been able to control the *who is it* thoughts, any attempt at sleep had instantly brought up old George's gray, peaceful face.

"That Facebook video of you—"

"It was nothing," Trick interrupted, gripping the arms of the chair. "She filmed me hugging the girls."

"And breaking a restraining order."

"My lawyer's dealing with it."

Cap let a beat go by, his stern expression indicating he didn't appreciate the interruptions and flippant replies. "I saw Eve on two national talk shows yesterday sporting a black eye."

Trick dipped his chin. "A friend overheard her boast exactly how she injured herself."

Cap froze for a second, then exhaled slowly. "Has your father-in-law made contact?"

"No. Pete told me you spoke to him on Tuesday?"

"I laid out a scenario of how much worse everything would get if he pursued his vendetta."

"It must have worked. He's been silent ever since."

Cap nodded, but the gravity in his face didn't let up. "Then there's this." He shuffled through papers on his desk and held up a form with the official Office of the Illinois State Fire Marshal header. "The state pulled your name from the Medal of Honor recipients."

Figures. Trick bowed his head, waiting for some blowback from within, fury, outrage, but his soul was numb. Exhausted from losing. "Can they do that?" he said. "For one Facebook video?"

"They can do anything they want."

"But it's for the Leeds Avenue rescue." A situation that had gone south as soon as he was in the building. Cap had ordered a defensive strategy, calling the men back, but Trick's intuition had found two kids under a bed on the third floor.

"Taken as a definition of pure bravery, that medal is owed to you, Patrick, but they also take into account the well-rounded life of a firefighter. For example, they'd never have given this to someone like Ted Barnett, who's struggling with addiction, no matter how heroic his act was."

On rote Trick tried running through the mettā Buddhist prayer of benevolence and good wishes to all. Nope. Didn't help. "So," he said through stiff lips, "Eve's defamation is affecting me with the top echelon."

"Ultimately, I think it was your behavior." Cap held up a hand as Trick sputtered. "Perhaps their initial motivation was based on the excess media attention that they and we have been buried under. But that video clearly displayed you thumbing your nose at the severity of your legal situation."

Trick's fingers cramped from gripping the chair arms. He let go and smoothed his palms up and down his jeans rhythmically. Was it worth explaining how necessary it had been to break the restraining order? Should he ask Cap to enlighten the Illinois fire marshals on the violating trauma of a gynecological exam for a little girl? Would airing his marital dirty laundry change anything at this point? "I had a critical reason to visit Eve."

Cap shook his head. "Not necessary to go into, son— it's a done deal, high above my pay grade. I'm sorry."

Trick swallowed past the bitter taste in his mouth. Who had believed Eve's lies enough to pull his name?

The answer registered loud and clear, jolting his tired brain awake. Horror bloomed in his heart. Should he confirm it, or let it go and get on with his life? There was no coming back from this.

But he had to know. "Was my father behind this?"

The moment's hesitation said it all. "That's some-thing you should speak to Connor about," Cap said. "I understand it took you most of the week to confide in him."

Trick bowed his head again, jaw clenched against the primal scream. He'd never tried to weasel his way out of trouble. Of all five sons, he'd always gone above and beyond to earn the old man's respect—which Cage sarcastically referred to as preferential treatment. But Trick earned every ounce of that admiration. His close relationship with Pop had been further proof of a life lived in luck. Now it too had imploded.

"Have you ever thought of therapy?" Cap avoided eye contact. "There's nothing wrong with talking to a professional."

Trick remained sullenly silent. If Cap had spoken to Pop, then these were Pop's words coming out of his mentor's mouth. Trick didn't need therapy to discuss something he hadn't done, for fuck's sake.

"Heard you went out on calls," Cap continued quietly. No doubt in the ten minutes since Cap had arrived, he'd been filled in on yesterday's fiasco. This lecture Trick deserved, but the job was all he had left, and the way things were going, Cap was about to take that away, too. Trick squared his shoulders and waited for the blow.

Ten minutes later, he cut out the back way to avoid the news vans and jumped in his truck, Cap's harsh reprimand still echoing in his ears. He still had his job, though, thank Christ, and he planned to take on those admin duties with renewed gratitude.

He sped down side streets until the I-90 ramp appeared. He swerved onto it and drove aimlessly in the early rush-hour traffic, listing all the things Eve had cost him in barely a week. A murderous fury finally coursed through him. Figuring out what spurt of craziness had taken her from a loving wife and mother to one so consumed with destructive hate was no longer his driving force. Now he needed revenge.

He needed proof she was fabricating these accusations, and he needed to protect his girls from that exam.

He exited the freeway and threaded through more side streets, fantasizing Eve's tearful confession in front of Pop and her parents. And the media. Trick legally going home to his girls. The Medal of Honor reinstatement. The luck returning.

A slamming bounce snapped him out of his daydreams, as his truck scraped over a speed bump. What the hell had possessed him to head to the supervision center? This was not the time to ask Zamira about tomorrow. Hell, his luck was so bad that just being here probably meant her answer would be no. And that would be strike three, game over on his patience with Eve.

He was circling to leave when, in a fittingly distorted version of his former luck, Zamira pulled in. The brilliance of her cobalt hijab made her hard to miss. He caught her surprise and tried a casual wave, but already a frown marred her usually serene face. She motioned to a pair of empty parking spaces nowhere near the building. He nodded, swearing silently, then reversed in next to her. He cut the engine and hopped out, pulse revving like he'd just finished a sprint. *Please. Please let it be yes.*

"Good morning," he said, but it came out artificially jovial, and he winced behind his sunglasses.

She returned his greeting, her expression equal parts shy and alarmed. "Do we have an appointment?" Her tone indicated they very definitely didn't. She was already hitching her enormous purse over her shoulder and taking a step away from him.

"Naw, I was in the area." He made sure his smile had extra wattage. "Thought I'd stop by and see if you'd heard back from your boss about the dance tomorrow." He leaned against his hood, hands in his pockets, like the outing wasn't the most important thing in his world. "You know how florists hate corsage orders at the last minute."

"No," she said, and his heart sank before the rest of her sentence filtered through. "I haven't heard back."

He nodded. "I just got off shift at the firehouse. I don't mind waiting out here. Or I can walk in with you...?"

"Patrick." She glanced around the empty lot. "I understand how important this dance is to you, but there's a lot of red tape, and the odds of it getting approved are slim."

His fake smile slipped. "I know." Before this week, he'd lived the holistic spiritual motto *you manifest what you desire*, and he desired this nightmare being over more than anything. But without the steady diet of meditation, luck, and serenity, bombarded emotionally on all sides, his thoughts were now stuck expecting bad stuff—which, for all intents and purposes, was manifesting it.

"I've done all I can, Patrick."

"I know that, too." He took off his sunglasses and folded them. "I heard you were at Seafood Harbor last night with Gretch and my brothers."

"I'll get in a lot of trouble if my supervisor finds out, but how could I not?" She squinted at the sun, then around the mostly empty parking lot again. "Blaming you for a self-inflicted black eye seems like only the beginning. What else has she done? Like to your girls, so the doctor will back up her accusations?"

Trick swallowed dust. Ever since he'd found Blaze choke-chained, that same thought was never far away. How extreme was Eve willing to go to get sole trusteeship? Before this week, he'd have been the first to tell anyone that she was the perfect mother. Now the only thing he could say for certain was he didn't know squat. What he'd thought was real, tangible truths in his life, wasn't. He didn't trust himself to know anything about Eve, his success or failure as a husband, or even about being in love.

And after twenty-four years of dating and marriage, that was a big, fat fail.

"I'm action-oriented," he blurted out of nowhere. "It's humiliating to need other people to solve my problems. But I can't get near her, can't see my kids, can't control what's going to happen to them..." He looked off in the distance. Why was he spilling his guts to this poor woman? He sighed. "I'm torn between wanting to get down on my knees and thank you for helping me with Eve and warning you to run. Don't get any further involved with someone so devious."

She crossed her arms, almost like she was hugging herself. Her luminous eyes held empathy, such a rare sight for him these days. "It can't be easy having your life turned upside down like this," she said quietly.

"I catch myself thinking, 'Maybe she'll snap out of it.'"

The sun was heating the asphalt quickly. Sweat prickled his temples and dampened his t-shirt. Zamira had to be hot. She wore a black long-sleeved shirt under a tan ankle-length dress, and the hijab was long enough to cover her torso. "Sorry to dump," he said, putting his sunglasses back on. He gestured to the center. "Don't let me keep you."

She shaded her face with a palm. "Have you ever considered the possibility that Eve is a narcissist? That your reactions are similar to Stockholm syndrome?"

His mouth went slack. "What?"

"It's a coping mecha—"

"I know what it is. Why would you say that?"

A Taurus turned in, and Zamira stiffened. "That's my boss. I've got to go." She hitched her purse more solidly on her shoulder and walked backward. "Look up the characteristics of a narcissist and how victims deal with a warped reality. See if it rings true for your marriage." She shrugged. "Could be I'm completely wrong..."

He barely got in a wave before she turned and hurried away. At the end of the row of cars, she waited for her boss, a short, thin man sporting John Lennon spectacles and a deep frown as he eyeballed Trick. After a brief exchange, the boss spun on his heel and marched toward him as Zamira rushed to follow and pull his sleeve. Her face was flushed, her expression pleading. No doubt with all the media, the boss had recognized Trick. Did he think Trick had come here to threaten Zamira? Or stalk her? Was it aggressive to show up without an appointment? To confront his supervisor as she drove into the parking lot? Hell yeah. Put like that, it went right in line with everything Eve was saying about him.

Trick lifted a palm in casual greeting, his grin easy, especially because it was meant for Zamira. Despite all the depressing topics they'd managed to cover, her serene manner fed his Zen side, which was so desert-dry that his spirit glommed on to these nourishing moments in her presence. If only he'd known her before this and in completely different circumstances. What would their friendship have been like? As it was, almost every exchange had been about him and his sick marriage. Besides her courage in the face of Islamophobia, what was her life like? What made her tick?

Trick got back in his pickup, tossed his sunglasses on the dash, and cranked the air. Even though he knew the word, he entered *narcissist* in his phone's search engine then clicked the top link:

Tricks That a Narcissist Will Use to Create an Imbalance of Power:

Manipulation, control, lies, distorting reality, gaslighting, winning at all costs...

By the time he'd read through examples of each, the breakfast he'd eaten at the station burned like acid. On a positive note, the darkness Eve had trapped him in all these years was now flooded with brilliant, hard facts.

CHAPTER TWENTY-FOUR

"He's still there." Andy peered furtively out the small window of the heavy door. "I'm going to notify Fred."

Just what Patrick needed: security to escort him off premises. "It looks like he's texting or something." Zamira wiped the perspiration from her upper lip. The rare humid morning this early in June paired with getting caught chatting with a notorious client who had no business being here had drenched her clothes.

If only she had the courage to confess her egregious overstepping and list the facts she'd learned. Patrick was being maligned, Eve was evil, and this case was clear-cut. Andy would be swayed.

And then write her up for getting involved.

"Honestly," she said, her annoyance at her cowardice making her sound curt, "Mr. Quinn is quite harmless. The press has spun innuendos into hard facts."

Andy turned from the window, scowling. "Then why is he lying in wait out in our parking lot?"

"I told you. He came to check about that father-daughter dance tomorrow night."

"And calling you wouldn't suffice?"

She waved dismissively. "He just got off work. He was in the area." Even though his station house was nowhere near here. It was hard keeping track of the lies. Belatedly, Zamira requested Allah's forgiveness. "Have you made a decision about the dance?" Her breath stalled at his hesitation.

He motioned toward the offices, and they fell in step. "If we'd had more time with this client," he began, and her heart plummeted, "we could've been more lenient. But deciding an offsite visit in a crowded auditorium based solely on one evaluation, amid those horrible accusations in the media... No. We can't risk something going wrong out in the community with no staff backup. It wouldn't be fair to whichever supervisor we assigned."

"I understand." Despite her wooden tone, she did. The problem was that Patrick wouldn't.

She stopped at her door as Alice flagged her down. "Mr. Tomball's already here," she called. "I put him in the playroom."

"Thank you." Zamira halted abruptly. Mrs. Tomball, forever impatient and put out, would be driving in any second with the kids. *Insha'Allah, I'm so late!* She muttered "goodbye" to Andy and spun back toward the parking lot she'd just left. The Tomball file was still in her car, the visitation progress forms hadn't been pre-filled out... What was happening to her? She should have excused herself thirty seconds after Patrick got out of his truck.

Zamira pushed on the heavy door and immediately sucked in a breath. Patrick still sat in his pickup, staring down at his lap. The hunched posture, tilted head, and position of his arms suggested he was still texting or reading his cellphone screen. Thankfully, Mrs. Tomball's car wasn't anywhere in the lot. This would be the perfect time to tell Patrick the dance was a no-go. Why make him wait or hope in vain any further?

Zamira descended the steps, biting her lower lip. Before sharing Andy's heartbreaking answer, should she remind Patrick she was solidly on his side? That at lunchtime she and Gretch were visiting one of Eve's friends?

She was halfway to his truck when Mrs. Tomball and the twins pulled in. Zamira waved brightly and held up an index finger to the mother, who slowed as Zamira raced by and halted at Patrick's door. His absorption in whatever he was looking at made her hesitate to knock on the window. Something was causing him great misery. Why add to it? She could call him after the Tomballs left. It would be a relief not to tell him the news to his face.

No. She owed him this moment. The dance was important enough for him to have driven all this way. Pulse pounding, she knocked on his window. He started and met her gaze so abruptly that she stepped back. There it was, the same intensity as when she'd first met him on Monday. She'd been incorrect perceiving it as a dark violence. Anguish all but throbbed off him.

He lowered the window. His face had a grayish tinge and deep lines bracketed his mouth. "You're right," he said in a gravelly voice. "All these years, I've been living with a narcissist. How could I not have known?"

Wow, there was so much to unpack in that question. A car door slammed and Zamira glanced over her shoulder. Mrs. Tomball stood beside her car watching impatiently, a squirming twin in each hand. "I'm sorry," Zamira stammered, turning back. "That's my appointment."

He looked over her shoulder. "Yeah. Sorry. I gotta go anyway."

"Wait," she said as the window began creeping back up. She exhaled in a rush. "Look, I've run into narcissists during my work here. I'd be happy to, I don't know... answer questions? Commiserate? Do you want to meet after I get off work?"

He blinked. "I thought you said that wasn't allowed."

It most definitely wasn't. Even worse than his non-Muslim status, she would be going unchaperoned. But how could she walk away from his sorrow and confusion? "The Starbucks on West Randolph," she said hurriedly. "Eight o'clock."

"Sure." He shifted in his seat. "Did your boss say anything about—"

"I'm sorry. Andy said no. I'm sorry," she babbled, unable to look any further than the tightening jaw causing a dimpled groove in his cheek. "Perhaps you can ask one of your brothers to go with Amy."

"Yeah," he said in a gruff voice. "Thanks for going to bat for me."

"Zamira," Mrs. Tomball called shrilly.

"I have to go, Patrick. See you tonight."

He nodded. His eyes... Oh, she shouldn't have looked! The pain there was unbearable.

AT THE ROAR OF AN ENGINE, Eve parted a slat in the vinyl blinds. Instead of the school bus carrying Amy home, her brother-in-law was climbing out of his monstrous black SUV. "Oh, great." This damn meddling family. She'd been avoiding her mother-in-law's calls for days.

Kicking some toys aside, Eve marched to the foyer. Too bad her parents had taken Tina to the park. Dad was lusting for some Quinn blood. She opened the door wide enough to stick her head and shoulder out, then blocked the bottom with her right foot. "Jace," she said curtly as he stepped onto the porch.

"You look like hell." He took off his sunglasses with the usual flourish and studied her puffy, multicolored eye and bruised mouth. "Guess you doubled down on getting people to believe your lies."

Jace always saw through her. It was one of the things she hated most about him. She waited a beat to make sure he picked up on her loathing expression. "I'm not going to dignify that with an answer. What do you want?"

He peered behind her, but she didn't budge from the threshold. The faster she got rid of Trick, the faster his family would get the picture that they were included in the purge.

Jace opened his blazer to stick his sunglasses in his breast pocket, but also to flash his gun and holster. So obvious. "Gotta couple of questions." His tone was cool, distant. The official FBI. Crazy that she'd once had a crush on him, to the point where she couldn't decide which Quinn brother she would marry. If only she could go back in time and kick her own ass on both counts.

"I'm expecting Amy any minute," she snapped. "If this visit has to do with Trick, keep your nose out of it."

"It's about your erratic behavior. The false accusations. The affair you thought no one would find out about until you got your hands on the lottery money and destroyed my brother."

Eve's blood surged in fight-or-flight panic so fast she barely maintained her icy exterior. How did he know? She'd taken such care of every detail. He had to be bluffing! "The press is going to love hearing how you're harassing the victim."

Jace snorted softly, his jaw tightening in a menacing way. He'd be a fool to act on impulse, but given his extreme alpha edginess, the effect was still formidable. Made for a great high school quarterback, Navy SEAL, and now FBI agent, but it sucked when he directed that underlying threat at her.

Best way to communicate with him was a preemptive strike. "Get off my property. This is all being decided by our lawyers, and you can tell your mother that too. I don't appreciate her calls."

She stepped back to slam the door in his face, but he surged forward, blocking the threshold with his boot. The flimsy door bounced harmlessly back at her.

"Not so fast, dear sister-in-law." He bodily nudged the door open. She'd forgotten how lightning-quick he could be, how he took what he wanted and did as he pleased without standing on ceremony or caring about manners. If only it didn't turn her the hell on.

She stumbled back without a fight. "Back off, Jace." Her tongue had thickened, and the words sounded garbled as lust snaked through her. It would take so little for her to reach for his belt buckle, and then all her carefully laid plans would bite the dust. God, where was Amy?

"See, here's the thing," he said, closing the door with a soft *snick*. He leaned against it, folding his arms. "I know ever since we were kids I've given the impression that Trick is annoying and we're rivals and shit. But he's family, and he's hurting." In the low light, his clear blue eyes almost glowed. "*You* did that." He shifted his weight ever so slightly toward her. "We both know he's a fucking angel. It clearly makes you want to puke, too. So to cut him down by claiming something he couldn't do if you put a knife to his throat was probably not your wisest move." His smile came slowly and never reached those eerie eyes. "In fact, honey, it's probably going to be your downfall."

Every cell in Eve's body that had been aching for Jace now perked to cautious attention. Seriously. Had she done something to give herself away, or was this more of Jace bluffing? The roar of the school bus pulling up and the squeal of brakes filled her with both relief and a bout of panic. Yes, she wanted Amy's presence as a buffer, but what did Jace know? "He *is* capable of violence," she blurted. "Remember when he beat up Tim Petroski?"

"Who'd messed with you because he misinterpreted your flirting? Yeah. I recall that's the one and only time Trick went batshit crazy—protecting your worthless virtue."

Footsteps pounded up the porch, and Jace slid smoothly to the side seconds before the door burst open. Amy flew in, braid half undone, one sock around her ankle, and her purple backpack hanging off her elbow. "Uncle Jace," she squealed, catapulting into his arms.

"Hey, kiddo." He bear-hugged her off her feet, then slipped the backpack off her arm, struggling with it and her wriggling weight before tossing it haphazardly in the corner. He tilted his torso wildly left and right so Amy's legs swung like a pendulum. She giggled raucously, the kind of rising hysteria where it would take forever to settle her back down.

"Enough," Eve snapped, squeezing her fists. Jace always did this: upended her girls then left her to deal with their overly high spirits. He started to comply, but when Amy wrapped her legs around his torso and clung like a little monkey, he danced in a tight circle, humming a tuneless waltz.

Eve stuck her hands on her hips. "Amy! Go get a snack."

Amy didn't even blink. "Are you taking me to the dance tomorrow, Uncle Jace?"

Ugh. She was so going to get it!

"What dance?" He dipped her low enough to conk her head on the floor, so dangerously close that Eve gasped and Amy shrieked in glee.

"Jace!" Eve screeched, but Jace, too, ignored her as he hauled her daughter back up.

"The father-daughter dance," Amy said breathlessly, "at my school. Mommy said Daddy can't go."

"Really?" Jace frowned and side-eyed Eve. "I heard your dad had the whole evening planned."

A look of confusion washed over Amy, followed by dawning hope. *Great.* "He can't!" Eve's voice edged toward hysteria. "He won't be there, so stopping getting her hopes up."

"But Mo-om," Amy whined.

"Don't Mom me," Eve said. "This is all your father's fault."

Jace studied Amy's crestfallen features. "She can go if someone else goes with her, right?" he asked quietly.

Eve gritted her teeth as her brother-in-law manipulated the situation to make her look like the mean parent. "It's a *father*-daughter dance, Jace."

"Why can't Daddy go?" Amy whined again, oblivious to interrupting.

"Because he's been bad," Eve snapped. "He *hurt* you. Remember?"

Jace pivoted so Amy's back was to Eve. He bent his head toward his niece and asked with false innocence, "Did your daddy hurt you, honey?"

Eve's heart jumped to her throat. "Jace! Keep out of it." She ratcheted up her mean-mommy voice, and thankfully, Amy stiffened. *Good.* She got that she was the center in this tug of war and that it came down to choosing Mommy's love or Uncle Jace's. Amy was no dummy.

When Jace repeated, "Did your daddy hurt you?" in a softer tone, Amy nodded, but the miniscule shrug that followed made Eve grit her teeth. Cyprian would have to insist the girls not take the stand. They were traumatized victims. They were too young. Loving their abuser made them unreliable.

"It's not fair," Amy mumbled, her lower lip trembling. "Everyone else's dad is going."

Jace set her down, crouched to her height, and kissed her forehead. "I'm sorry, sweetie. I would go in a heartbeat, 'cause you're my best girl—you know that, right?" At her dispirited nod, he added, "But I've gotta work late catching bad guys."

Another nod as Amy stared at the ground.

"Hey, you know what? I bet Uncle Sean would love to take you. Your mom's okay with that, right?"

They both looked at Eve, a small, hopeful face and one full of deadly challenge. The fucker had boxed her into a corner. Screw Jace for coming here and causing all this drama. For forcing her hand and undercutting her authority.

He cocked an eyebrow. "Right, Mommy?" he said in such a mocking voice that Amy glanced curiously between them. Eve gripped her fingers together to stop the trembling. God, he was messing up everything!

She had to calm down. Jace always had a knack of reading her thoughts like they were tattooed on her forehead. Eve shrugged. "Sure." It would never get to that point. She'd take the girls out for the evening or not open the door to Sean, but if it got Jace out of here, she'd say anything.

Jace turned back to Amy. "I'll have Uncle Sean call your mom for details, okay?"

Amy shrugged dispiritedly. Sean came in a distant third to Trick or "fun Uncle Jace."

"Gotta get back to work." Jace tugged Amy's braid. "I promise, as soon as work lets up, you and I will do something cool, like batting practice at Wrigley Field, okay?" She brightened immediately. He stood, jerking his chin at Eve. "Walk me out."

She shook her head. Like she was stupid enough to be alone with him again. "Too busy." He leveled such a dangerous scowl over Amy's head that Eve's heart stalled before drumming extra-fast beats. She hated his guts and craved the contest of wills. It had always been this way with him. Probably why she'd chosen the safer brother. Her nostrils flared at the challenge before her: getting him the hell out of this house.

"Amy," she said firmly without breaking eye contact with the bastard, "say goodbye to your uncle and go get a snack."

"Nuh uh," Jace said immediately, in a falsely cheery tone. "Not without goodbye hugs. One for Ames"—he leaned down and embraced his niece again—"and one for you."

Before Eve could careen away, he snatched her, his grip unbreakable steel. He crushed her to his chest, a rigid wall of muscle. "Pay attention." His breath came hot in her ear, his voice a harsh rasp. "If you continue this bullshit, I'll do everything in my *considerable federal power* to make your life a living hell. That goes if you cancel on Sean, too." His embrace, which had ignited sparks in her brain from lack of oxygen, ended as abruptly as it had begun. "Got it?" he said in the fake-friendly tone.

Amy turned toward the kitchen as Jace blindly grabbed the door handle behind him. "Got it?" he repeated, low and menacing. The threat and icy stare triggered such a rush of tingles between Eve's thighs that her legs went numb. She was so going to lock herself in the bathroom with Mr. Happy the second his car pulled away.

"I'm not afraid of any of you," she said with a sneer as he stepped outside. "And don't bother calling Sean. She's not going to that dance."

"She goes or I come ba—"

She slammed the door and bolted it, then waited a few seconds and peeked through the peephole. Jace slowly got in his SUV and backed down the drive. Eve breathed out a shaky sigh of relief and spun around. "Amy, when you're done with your snack, you sit at the dining room table and do your homework. Understood?"

"But Mo-om..."

"Or you're grounded for a week."

"Okay," Amy whined, and muttered something.

Any other time, Eve would have forced the backtalk out of her daughter, but the hormones flushing through her were in full command. She dug through her purse for the burner phone, bolted up the stairs, and locked herself in the master bath. She hit redial, her fingers spastically pushing her yoga pants down.

"What's up?" came the gruff voice. She squeezed her thighs in agony.

"Phone sex," she said. "Tell me what you're doing to me right now."

"What?"

"Hurry." She lay on the bath mat, rubbing herself, too agitated to go get Mr. Happy in the next room.

As he murmured filthy suggestions and a pose that even in her wildest fantasies she would not have come up with, she closed her eyes and dredged up Jace's take-no-prisoners stare, the way his mouth curled into a cruel sneer. She orgasmed violently, without pleasure, her cries loud enough that Amy called up the stairs. Eve gasped as the tingles began to subside, ignoring her daughter and the gruff voice asking her what this was all about.

Jace was turning into a wild card she hadn't factored in, and she was not about to lose. "We have a problem," she said into the phone.

CHAPTER TWENTY-FIVE

"This is damaged," Gretch said loudly enough to attract the boutique owner, Marisol Cruz, who hurried over. Zamira stepped aside and fingered the fringe of a silk shawl that cost more than she made in two months. The first half of their lunch hour, Gretch had rolled out a plan: start up a conversation with one of Eve's best friends and see if there was any information she could shed on Eve's motivation or the other man's identity.

Gretch carefully held up an antique pendant by its chain for Marisol and pointed out a nick.

"That's part of the design." Marisol's worry morphed to relief then exasperation. "You see it's repeated there too."

Gretch tilted one formidable eyebrow. "What's it made of?"

"Cast gold and opalescent enamel. It's an art nouveau piece from the turn of last century."

Gretch nodded. "I thought so. You see the discoloration in both places? It's chipped." Zamira stepped closer, unable to see any irregularities. If Gretch was acting, she was very good.

The worry was back on Marisol's face, and she squinted hard at the pendant.

"Given its price and your boutique's great reputation, you should probably have it checked to be sure." Gretch held up a business card. "I'm the restoration manager at Moore and Morrow. Even though it says art, we repair artifacts too. This is my direct line, and I'll make sure to give you a good price."

Zamira pressed her lips tight to control the smile. For sure Gretch was bluffing; she was the receptionist. That card listed the main number.

"Thank you," Marisol said distractedly. "But I'm happy with the firm I use."

"Really?" Gretch's smile was condescending. "We're contracted with the Art Institute, and last fall, Harrison Wickham hired us to repair the art in his private galleries after his house fire. You remember that from the newspapers? Quite a bit of smoke damage. We were there for months."

The name-dropping of Chicago's famous billionaire did it. "Thank you." Marisol tucked the card in the pocket of her sheath dress and studied the women with interest. Zamira knotted her fingers together behind her back. As much as she wanted to be a part of this adventure and help Patrick in some way, she knew nothing about art and always got caught in lies.

Gretch pirouetted slowly as she gazed at the merchandise. "Eve Quinn recommended your shop to us."

"Oh, she's a great friend."

"Yes." The catlike smile was back. "She mentioned that. So you know the whole Trick debacle?"

"Isn't it tragic?" Marisol's voice dropped. "You could've knocked me over with a feather. He's always looked so gentle. So in love with her."

Gretch gave a dismissive shrug. "But you know she's seeing someone else, right?"

"I—I don't know who," Marisol said. She ruined the lie by glancing away.

"I do," Gretch said. "Someone who knows Trick well. But I've been sworn to secrecy."

Marisol tilted her head like she was assessing a new rival. "Does Trick know?"

Thankfully, this answer was not a lie. Zamira shook her head, capturing Marisol's brief attention. "No, he doesn't."

"So Eve didn't tell *you* about her new guy?" Gretch asked, her lilt of disbelief smoothly redirecting the shop owner's attention.

"Well." Marisol seemed to flounder at the sudden competition of who was closer to Eve. "I know they've been together four months. I've been her excuse when she went out on date night."

Zamira swallowed her gasp. The shop door opened, initiating a two-toned chime, and a couple of women entered. Gretch handed the pendant back with care. "You make sure to repair that before you put it back on display," she said. "And when you see Eve, tell her Gretch says hi."

TRICK SLUMPED onto Pete's ancient sofa and answered the videoconference ring. His brothers' faces popped up: Sean's perpetual sulk, probably at having his work interrupted, and Jace's mug flushed with triumph. "What's up?" Trick asked, stroking Blaze's silky fur.

"I went over to your house this afternoon and dropped a listening device into Amy's backpack." Jace grinned smugly. "It's state of the art. Even if Eve is upstairs, it'll pick up most of what she says. If she's outside, it picks up several thousand feet. And I've got a friend at the agency tracking Eve's GPS. He's back-tracing every place she's been this past week. His app will pick up pings even if she turned her phone off. We've got her."

"Unless you've got a warrant," Sean piped up, "you don't have her. That's illegal in Chicago."

Jace waved impatiently. "We're not submitting anything as evidence. We're just trying to figure out what she's doing, who's she's with. Why she's a psychotic liar."

"Money," Sean said emphatically.

"How do you know it's not the affair? I heard their raunchy phone sex minutes after I left."

"Jesus." Trick's heart lurched as painfully as the first time he'd heard of another man. His imagination immediately began playing the phone-sex scenario in lurid detail. He shook his head until his brain rattled. "It's both," he said dispiritedly. Blaze pawed him sympathetically.

"I got a really weird vibe from her," Jace said, "almost like she was egging me on, hoping I'd get physical. There's no one home behind her eyes. Even when it came to Amy and the dance."

Trick rubbed his dry, itchy eyes while he collected himself. The dance had become such a sore point. Fuck the restraining order. "I'm going. I just haven't figured out how."

"And let your daughter witness you handcuffed?" Jace countered, cuttingly unsympathetic. "And dragged off in front of her friends?"

"Jace—"

"This is how it's going down. *Sean* takes her to the

dance"—Jace spoke over Sean's sputter of protest—"then back to Mom and Pop's for ice cream, where *you* will be. Mom can put on an old-timey slow song and you dance with Amy before Sean takes her home."

There was a fatal flaw with that plan: it meant spending an evening with Pop. After he'd had Trick's Medal of Honor pulled, the bitterness and betrayal would be too difficult to hide.

"I think Gretch already made plans," Sean said.

"Cancel them," Jace barked. "Or bring her along. You know she'd agree to this. Stop thinking about yourself for once."

All three of them grinned, which was no doubt what Jace had been going for. Of all five boys, Jace was the one whose instinct was to think only about himself. Ordering his brothers around, disregarding their wants and needs, was second nature. Doing so to help one of them? Definitely not.

"What do you think?" Trick asked Sean.

"I'll sacrifice my date night for the cause."

"And I'll report back where Eve's been all week," Jace said. "If we can't get through to her, we'll get lover boy to see reality."

Trick cringed. Eve entwined with another man... How had she hidden her secret life so adeptly? Not shown one sign of this fathomless hatred for him or the lack of concern for what she was putting Amy and Tina through?

"If you don't need me anymore..." Sean said, and let the sentence hang. He was looking off screen. Probably had been restoring art the whole time.

Jace nodded. "Call Eve and get the details. The first thing she'll do is give you hell and try to forbid it. If so, mention my name as many times as you have to. And whatever time she tells you to show up, go an hour earlier."

Sean frowned into his camera. "Why?"

"I wouldn't put it past her to take the girls out before you get there."

"Why?" Sean repeated.

"Because she hates to lose."

Trick gaped at his older brother. Of course she'd do that. Or something similarly devious, and then tell any outraged Quinn that Sean had gotten the time wrong and she'd taken Amy out to console her. Jace had predicted and countered her gaslighting so effortlessly. The dozens of articles on narcissism Trick combed through had been like finding the Rosetta Stone to interpret his marriage, yet he still wouldn't have seen the big picture just now. The only reason he didn't consider himself a grade-A chump was because Sean looked just as astonished.

After Sean muttered goodbye, his screen image disappeared and Jace's instantly enlarged. "I know you tagged Eve as manipulative," Trick said, "but would you call her a narcissist?"

"Hell yes. Welcome to reality, Mr. Magoo." Under the circumstances, the reference to the befuddled and mostly blind cartoon character was so adept that Trick didn't even flip Jace the bird.

"How could I not have seen it?"

"Maybe you did on some level." Jace circled a finger around his temple in the universal sign for cuckoo. "Maybe that's why you got all obsessive about meditating. You started all that woo-woo stuff right after you got married."

"There's no correlation."

"Subconscious escapism?"

The surprises were coming in fast and furious today.

Jace having insight into the human psyche? "All the more reason my higher self should have been in tune with what was in her heart."

"Not necessarily." Jace shrugged. "Being in the thick of battle would've given you tunnel vision."

"Marriage to her wasn't a battle."

"Man, you are like a newborn babe." The pity in Jace's expression didn't have the usual underlying satisfaction. "Think about it. She had a career that stopped almost the instant you guys got married—"

"Because the doctor told her the stress was keeping her from having a baby—"

"Which *she* told you, right? You weren't at the appointment."

"I'd wanted to go." Trick scraped fingers through his hair. "She was furious. Said the only reason I was offering was to make sure the infertility wasn't my fault. Do you think she lied about the work stress?"

"Wouldn't put it past her."

Trick never did speak to the doctor. Could she have even lied about her inability to *conceive*?

No. IVF was way too expensive. The painful shots, the crazy hormone cocktail... The pendulum had swung too far in the other direction—he was getting paranoid. "She wouldn't do that," he muttered.

"She made you buy a house you couldn't afford, so you held down two jobs *while* taking college courses at night."

"A lot of couples have a spouse that stays home."

"Not when the spouse staying home is so money driven." Jace gestured impatiently. "And the second you got the pay raise, she wanted a bigger house. Then you won the lottery, and bam! She goes all in trying to take everything and destroy your reputation in the process."

Jace's words seeped into Trick's brain and grew roots.

Memories tumbled forth and rearranged into new perspectives. Eve's way of turning the tables on any issue. How it was just easier to accept the blame than fight her reasoning because the payback was always such a bitch. Like five years ago, during that epic polar vortex, when he'd driven off after an argument to get his head on straight, and his truck had broken down twenty minutes away. Nothing like negative wind chill and no heat to shift priorities. He'd called Eve, apologized, and asked her to come get him. She'd immediately turned lovey-dovey, the perfect courageous rescuer, saying she'd ask the next-door neighbor to sit with the girls and be there in a jiffy. Only it had taken her hours to arrive, and when she had, the girls were bundled in the back sleeping and her savior persona had vanished. She'd railed at him for the hazardous driving conditions, the damn neighbors on either side not being home, and the danger of the kids being stuck in the cold. What if something had gone wrong with *her* car, she'd screamed. If only they could get new cars, none of this would've happened! She'd repeatedly accused him of giving her the wrong location and potentially harming all four of them with his "running away stunt."

Hypothermia had set in, and he'd been too cold, too tired, too defeated to respond. The ride home had been a blur except for one certainty: he'd been an Eagle Scout, an Army corporal, and a firefighter—he'd given her the exact coordinates. And when they'd finally turned into the driveway, almost every home on the street had multiple lights on. He hadn't pointed any of that out. Why dig the trench deeper? Then the next few days she'd love-bombed and cared for him like they were newlyweds, and he'd let the memory fade into the mist. Until now.

He mustered the courage to ask his brother the

vulnerable question that had haunted him all week: "Why did she stay? Twenty-four years is a long time to pretend to love me."

"Because she loved what you could do *for her*," Jace said quietly. "Now, you're expendable."

CHAPTER TWENTY-SIX

Gretch should have been the messenger. Zamira squirmed in the coffeehouse's wooden chair, fingers knotted in her lap. Or maybe this information shouldn't be delivered so soon after refusing permission for the father-daughter dance. Patrick sat across from her, broad shoulders slumped, thick black hair unkempt, turning his coffee cup in listless circles. Such a contrast between alpha competence and wounded vulnerability. He must have lost weight since Monday, because his lean cheekbones looked razor sharp now, the creases bracketing his mouth deeper, the violet shadows under his eyes puffier. When was the last time he'd slept? Or smiled? Yes, Gretch should've been the brave soldier to deliver this news.

"According to Marisol," Zamira said haltingly, "Eve started seeing the other man four months ago."

Patrick flinched like he'd been slapped. "That's a month before the ER visits began. He's got to be in on this with her." He scowled so fiercely her breath stilled. "*Four...* Who is it? Who hates me as much as she does?" His gaze drifted around the near-empty coffeehouse.

Zamira stayed silent. The questions weren't meant for her. She used the brief reprieve from his attention to collect herself. Outwardly, she was pretty sure she looked the part she was playing: the court-ordered provider worried enough about her client's string of catastrophes that she'd reached out to check on him. Inwardly? Her nerves hummed. She was seconds from hyperventilating.

The magenta streaks of sunset sparked more jitters. It was hard to keep convincing herself this was a professional meeting when the world outside was at its most romantic. This was a ruse to see Patrick again, another pathetic attempt to explore why her feelings went so haywire in his company. And every minute she sat here was another rebellious step away from the halal lifestyle she'd been taught to lead. Such a contrast from when his arrival at the Thai restaurant had shocked her senseless. This time, *she'd* instigated being with him. And *alone*. She'd used vague enough language for her parents to think this outing was with Gretch. And the too few times Patrick had glanced away in these last six minutes, she'd instinctively zeroed in on his lips. What would they feel like on hers? How did he kiss?

She blinked back to attention as his slow contemplation of the room ended on her again. Her pulse fluttered under the intense scrutiny. "Maybe the guy's the mastermind behind this," she stammered. "And it's Eve who's being coerced."

Patrick shook his head. "Naw. You tagged her correctly this morning. She's a narcissist, and I've been nothing but a marionette." He curled both palms around the cardboard cup as if warming them. "The guy might be the catalyst to speeding up her goals, but I doubt he has any more control over her than I did." He took a sip, eyeing her tea across the table. "It should be cool by now."

Zamira nodded. There was no way she was lifting these trembling fingers out of her lap.

"Are you— Have you come to terms with— I mean... How are you?" She almost slapped her forehead at the botched attempt to turn the conversation to his wellbeing. "This morning in the parking lot... I know you're dealing with a lot. And I saw yesterday's news about the victim dying..."

Patrick closed his eyes briefly. "It was bound to happen sooner or later. Besides, my save record was such a weird thing to be famous for. Better than being known throughout the world as a depraved lunatic, but still..."

She ached to comfort him. "Sometimes when something gets me down..." How to say this without sounding trite? Or naïve. *Who cares?* If it would ease his agony, her simple philosophy was worth sharing. "I try to find the positive angle. It can be hard, but there's always a different way to look at any event."

His eyes crinkled half a second before a devastatingly sexy smile bloomed. Her breath stilled as she tried to memorize this heart-stopping moment. "I need all the help I can get," he said softly, palms clasping in prayer. "Teach me your magic, Zamira."

She shuddered an inhale. "My underlying philosophy is that people's thoughts and words create their reality. Like, if you say a task or a conversation is going to be difficult, then it becomes difficult. Your focus was on the negative, so you wrote that negativity into your life. Or if you say, 'I bet this guy will cut me off in traffic,' and seconds later he does, it wasn't a premonition, it was you. I know it sounds crazy—"

"Not at all." Patrick crossed his forearms on the table, the coffee forgotten. "I believe it too, but I *know* I didn't write this toxic shit—excuse me—stuff into my life. I didn't even see it coming."

"A lot of times, our ego doesn't see what our subconscious mind orchestrates." She ducked her head at his startled expression. "Anyway. My method goes one step further. If something awful does happen, I rewrite my thoughts on the event or find the positive angle in it and then make myself *feel* that the outcome I want has already happened. And then it does."

"Walk me through the death of that fire victim," he challenged. "How do I change that?"

"What's the negative thought you can't get out of your head?"

He waited a beat. "That I'm to blame."

"Now find a way to think about the event with a positive spin on his death."

He pursed his lips, staring at the table, and she indulged in her favorite pastime: fantasizing about his kiss. His mouth would be soft...the pressure firm. Commanding. He'd cup her chin first...

"How about," he said haltingly, "George was staring down a disease, maybe cancer or something. And this fire that brought on a heart attack or the heart attack that brought on the fire was actually a quicker and more merciful way to go."

Zamira nodded. "And?"

"And...that reviving him would've meant him facing his disease and the pain and the downward spiral of months going through toxic treatment?"

"So it's a blessing he is not suffering."

Patrick studied her raptly, as if he was trying to see into her soul. "Well, I do feel better," he admitted, "but that was just me making up a story."

"Now it becomes how fervently you believe in it. Make it your truth." She gestured with a hand that was strangely no longer trembling. "They showed a picture of him on TV; he was in his eighties or nineties. His time on earth was clearly drawing to a close. And I know you did the very best you could. So write that you helped him not to suffer the indignity of a disease. You also saved him from the flames so his wife could give him an open-casket funeral. Find the positive aspects and rewrite your perspective."

He exhaled a long breath. "You're very good at this—the way you come up with stuff so fast."

"It's a secret my sister taught me when we were little. I swear it works. You feel better about the event, right?"

He nodded mutely, shrugging. To him, it was still a story.

"And now," she said lightly, "you won't fear your next rescue."

He started. "Whatever made you think I'd be afraid?"

"This morning in the parking lot, I could almost feel your pain. Same thing as when you blamed yourself just now. If you don't stop owning it, you'll carry that darkness into the next rescue."

"Darkness?" He sat lost in thought, and she daydreamed of a parallel universe where she leaned forward and smoothed the frown from his forehead. In reality, her spine had been plastered against this hard chair so long that she ached. "I guess you're right," he said finally, his expression clearing. "Has anyone ever called you an empath?"

"No." She puffed a soft laugh.

"You've got this otherworldliness about you. So calm and self-possessed." His gaze had that intense searching quality that made her want to squirm.

"I'm nothing like that. I have inner battles like anyone else."

"Name one." His insolent grin dared her.

She clenched her palms together. "I...I can't. I'm just your—"

"Yes, but see, you're not just my supervisor, are you, Zamira? Not anymore." Although his smile was still in place, his eyes burned with intent. "You've rallied to my side. You're helping Gretch and my brothers. You know so much about my battles, and I know nothing about you."

Did she dare? She licked her lips, her face in flames at the haram way this meeting had grown so personal. "Tomorrow at Mosque Mohammed, after the prayers and celebration, I...I may be getting engaged." Her breath stuck in her throat. "To a man I despise."

"Jeez."

"It's my father's wish," she added quickly, "and, of course, he is guided by Allah." She turned her palms up helplessly. "So..."

He waited for her to continue, but she was struck dumb by her confession. Only Shadi knew this secret. Cold sweat dampened her skin. How fast could she say goodnight and flee?

"Let me guess," Patrick said like he was trying not to scare off a child. "Your positive thinking works fine in any situation except when your religion overrules that instinct."

And in a nutshell, he'd identified the two warring sides of her: her independent life of positive thinking, and the self who found comfort obeying Allah and her parents. Which side was right? Why couldn't there be a seamless merge of accepting her parents' choice of a husband because she wanted it with the same enthusiasm? "Yes," she whispered, her throat thick with tears. "I cannot defy my father."

"I know all about fathers and expectations." His smile had a sad quality. "I wish I had some advice." His sigh was deep and tinged with weariness. "I'm sorry for your unhappiness. It brings out this firefighter need in me to protect you."

"I'll be fine." The tone sounded false even to her ears. But she *would* be fine. Tomorrow, the struggle between her divided selves would be over, her path in life set. Surely getting rid of that turmoil would be a relief. And she still had tonight, where she was free and rebellious and sitting across from Patrick Quinn. A furtive glance at the now empty coffeehouse solidified her determination. To have this one last memory... "May I shake your hand?"

He blinked to attention. "I thought—"

"Just this once." Her words came from far away. "To thank you for this evening."

"It was my pleasure, Zamira." He held out his palm. She released the bunched fabric of her kaftan, her palm cold and clammy. It didn't matter. She clasped his hand, immediately engulfed in the large, callused grip. So warm and strong. So...intimate. "You're trembling," he said softly.

"Yes." Later there would be endless opportunities to recollect his observation and cringe into a fetal position, to pay for this haram act with extra duas. Right now, she was touching Patrick Quinn. Shivers tingled through her as she boldly held his gaze. His midnight-blue irises were ringed with black on the inside, amber on the outside. His dark lashes were incredibly long and thick. The spider-web wrinkles in the corners of his eyes were shades lighter than his tan face. What was he thinking? Was this a simple handshake? He seemed to be studying her just as deeply.

His lips opened to say something, and her fantasy roared back to life. *Right now!* With his lips parted, he'd lower his head. The kiss would start lightly, and he'd be very patient coaxing a response from her... Then his mouth would slant and widen, encompassing hers, and the kiss would turn into an achingly slow exploration.

She sucked in a shallow breath as he said, "This evening is exactly what I needed to recharge me. Your serenity quiets the chaos in here." He tapped his head, then wrapped his other hand around their clasp. "And thank you for teaching me your strategy. I'll give it a shot."

The rich timbre of his voice washed through her, igniting a quiver in her lower belly. If only their circumstances were different. If only there was a way to bridge the vast disparities in culture and religion and who they were eternally promised to. They were both in exactly the same crazy moment in their lives: helpless bystanders entangled in someone else's agenda for them.

She glanced at his two-handed grip. They were holding hands. If only she had the courage to bring her other palm into this embrace, but it was too much. "You're a good man, Patrick," she said, and again, it seemed to come from far away. "I hope...I mean, I *know* things will work out for you."

"The same goes for you." He squeezed gently before letting go. "Let me walk you to your car."

Their chairs screeched as they pushed back and stood. Her full cup of tea would never be drunk. The empty coffeehouse was dim, and the lone barista wiping down a table at the far end paused to wish them a good night. She probably thought they were a couple.

For a split second, Zamira allowed it to be true in her alternate universe. Rewrote her story so that this evening she'd gone after what she wanted and was living the joyful life her deepest self had always craved.

CHAPTER TWENTY-SEVEN

"As-salāmu ʿalaykum," Faisal Abdul murmured, and although he was the same height as Zamira, he managed to look down his nose at her.

"Waʿalaykumu as-salām," she responded demurely under her parents' watchful gazes. Was she pulling off the false enthusiasm? Her skin crawled, and it took everything not to shiver in revulsion. The goiters on his neck seemed to have multiplied since the last time she'd stood this close. And now that she'd experienced all the visceral sparks of touching Patrick, it was impossible to stop her imagination from hideously fast-forwarding to a future of lying beside Faisal and his lumps...soft and squishy under her fingertips. She jerked her gaze away, her breath so shallow that oxygen wasn't reaching her brain. Her brother had woken this morning with a fever and was home with Jaddi. If only Allah had allowed her to trade places with either of them.

Around them, the giant foyer of Mosque Mohammed grew noisy with clusters of families emerging from Eid and the sermon celebrating sundown's end of Ramadan.

Quite a few people studied the foursome, and it wasn't lost on Zamira that she and her parents had been embraced by many when they'd arrived. Perhaps it was the spirit of generosity and charity this holy holiday dictated. Or perhaps it was the revered and respected Faisal Abdul's personal attention. Zamira ignored the gawking crowd, maintained her shy smile, and avoided the traitorous impulse to stare at his goiters or bulbous nose. She beseeched Allah to endow her with gratitude and generosity of spirit. She would please so many if she could just embrace her future with the same happiness it was instilling in others.

"I must go outside for a moment to assess the state of the protesters and the final preparations for the fireworks," Faisal Abdul said in a pompous tone, and turned to Babi. "May I entertain the thought of joining you for the feast?"

Babi gushed his approval, and Mami bowed her head, the drape of her hijab falling forward, which still did not hide her beaming smile. Faisal Abdul made his way to the entrance, his path cleared by clusters of people parting before him. "A fine man," Babi murmured, his smile widening as someone called out a greeting.

Soon her parents were surrounded by previously standoffish friends. Unable to maintain demureness in the face of such hypocrisy, Zamira escaped into the enormous central washroom, which was blessedly empty. Maybe if she hadn't met Patrick last night, hadn't experienced all those quivering urges, she wouldn't have anything to compare with this current abhorrence. She sat on one of the stone benches surrounding the ornate fountain and bowed her head. "I cannot bear this task," she whispered. "I've tried so hard to respect my parents' wishes all my life, but in this I cannot. Please, *please* find a way to get me out of this match."

As if on cue, the ground trembled beneath her feet. Tiles jittered as a deafening blast rocked the room, flinging her off the bench. She shrieked as her shoulder slammed against the side of the fountain and clumsily clung to the edge. What was happening? Water splashed over her forearms. Chunks of ceiling rained down. She huddled in a fetal position, covering her head. Another earsplitting *boom*, somewhere close to the mosque, created more tremors that rocked the washroom. More concrete and dust fell upon her. Her parents! How could she escape?

Zamira rocked to her knees, coughing and choking on the debris. The entire room was a thick haze of gray powder and particles raining down. Her ears rang like a shrill bell was lodged in her head. Draping her hijab around her nose and mouth, she rose on trembling legs, eyes stinging. Way in the distance, a soft red exit sign glowed in the haze. She staggered toward it.

A third prolonged explosion, much closer, blasted her off her feet, and a crushing weight of concrete landed on top of her as she hit the ground.

TRICK'S PHONE DINGED AGAIN. He swiped the message open and grinned at another photograph Sean had texted. Amy was having the time of her life, and that was a balm to his soul. He texted back the thumbs-up icon and chucked his phone next to the portable radio that had been intermittently squawking all evening.

The school grounds were well lit, and a thumping bass came from the gymnasium. Shifting into gear, Trick circled the packed parking lot again, at war with whether to park on the grass and sweep into the gymnasium to take his rightful place at Amy's side or live to legally fight another day. He should leave. He'd figure out a way to make this up to her—maybe Zamira could help find something that wasn't against the center's rules.

He sighed. It wasn't the dance; it was the point of the matter. Him sitting out here like a powerless chump. At every helpless turn, he was letting his daughters down. "Find the positive," he muttered, visualizing Zamira's encouraging smile last night. Let's see... Amy had ended up going to the dance. She was clearly having a blast.

The portable radio sent out an elongated tone. Trick frowned at the device, the hairs on his neck prickling. That was the all-hands signal—a *massive* disaster. "Shit." Trick cranked up the volume.

"All hands be advised," came dispatch's disembodied monotone. "A series of explosions at Mosque Mohammed on South Wabash and East Sixty-sixth Place. Responding units proceed with caution due to the possibility of additional explosives. Potential MCI."

Mass-casualty incident. Trick spun the wheel and roared out of the parking lot. Jesus Christ. *Zamira!* That was her mosque—her engagement was there tonight. Sweat trickled down his back as he stomped the gas and took the corner on two wheels.

Dispatch went silent, the norm for the preparation of task assignments to follow. His station was on the other side of town, but MCI... No doubt they'd be included. The list began, organized by battalions, the monotone drone making it all the more gruesome. "Engine Thirteen, Truck Six, Ambulance Seventy-Four, Engine One..."

Trick gunned it onto the freeway as dispatch called the six mass-casualty units, the entire Central and East Districts' rescue, BLS, and ALS medic units, engines, and trucks. There was the appropriate command assignment, then medic units from neighborhoods were toned out, all mutual aid protocols for a mass-casualty incident. Finally, Trick's unit in South Shore was called, Engine 126, Truck 9, Ambulance 50.

Trick careened into the far-left lane and leaned on his horn, tailgating vehicles into swerving to the right. Pete was on as acting lieutenant tonight. Cap would've gone home by now, but he'd be there. Something this big usually brought out even bigger fish than battalion chiefs and their boss, the district chief. Someone like the assistant deputy fire commissioner—Pop—would assume command. Trick's gut tightened at the bad blood between them.

"Main, Engine Eleven on scene. MCI! MCI! Setting up triage on the east side of the parking lot. Entire west end of the building is gone. Eyes on walking wounded. Bodies everywhere." The voice trembled on the last two words.

Each apparatus began announcing their arrival, describing the daunting casualties they were witnessing. Saliva evaporated from Trick's mouth as the body count continued to grow. The ride seemed interminable, the radio chatter ceaseless in conveying horrific updates.

He wove around cars jamming the streets with rubbernecking citizens, aggressively merged in front of media vans, and passed antagonized cops trying to clear the road. Each officer let him gain a few more feet after he flashed his CFD badge, until the road ahead was fully blocked by CFD apparatuses and laid hose lines. He double-parked, grabbed his flashlight and gloves from the console, and jumped out. Thick layers of ash and debris rained like soft, warm snowflakes, gagging his airway. Even from here, it was obvious that a third of the mosque was reduced to rubble.

As Trick bolted down the sidewalk, industrial-strength spotlights lit the scene and the swirling particles. The gruesome reports hadn't done the mayhem justice. The sheer number of victims sitting or lying on the colored tarps stole his breath. How would he ever find Zamira? Shrieks of agony or cries for family members could be clearly heard over the shouts of first responders and intermittent wails of sirens still arriving.

Trick ran from the green tarp, the walking wounded who had BLS units checking pulses and applying bandages, to the yellow tarp. No sign of her there, among the women crying or lying unconscious. Trick bellowed her name as he crossed to the red tarp, the severely wounded—the compound fractures, open wounds, and traumatic head injuries. Here the animalistic moans and gasped prayers mingled with the curt communication of advance life support crews squeezing IV bags, intubating and scribbling vitals on color-coordinated tags attached to each victim.

Trick ignored the cacophony as he made his way past each victim, scanning the faces of the half-burned women. No Zamira.

His relief was short-lived as he steeled himself and glanced at the black tarp. Motionless bodies lay in rows as a lone firefighter covered them with sheets. Trick's heart flipped in his chest. *Not her. Please, God. Not Zamira.*

"Quinn!" someone called, and he spun around. Kevin Needham from Truck 62 was waving. "We need help evacuating. There's a spare helmet and SCBA in the truck." He jerked his head toward his apparatus. "It's bad in there. B side isn't structurally sound enough. Go in through D."

Trick nodded, hustled to the truck, and grabbed the gear. Passing half-destroyed cars with shattered windows or no top, he scanned the newly rescued victims being carried out by crews. Still no Zamira. As he got closer to the smoking gap in the mosque, he skirted around blackened, severed body parts that littered the asphalt. The stench of burned flesh and the metallic tang of blood was so overpowering he fought not to retch. Quickly adjusting the borrowed SCBA mask over his face, he strode inside.

The atmosphere was surreal. In the glow of lamps, floating dust rained on silently moving first responders. A firefighter wearing a chief insignia pointed to him, then down a branch of what looked to have been a giant foyer. Trick raised his thumb and threaded his way carefully over the rubble.

Another firefighter emerged from what looked to be a kitchen area and flashed the all-clear sign, pointing to his right, further into the structure. Trick threw him a thumbs-up too and trudged on, sucking in the compressed air, sweeping his flashlight in an arc. Within ten feet, he spotted a closed door with the standard female stick figure and carefully pulled the handle. Splashing water and the sounds of rain and falling debris filled the air. He lifted the mask and hollered, "Hello? Anyone in here?" Nothing but dripping water. He propped the door wide with a chunk of rubble and stepped in.

It had been a grand bathroom with cement benches circling an imposing center fountain. Water continued to cascade from the top, but the cracked foundation gushed water in several directions. Multiple pipes from the sinks that surrounded three sides of the bathroom had burst, shooting geysers that poured onto the tile floor. Drains somewhere nearby gurgled loudly. He crouched and haphazardly shined his light under the stall doors. The place seemed empty. Just a few feet farther around the fountain to be sure, and then he'd continue down the hall.

There. A figure in a yellow hijab lay in an impossibly small fetal position on the tile. Trick hurried over, careful of the wobbly concrete and pooling water. She lay on the wet tiles, a slab of concrete on her hip. One arm covered her head, no blood visible. He moved the arm covering her face and his heart shot to this throat. "Zamira!"

Be alive, he prayed, yanking off a glove and feeling for a pulse. Thready. He swept his palms along her body, searching for any compound fractures, sidetracked for a split second at how small and curvy she was. Those shapeless dresses had completely disguised her figure. No detectable external injuries. "Zamira," he called loudly, and grasped her shoulder. The muscle twitched, and she groaned. Barely audible over all the splashing water, but the best sound he'd heard in ages.

He rolled her gently on her back. One side of her face was wet and clean, the other caked in ash. Lush, dark hair peeked from the now-loose hijab, and he tugged it off, swiftly feathering fingers through her scalp. No visible damage anywhere. "Let's get you outside."

He shoved the scarf in his belt and lifted her in his arms. She was even lighter than Eve. Her hair cascaded down his arm, and swept the wet tiles. Nothing he could do about it now. Wrapping her back in her hijab was precious time wasted. He carried her from the bathroom, down the hallway, and across the damaged foyer. Outside, the blinding rescue and media spotlights and the commotion of shouts, sirens, and helicopters were jarring, but Zamira didn't stir.

Although she showed no outward signs of injuries, her loss of consciousness and threadbare pulse made it a no-brainer. Trick headed for the red tarp and immediate ALS care.

He laid her down gently and ripped off the helmet and SCBA. "LOC, probable BP issue," he called, and out of the mass of first responders striding around him, a vaguely familiar paramedic dropped to her knees by his side.

"I know her," Trick said, and to his horror, his voice caught. "I'm going back in, but if you could do your best..."

"Always do," came the curt reply.

Of course. What a stupid thing to say. As the paramedic Velcroed on a blood pressure cuff, Trick brushed away the wet strands of hair sticking to Zamira's damp cheek and cupped her face. "You're going to be okay. I'll be back." He shook out the yellow silk and covered her head, then gathered her flowing mass of hair, scooping and tucking several times before it was all beneath the material. He tied the ends underneath her chin. The result looked ridiculous, but her modesty was secured. On impulse, he grabbed her hand and bent his head over it. Spoke his pleas to God, Allah, and the universe. Whoever was listening. The contact with her was all too brief—he had to get back inside—but, as always in her presence, something in his soul fell into place. They must have loved each other passionately in a prior lifetime. One day soon, he'd contemplate the meaning of that.

Trick stood, wiping the sweat from his forehead as he surveyed the entire scene, the shocking destruction. Over by the first engine on scene, and flanked by various battalion chiefs, Pop issued orders through a walkie-talkie held close to his lips. His gaze, though, was on Trick. Trick waved the helmet, but his grim-faced father didn't acknowledge the gesture. No doubt he'd caught the insanely unprofessional delay of rescuing others to cover a woman's hair and pray over her inert form. Other lives hung in the balance. Too bad. Trick lowered the helmet. Given a reset button, he'd do it all over again.

"Lieutenant Quinn."

Trick pivoted right into the spotlight glare of a media camera.

"Is that the other woman?"

CHAPTER TWENTY-EIGHT

"Authorities are still searching for the source of the bombing that rocked Mosque Mohammed at eight-oh-seven this evening," the newscaster stated, "but the massive amounts of fireworks also found in the area caused added destruction, according to a spokesman for the mosque. At this time, forty-eight are confirmed dead and hundreds are injured or missing."

"Turn it off; they're not saying anything new," Eve said irritably, but her parents, seated on either side of the sofa, remained glued to the chaos onscreen.

"Such a shame," Mom murmured.

Dad grunted. "An eye for an eye."

"This mosque had nothing to do with last week's bombings, Jeb."

"Did any of these Muslims speak out against that jihadist? No." He gestured to the TV. "So even if they weren't physically involved, their silence implicated them."

Eve rolled her eyes at the predictability. Her parents staying here for the fifth day was on her last fucking nerve.

"There's Trick." Mom pointed at the screen before she caught herself and clapped the same hand over her mouth. Eve ceased to be aware of anything but her thudding heartbeat. Onscreen, Trick, in profile, was playing with a Muslim woman's hair and fussing with her scarf. Then he curled over her hand. Was he *kissing* it?

"What the hell?" Dad muttered.

The pain in Eve's chest was crushing and all-consuming. How *dare* he?

"Lieutenant Quinn. Is that the other woman?"

Eve stared at the screen, willing him to answer no, to say Eve would always be his true love, but Trick just stuck his helmet on his head and trudged toward the mosque. His shoulders sloped forward, a clear sign he was on his last ounce of energy.

Eve turned abruptly from the screen, pulse pounding. Her parents were watching her wide-eyed and, if she wasn't mistaken, holding their breath. Like, what? They were waiting for her to freak out? She blinked away stinging tears. Who cared that Trick had another woman? A *Muslim*. Wasn't that totally heretical for them anyway? May she rot in hell!

And who cared if Trick was exhausted past his superhuman level? He was cheating on her!

"Well, this should help your case," Mom huffed.

"Shut up." Eve squeezed her fists. "Just shut up!" Unable to bear another second of their cloying attention, she jumped to her feet. "I think it's obvious he's too busy to come beat me up. You guys can go home. *Please.* Give me one night to myself already." It was so like them to not know when to quit overprotecting her. As soon as the detail of them staying here for her safety had been fed to the national media, their gesture had lost its value. Now it was just fucking torture.

"Evelyn Grace!" Mom sputtered, but Eve held up her palm.

"I'm going to check on Tina, and when I get back downstairs, I want you both gone."

As she stalked by the television, she couldn't help but glance at it once more. Although Trick was no longer onscreen, his betrayal still stabbed her heart. It wasn't that she was hurt. No, she wasn't *hurt*. She couldn't care less. It was hate that welled. To think, all week she'd assumed he was crushed and brokenhearted, when he'd obviously been hiding his own affair right under her nose. Boy, was he going to pay.

Eve started up the stairs, her mom's voice drifting after her. "She's not herself, Jeb. I think we should sit tight."

The lack of an immediate answer slowed her steps. She spun around, ears pricked for a response. Dad should be adamant about staying and protecting her! Why this silence? "No," he finally said, his tone resigned. "Let's give her some time and distance. I think we could use it too, to get some perspective on what's really going on around here."

What's really going on around here? Eve stomped upstairs, lips trembling. She'd already spelled it out with the bruises. No way could Dad be questioning this again. She clenched her teeth and followed the sound of tuneless humming. In the girls' room, Tina lay on her stomach, coloring. Eve walked on, in no mood to engage. All this week it had been "Daddy this," and "Daddy that," and so help that child if she mentioned him right now!

In her bedroom, with the door firmly shut and locked, Eve breathed out a shaky sigh. She reached into her underwear drawer and withdrew the burner phone.

He answered in one ring. "I absolutely can't talk now."

"Evidently, I haven't taken enough drastic action," she snarled.

"I think you have, babe. You're taking everything he's got."

"He has someone on the side!" she shrieked. "One of the Muslims there. Did you know about her?"

"No. This is the first I've heard, I swear."

She paced, clenching and unclenching her fist. "He just humiliated me on a hundred channels. I want him to pay for this."

He snorted. "Pay how? He won't have a cent left. And I've heard his father is siding with you."

She halted abruptly. "Really?" Connor Quinn siding with *anyone* over his golden boy? Some of the trembling subsided. Her father-in-law had a spotless reputation in this city. His word held weight. Maybe she could think of a way to use his opinion to her advantage. But this issue had to be dealt with first. Trick had hurt her! "Still."

"Don't fuck anything up at this stage of the game, girlie."

She was in enough of a mood to chew him out for the "girlie" comment but held back. She needed him. He knew too much. "I want Trick to have an accident."

"Are you out of your *mind?*"

His increasingly disrespectful tone set her teeth on edge. "I'm not saying a fatality, but he needs to get a clear message."

"You've given him four million messages, sweetheart. Stop kicking the dead horse."

"You want my money? You want my VJ? *Do it*," she snarled, and hung up.

CHAPTER TWENTY-NINE

Zamira awoke to a sledgehammer sensation in her head. She moaned at the immediate urge to vomit and squeezed her eyes shut.

"Hello, dear."

Too afraid to move, Zamira swallowed her thick saliva and carefully squinted left. An elderly nun stepped up to her bedside. A bed with rails.

"My name is Sister Agnes."

"What...?" Zamira whispered. Even before the nun grasped her hand, the events flashed back. The mosque washroom trembling like an earthquake. The explosion that still rang in her ears. "Mami...Ba—" It was too much effort. She silently recited a dua for her parents' safety, a tear trailing out of her eye.

"Now, now." Sister Agnes patted her hand. "Give thanks to God that you're all right."

"Where...?" Zamira squinted at the brightly lit ceiling to finish the sentence.

"You're at Evanston Hospital. It's quite a ways from your mosque, but all the hospitals were filled by the time they got you in one of the ambulances."

"What...?"

"A bomb, dear. They think it was one of the protesters."

"My parents..."

"Give me their names and I'll try to find out where they are, all right?"

With breaks for shortness of breath, Zamira said and spelled her parents' names.

"I'm still making rounds to everyone on this floor," Sister Agnes said, "so give me a little time and I'll call other hospitals."

With a final gentle hand squeeze, she placed the call button in Zamira's palm, said a soft prayer to Mother Mary, and bustled out. Zamira trailed her free hand slowly up her aching body and touched her throbbing head. Her hair streamed freely on the pillow. *Forgive me, Allah, I cannot cover it just now.* More tears flowed.

A bomb? Why them? Where were her parents, her family's friends? What had happened?

"Hey." The soft male voice made her start and wince once more. Patrick loomed above the bed, blocking the bright light. He smelled of bay cologne and smoke, and most of his raven hair was gray with debris. Oily streaks smudged his face, darker in the spider wrinkles around his red-rimmed eyes. His expression was grave.

On instinct, she inched the sheet upward to conceal her hair. He frowned at the strands. "Guess I didn't tie it tight enough," he murmured, and strode out of sight.

What...?

In seconds, he was back with a thin white towel, which he draped about her head. He pressed the cloth gently around her ears and skull, and tucked her hair underneath. The intimacy of the gesture quickened her pulse, which aggravated her pounding headache. She shut her eyes to distance herself. What was worse? Lying here without hijabing, or having a man who was not family take such liberties?

She was overthinking again. The will of Allah was for Patrick to do this favor. She relaxed and concentrated on the exact points of contact to relive it when she was safely alone. His shadow withdrew, and she peeked up at him. The ash and filth covering him enhanced his dark angel looks. Her heart shivered a beat.

"How did you know...I was here..." Again, her breath ran out. Her lungs felt clogged, like she could cough forever and not clear out the grime.

He pulled over a chair and sat down with a weary grunt. "I found you in the bathroom."

She searched his face. Of all the victims in that mosque and all the first responders... "*You* saved me?"

"Your hijab had come off, so I tried to retie it." He gestured helplessly, his chuckle a short, swift burst. "Give me fire suppression maneuvers anytime."

"Thank you..." she whispered, "for saving my life."

He nodded, shrugging like: *this is what I do.* "The EMT who transported you made sure to tell me where he'd taken you."

She licked parched lips. "I need to...find my parents..."

"I know." He propped his forearms on the railing and gripped her hands. Goosebumps prickled through her. The comparison to last night in the coffee shop was inescapable. There they'd cloaked the physical contact under the disguise of shaking hands. Here he'd assumed control, and, although haram, it was exactly what she needed. She didn't pull from the comfort. "Try not to worry," he said. "Sister Agnes will find them. You just concentrate on getting better."

She seized on his odd tone. "How many dead?"

"Too many. I pray to God this insanity stops tonight."

Unable to hold back any longer, Zamira wept openly. Even if her parents escaped unscathed, which now sounded impossible, her world would never be the same. "Why us?"

He shook his head. "The FBI is investigating. The National Guard has been called out to protect the other mosques." He sighed. "Get some sleep. It's almost dawn. They gave me a few hours' break, but I'm going to go clean up and head back. I just wanted to see you—make sure you were all right." He squeezed her hands and stood.

"I'll live." The phrase brought another gush of tears, and after a split second of hesitation, he wiped them with his thumb. Despite all the aches and pains, her heart fluttered at his touch. More intimacy that awoke a roaring craving inside. Why continue to pretend Patrick didn't mean something to her? And yet Allah saw all, and he was clearly displeased. She'd lied to her parents after inviting Patrick for coffee unchaperoned. They'd touched, were still finding ways to touch. She'd been thinking of Patrick the entire time she'd been in Faisal Abdul's loathsome presence. Then prayed in the washroom for an immediate intervention to the engagement. The timing of the explosion was a little too coincidental not to take seriously. All of this haram behavior had caught up with her.

He smiled sadly. "I'll visit again tomorrow, okay?"

Say no. End what can never be. "Okay."

"Oh, I recognize you now, dear," Sister Agnes said from the doorway, which was not in Zamira's field of vision. Who was she speaking to? A few seconds later, the nun stood beside Patrick, looking from one to the other with a bright expression. "You're the firefighter that kissed her."

Every cell inside Zamira froze. Patrick blinked in pure confusion.

"Patrick?" Zamira asked in the prolonged silence.

He glanced down at her. "I held your hand and prayed..."

The nun patted his arm. "They're replaying the segment over every channel. I suppose one could interpret it as praying, but not from the angle they caught. Some reporters see it as a symbol of how we can all care for one another, no matter our beliefs. Others say you two are having an affair."

"What?" Zamira sputtered.

"We're not having an affair." His casual tone meant Patrick clearly missed the depth of this disaster. If her parents were still alive, if they were conscious and watching TV, this would kill them. Andy would recognize Patrick and *know*. He'd have her job for engaging in intimate contact with a client, an alleged pedophile. And Faisal Abdul's reaction! Yes, Allah had given her a sign, all right.

She tugged her hand from Patrick's grasp. "Go," she whispered.

"Zamira, I'll explain to the press—"

"Thank you for saving me." She paused and gathered more breath. "Please don't visit again."

"I—"

"*Go.*"

He squinted eyes that were bright with pain. Sister Agnes patted his arm again. "Go get your own sleep, son."

Patrick nodded once and left without a backward glance. Zamira gulped air like she was drowning. There were too many catastrophes happening too fast. Her mind swirled and the nausea returned.

Sister Agnes sidled to the right and took his place at

the rail. "My dear, I cannot find your parents in the admitting lists so far, but I'll keep trying. It's all very disorganized, you see. The whole city is in chaos tonight."

"Thank you, Sister Agnes." If only Jaddi spoke English or someone knew to use a TDD device to communicate with Aakil, they might have heard some news. It was time to reach out to the one member they were forbidden to ever speak to again. "Could you call my sister? She lives in California."

CHAPTER THIRTY

T rick pulled into Pete's driveway as the sun broke over the horizon. As much as his body pulsed with exhaustion, his mind buzzed like he'd drunk a half a dozen espressos. The thing about a mass-casualty incident was no one stayed on admin duties. He was easily looking at a forty-eight-hour shift before his next day off.

As he reached for the door handle, his phone vibrated. *Jace.* "Are you still on scene?" Trick asked, the dust lodged in his throat making it come out like a croak.

"Yeah. Just got assigned to the task force."

Trick grinned wearily, climbing stiffly out of the pickup. "Of course you did." Jace weaseling his way onto the most important investigation in Chicago's recent history? No surprise there. "I'll be heading back there shortly. What's up?"

"Quick update, 'cause I won't have a chance to later. Sean got squat from that trainer you talked to. Gretch and Zamira found—"

"I know. The guy came into the picture a month before the ER visits began." He hadn't had a chance to do much with that information and wouldn't for the foreseeable future.

"And that listening device I put in Amy's backpack?"

Jeez. Thursday seemed so long ago. "Yeah?"

"Luckily someone moved it upstairs, so when Eve made a phone call last night, her words were crystal clear. And it wasn't on your home line or her cell, so she's using the burner Gretch overheard the guy bring her Wednesday."

Trick rubbed his gritty eyes, another rock-solid perception dissolving. The Eve he knew didn't know about burner phones. "Was the call to the same guy?"

"Seems so. No way to prove it yet. Evidently you kissed a Muslim's hand on live TV—"

"I didn't—"

"—and Eve flipped the fuck out. She wants you to pay, her words, and insists this guy do the dirty deed."

In the pink-tinged morning light, Pete's neighborhood looked safe and deserted. "I gotta admit, I'm surprised she cares enough to be jealous."

"Colleague of mine says it's a classic narcissist's reaction. Whatever *you* do reflects on her. In that light, her reaction makes sense. She doesn't want you, but no one else can have you either."

Eve did react to others in that tunnel-vision approach. Like instead of a sympathetic response to Amy or Tina getting hurt, her first instinct was to worry their blood would ruin her clothes. All these years Trick had passed it off as Eve not wanting to admit that the sight of blood made her queasy. He grimaced. In his blindness, he'd exposed his girls to this.

"In her eyes," Jace went on, "you live to serve her. And when you don't, you become expendable. She's gets another supply source—that's the lingo they use for the new guy. And he has orders to hurt you."

"I'm pissing in my pants."

"You need to take the threat seriously," Jace snapped. "You of all people know how good she is at gaslighting people into blindly following her down the rabbit hole."

Yeah, Trick was a poster boy for living a life of epic self-delusion. If only he could feel sorry for the new guy. Trick scratched his itching scalp, dislodging dust and debris. "Any way to trace this guy?"

"You've gotta come up with some names on your end. One of your friends hates you enough to help her. Eve asked him who the woman was that you were kissing, so it's someone close enough to know the answer."

Trick's heart lurched so painfully he leaned against his cab. "No one hates me, man. Not counting her. I'm friends with everybody." Except Sam, and that guy was too busy pulling extra shifts to orchestrate this much damage. "Maybe it's someone who knows *of* me, you know, from when my lucky status kept making the papers?" To think that cloying, *positive* coverage used to annoy him.

"Do you have close buddies outside of work that would know an intimate detail like you cheating on Eve?"

"No! And for the love of God, I'm not cheating. It wasn't a kiss. Haven't you seen the footage?"

"I'm a little busy for TV, bro."

Trick opened his mouth to explain, then shook his head. He'd caught the segment in the hospital lobby, and it was pretty clear to him he'd been praying. The news anchors kept referring to Zamira as the other woman, though, instead of the nun's interpretation of a moment of hope for humanity. It was like the media wanted the world to believe the worst in him. Everything he did was filtered through a distorted lens of defending Eve the martyr.

And now he'd dragged Zamira's reputation into this.

They'd find out her identity. It had taken seconds for Sister Agnes to connect the dots. Trick sighed into the phone. "It was Zamira. I was praying over her hand." Touching her. Touching her hair. Intimate contact. On camera. Her horrified expression popped to the forefront of his mind, and he winced. What had he been thinking on that tarp?

There was a sharp obscenity on the other end. "That was her mosque? Is she okay?"

"She's conscious. Probable concussion and either bruised or broken ribs. I just came from Evanston Hospital—went to check on her."

"Sooo..." Jace said. "You're not having an affair, but she teams with us to help you, and you, with your life in the pisser, go visit her bedside. What exactly is going on?"

"Nothing."

"Trick, you can't afford to fuck this divorce up any further. Eve already holds the winning hand, and you just handed her another ace."

"Zamira's just a friend." Hopefully they were still friends. The look on her battered face would haunt him for a long time.

A loud metallic bang rent the stillness, and Trick spun toward the noise. Just a garage door jerking up on its hinges. A middle-aged woman in a peach bathrobe emerged, wheeling a blue recycling bin down her drive. *Jeez.* Trick steadied his heartbeat with a deep breath. Apparently the gravity of Eve sending someone to hurt him was sinking in.

"Anyway, watch your back," Jace said. "I have to take a back seat helping you figure it all out. If I thought cleaning up last week's bombing made for long days, this investigation is going to be ten times the pressure. I know a PI, though, so I'll text his number, and when my associate finishes backtracking Eve's cellphone pings, the

PI can follow those leads." There was mumbling in the background, then Jace's muffled voice in response. "I gotta get back to the site," he said wearily. "Don't do anything stupid."

Trick hung up and stumbled up the walkway. He'd been stupid underestimating his opponent. He'd been stupid fighting fair and playing by the rules of decency because he'd expected rationality from his wife, the mother of his kids. But the more he read up on narcissism, the more it became obvious Eve wasn't wired for those human instincts; she was wired to win at any cost. So now that she was in this jealous rage, if she couldn't take it out on him, would she turn to Amy and Tina? Or Zamira, once the media broadcast her identity? There were so many things he needed to fix immediately his head spun.

He dug in his pocket for the key to Pete's house as his cellphone dinged with Jace's text. First up: hire this PI to find out the lover's identity. *Who* was the friend?

EVE WAVED after the car carrying her kids to Saturday soccer practice, then shut the door with a groan of relief. Her parents had left early this morning, pinched-lipped and worried. The girls were gone until after lunch. She could openly engage in her favorite activity. Making. Trick. Pay.

She got out her legal pad of questions and called Cyprian.

"I'm unavailable at the moment, my dear," he said instead of a greeting. "Why don't we coordinate a time to speak after the court hearing?"

"This can't wait that long," she snapped. "Did you see my husband kissing a Muslim?"

"The whole world saw it. This can only help our case."

His patronizing tone rode right up her spine. "Something needs to be done right *now*."

"What do you suggest?"

She rolled her eyes. "You're the lawyer."

"And as such, I suggest we wait until Monday."

He wasn't taking her seriously. She was paying top dollar for nothing getting done. "Why was he never arrested for breaking the restraining order?"

"It's up to Judge Price if there will be jail time."

Goddamn it, Trick would get away with this! "You make sure there's jail time."

"Mrs. Quinn—"

Mrs. Quinn now, instead of *my dear*. Her fingers tightened around the phone. "I hired you to protect me. Now you're on his side!"

"Please stop putting words in my mouth," Cyprian said. "I'm trying to get across two points: I will not be discussing your case with you today, and I am not responsible for deciding your husband's jail time."

He was treating her like an idiot. Her mom and dad had deserted her. Gretch was nosing around Marisol, blatantly thumbing her nose with the "say hi to Eve" remark. Her entire support system was turning against her!

"I don't appreciate being talked down to, Cyprian, although I guess I shouldn't be surprised because of *these* two points: you're a man, and you're protecting your own. Big surprise. I've shown you the bruises, I've videoed him breaking the restraining order and marching right into my house, yet it's always someone else's decision to punish him. What does he have to do, kill me?"

The silence on the other end lasted long enough that she would have thought he'd hung up except for the telltale rattling of a smoker's breathing. Which, by the way, drove her batshit crazy.

"We have a solid case, Mrs. Quinn," he finally said in a chilly tone. "We'll discuss this after the hearing Monday."

"I have a legal pad full of ques—"

The line clicked, and Eve gaped at her phone. Who did he think he was? How did this prestigious lawyer not understand he was at her beck and call? She was the one with *millions* at stake.

She slammed her phone on the counter, where it bounced once and fell on the kitchen floor. The plastic casing cracked. Great! She was totally billing him for that.

The burner phone upstairs, so she threaded past spilled cereal toward the wall-mounted landline that had come with the house, cord dangling like something out of an eighties sitcom. Her knee caught the hard corner of Tina's chair, and she stumbled against the refrigerator, howling. That damn child, never pushing her chair in!

Gasping, Eve hobbled the remaining feet, grabbed the receiver, and pressed the small, square buttons. Her trembling fingers misdialed, so she started over, this time stabbing the buttons. He'd make things right. The last person in her corner. He'd had twelve hours to come up with a plan to defend her honor.

It rang four times, then his voicemail started, chilling her to the bone. He *always* took her call. This was him choosing not to speak to her. He was the reason she'd started all of this! At the beep, she hung up. He'd see the caller ID. Let that be the message.

She glared out the window. Fuck all the people who kept letting her down. Somewhere out there was a real man who'd appreciate all she did for him. Someone capable, who'd take care of her.

CHAPTER THIRTY-ONE

Zamira woke to warm fingers clasping her hand. Slowly she opened her eyes, then let out a soft squeal. Shadi sat at her bedside, beautiful hair in a ponytail, eyes filled with tears. She bowed over their grasp. "Allah has answered my prayers. As-salāmu ʿalaykum, Zamira."

"Waʿalaykumu s-salām, sister." Zamira cautiously touched her own head. The lump on her forehead felt smaller, and she breathed a sigh of relief at the cool slide of silk. Someone had hijabed her while she'd slept. "What day is it? When did you get here?"

"It's Saturday. As soon as I saw the news about our mosque, Martin drove me straight to the airport."

Zamira's heart swelled. "Mami and Babi?"

"They're in ICU at Northwestern Memorial, critical condition and not conscious yet." Shadi's lips trembled. "They found Mami under his body, so he got the brunt of the blasts. Both have multiple fractures, and they are not optimistic about saving Babi's legs." She bowed her head again, beginning to sob, but still recited her best dua for Allah to shower His merciful blessing upon their parents.

Zamira recited the same words quietly to herself, incapable of tears or finding any positive angle in any part of her life. Babi and Mami critically injured. Patrick impulsively touching her in front of rolling cameras. Zamira was the sole breadwinner now, but her job had to be on the line. "Who will be the head of the household?"

"You, of course," Shadi said emphatically. "And you'll rock it." She dug a tissue from her purse and blew her nose. "You'll easily bridge our cultures like I did."

How effortless words were. "Are you unaware of the hatred blanketing this city? How everything Babi feared not only came to pass, but struck him, Mami...all our community down? How do we move on from this? Where is Allah's blessing?"

"He is here, and the answer to the rest is self-reliance. From this day forward, we honor Allah and our parents by leading our own lives, making our own decisions."

As usual, a part of Zamira shrank at the haram ideas not espoused by the Quran, while the other side of her flickered to life. To use this opportunity to seek the freedom to live without guilt, to find answers inside herself instead of turning to Babi and the imam for direction... To choose whom to love. "What happened to Faisal Abdul?" she whispered.

"They haven't found his body and don't expect to." Shadi lowered her voice. "A witness said he was closest to the area where the bomb went off. He'd been checking on the fireworks display."

Zamira closed her eyes as nausea shuddered through her. She would never get over this. Allah had taught her a hard lesson for wishing someone ill.

"Zamira, what is it?"

"My prayers," she whispered, "are the reason for his death." Shadi laughed so loudly that Zamira rose on an elbow. "What could possibly be funny about that?"

"Your confidence in your superpowers." Zamira fell back in a woozy lump, and Shadi squeezed her arm. "You silly girl. We are not to question Allah. I can assure you He didn't guide the bomber to decimate our community just to grant you your prayer."

"It's more than that. I despised Faisal Abdul. I would have done anything not to become engaged. Obviously you did too."

Shadi's smile slipped a little. "Yes, of course I had those same thoughts, but I took action. I didn't sit around dreading my life and praying for Allah to intervene. That impending marriage forced me to choose the independent path, and I've never looked back. Look at me." She swirled a hand through her ponytail. "So I'm not a traditional Muslima anymore. But I don't question Allah's love, and I love Him the same, if not more, for every day I spend with Martin."

"But you left us to pick up the pieces. That's something I could never do."

Shadi turned her face away, such a familiar reaction when her impulsive nature was called into question.

Zamira reached through the railing and grasped her hand. "Listen to me." It was time Shadi understood that her headstrong stubbornness had far-reaching consequences. "Babi and Mami have been so hurt by your actions. The community's reaction has been horrible. We were all punished because of you. While you've been loving your independence and Martin and California, we've taken the brunt of the shame. We were as ostracized as if we carried a disease. Only Khalti has acknowledged us all these months. And worse, your leaving meant I would have to marry that horrid man. So now knowing all this, can you honestly tell me your choice is the better path?"

Shadi bowed her head, her lips moving silently. She

should pray for forgiveness. How could Allah have punished the family and not her? Not at all. She was so happy. How was that possibly fair? Look at the disaster that lay in the wake of Zamira's infractions.

Shadi opened her eyes. "I will never believe that Allah was behind the ostracism in our community. It is they who committed the sin of not adhering to his teachings." She paused, her gaze traveling the length of the hospital blanket. "I've tried many times to talk to Babi," she continued softly, "but he won't answer my calls. It's a blessing I came out here; I see that now. Allah had given me this chance to show Babi, Mami, and the community that I can love Allah, live a life true to the Quran, and still love someone who is not Muslim. Watch me fix this."

Zamira smiled sadly. "Don't tell me. Positive thoughts create positive events?" *Because toxic thoughts can create a bomb blast.*

"Exactly," Shadi's bright smile returned. "Which leads me to the firefighter on TV kneeling over you."

Zamira's breath hitched at the unexpected shift in conversation. "I don't want to talk about him."

"I'll need to know how to defend you in the community."

Yes, she would. It was now Zamira who brought shame to the Bey family. Haltingly, she recapped the incredibly long week that Patrick had been in her life. The court-ordered supervision, the growing signs that Patrick was being set up by a cunning wife, and Zamira's small role trying to find evidence. No one needed to know about the Starbucks on Thursday night. "There is nothing between us," she ended, overcome with a hot blush at the wistful tone. "I know it looks bad, and I'm certain my boss won't tolerate how many rules I've broken to become that familiar with a client."

"Then you quit," Shadi said forcefully, gesturing with

wide arms. "And find a job that feeds your passion. Live your life the way you want, Zamira. Look at how fast it can all end."

Zamira closed her eyes, suddenly weary of the choices in front of her. The struggle between not wanting to create waves and her desire to be as carefree as Shadi. Was that even possible in Chicago anymore? Even before the bombing, they'd been hounded by mass protestors. "Did they find who committed this atrocity?"

Shadi shook her head. "According to the news, the FBI has agents from all over the country investigating. So many Americans are reaching out to us, though. As senseless and tragic as this was, the outrage from all religions across the world will begin healing the divide we've felt since nine-eleven. This is a turning point, sister, and I know you'll creep out of your shell to grasp your new role proudly."

A nurse's assistant came in to take Zamira's blood pressure, and Shadi stood. "I've got to go. Aakil and Jaddi are making dinner, then tomorrow morning I'll be back at the ICU." She picked up her purse. "I'll bring Aakil by tomorrow." With kisses on both cheeks and parting *salaams*, Shadi left.

"You're doing just fine." The CNA smiled as she released the cuff. "Someone named Gretch stopped in earlier, but she didn't want to wake you. She said she'll come back later. And is your scarf tied okay? I wasn't sure how to do it."

"Oh." Zamira clasped her hands to her chest. "It was you! Thank you."

"That man who'd visited you gave me money to buy a scarf. I found this in the gift shop when they opened this morning. I hope it's okay."

Zamira's pulse tripped at Patrick's gesture. At the

look on his face when she'd asked—no, ordered—him to go. "It's...it's perfect. I appreciate this so much."

When the CNA departed, Zamira touched her hijab again. Patrick had paid for it. Covered her hair with a towel. Even tried to retie her own hijab in front of national cameras. All to honor her modesty. Her reaction had been so wrong last night. In fact, these examples of his thoughtfulness and consideration, the way he listened to her so intently... If she were to list qualities she looked for in a future relationship, these would all be at the top.

If only she had his phone number to thank him. It was doubtful she would run into him again. Even if Allah blessed her with keeping her job, Andy would make sure Patrick was reassigned. Zamira bit her lip. She couldn't bear never seeing him again. When she got out of here, she'd find a way to meet him, to tell him about Faisal Abdul's death, and her parents' dependency, and this new and scary crossroads she faced. He'd probably challenge her the same way she'd challenged him. *Scary? Positive thoughts, Zamira. Rewrite your reality.* She closed her eyes, despair filling her heart. Her positive thoughts lay among the washroom rubble.

CHAPTER THIRTY-TWO

"We've proven the respondent recklessly disregarded and violated the protection order you issued nine days ago, your honor, and we're asking the court to assign jail time accordingly."

Judge Price scanned the plaintiff's document proving Trick had phoned Eve several hours after the last court case, which was the first violation of the protection order. He then scowled at the large screen across the courtroom, where the last frame of Trick walking out of the kitchen was frozen. A quick glance over Trick's shoulder confirmed the room full of lawyers, clients, and rows of reporters were gaping at the screen too, the air charged with anticipation. Trick hunched his shoulders, squeezing the tremor from his clasped hands. Thank God Mom and Pop weren't among the throng. Sean was in the back row, both for support, per Jace's order, and to lend money should Trick face a fine.

At the next table, Eve sat ramrod straight, her expression the entire time a blend of fear and martyrdom. During the video she'd held a tissue to her mouth as if to ward off a scream. It was fantastical, really. If there was one upside to this horrific charade, it was the relief that years of doubting his self-worth as a husband were over. He'd done all he could to be perfect amid the crazy mixed messages and her Dr. Jekyll–Mrs. Hyde personalities, like this cunning act to sway everyone in court in her favor.

Judge Price peered over his glasses. "Let me ask you, Mr. Quinn, what part of 'respondent shall not initiate or have any contact with the protected persons' did you not understand?"

A murmur rippled throughout the room; the press had their sound bite. On Trick's right, Morgan popped to his feet and gestured for Trick to stand and answer. Trick rose stiffly, his tight shirt collar and tie restricting his breathing.

"Your honor, I, uh, needed to speak to my wi...the, uh, plaintiff on a critical issue concerning our daughters. I believed it was essential to conduct the conversation without lawyers present. Before we had a chance to resolve the matter, my daughters came downstairs and suddenly I was being taped. I didn't go there to harm anyone, I swear. I wanted to make sure my daughters' *safety* was being considered a priority over our marriage." Did that make sense? Based on the judge's blank expression, he wasn't buying it. While awaiting the case to be called, Morgan had been brutally frank on the seriousness of this violation, the looming possibility of jail time. He'd ended with a final "I'll do my best, but you're on your own" lecture. The onus was a hundred percent on Trick, and that fear lodged in his throat as he gurgled out, "I apologize to you, the court and...my, uh, wife for the violations. I promise they won't happen again."

The judge's face turned baleful, like he'd heard that line a million times. Dank sweat streamed down Trick's back, making his shirt cling, adding to the current claustrophobia and overall fear of imminent confinement.

The next minutes were the longest in his life as the entire court watched Judge Price contemplate the evidence and Trick's punishment. Had Pop come through with a phone call? Doubtful. If he had, would Judge Price take this long? Look this serious?

After clearing his throat and pushing the documents aside, the judge took off his glasses and eyeballed Trick with the severity of a drill sergeant. "The court finds you in contempt of court for violating the protection order issued on May twenty-ninth of this year and hereby fines you five hundred dollars. Pay the clerk." Judge Price banged his gavel and pointed it toward the sleepy-looking woman behind a tall desk. "If I see you in my court for contempt charges again, Mr. Quinn, the hammer comes down. Am I clear?"

"Yes, sir, your honor."

"Next case."

Immediately, blinding flashes lit the room as cameras clicked and questions were shouted. The judge banged the gavel again as he bellowed for order. Ignoring the circus and Eve, Trick crossed the room on quivering limbs. Sean was already at the tall desk, pokerfaced as usual, wallet in hand. It was an added humiliation to ask his brother for a handout, but Trick had canceled all the lines of credit last week after Eve had drained their accounts. He was existing on Friday's measly paycheck and faced a mountain of bills.

Sean withdrew a wad of cash.

"Thanks," Trick murmured. After a lifetime of playing the hero with such ease, he'd stood by twice now, as his introverted baby brother saved the day with his surrogate role in the father-daughter dance, and now forking over his hard-earned money.

Morgan had his back turned, his focus on Cyprian and Eve whispering as they walked up the aisle. Before being ushered out the door held open by a clerk, Eve shot a murderous glance their way. Morgan turned back to Trick, scowling. "The press is right. You *are* lucky. Or else you've put out a fire for someone Judge Price knows. It's highly unusual to get such a soft ruling."

Pop must have come through. A lightness of spirit briefly washed over Trick, even as he half expected Judge Price to hammer that gavel and call out a change of mind. "Let's go out the back way," he muttered to Sean.

Out on the sidewalk, Gretch sidled up in dangerously high stilettos and bling-covered sunglasses. "Were you in there?" Trick asked, baffled he'd been so focused that he could've missed her in such a blindingly bright fuchsia dress.

She shook her head, her cool expression and movie-star pose attracting every male gaze for a block and a half. Even Morgan stood there with a stupid look on his face. "I only peeked my head in to hear the judgment," Gretch said. "I wanted to surprise Eve when she walked out."

"Well, thanks," Trick said politely, "but you didn't need to come."

Sean snorted. "Asking her not to show up today would've been a waste of breath."

Trick glanced from her to his brother. What was he missing?

Sean cocked his head. "The more crap Eve puts you through, the angrier Gretch gets for being duped into helping set you up."

"Angry?" Gretch snarled. "It's a goddamn travesty that a system designed to protect women can be so easily sabotaged. Eve's tricks are causing irreparable harm to women who truly need this kind of help."

"What did you say to her?" Morgan asked in a

subdued tone. He still seemed puzzled that such a bomb-shell would be holding hands with Sean, the king of nerds.

"I told her I was on to her, and that I'd be contacting you to testify against her." She whipped off her sunglasses and eyed Morgan. "I'm Gretchen Allen. I helped her escape her so-called *violent* home life and check into a women's shelter."

"Oh yes," he said vaguely, "I've heard about you. You were Cyprian's strongest witness."

"Not anymore."

Trick rubbed his eyes as his sluggish brain tried to recall when the subject of Gretch had come up. Maybe Morgan had gotten wind of her from all the inaccurate newspaper accounts or Eve's drama-filled lies on national morning talk shows.

"I would very much like to hear your account, Miss Allen." Morgan dug out a business card and handed it to her. "If business hours are a problem, I can meet evenings, too. I'm at your disposal."

The prolonged and meaningful look he gave her struck Trick as a blatant come-on, but Sean didn't bat an eye. Gretch hid behind her sunglasses again. "Whatever I can do to prove she's a liar," she answered shortly. "I'll call with my schedule once I get back to the office. Come on, Sean."

Once they left, Morgan shifted his briefcase to the other hand. "You have some time to come back to the office and discuss strategy?"

Trick glanced at his watch. He had an hour to kill before meeting with Jace's PI friend. "Sure. What comes next?"

"We need to file responsive declarations. One to dismiss the TPO, which will be hard, given you violated it twice already. And the other to seek partial or full child custody."

"Let's start with the custody," Trick said firmly. "This whole supervision thing is bullshit." His thoughts turned to Zamira lying in a hospital bed. He'd respected her wishes and hadn't visited, but no way was their budding relationship dying. Until he had the upper hand in this marital battle, though, his focus had to stay on outmaneuvering a narcissist's mind games.

CHAPTER THIRTY-THREE

Zamira picked up the small overnight bag Shadi had packed for her and hobbled across the hospital room. There was still a pinching impingement in her hip where a chunk of the washroom fountain had collapsed on her, but the doctor had assured her that, after a six-week course of physical therapy, she'd recover full function.

Halting in front of the small mirror, she smoothed her new hijab and gently caressed the bluish-yellow bruise on her right cheek. The puffiness made her face look lopsided, but Insh'Allah, if that was all she had to complain about, then she was blessed. So many weren't as lucky. The first responders had found the remaining bodies, and although not all had been identified, the casualty list was closing in on one hundred, with about twice the number sustaining injuries.

Shadi popped her head in, flashing her sunshiny smile. "Ready?"

Zamira nodded, trailing her sister slowly toward the busy nurses' station for discharge instructions and a prescription. A few feet into the journey, her heart hopped into her throat. Patrick was leaning against the counter, head bent as he scrolled through his phone. Beside him lay a cellophane-wrapped bouquet of daisies. Despite the hectic bustle, he seemed deaf to the chatter and blind to the parade of nursing staff ogling him. Zamira limped forward, knees quivering. He'd come back. Her rudeness on Saturday had no lasting effect. She sent a prayer of thanks.

"Patrick?"

He glanced up, shoving the phone in his pocket. His smile was slow and lopsided, his bashful expression tinged with uncertainty. "Hey, Zamira."

That bay woodsy scent settled around her like a favorite blanket. She searched for words vague enough not to draw Shadi's attention that would let him know she welcomed his presence. "What a lovely surprise."

His features relaxed, and he handed over the flowers. "I heard you were getting discharged and didn't know if you needed a ride."

"How sweet, thank you." She cradled the crackling cellophane, then gestured to Shadi, who was regarding them with avid interest. "I have a ride. This is my sister, Shadi. This is Patrick Quinn, the firefighter who pulled me from the rubble."

The two shook hands. "Sure, I've seen your picture on Zamira's desk," he said. "Nice to meet you." As Patrick's grin deepened, Shadi looked downright dazzled.

"I recognize you, too. You're taller than you look on TV, though. Allah's blessings upon you for saving my best friend." She slung an arm around Zamira.

"Your sister kinda saved me first." Although this was said to Shadi, Patrick's warm gaze shifted to Zamira. The intimate coffeehouse conversation roared back, as did the haunting memory of those profound tingles when they'd touched. Thursday seemed so long ago, her complaints that evening so overly dramatic in light of this tragedy. Even the media misinterpretation at the rescue site seemed trivial.

Zamira fingered the hijab. "Thank you for this."

He perused the fabric with a critical expression. "Definitely beats the hospital towel."

"White was never her color," Shadi said with a mock shiver. They shared another mutual grin.

A harassed-looking tech pushing a gurney with a zigzagging wheel drew close, and Zamira shifted toward Patrick to give it room. He pressed against the counter to provide as much personal space as possible. Thoughtful acts like this were why she stayed so smitten. Guide him in what was permissible and he did his best to respect her boundaries. "Are you still working at the mosque?"

He shook his head. "I worked a forty-eight, then had a court appearance this morning."

Oh yes, the contempt of court charge. She swallowed the urge to ask about the outcome. These few days in the hospital had cured her of her compulsion to entrench herself in the middle of his fiasco. When Andy had visited yesterday, his troubled expression had never cleared. Any attempt to broach the subject of Patrick bending over her hand in *prayer* though, had been swiftly interrupted with chitchat about colleagues. There must be something in Andy's beloved policy manual pertaining to not firing employees while they lay in hospital beds, so as of now, she still had her job. She smiled up at Patrick, redirecting her attention to the grueling forty-eight hours he'd worked helping out her community. "Is it appropriate to say 'thank you for your service' to first responders, too?"

He gave the one-shouldered, *It's what we do* shrug. "You're welcome. And you? Are you okay to return to work?"

"Yeah." She gestured to Shadi holding the discharge order. "Although I don't report until next week." At his dismay, she assured him another provider would take his case, which didn't clear the look on his face.

"Say," he said with a swift glance at her sister, who was pretending to read the paperwork, "I was wondering if, um, I could buy you and Shadi a cup of coffee."

"Perhaps soon," Zamira hedged. Why not give herself more time to think this forbidden attraction through? "We're about to go see my parents in the Northwestern ICU." They were conscious now and refusing to see Shadi, but she stubbornly returned each day to try again. Their reaction was no surprise, but in light of the tragedy and shocking fragility of life, their refusal to acknowledge their firstborn seemed petty and obstinate. Zamira's goal today was to run interference as the voice of reason.

"We can visit them this afternoon," Shadi said, eyes widening in matchmaking excitement. "Coffee sounds excellent."

Zamira bit her lip at the temptation, but shouldn't one Bey daughter uphold the family traditions and expectations? It would take a long time for her parents to be well enough to arrange another marriage for her; why add to their worry and burden by daydreaming of following in Shadi's wayward tracks?

Zamira steeled herself to say no as she turned to Patrick. The hopeful expression on his handsome face melted her heart into goo. "Yes," she murmured, "I'd like that very much."

———

"ARE CHAPERONES SUPPOSED TO DO THAT?" Trick gestured to Shadi out at a patio table, cellphone glued to her ear.

"It's a sneaky way to get around the rule." Zamira said. "And if know my sister, rule-breaking is her superpower."

With Shadi's dark ponytail and the animated way she chatted with whoever was on the other line, she blended with every other Chicagoan. Passing men sent interested signals like smiling or the more aggressive full-body perusal. Women scrutinized her red heels or dramatic gestures as she laughed. No way would any of that attention happen if she were covered up in loose clothing and a hijab. "I see what you mean about the more fabric you wear, the less you're noticed."

"Except when we're noticed by people who consider us a threat."

Way to open that can of worms. Trick turned his back on the wall-length window and faced Zamira. Her complexion was wan, eyes etched with worry. She'd mentioned that her income would have to carry her whole family, and yet her boss was upset at the unprofessional relationship that had resulted in the prayer debacle. Trick ignored the impulse to reach across and clasp her hands. Like he hadn't learned that lesson. Yeah, they hadn't been overtly recognized in this public place, but that didn't mean someone wasn't covertly filming this interaction for TMZ. He leaned on the small table, putting all the tenderness he felt for her in his tone. "I'm sorry I made things so much worse for you."

"Enough with the apologies." She cradled her tea in both hands. "The media caught a bad angle. Besides, we're yesterday's news. They've moved on to the governor's scandal." Her smile didn't reach her eyes.

"I'm pretty sure my court case will get a mention." He brought her up to speed, including hiring a PI, but kept it short and sweet. All they ever did was talk about his fiascos, and here she was dealing with a mass disaster and critically injured parents. "How are you really holding up?"

She traced the rim of her cup. "Physically I'm on the mend, but mentally I'm not holding it together too well."

"What happened to those positive thoughts?" he joked, but by her stricken expression, it was another blunder.

"It's like I never knew how to do it," she said softly. "My mind draws a blank whenever I try. I can't move past this overwhelming negativity. My prayers have suffered too. Something inside me is severed, and I...just feel empty."

"You've been through a huge trauma, Zamira. Give yourself a break."

"The man I was supposed to marry died in the blast."

The subject change was so abrupt Trick blinked. Her wide brown eyes grew luminous with tears, and his muscles twitched to comfort her. He hadn't known he was such a physical man until he was forbidden to touch the people he cared about. Cursing his circumstances all over again, he tucked his hands under his thighs.

"I'm sorry for your loss." He made it come out like a question, because her dread at the match was starkly fresh, along with his dumbfounded reaction that she'd willingly sacrifice her independence to obey her family. Sure, the man's death was tragic, but her freedom was intact. Why was she near tears?

"My last thoughts in the washroom were beyond negative," she said in a shaky voice. "About him, my circumstances... And ever since then, my thinking is all..." She gestured in loopy circles.

Monkey mind. He nodded. "I've been there."

"I thank Allah I'm alive and that my parents are on the mend, but going through the bombing makes me question the certainties in life. Like hard work pays off, or obeying rules keeps you safe. Now I feel like my only accomplishments have been trying to mold myself to someone else's edicts. And for what? Where has being the perfect daughter and perfect employee gotten me? Our lives could end tomorrow. Why are any of us doing anything in life that makes us uncomfortable or unhappy?" She swallowed hard and gestured helplessly. "But these thoughts aren't like me either and I feel like a misfit."

She definitely had symptoms of PTSD. And if she did, that meant he did, because he identified with every word. He jerked in his chair at the epiphany. "Sorry." He chuckled at her alarmed expression. "You brought up some great points." How had he not seen this in himself before? It was his pet project to keep his crew mentally healthy; he *knew* the signs. "It's pretty normal," he said slowly, "to feel anxious and unmotivated after a physical or emotional trauma. Even though the danger is over your mind is still in fight-or-flight mode. It happens a lot in our profession."

"How do firefighters deal with this kind of trauma as a job?"

He spread his hands. *Sometimes not well.* "Talking it out helps, like individual therapy." Even though he'd refused Pop and Cap's recommendation. In hindsight, it was a hundred percent self-sabotage. "We also implemented a group support and a twenty-minute meditation after each active callout. That's gone a long way to combat the crew's stress and squirrelly thoughts."

She nodded absently. "You mentioned meditating before. Maybe I'll look into it."

He was an expert in guided meditation. This was the perfect opportunity to help her seek solace, to release the constricted awareness of her trauma. But the exercise held little appeal. He was still fighting his own trauma.

Trying to pick up the pieces. Not knowing what pieces were even important anymore. And yes, this apathy was disturbing. No matter how Jace or Pete urged him to anger and action, here he was...

He frowned at his coffee. Damn if Jace's escapism remark wasn't right on the money. The reason meditating had become near impossible was because ever since Trick got married, he'd used it as a coping mechanism. And when the shit hit the fan ten days ago and Eve was no longer a fixture in his life, that kind of escapist meditating had ceased to be effective. "I think I've been meditating all wrong."

"There's a wrong way?"

He chuckled. "I mean it's time I tried a different approach." Stop contorting himself to fit everyone else's expectations, and expand his consciousness through self-love instead. Self acceptance. It would be hard, but he could do this.

The impulse to drop everything and find a quiet place surged through him. "If you're free today or tomorrow, I'd be honored to show you how it's done. See if it'll lead you back to your positive outlook or reconnect you with Allah?"

She shrugged skeptically. "I suppose it can't hurt. You realize Shadi will have to come along."

He mimicked the shrug right back. "She's going to have to be quiet and still for twenty minutes."

Zamira tilted her head and laughed. The carefree sound and sheer joy on her beautiful face made his chest ache with longing. No matter what happened to either of them in the days ahead, he'd find a way to get her to laugh again and again.

CHAPTER THIRTY-FOUR

A stranger was at the curb, rummaging through her trash can. "You have got to be kidding me," Eve muttered, strapping the belt of her robe tighter. "Girls," she yelled, "this is the last time I tell you to get up! You're going to miss breakfast."

Still no peep from upstairs, but her attention was fixed on the trash digger. He didn't look homeless, so what the hell was he doing? She wouldn't put it past Trick to use this kind of ploy to get under her guard. She unlocked the front door and eased onto the stoop. Only Steve Nelson was out this early, trying to open his car door while holding a briefcase in one hand and thermos in the other. That wasn't going to end well.

Eve ignored him and, leaving the door slightly ajar, marched down the drive. The ginger-haired man was transferring her garbage into a black trash bag. He looked to be around her age and sported a nice physique under clean jeans and a t-shirt. "Hey," she called shrilly. "What do you think you're doing?"

The man glanced up, a pleasant smile in place. "Mrs. Quinn?"

She paused, her brain leaping to red-alert mode. "Yes?"

"Bob Marino." His smile widened. "I'd shake your hand, but I'm a bit of a mess. I'm a private investigator."

PI? Going through her *trash*? "Are you effing kidding me?"

He nodded at her bin. "Once you put it out on the curb, it's no longer your personal property." His tone was easygoing, like he was soliciting door to door. "It doesn't require a warrant or anything. I tried not to make a mess."

Her mouth dropped open. What was Trick's game? Why would anyone want trash? She began to sputter an objection, but there was nothing incriminating in there. The PI definitely got points for audacity, though. "You're welcome to the filth." She eyed the goopy applesauce, last night's dessert, which she'd thrown out when Tina had given her lip. "But tell my bastard husband not to waste *my* money like this."

"It's not just collecting trash." Bob straightened and snapped off his gloves, adding them to his black bag. "We know about your soup-can-falling-from-the-pantry-shelf trick"—he eyed the bruising on her face like he was admiring it—"and we know about your affair. Just trying to wrap up the extent of your lying and betrayal to hand over to the judge." He pulled the bag's handles, sealing the garbage inside, and hefted it over his shoulder. "You had a good run, Mrs. Quinn, but I'm on the case now."

He saluted with two fingers and walked across the street, popping open the trunk of a nondescript beige sedan. A horn toot-tooted, and Steve Nelson waved to her as he drove by. Like an automaton, she waved back, then cursed herself.

The soup can trick? Her heart fluttered like she'd finished a hundred-yard dash. How had Trick found out about the soup can? No one had been in that kitchen!

Bob slammed the trunk.

"Hey," Eve called, her voice squeaky.

He spun toward her, that pleasant smile on his face seriously creepy given the threat he'd just hurled.

"I'm the one who's been abused, and now I have to suffer through your intimidation too? You'll be hearing from my lawyer."

His agreeable expression didn't flicker. "Nothing I said can be construed as intimidation, Mrs. Quinn." He patted his breast pocket. "I've been taping our conversation just on the off chance you misheard or accidentally misinterpreted the facts."

Was that legal? Shock kept her silent.

"Have a nice day." He slid into the front seat and revved the engine, the smile finally slipping from his face. The look that replaced it was chilling.

Long minutes after he'd driven off, she stood next to her empty trash bin, her trembling fingers holding the flaps of her robe at her throat. There was only one person she'd told about the soup can, and he was supposed to be her *partner* in all this. The ramifications caused a shiver to snake up her spine. What the fuck was she going to do?

ZAMIRA OPENED her eyes at the sound of a soft bell. Patrick sat cross-legged on her parents' living room rug, facing her and Shadi. "Namaste," he said solemnly, bowing over his prayer hands.

"Namaste," they chimed together.

"That was lovely, Patrick," Shadi gushed.

Zamira nodded, unable to describe the profoundly euphoric experience. She was humbled. Awed. Who would have thought, only days after her world fell apart, she could feel this tranquil? Sure, it would probably only last a few minutes, but in *this* moment, she was uplifted and grateful. Even more incredible, she sensed her positive vibe again.

"Thank you," she said softly and so inadequately, but he seemed to know the fathomless layers she meant underneath, because his expression went from serene to euphoric.

"It was my pleasure." He eyed Jaddi seated on the sofa, watching all of this suspiciously, and bowed again with a hand over his heart. "As-salamu alaykum." The accents were in the wrong places and his tongue had tangled in the middle, but the meaning was heartfelt. *Peace be upon you.*

Though she didn't respond, Jaddi's face softened.

"Please say you'll stay for dinner," Shadi said, completely at ease extending invitations and making people feel welcome. Perhaps it was this awakened feeling in her soul, but Zamira swallowed back welling tears. How she'd missed having her older sister's strength and sociability to lean on. Life had been fun and adventurous under her wing.

"Sure. If I wouldn't be intruding." Patrick's laidback smile swept from sister to sister to grandmother. "Something smells delicious."

"Kushari," Shadi said, leaping to her feet. "Egyptian pasta."

Patrick rose too. "May I help? I'm pretty good in the kitchen."

Zamira stifled a giggle as she went to help Jaddi off the sofa. Pretty good in the kitchen? Babi and Aakil wouldn't know how to cook a meal if their lives depended on it. "I imagine you have to be self-sufficient at the fire station."

"Yes, that," he said, slowing his stride to stay next to

her and Jaddi, "and when I got home, I'd spelled Eve from holding down the fort by herself."

They exchanged a look of cautious acknowledgement. The supervisor-client relationship was settling into something new and as yet indefinable. He'd texted a few times during his last twenty-four-hour shift, checking on her wellbeing, even mentioning his squad's suggestion to adopt the Bey family in the new citywide initiative: Adopt a Muslim Family. The crew was insisting on helping with errands, chores, and handyman tasks until Babi got back on his feet. These last few days Patrick and Zamira had been carefully paving a new friendship of mutual respect, and neither seemed willing to dredge up Eve's name or analyze Patrick's slow-moving legal problems.

They all stepped into the kitchen. Aakil must have come downstairs while they were meditating and was at the breakfast table, engrossed in homework. "This is my brother, Aakil," Zamira said, depositing her grandmother in a chair across from him. The movement caught his attention, and when he looked up, Zamira signed and spoke simultaneously. "This is my friend Patrick Quinn. He's a firefighter."

Patrick's face combined surprise with enthusiasm. "It's nice to meet you," he signed clumsily.

"You know ASL?" Zamira asked, as Aakil rapidly signed questions about firefighting.

Patrick held up a hand, laughing. "I know some basics. It's a course offered to first responders." He signed *fire, stop, pain,* and *help.* "I'm very rusty." He seated himself at the table and pointed to Aakil then himself. "You...teach...me?" he said, although he signed, *You know me.*

Zamira turned her back on her brother's excited nod and shared a contented smile with her sister, already at the stove. Imagine Faisal Abdul asking to help in the kitchen or laughing at himself as he imitated signs from an eleven-year-old?

"I fully recognize the feelings you're struggling with," Shadi murmured.

Zamira pretended not to hear. Her boring, predictable life was nothing like Shadi's all-encompassing happiness. A Muslima and a Jew transcending clashing religious beliefs and family values for love was hard not to romanticize. So, yes, while Patrick was idyllic for Zamira's daydreams and perfect for the American-pop side of her, and while she appreciated his company and the journey into meditation tonight, she was in no hurry to choose her future.

She turned from stirring the lentils to face Jaddi, who'd intuitively known of Zamira's dread at being trapped in an arranged marriage and had nipped that rebelliousness by calling her "the good daughter." Perhaps the decimation of their family unit or Zamira being the sole breadwinner and temporary head of the house had skewed her grandmother's lifelong beliefs, because from across the kitchen, Jaddi nodded in under-standing, maybe even support, and went back to watching the spirited exchange of signs with a sad half-smile.

CHAPTER THIRTY-FIVE

Trick handed over the list Jace's friend had emailed. "Sorry this took so long. The FBI is up to their necks with the bombing investigations. These are the places where they were clearly able to trace Eve's phone pings."

Bob Marino perused the sheet. "Why are so many highlighted?"

"Ones you probably don't need to check." Trick pointed to a few he recognized upside down. "The elementary school, the gym, the park, the hairdresser, the grocery store, her friend Marisol's house..." Many weren't highlighted, like the last address, in a residential neighborhood. An internet search had only brought up the property appraiser information, the owner was listed as a corporation. "I don't know that one."

"Hmm. West side."

"We have no friends anywhere near there." And yet Jace kept insisting the other man was Trick's friend.

"Thanks for this." Bob folded the list and stuck it in his wallet, then flagged the waitress for a coffee refill. "Tuesday, I made inquiries with my contacts in banks and credit card companies. Eve's opened several accounts with Chicago Trust. Wednesday, after I made sure she saw me take her garbage, I started surveillance that lasted just under twenty-four hours." He waited until the waitress poured and left. "I was sure it'd force her to either call the guy or visit, but she hunkered down and went radio silent. Not even a grocery store run."

Trick frowned. The Eve he knew wasn't afraid of anything. "Wednesday evening is peewee soccer practice. They never miss that."

Bob shrugged. "They didn't go."

"She's not answering the calls from the new court-ordered supervisor, so I haven't been able to see my girls since last Tuesday." *Ten days.* Trick clenched his jaw. "We've gotta force her hand and end this."

"I checked out the firefighters you listed from your station... Sam, Chad, and Danny. Not a trace of them have entered her orbit. Are you sure there's no one else?"

Trick scratched at the dull gold dots in the diner's Formica table. "Guess you could check out the married men." He hated suspecting any friends he trusted with his life, and pointing the finger at *married* friends really made him sick. Friends whose weddings he'd probably been groomsman at, or at least attended the bachelor party. On the other hand, when Eve wanted something, nothing stopped her from going after it. It stood to reason the guy's marital status wouldn't mean squat to her.

Bob sipped his coffee and winced. "Ugh, this is worse than the last batch." He pushed it away with a sigh. "What about the guy you're staying with?"

"Pete?" Trick glanced up for a nanosecond then refocused on the dots. "Not worth your time. He's been my best friend since we were kids."

"All the more reason to check him out." Bob reached

into his sport coat and retrieved a pen and small notebook.

"It's someone else," Trick said firmly, and thumped a palm over his heart. "I'd know it in here if it was him."

"Which means you can hand over his last name with a clear conscience, then, right?"

Still Trick hesitated. Bitter coffee churned in his gut, his cleansed spirit from yesterday's second meditation spiraling back to the dank, polluted one he'd lived with for two weeks now. Yes, of course he wanted to know the guy's identity, and yet somehow, now that Bob was ready to lead the charge, it was also a bridge Trick dreaded crossing. Knowing who'd betrayed him would be one more reminder of his colossal inability to judge character. And if that friend turned out to be Pete? There was no coming back from that kind of treachery—and it also meant Eve would win this massive legal battle. She'd have Morgan McNally's entire strategy and every vulnerable word Trick had vomited to Pete about his love for his wife... And she'd have Pete, his best friend, who'd never survive her narcissistic games. *Please, God, not Pete.*

"Dobson," Trick said softly, sliding out of the booth. "He gets off shift tomorrow morning at seven."

THE FOURTH AFTERNOON of persuading and cajoling, Zamira convinced her parents to stop banishing Shadi to the waiting room. Now the girls sat in the small space between both hospital beds, Shadi as meek and quiet as any of them had ever seen. Yesterday Babi had been transferred out of ICU, legs intact, thank Allah, and seemed in good spirits as he smiled at his wife in the next bed. Although prayer on mats was impossible, he had just led Asr, and the miracle of Allah's healing had renewed Zamira's positive spirit a little more.

"I visited Gufran Menjarra this morning," she said to Mami. "She was released from the hospital yesterday, and naturally, not a moment too soon. She has a list of grievances against the staff, the side effects of her pain medication, the cost for critical care... I think they're glad to see her go."

Mami laughed softly. "I can hardly wait to share a cup of tea. I pray Allah will bless me with a discharge, too."

The sisters traded a quick glance. Although still alarmingly weak and easily tired, Mami was determined not to complain so she could be discharged to care for her family. No matter the assurances that everything at home was running smoothly, Mami kept insisting she'd almost regained her strength.

Zamira leaned forward and clasped her hand. "I'll arrange to drive Khalti here with a thermos of your favorite tea tomorrow afternoon. How's that?"

"Isn't that when you meet your boss?" Babi asked.

Zamira stiffened and withdrew her hand. "Yes. I mean I'll drive Khalti after work." *If I'm not fired.*

His stern expression remained. "Have you prepared what you will say?"

"Allah instructs us to answer honestly, so I will." She smoothed the bedsheet with her thumb. "I'm a very good employee, but I became too engrossed with one client because I believed in his innocence. And I still do." Babi had been outraged at the mosque video footage, and Zamira had finally confessed most of her haram behavior. Her father seemed torn between his suspicions of Patrick's intentions and thankfulness that Allah was orchestrating an entire station company to watch over his family.

"Insha'Allah that you keep your job," he said firmly. "We're relying on your salary for the foreseeable future."

Zamira swallowed hard. The burdensome knowledge rarely left her thoughts. "Yes, Babi." She'd been praying to keep her job, while, on the other hand, refusing to regret the choices that had led her to this exact spot. Surely Allah had meant for her to break rules and become involved. From blurting the details to Gretch to following her instincts that something wasn't right in Eve Quinn's accusations... Hopefully she'd helped right an egregious wrong, and wasn't that in His teachings? All of her actions would be worth the cost if the end result was Patrick reuniting with his daughters. Yes, tomorrow she'd face Andy's decision without regret and, if need be, find another job.

"I can always persuade Martin to move back here, Babi," Shadi said. Silence lengthened like a murky shadow in the room, and Zamira homed in on the emotions swirling about as her parents avoided looking in Shadi's directions.

"For now," Babi said formally, "we will count on Zamira."

If they had castigated Shadi for chasing her happiness at the expense of her family's standing or not hijabing, Zamira had not been present, nor in her sister's confidence. But despite all her sins, Shadi had dropped her happy life in California to come help. Was offering to move home. And yet, in the middle of a family and community crisis, her parents were rigidly stuck in their ways.

Zamira shook her head, regret and wonderment swelling so suddenly they choked off words. *Neither* side was right. Here, finally, was Allah's sign for choosing which part of herself to honor. It was so obvious which path offered happiness.

CHAPTER THIRTY-SIX

E ve paced the living room, biting her thumbnail. What was she going to do? Everything she'd worked for was imploding. She was also stuck in her house like a trapped rat.

This was her favorite day of the week. She got tremendous attention as the booster club president for peewee soccer, but she'd spied that beige sedan down the block again this morning and freaked. Had ended up calling Chelsea's mom to carpool the girls to their game instead. That PI wasn't going to get one glimpse of her.

Eve went to the front door again and peered through the peephole. The car was finally gone. She shivered in relief. Now what? She couldn't call her parents. Not after the ugly way they'd finally left her house. Couldn't talk to Gretch the betrayer. Eve slammed a palm against the front door panel, causing a jarring pain to shoot up her arm.

Did she dare use the burner phone? She hadn't spoken to *him* all week, partly to punish him for not answering when she'd wanted to update him about Cyprian's audacity, partly because something didn't feel right. He was either betraying her secrets to the PI, or the phone was somehow tapped. Maybe she'd gone too far demanding he hurt Trick, but how could she even start damage control unless she talked to him? Gauged his mood?

Fuck it. Eve stepped over the open coloring book and crunched through a pile of crayons on her way to the stairs. This place was a mess! Damn Trick for his holier-than-thou attitude about hiring a cleaning woman. Just because his mom used to clean for wealthy families in the North Shore... "We don't put on airs," he used to say. "*We* are the cleaners and the fixers."

Eve *tsked* as she headed into the bedroom. All these years she'd tried to kick-start his desire to become one of those affluent families, but he'd wallowed in this blue-collar existence like a happy pig. Then his bright idea to hide the lottery winnings in a personal account. Money that was just as much hers.

Luckily, Illinois divided marital property "equitably," which was not the same as fifty-fifty. If Cyprian's strategy worked, she'd get what she was due out of this godfor-saken marriage. Let Trick drown in this working-class muck.

Eve yanked open the bureau drawer and snatched out the burner phone. She breathed in deeply. It all came down to this call. She was disenchanted with this rela-tionship, to say the least. If he wasn't all in and begging her forgiveness, he was getting dumped on his ass. She could find someone else in a heartbeat. She hit redial.

"I'm working," he said instead of a greeting.

"I don't care," she said in the same tone. "Why haven't you called?"

"Have you cooled down yet?"

She reared back like he'd slapped her. "*Me?*"

"After Trick kissed the Muslim woman."

"I couldn't care less." She didn't appreciate the reminder. Her pulse spiked with wrath that had taken her days to control. "Are you spilling my secrets to the PI?" she asked bluntly.

"PI?"

"The guy was taking garbage out of my can Wednesday morning."

"And this is the first I'm hearing about it?" The fear in his voice was unmistakable. "Why did you wait so long to call?"

"Because he knew about the soup can."

"What?" His voice rose to twice the volume. "Who else did you tell that trick to?"

"Just you. Why haven't *you* called me?"

He huffed out an exasperated breath, like this was her fault! "Did this guy say anything to you?"

She summed up the visit, making sure to emphasize her vulnerability and fright at being threatened on her own property.

"All right, let me talk to Trick and see what they've found out."

Eve sighed inwardly. She shouldn't have waited this long to take control of the situation. "And call me right back."

"I've told you I can't, Eve. Just lie low for a while. We've done all we can."

"Except punish Trick for cheating on me, but I guess that's not important to you."

"Not in the scheme of things, babe. You're cheating on him."

Which was not the same at all. Why couldn't he understand? Eve dropkicked her makeup stool. Her bedroom was such a mess that it bounced harmlessly onto piles of clothes. "When will I see you again?" she snapped. He wasn't acting right, but maybe after a good round of fucking, he'd see things her way.

"Until I know how this PI is getting his information, we won't have any communication, got it? Get rid of this burner. I'll contact you again when it's safe." He hung up.

She gaped at the phone. "Are you *kidding* me?" Like *he* was in control of this relationship? Like he would waltz in *after* all her hard work and anguish and expect to share her millions?

She threw the phone against the wall, reveling in the loud crash, the exploding fragments, the dent it left, and the fact that nobody was here to tell her what to do. Screaming obscenities, she swept the perfumes and cosmetics from her table. The stink of her fragrances quickly became too much, so she stomped downstairs, where the plates piled near the sink were just begging to be smashed into shards, one by one. Her body trembled in equal parts exhilaration and anger. She circled the kitchen on unsteady legs, flinging everything off the counters as she swore at all the people who'd betrayed her.

Out in the living room, she whipped pillows onto the floor, one on top of the other, then rounded the cocktail table to kick some toys. Her ankle caught the edge of the table, and she shrieked, hobbling in pain. Tears streamed down her cheeks. She hated her life. Hated this goddamn mess. It was all Trick's fault!

The memory of him bending over that woman's hand reared its ugly head again. Eve howled in helpless fury. He'd humiliated her, and no one was doing anything to pay him back. "I will *kill* you!"

She ripped pages from a coloring book and flung Tina's stuffed lamb into the darkened mouth of the fireplace. If only it were winter and there was a fire lit. She spun about, panting and sobbing. What else could she destroy? Basically everything in this fucking decrepit old house. As soon as she'd moved in and realized it wasn't the charming cottage she'd imagined, seen how cluttered everything was, this heap had been a thorn in her side. The first of many issues tight-fisted Trick would take a stand on, and the beginning of the end.

Inspiration struck, so brilliant she gasped. Since he loved the place, it was the first thing to go. She limped back to mantel and snatched the lighter. Yes, *this* was how she'd repay him. Burn the firefighter's house down.

Then she'd call nine-one-one and tell them she'd just seen Trick's pickup roaring off.

Eve held the flame to the corner of the upholstery pile littering the floor. Grinned as the spark caught. Stupid furniture was so ancient it wasn't even flame retardant—how fitting was that?

She hurried to the dusty floor-length draperies, an eyesore all these years. The fire zipped up the thin fabric with a *poof*, then ignited the dusty valance in a burst of flames. Eve squealed as she jumped back, slipping on the coloring book, which made her stagger backward and trip on the upended fireplace tools. Her forehead cracked against the mantel, and all went dark.

CHAPTER THIRTY-SEVEN

"What do you mean someone just tried to kill Eve?" Jace demanded. "Where are you?"

"In front of my burned-out house." Trick's voice cracked, and he shuddered in a breath. Losing it now would only be fodder for the media. He gunned the engine and pulled out of the Farnsworths' driveway. In the safety of his rearview, he glimpsed the milling reporters filming B-roll footage of his smoking home and his pickup leaving the scene. Nearby, the squad from 74 ignored the distraction and continued securing the hose. Trick headed down the block. "She's en route to Chicago General... She looks bad, Jace—we're talking second and third-degree burns over half her body."

"Jesus."

"I saw a knot on her forehead, too. Someone hurt her, then tried covering it up with arson."

"You think someone tried to *murder* her?"

Trick stopped at a red light. Jace knew what she was capable of—the lengths she was willing to go in this divorce. Here was the chance to float the crazy theory that she'd started the fire herself. Maybe to blame him, which was exactly what the media had done when they'd arrived. Trick opened his mouth.

No. It was too insane. *Someone* had given her that knot on her forehead. "The only reason she's alive is the neighbor across the street saw the smoke and called it in." And she was barely alive. What would happen if she died after accusing him and videoing him and going on national talk shows? Sweat beaded his forehead. If he thought his life was shit now...

"I wish I had the time to help you, man," Jace said. "Call Marino. He's an ex-cop; he'll have contacts with the arson investigators."

So would Pop, but after these two weeks, the idea was beyond a dead end. Chest aching, Trick signed off and called the PI.

"Hey," Bob said, "I was just about to call—"

"I think someone tried to kill my wife." Trick quickly described the last forty minutes.

"When was the call?"

"The dispatch went out at seven thirty-three."

"I literally departed the premises seven minutes earlier, Trick. I noted the time. No one was there besides Eve." Bob's exasperation came through loud and clear. "I'd been running surveillance again since eight o'clock last night." The sound of pages turning. "A minivan stopped at your home at oh-seven-hundred, your kids walked out in their little soccer uniforms, your wife waved goodbye, glared at me, and slammed the door."

Trick thumped his palm on the steering wheel. There was no way she'd hit herself over the head. "None of this makes sense. She never misses their matches. Maybe she was waiting for someone who was watching you, and he went in after you drove off."

"Well," Bob answered doubtfully, "it's a theory."

"Will you touch base with whoever's assigned as investigator?"

"Sure. Also, I have a bead on the guy's identity."

Trick's heart stalled. "Pete?"

"Gotta check one more lead. Are you available to stop by later today?"

Too much was happening too fast. Trick's focus was still on this medical emergency. "Yeah, maybe. Late this afternoon? Obviously I gotta call off work and go pick up my kids. I'll drop them at my parents, then check on Eve at the hospital."

"You're under a restraining order and child supervision, Trick."

Bob's bluntness brought him up short. *Shit.* How in the name of sanity had he forgotten this? He slowed for a red light, thanking the universe for the extra time. The park was two blocks up.

"Don't get on the wrong side of the law now," Bob warned. "Can someone else pick up the girls?"

"I don't know." Maybe Mom or Sean. The thought sat like a nugget in Trick's gut, reigniting the parental impulse to ignore the law. Shouldn't he be the one to break the news about Eve and comfort their fears? And even if Mom or Sean picked them up, where would the girls stay long term? No parents, no home... He needed to call Morgan McNally immediately. There had to be an emergency provision to the supervision order when the primary parent was critically injured.

The onslaught of nitty-gritty details and the herculean tasks required to do right by his girls made his head swim. The car behind him beeped, and he coasted blindly through the green light. "I don't know what to do first," he confessed to Bob.

"Get someone to pick up your kids. I'll check on Eve

and call you with an update. Stop by my office when you can. I should have the guy's identity wrapped up soon."

They signed off, and Trick parked a safe distance from the soccer games. He watched his girls on the field as he called Mom, who immediately agreed to not only pick them up, but have them stay with her and Pop for the foreseeable future. She also agreed to hedge on why they were staying with Grandma and Grandpop until Trick could go over and break the news.

CHAPTER THIRTY-EIGHT

Trick headed into the station to use his office as command center and begin the massive coordination of dealing with Eve's insurance, filing damages with his homeowner's policy, and arranging for fire cleaning services in the near future. Cap had given him extended leave, which was generous, given the team was critically short-staffed and overworked.

Trick skirted past the doorway to the break room, where the rapid-fire sounds of videogame AK-47s emanated. Pete was probably in there. Ever since divulging his name to Bob, Trick had avoided his friend like the plague—quite a feat, given they lived and worked together. If only Bob had ripped off the bandage already. Trick sat heavily, reluctant to begin the tedious insurance duties when his scattered brain was stuck wondering about the man's identity, worrying whether Eve would pull through, and obsessing over the caretaking decisions for the girls' immediate futures. He thumped his elbows on the desk and held his head in his hands. "Shit."

A short knock. Pete poked his head in. "Cap told me about the fire."

"Yeah. I'm waiting on word of Eve."

Pete eased in and shut the door. "Are we all right? You've been kind of distant."

Trick shuffled papers to avoid eye contact. "Got a lot of my mind, what with the girls' welfare."

"Yeah, but before that."

Within hours, Bob would reveal the name of the friend who'd betrayed him. The dreaded anticipation shortened Trick's temper. It seemed light years since he'd been Lieutenant Yogi, at peace with the universe, at one with his fellow man. Had his innate trust in friends made him a rube? There was only one way to find out.

"You got anything to tell *me*, Pete?"

His best friend blinked once. "Just that I'm here for you. I don't think I've got the room or temperament to house your girls, but I'll help you look for another place."

That did it. How could it possibly be Pete? Trick exhaled heavily, slumping back. "The PI is about to tell me the identity of Eve's lover. Jace insists it's someone I know well."

"Shit, that bites." Pete leaned against the door. "You want company to soften the blow?"

See, if it were him, would he offer to come along and hear himself tagged? Trick shook his head, both at Pete's invitation and his own broken-down capacity to read people.

Belatedly, Pete's eyes widened. "Wait... You don't think it's *me*?"

Trick grimaced, face heating. "I don't know, Pete. I don't know anything anymore."

"But my name's on the list?" The stricken tone knifed through Trick.

He nodded reluctantly. "I insisted he eliminate all the other single guys first, and...everyone checked out. I hated giving your name. If it was you, it would've killed me."

"If it was me, I would have killed myself first." Pete thumped his chest. "Why didn't you just ask me outright, man?"

The million-dollar question. "Because," Trick said, "these last weeks have shown me over and over that I can't spot lies worth shit."

Blotches stained Pete's cheeks. His chest rose and fell rapidly. On some level, Trick's treatment of his best friend was similar to what Pop had done to him. He wholeheartedly connected with Pete's stupefied disbelief. There was nothing to do but man up under the silent accusation of betrayal and disappointment.

"It's like..." Pete struggled for words. "It's like I don't know you anymore, man."

Trick pushed back from the desk and walked toward him, stopping a foot away. "I'm sorry. I should've trusted my soul. Of course it couldn't be you."

Pete shifted his weight, the mulish expression fading. "What I hate Eve for the most is taking away the carefree guy you used to be. You don't deserve any of this mind-game shit. I hope when it's all over, you can get back to being the lucky guy who loved life."

"Thanks." Great vision to work toward. They bear-hugged, and a lightness seeped into Trick's veins. Find the positive in a negative event and turn it around. The other guy wasn't Pete. Trick's parents would keep the girls safe, and hell yeah, he'd rise above all of this and manifest joy and luck again.

CHAPTER THIRTY-NINE

"They have Eve on a ton of painkillers, and her parents are sitting vigil," Bob said, taking a seat behind his desk. "The nurse says she has moments of lucidity and is scheduled to begin initial skin grafting tomorrow."

Trick kneaded his forehead where a headache was forming. The sheer range of his emotions was too thick to parse, and some—like relief she couldn't hurt him further and the vindication of karma—were downright shameful. He dropped his hand. "Did she say who did this?"

Bob shook his head. "She hasn't spoken about it to anyone. Aaron Benedict is the arson investigator assigned to the case. You couldn't ask for a better man."

"I'm familiar with his reputation."

"He did a preliminary walk-through and says it looks like Eve started the fire. Point of origin is the sofa cushions, which she piled together like bonfire logs."

Trick clenched his hands. So his instinct—the one he'd immediately discounted as too crazy to even tell Jace —had been right. "I still don't get the motivation. It wasn't to commit suicide; she had everything to live for."

"That's something you'll have to ask her. Aaron said the place went up so fast it could be she knocked herself out trying to escape. There would've been only seconds to react."

Trick nodded. It was definitely possible, what with the incendiary old materials and Eve's inherent clumsiness. Still, if she'd been incapacitated but not unconscious... The horror she must have faced... He shifted uncomfortably in the chair.

"So, the other man." Bob opened a file and slid a photograph across the desk.

Trick stiffened. "Jesus..."

"You know him?"

His breath left in a rush. "I sure do." His pulse thumped in his ears, causing his voice to sound far away. "He's my divorce lawyer."

"Shit. If that don't beat all."

"How is it possible?" Trick sputtered. "He *represents* me."

Flipping open his little pocket notebook, Bob read a few pages in silence then said, "She first met him through her friend Marisol, who evidently used his services when she got divorced last year. His neighbors mentioned frequently seeing someone who looked like Marisol slipping out of his house early in the morning, so it could be his MO—when he handles the wives' cases, he also helps himself to the wives. Anyway." Bob placed the Quinns' February bank statement on top of the photograph. "Your wife paid his hourly fee in cash on this day." A two-hundred-dollar ATM withdrawal was circled in red.

Fresh horror washed over Trick. "I remember that. Eve claimed the money was for a fender bender she didn't want to file with our insurance. I even hammered out the dent that had white paint on it."

"Easily made, too." Bob swiveled his laptop around so

the screen faced them both. "Courtesy of your local branch." The security video showed Eve beginning to pull into the ATM drive-through, then angling her Kia so her front bumper smacked into the white cement pole protecting the side of the ATM. "The branch manager told me they decided not to pursue any charges, given your hero status back then." Onscreen, Eve was reversing and correcting the angle, her face expressionless. She withdrew the cash and left. The date and time were stamped at the top right and coincided with the bank statement before them.

Hair pricked up the back of Trick's neck, as his mind replayed the vandalism. A part of him didn't recognize her coldly meticulous act, while another—the tiny part of him he'd ignored for years—identified with every ruthless detail. Bile rose in his throat. He hadn't been blind to her gaslighting after all. He just hadn't trusted his gut enough to listen.

"Finally," Bob said, drawing Trick's attention to a copy of a parking ticket he pulled out of the file, "this is what I had been waiting for." He slid it across, and Trick read the license plate and date issued—the Wednesday in May she'd convinced Gretch to check her into the women's shelter. Gretch had done so at eight in the morning. This ticket was issued six hours earlier.

It took Trick a few seconds to process the address. "This is one of the locations Jace's friend tracked her phone to."

"Correct. It belongs to a shell corporation that took a while to trace back to McNally. Must be some kind of tax dodge."

Trick stared out the window, his hand rhythmically scraping his mouth. This was so freaking surreal. Eve had hired Morgan, then had an affair with him, then manipulated him to join her side, even while Morgan represented Trick. Why hire Cyprian at all? Morgan could've easily remained her counsel and taken Trick to the cleaners. What was their end game here?

"That's all I have," Bob said. "I can get more if you give me time."

With the disbarring-worthy evidence—unethical conduct and gross misrepresentation, for starters— Morgan might bargain with crucial information or proof that could clear the allegations and restore Trick's name. At least explain the motivation behind why the hell any of this had happened. He texted Morgan: *Urgent. Where are you?*

A text immediately dinged back: *At office catching up on work. Come on by.*

Trick dragged his gaze back to Bob. "I think I can handle it from here. How much do I owe you?"

"Nada. Jace took care of it."

TRICK STRODE into his lawyer's plush office, with the same trembling need to punish as when that client had torn off Zamira's hijab. The secretary smiled professionally and waved him down the hall. "He's expecting you."

Unable to form a civil response, Trick swept on by but halted outside the closed door. Anger would get him nowhere. He needed to tap his Ajna instinct to identify truth from lies, and channeling the mysterious energy of the universe required a peaceful soul. Trick breathed deeply, mentally collecting himself until his tension deflated and his spirit grew still. He could solve this and clear his name. On some cosmic level where time was meaningless, this had already happened. He rapped on the door and walked in without waiting for a response.

Morgan was sitting behind his desk, glasses perched

on his nose, reading a document. He looked up with a smile. "Glad I could squeeze you in."

"Eve's in ICU," Trick said. "She almost died in a fire at our house."

"What?" Morgan ripped off the glasses. "When?"

"This morning."

"Is she...is she going to live?"

There it was, written all over the lawyer's face. No further confession needed. "You're awfully concerned for the plaintiff, Morgan."

"Well...burned in a fire. My God, I'm not a monster."

Trick clenched his jaw. Mind games were awakening his anger. "Her cellphone's GPS pinged your personal home as a location she visited almost three weeks ago. She received a parking ticket there at two in the morning. Why would she visit my future divorce lawyer at that time of night, Morgan?"

Morgan sputtered something incoherent, his face a crimson stain. "She—uh—stopped by that evening to talk about hiring me, but she'd been drinking heavily, so I—"

"Bullshit, Morgan. The FBI heard your conversations on the burner. Even the phone sex."

Morgan straightened in his chair so fast it squeaked. "FBI?"

Trick braced his knuckles on the desk and leaned in close. "Why were you fucking my wife? And whose plan was it to rob me of everything, yours or hers?"

Silence descended as Morgan gazed at him open-mouthed. As if it never occurred to him he'd get caught. The mastermind behind the mastermind.

"Mor—"

"Hers!" Morgan burst out, leaning back in his chair. "Aw, hell. Eve came to my office in early February, wanting to hire me and start divorce proceedings." He flapped an arm in exasperation. "As soon as she mentioned your name, I was like, 'No way.' With your stellar reputation? Chicago's golden boy? The way no one died around you? I told her she didn't stand a chance at even a fifty-fifty split of your marital holdings. The only way to get what she wanted was to lay some groundwork. Systematically topple you in the public eye, and to do that, she needed convincing proof."

Trick drew in long, slow breaths, but his control was slipping. He itched to deck the motherfucker. Morgan side-eyed those clenching fists. "Trick—"

"I'm not going to hurt you," he said woodenly. "Go on."

"She asked me to lead her through the process of providing irrefutable evidence, or at least enough of a 'he said/she said' murkiness that we could tap people's biases. It took months. When she was ready, I told her to go hire Cyprian."

Trick scrubbed a hand through his hair. This still made no sense. "You groomed her. Why not represent her?"

"Because Cyprian Hunter is the best. If Eve hired me, it left him on the market to represent you." Morgan waved a hand like Trick was slow on the uptake. "Again, back then, you had Chicago eating out of your hand. Cyprian would've probably sought *you* out as a client."

Trick paced to burn some energy, mind reeling with the sequence of events. "So then... You came to court after Cyprian torpedoed Gina, and offered to represent *me*."

Yeah, there was guilt on the man's face, but a thread of pride, too. Morgan eased back in his seat. "Takes a good lawyer to know how to strategically screw up a divorce case. No matter who you'd have hired, Cyprian would've taken you to the cleaners, but I was Eve's insurance to make sure the trust definitely fell into a sole trusteeship."

Trick halted. "You weren't her insurance—you were her lover."

"Things have been waning." The crimson stain blotted Morgan's cheeks again. "I don't have to tell you what a dynamic force she is. Was, at least." A flash of grief crossed his face. "I am sorry to hear about the fire. Is she going to recover?"

Trick stayed silent. It was a phone call he was reluctant to make. So far, her updates had been provided by Bob or Jace. Eventually, though, Trick would have to confront the ugliness head-on, encounter his in-laws, confer with doctors, make decisions in Eve's best interest. She was still legally his wife, and some part of him still cared for her wellbeing.

Morgan squirmed in his chair. *Wait.* Things had been waning between them... And she'd been pulled out of the blaze with a knot on her forehead. "Did you set the fire, Morgan?"

"Me?" His mouth dropped open. "I'd never harm another person."

"You've done a number on me," Trick said succinctly.

"I mean physically." Morgan waved a hand. "She wanted me to injure you after the segment aired of you and that Muslim woman. That's when I got a glimpse of someone riding the third rail."

"And the delay approving my family as supervisors?"

One shoulder lifted in a half shrug. "Eve insisted."

Trick let a moment go by, grappling for composure. "Did you or my wife do anything to the girls so that the gynecologist..." He couldn't finish.

Luckily, Morgan was already shaking his head.

"We hadn't gotten that far along. And for what it's worth, I would've been adamantly against anything she came up with. I didn't want your kids and was quite clear about it. She didn't seem to want them either, so I figured she was just sticking it to you for maximum pain and would withdraw the sexual predator charges before a doctor's exam proved her wrong."

Trick opened and closed his fists, his inner peace shredding. Beating the cocky man senseless wouldn't do any good, might even bring new charges. "You'll be disbarred, Morgan, you get that, right?" he bit out. "You'll probably be arrested and charged. After that, I'll sue you penniless. If it takes to my dying day, I'll make sure your life is as wrecked as mine."

Morgan sat forward. "I suggest you think long and hard before acting in revenge. I'm your only hope in getting those charges dropped."

Murderous fury coursed through Trick. That this lawyer could use his credentials to rob him of his life and then casually say he was the only one with the bread-crumbs to lead him back to that life?

Still, if the rat could undo the damage, Trick would be an idiot not to take him up on it first. Once Trick had the girls and his reputation back Morgan would pay.

"I want all charges dropped," he said calmly. "I want a quiet, uneventful divorce, and I'll split everything fifty-fifty except the girls' trust fund. I want sole trusteeship and full custody of my daughters immediately, with supervised visits for Eve after her discharge. I want proof sent to all national media outlets that I'm innocent of any abuse, and I want to make *sure* my daughters aren't caught in some red-tape snare where they're still forced to go through with that exam. Everything hinges on this last point. Are we clear?"

"Yes." Morgan nodded vigorously. "Yes. Leave it to me."

"If they go through with that appointment, Morgan, I

will rain hell down on your life. I will make sure the FBI investigates all the way up your asshole."

"Don't worry. I can fix this." Finally, a trickle of sweat ran from Morgan's temple to his chin.

Trick jabbed a finger at him. "You have two days to start showing me results."

CHAPTER FORTY

"Then Eve's lawyer called me late this afternoon," Trick said, his voice hoarse from all the talking. "During a short period of lucidity, she told him she's dropping all charges and, quote, will take me back, unquote. She wants to speak with me as soon as possible."

"What did you say?" Mom asked, her dinner forgotten.

"I declined. I'm going for the quickest divorce possible—whether it's amicable is up to her. But I want full custody."

Mom mumbled, "I just can't believe all this," for the twentieth time. Pop stared into the beer glass he was rotating on his place setting. In the living room, Amy and Tina colored homemade get-well cards, with Blaze stretched between them and pawing one or the other to continue petting him.

The hospital would not allow the girls to see Eve yet, probably not for a while, so they were morose and confused. Tomorrow Trick had a full girls' day out planned to distract them. Pancakes, soccer, the new Disney movie, then the children's bouncy house arcade on West Eastman Street. No ideas for the next day, given he planned to work, but Mom was looking after them, and he was okay taking it one day at a time right now.

Pop wiped a hand across his face and sighed. In the last couple of weeks, he seemed to have aged ten years. The strain from the disaster he'd thought Trick had brought upon the family and the pressure of having scene command during the city's worst mass-casualty bombing had taken a toll. "I'm sorry I didn't see any of Eve's machinations for myself."

"She fooled me too, Pop. For years. Jace says he always saw through her, but..." Trick chuckled, spreading his hands. "That's typical for Jace." He sobered. Strange; his brothers were the only people in his life he hadn't striven to be perfect for, and yet they were the ones who'd supported him the most through all this. "I'm lucky he and Sean had my back, though, along with some friends and the crew, and a kickass PI."

"I should never have blamed you without investigating the facts."

Trick wasn't about to disagree. "I would never hurt them. I would never lie to you."

Mom nodded, throwing Pop a reproachful glance.

Pop squared his shoulders. "I'm so sorry, Patrick."

A selfish part of Trick wanted Pop and the rest of the world to do more than apologize for putting him through this, but bitterness would only hold him in the past. This horror was almost over. And abject misery aside, falling from Pop's grace had actually gone a long way to helping gain this newfound insight that he needed to learn to love himself. It was a crazy waste of life trying to live up to anyone else's expectations. The healthiest option was to move forward and gratefully embrace the only part of time that held any meaning: this moment right now. "I forgive you, Pop. We're good."

"Well, what are your immediate plans?" Mom asked.

"Work. Find a place to live while Mark's crew helps me rebuild. Deal with the divorce." See Zamira as often as possible. He stretched back in his chair casually. "I'm also thinking of attending some counseling next week. Check into it for the girls as well." They could all use help embracing the changes in their new lives.

"That's wise," Pop said shortly. "And I'll see if I can reinstate the Medal of Honor."

Trick held up his hand. "Under the circumstances, it'd be really inappropriate to celebrate anything right now. Besides, I've got a to-do list a mile long that'll take all my downtime."

"Well, you and the girls *have* to stay with us until you find a place," Mom declared, standing and reaching for the dishes.

"Thanks." Trick rose too. "Here, Mom, let me."

"You spend time with your girls. It'll be a long time before they see their mother again."

He glanced furtively at the trio lounging on the carpet. "I don't know what to say to them," he said quietly. "How will I commiserate with them without it coming off as false platitudes?"

Mom smiled. "You don't need to commiserate, just acknowledge their emotions and support them through this."

"But I want to get this right—"

"There is no right in fatherhood, Patrick," Pop interrupted. "There's only instinct and good intentions, and believe me, while I've been the embodiment of neither, you've mastered both this month. No one should've had to endure what you did with so little support, yet through it all, you remained true to your principles and did your best to protect your daughters." He rose with a grunt and patted Trick's shoulder. "No one can ask more of them-selves. You did a fine job, son. I'm proud of you."

Trick swallowed past the thick swell in this throat. "Thanks, Pop." He walked into the living room, his heart so full it seemed to expand his ribcage. He'd waited a life-time to hear this kind of validation from Pop. But as much as he appreciated the words, things had changed. Trick's priority was learning to trust his own measure of good enough.

He leaned down and hugged his girls. Doing right by them was the perfect start.

SHADI RUSHED INTO THE KITCHEN, eyes shining. "Patrick is at the door," she whispered.

Zamira set down the dish she'd been washing and glanced at the clock. Nine-oh-seven. She frowned at her sister and swept a hand through her loose hair. Her hijab was in the other room.

"I'll get it," Shadi said, swiveling toward the den.

"Wait."

Shadi turned back, an eyebrow cocked. "Is my baby sister crossing to the dark side?"

Zamira ignored the mocking tone, her thoughts swirling. The realization that her parents' unbending principles were definitely not the way she wanted to live her life warred with the ingrained modesty of wearing a hijab all these years. No, she wasn't quite ready for such a radical shift. "Yes, go get it."

Once she'd hastily covered her hair, she ran her hands down her loose-knit jersey dress. It was drab gray, old as the hills, and immensely comfortable. She'd tried to meditate by herself this evening, and it had seemed appropriate to wear. Not so when being visited by a fire-fighter who took her breath away.

Still she raised her chin, straightened her shoulders, and swept into the foyer. Immediately her heart skipped a beat at the devastatingly handsome man standing by the closed door holding a dozen multicolored tulips. Although his eyes looked exhausted and evening stubble darkened his jaw, his smile was dazzling. "Sorry I'm here so late," he said. "I got your text." He held out the flowers. "A promotion? Way to misread a firing."

She burst out laughing and accepted the bouquet. "Andy said the center has gotten tremendous press in the aftermath. Thank you. These are lovely."

"I wasn't sure what your favorite color was, so I covered my bases."

"Yellow. The color of happiness." She gestured to the kitchen, and he waved her off.

"I don't want to keep you."

"Nonsense. Come tell me about your day while I put these in water."

He followed her, and after they were seated at the breakfast table, glasses of water and the vase between them, he told her everything, from the fire, to Morgan's confession finally putting all the pieces together, to Trick's personal realizations.

"Wow," Zamira said softly, still trying to wrap her head around the multiple betrayals. "I don't know if I could have withstood that myself."

"It was maddening." He scraped a hand through his messy hair. "I did my best to be the perfect husband, always gave her the benefit of the doubt that I was in the wrong and wasn't good enough. It'll take some time to untwist this view of myself and the world." He crossed his arms on the table and leaned in. "But taking a page from your philosophy, I've also come out the other side stronger than ever. I don't want to waste another minute trying to be somebody I'm not just to please others. I can see now I used meditation as an escape. It was the only time I touched base with my real self, like this quick daily visit was all I allowed before the delusion set back in."

He lifted his glass, his t-shirt sleeve riding up to accommodate the pop of his flexed bicep. In two gulps he guzzled the water, his pronounced Adam's apple rising and falling, a droplet of water trickling from the side of his mouth. Zamira's breath caught at the primitive, greedy display. Unapologetically embracing life like this, even in a task as simple as drinking, was not in her wheel-house. But oh, how she wanted it to be.

"Where do you go from here?" she asked, as he swiped a hand across his lips.

His gaze drifted over her shoulder, unfocused as he contemplated her question. "I'm going to embrace my imperfections. Listen to my inner self instead of relying on other people's truths."

Everything she wanted, too, in her goal to weave together the worthy parts of her radically different cultures into one positively perfect life. *Take me with you on this journey, Patrick.*

"Right now," he added softly, "my inner self would like to take you out to dinner this week. And Shadi or Aakil, or both, are more than welcome to come along."

She dropped her focus from the desire in his eyes to the hands clenched around his glass. He was nervous. How adorable.

Zamira reached out and lifted one hand off, shivers coating her at her boldness and the warmth of his palm. "I think, Patrick," she said with a smile, "our inner selves are on exactly the same path."

EPILOGUE

"Labor Day is a big deal in this house," Trick warned, killing the engine. "We Quinns embrace our blue-collar roots."

His joke fell on deaf ears. Zamira snapped off the seatbelt and lowered the visor. She twisted her head left and right, fluffing the folds on her pale pink hijab and skeptically checking the mirror. "Do I look all right? Does this color make me look too young?"

"When have you ever been self-conscious about the way you look?" He tilted his head, smiling. "And you've met everyone before."

"Not all at once. Not your other two brothers."

Trick scoffed. "The last time they had leave, Cage was a drunken rebel and Kevin prowled for a new woman every night. You do *not* need to impress them."

Her eyes gleamed impishly. "Maybe I should pretend I don't speak English."

"See now, if *I'd* said that—"

She laughed in that wonderful, musical lilt. He snapped off his belt and hauled her close. "You're so easy to tease," she murmured, caressing his cheek.

The sudden burst of joy rendered him speechless. He traced her mouth with his thumb, his lids dropping with the desire to kiss her senseless. Nibble on the pert upper lip. Usher her into the house with that bee-stung look. Or hang a "keep away" sign around her neck to warn off his reckless younger brothers. Trick settled for a quick, soft kiss because they were parked at the curb, and she was still ill at ease with PDA. He also wanted to respect Mr. Bey's remaining unease about Zamira dating a Catholic. The restraint was killing him.

"Come on," he said, reaching for the bag of *Kahk* cookies she'd made for the event. "Let's storm the picnic."

The aroma of barbecued meat filtered in as Trick led Zamira through the still house. The boisterous party was in full throttle out back, the yard filled with extended family. Jace was in the center of a group of male cousins, beer bottle in one hand as he grandly gestured with the other, no doubt regaling them with a SEAL tale or an FBI case, like the return of the infamous Gardner Museum painting. Even though he wore sunglasses, his haggard features were clear from here. The Bureau hadn't found much on the Mosque Mohammed bombing suspects, and Jace took it as a personal failure. The trailblazing task force he'd clawed to be in on had gradually thinned out until only he and two other agents were assisting the lead investigator. Which was actually perfect for Jace. The harder the mission, the more he rose to the occasion. Like a dog with a bone, he was determined to find the individuals responsible.

Sean and Gretch were in the rocker-sofa on the deck. No surprise—Kevin was seated at Gretch's feet, braced on fully flexed biceps, talking to her, while Sean side-eyed him in amusement. Around the trio, shirtless male cousins, of the teenage variety, were roughhousing in hopes of catching Gretch's attention.

Mom was seated with her sisters in the shade of the hundred-year-old elm, all of them drinking lemonade and fanning their flushed faces.

Trick had picked up his girls from their first night's stay at Eve's apartment hours earlier and dropped them off to help their grandparents set up. Now the girls splashed in the pool with the smaller cousins, all screeching at an anxiously pacing Blaze to jump off the pool deck and join them.

Pop grilled the burgers—halal beef, per Trick's request—with his brother and two brothers-in-law, all talking over each other around the original red Weber charcoal grill. Even through the dense smoke, Pop's pained smile betrayed his introverted longing for peace and quiet.

No sign of Cage, but that didn't mean anything. He could be out partying with high school friends, or already passed out drunk in the guest room upstairs. Trick turned to Zamira, who was watching the scene with a nervous smile. He held out an arm, encompassing the masses. "Ready?"

"There are four times more men than women here."

Trick nodded. "I'm the only one who had girls."

"Wow." Zamira's eyebrows wrinkled. "That's quite a..."

"Trick?"

"Ha, ha." But his corny joke worked, because her mouth relaxed into a smile.

"Zamira," Gretch called, patting the cushion beside her, "come sit here."

"Zamira," Tina shrieked, and began splashing her way to the ladder. Amy, unable to bear not being first at everything, pumped her arms and legs, determined to overtake her sister and greet Zamira first.

"Dry off," Trick called, drawing Mom's attention. She

brightened and waved, excusing herself to make her way over. Zamira was once again about to be thoroughly, noisily adored.

Trick squeezed her hand. "Go on, beautiful soul. I'll bring you some lemonade."

He headed for the supersized cooler, heart swelling with love for this unique woman. Their summer had been an amazing journey of creating new traditions and embracing change. For him, it was also recognizing that the power of self-love was the universe's not-so-secret secret to the perfect life—no luck needed.

ACKNOWLEDGMENTS

My heartfelt thanks to the following friends and professionals who helped shape this novel:

Anya Kagan of Touchstone Editing, for the exceptional skill, patience and hand-holding.

Christa Holland of Paper and Sage, for another poignant cover of a damaged hero.

Arran McNicol of Editing720, an extraordinary copy editor who probably never foresaw reading this many romance novels. I went with Legos. I know you're cringing...

Aneela Iftikhar, sensitivity reader-editor, for your helpful insight and feedback into Muslim-American culture.

Ivy Arbuckle, retired juvenile court referee, Jackson, Michigan, for clarifying court procedure and your total lack of surprise at the twisted motivations of my characters.

Mary E. Morrison, MSW, for explaining the heroic work you did for Child Protective Services. Heaven is naming angels after you.

Cheryl Harrison, for keeping me sane these two long

years and helping me dream up these subplots. "Love and joy, badass, love and joy!"

Caroline Jones Silva and Catherine Hunter, for your friendship and answering questions that were completely none of my business.

My brother John, for recalling your experiences as a volunteer firefighter and answering all my dumb questions without pointing out exactly how dumb the question actually was. That must have been hard!

Firefighter Terence Keenan, aka "Kristan's husband, McIrish," for answering a long list of firehouse and crew questions that I later realized were basically a handful of questions that I then asked over and over in different ways. You get that you're famous in our world, right? I guess I was nervous.

Amy Atwell of Author E.M.S., for taking a huge burden off this self-professed techno-tard by uploading this story to retail stores and fixing all those annoying glitches. Your tech and organizational skills are priceless.

And you, Dear Reader, thanks for picking this up. Don't forget: this is a work of fiction, meaning I spent months researching facts to bend into this plot. All errors are mine. If you're coming directly from reading the previous novel, *Capturing the Queen*, you'll notice tiny deviations in days. I couldn't find a way around it, so please suspend your disbelief and just enjoy!

ABOUT THE AUTHOR

ROMANTIC SUSPENSE THAT KEEPS YOU UP ALL NIGHT

Sarah Andre is a RITA® finalist, which is Romance Writers of America highest award of distinction. She lives in serene Southwest FL with her husband and two naughty Pomeranians. When she's not writing, Sarah is either reading or coloring. Yes, you read that right. She's all over those coloring books for adults.

For more information please visit:
www.SarahAndre.com

facebook.com/SarahAndreNovels

twitter.com/SarahRSWriter

goodreads.com/Sarah_Andre

bookbub.com/authors/sarah-andre

ALSO BY SARAH ANDRE

Locked, Loaded and Lying

DAMAGED HEROES SERIES
Tall, Dark and Damaged
Capturing the Queen

EXCERPT OF TALL, DARK AND DAMAGED

DAMAGED HEROES, BOOK ONE

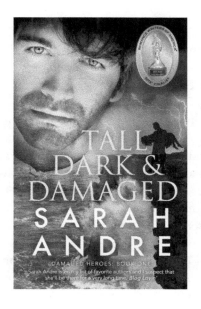

CHAPTER ONE

Devon Ashby cut the engine. "I can't believe someone tried to torch the place."

On the other end of the Bluetooth earpiece, his cousin grunted. "Happy fucking birthday to your old man, right?"

Devon climbed out of the rental car, and inhaled the chilly night air. Yep, overlaying the scent of Lake Michigan and decaying fall foliage was the distinct whiff of acrid smoke. If it hadn't been for the foolish risk of his siblings' lives, he'd have shaken the perpetrator's hand. "Gotta go. I'm about to walk into the lion's den."

"Don't screw this up," Eric said. "Go in, make nice, get out."

"Relax. I'll lay that olive branch right on a Wickham silver platter. *After* signing for the trust."

"I'm popping the champagne now."

Devon clicked off and stuck the earpiece in his overnight case. Wind buffeted his coat, its high-pitched whistle and the swishing clack of tree limbs the only sounds in this sleepy suburb. Fine gravel crunched underfoot as he headed toward his childhood home, majestic and formidable in the strategic landscape lighting. Christ, how he used to despise this mammoth symbol of wealth and power and success. Now the thick stone veneer and white-trimmed windows tantalized his adult sensibilities. He'd own a mansion like this one day—only in White Plains or New Canaan. He'd come a long way since leaving Chicago, and after tonight, he'd have it all.

Crisp leaves skittered past his ankles as he passed the Poseidon fountain centering the stately circular driveway. The statue's trident was raised in triumph at the harvest moon. Talk about symbolism. Devon saluted the sea king, and bound up the marble steps guarded by life-sized stone lions. He vigorously pressed the doorbell. The deep, gonging chime—so familiar—raised goose bumps. *You shouldn't have come. Go home and have the documents express-mailed.* As if in agreement, a gust swirled in off the lake, slicing icy talons through his wool coat. Devon scowled at his thoughts and swiveled so his back took the force of the wind. Still, a thin shiver rolled through him.

The massive oak-and-wrought-iron door slowly opened. Golden light and warmth spilled out onto him, like the first rays of a spring sun. At the sight of the ageless butler, Devon broke into a wide grin. "Hey, Joseph."

"Good evening, sir. It's a great pleasure to see you again."

Devon stepped past him, fighting the childish urge to embrace the man who'd adopted his father's role too often to count. "It's been a long time," he said instead, as if the older man wasn't aware of his twelve-year absence. *Talk about lame.*

The door closed with an echoing *thunk.* He should

unbutton his overcoat and comment on the weather, but the words died on his lips. One glance around the vast hall evoked memories that crushed him like a steroid-laden linebacker.

The Christmas mornings he'd flown down the sweeping staircase into the formal living room where his presents lay. The black-and-white art-deco tiles, and that dumb game of all-white-tile hopscotch Frannie used to coax him into. Or how they'd race each other past these glowing wall sconces to a dinner as abundant and comforting as his mother's smile. The ache he thought he'd conquered almost doubled him over. Who'd expect to be ambushed by *good* memories?

Behind him, Joseph coughed discreetly. Devon consciously steadied his breathing and fumbled with the coat buttons. "How is Mrs. Farlow?"

"She's well, sir. Very busy with the festivities tonight. May I wish you a happy birthday?"

"Thanks." Devon grinned as he handed the coat over. *Happy birthday.* The phrase restored the confidence he'd had climbing out of the car. "I'll try to stop in the kitchen later and see her myself. I've missed her apple pie something fierce."

The butler bowed, a shadow of a smile touching his lips. "She'll enjoy seeing you again. I'll put your bag in your mother's old bedroom, if that's all right with you."

Devon nodded. "Any news about the fire?" The question clearly caught Joseph off guard; family members would never have asked the help, but Devon had long ago parted from the Wickham ways.

"No, sir. Very little damage to the theater itself, but your father's art gallery needs restoration."

"Do they know who did it?"

Joseph flushed and swallowed. "I don't believe so, sir. An arson investigator was here most of today."

Devon nodded. It wouldn't surprise him if the investigator found multiple people with a motive. In fact, if he'd been here Tuesday night, no doubt he'd be the number one suspect. "I'm glad no one was hurt." He gazed around the foyer again, seeing the opulence instead of the memories, and his shoulders relaxed. "Are they in the dining room?"

"The party moved to the formal library for dessert and coffee. Dinner was served at eight." Joseph's dry tone held volumes of warning.

Devon glanced down the long hallway at the arched doors gleaming in high polish. Even after all this time, he knew what lay in wait. Just like with Henry VIII, when one person displeased the old tyrant, they all got punished. And Devon was an unavoidable hour and a half delayed. He broke into a grin at the challenge ahead. The fearlessness he displayed in the boardroom was a direct result of growing up here. "I'll handle him."

"Yes, sir."

He headed swiftly toward the living room, elation growing. Tonight, on his thirtieth birthday, the provisions from his mother's trust came into effect. It had been a long, difficult twelve years, scraping and clawing his way from a broke and homeless eighteen- year-old to an up-and-coming force in Manhattan. This gift from his mother couldn't come at a more perfect time in his career. He'd already signed over the inheritance to secure a business loan. The high-risk venture had required the personal guarantee; banks were still too cautious. But the property was a steal, the value from developing mixed-use dwellings too substantial not to snap up. And he wasn't nicknamed Renegade because he invested cautiously. This deal would ensure his status among corporate giants.

At the arched doors, Devon straightened his tie and

shot his cuffs. Soft strains of classical music wafted from within, one of Mozart's violin concertos. A woman laughed, throaty and melodic. He inhaled deeply, grasped the century-old crystal handles, and thrust both panels open. The laughter died mid-note. Time came to a freeze-frame halt, as if the guests posed for a portrait. His sister, Francine, hair shorter and darker than he remembered, held a china cup to her mouth. Beside her, his half-brother, Rick, had a chokehold on the slim neck of a Château Latour. Across the room, two men sat in wing-backs, their backs to the door, profiles turned to the platinum blonde—the source of the laughter—her mouth still open. And beside her, too close for any misinterpretation, sat his father: majestic, patrician, and grim. No one would ever confuse the etched wrinkles on his face for laugh lines. An expression flashed across his face, too quick for Devon to catch. *Regret, maybe?*

The old man broke the spell by glancing down his hawk nose at his Rolex. "Ah, the grand return of the prodigal son. My eldest, who goes by a different name..."

Nope, not regret. Devon managed a half-smile, but already his olive branch goal was faltering. "Happy birthday, Harrison." The irony that his father and he shared a birthdate when they had nothing else in this entire world in common...

Someone cleared his throat, and Devon's gaze swept over the men again, who'd turned in their seats to face him. He nodded to George Fallow, the family lawyer. He hadn't aged well by the looks of his sunken cheeks and hunched posture, but the fact he was still here even though Devon was so late was a great sign. Hopefully the trust business could be concluded tonight.

"Honey, Wesley," Harrison said, "this is my eldest son, Devon Wickham." *Really?* "Ashby," Devon corrected.

"Grown men don't use their middle names—unless they're rednecks from the South." The condescending tone baited, and Devon's muscles tensed.

"Ashby is my mother's maiden name." He looked pointedly at his father. "Or had you forgotten?"

Those ice-blue eyes sparked with animosity, but when Harrison continued, his voice remained affable. "This is Honey Hartlett and Wesley O'Brien."

A second passed as Devon waited for how they related to the Wickham birthday dinner to be disclosed, but no explanation came. He nodded once to each of them. Honey responded with a thin-lipped smile, and the young blond guy studiously ignored him.

"Sit down, Dev," Frannie said sharply. She patted Rick's arm, and he rose with a grumble. Devon clapped him on the shoulder, murmuring a greeting as he passed by. The last time he'd seen his half-brother, Rick had been a chubby nine-year-old. Their communication over the years had been infrequent and stilted, a shattering example of the collateral damage from that horrific night exactly twelve years ago.

Devon sat beside his sister, and they exchanged a hug. They, at least, had kept in touch through email and holiday video calls. She was thinner than her screen presence, her skin the kind of bluish pale that came from exhaustion. The divorce must not be going well. He grasped her hand, ice-cold and twig-like in his, and squeezed.

An enormous silver tray on the cocktail table before them held coffee and Wickham china. "My dear," Harrison murmured, and Honey immediately leaned forward, pouring coffee with an elegant tilt of her wrist. She looked about the same age as Frannie. How long had she and Harrison been dating? Frannie hadn't mentioned her the last time they'd spoken.

When Honey handed Devon the coffee, her corn-flower-blue eyes regarded him coolly. Clearly she knew about his black-sheep status. He thanked her, though he didn't intend to stay at the party long enough to finish it. "I'm actually here for—"

"Drink your coffee," Harrison interrupted. "If there's one thing I've learned in my vast years, it's to enjoy the company of loved ones over business."

Devon sipped the piping-hot liquid to stifle the abrupt laughter rising up. Never had a man less deserving of the title "father" walked this Earth. He was pretty sure Harrison knew it, too, and couldn't give a shit. Not to mention the man had run through three wives... *Loved ones over business.* Yeah, right.

Still, Devon was in his father's house, and an olive branch could turn into lucrative business contacts or part-nering on future ventures with Wickham Corp. Why not take the high road and try to build a bridge across the great divide? "Frannie told me about the fire last night," he commented. He didn't tack on Joseph's update about the arson investigator.

"Yes, last night was quite dramatic," his father answered, his tone lacking any drama.

Interesting. The fire had been in the old-fashioned theater, but it shared a wall with Harrison's climate-controlled art gallery, filled with masterpieces. "Is your art damaged?"

"There's too much oily soot covering the paintings to be sure." Another clipped response. His father wasn't the kind of guy who kept his displeasure under control like this. And back in the day, a three-degree temperature malfunction in either of his two galleries was considered catastrophic. This was a freaking *fire.* What had changed? Maybe it was the fact that the perp might be in this very room. Devon glanced at the faces surrounding him, all filled with the usual tension associated with just being in his father's presence.

Francine crossed her legs. Her foot nudged Devon's twice. "I saw workers in the gallery this afternoon," she said to Harrison, then threw Devon a pointed look.

So? He gave her an imperceptible shrug. His disinterest in art was in direct proportion to his father's obsession for it.

"Some woman with red corkscrew curls," she added sharply. A buzzing began in Devon's ears.

"I hired Moore and Morrow Art Restoration." Harrison poured himself more coffee.

Corkscrew... Moore and Morrow...? *Hannah* Moore? *His* Hannah? Something must have registered on his face, because his sister widened her eyes like: *Yes, idiot, that's what I've been trying to tell you!*

The buzzing grew louder, and goose bumps covered Devon's arms. Hannah had been *here* today? Regret at missing her flashed through him a second before his heart squeezed so hard he squinted. Yet another "twelve years ago tonight" memory, the wreckage he'd left in his wake... *Jesus.*

His hearing returned in time for the tail end of his father's remark: "—company that discovered those Rubens forgeries."

"I heard the Art Institute almost closed down after the Rubens scandal," Francine said.

Devon pulled himself together, focusing on three details. Based on the name of the company, Hannah didn't just work for a restoration firm; she owned part of it. Second, he'd heard about that forgery scandal at some exhibit Nicole had dragged him to. The well-respected Art Institute of Chicago had unknowingly hung three forged paintings, and the discovery sent the staid art world into a frenzy of paranoid speculation over their own works. Third, his father had unwittingly hired Devon's high school sweetheart yesterday. Harrison had never met her; Devon had gone to great lengths all senior year to make sure of it.

"The restoration firm is gaining a remarkable reputation," Harrison said. "Next subject."

Devon sank into the cushion, a warmth settling in him at Hannah's accomplishments. Followed instantly by the warmer memory of her soft lips, perfecting the art of French kissing. He inhaled unsteadily. *What the hell?* He was engaged. All that grand passion, roller-coaster crap was well left to his teens.

A discreet cough captured everyone's attention. Joseph stood in the doorway holding a white, frosted cake piled high with strawberries. "Don't sing," Harrison ordered, and nobody did.

Devon reluctantly shook off the remaining Hannah-daze as his father's girlfriend cut and plated the perfectly proportioned wedges. Honey had the kind of finishing school grace even Nicole and her aristocratic friends couldn't pull off. An aura of mystery surrounded her—someone so flawless suddenly appearing in his family. He made a mental note to Google her, because although he shouldn't care whether she'd snagged a sugar daddy, and Harrison was gullible enough to fall for it, something wasn't right. The father he'd left behind wasn't that stupid.

Honey passed Devon his slice, and although Harrison didn't make eye contact, the old man smiled grimly. This wasn't an innocent cake choice on his father's part, and they both knew it. Harrison had been aware a month ago that Devon would arrive on *their* birthday to sign the requisite papers; the Wickham executive secretary had even insisted Devon stay for the small dinner party. And yet eating even one of the strawberries would cause Devon's throat to swell up. Part of him felt the intended insult like a shank to the gut, while another side was amused at the calculated lengths Harrison had gone to tonight to ensure his complete discomfort. *So much for the sapling olive branch.*

With scalpel-like precision, Devon separated the berries and any frosting that even remotely came into contact with them, keeping his expression carefully blank. He was certifiable to even engage in this double dog dare to eat the cake, but he wasn't going to give his father the satisfaction of refusing the slice. Besides, he'd been so busy working throughout the private flight, he was freaking ravenous. He waited for Honey to lower the cake knife and raise her fork, and then all but shoveled the dessert into his mouth. And felt no remorse helping himself to seconds while his father opened presents.

When Harrison lowered the Jag XKR keys Honey had given him back into the little heart-shaped box, Devon shot a look at George Fallow, who had his briefcase by the clawed leg of his armchair. *Good.* Devon swallowed the last bite and slid the plate onto the cocktail table.

"I have several announcements," Harrison's said, his cup hitting the saucer with a clinking flourish, "which will cumulatively affect everyone here."

Rick jerked like a puppet on strings, almost spilling the new glass of wine he'd poured. The birdlike clutch returned to Devon's arm, and when he glanced at his sister, her profile was a study in dread. He frowned at his siblings and redirected his attention to the supremely smug man across from him. What the hell was his father up to?

Harrison smiled at Honey as his gnarled hand

reached for hers. Her return smile held the contentment of a purring cat. "First, Honey has agreed to become my wife."

Devon blinked at the pair. The simmering gut reaction of something not being right boiled over. Why the rush? Jesus, if he had another half-sibling on the way... But maybe he was looking at this all wrong. Maybe he should feel sorry for Honey. *Welcome to the circus, wife number four.*

As he added his congratulations to the subdued chorus, he covered Frannie's hand and squeezed.

"Second," Harrison continued, "she'll inherit all the cash, stock, and property I own except for the trust I set up for my grandson." His gaze flicked to his fiancée, before focusing on Francine. "Provided you both remain under this roof until you finalize that disastrous divorce."

At her audible inhale, Devon clenched his jaw and stared into the crackling fire.

Clearly Harrison was still a smothering control freak with Frannie. It was one thing when their mother died, but his sister was an adult with her own child. To force her and Todd to live here with the soon-to-be newlyweds was downright offensive.

"Third, I plan to retire immediately. Wesley here will be promoted to CEO of the Wickham Corporation tomorrow." Pretty Boy gasped. "Fourth. Once I'm gone, the entire empire is his to run. None of my three children has ever shown the slightest interest in my businesses anyway."

Devon heard Rick's weight shift on the creaky floorboards, somewhere behind him. "Why?" his brother sputtered. "Why would you disinherit us?"

Those arctic eyes focused like laser beams over Devon's shoulder. "It's time for you to make your own way in this world, son. It's time for you to stop gambling on every sport game or horse race, and using *my* money to pay off your debt. Your credit cards are one big bar tab. You want to engage in those debasing activities, fine. Pay for it yourself." Harrison sipped coffee without breaking eye contact with Rick. He set the cup in the saucer. "You're welcome to stay in this house while you make other arrangements, but by our wedding date...when is it again, sweetheart?"

"A week from Saturday."

He kissed Honey's hand, his demeanor relaxing. "I expect you to find a job and vacate the premises."

Rick didn't respond. The fingers on Devon's arm had him in a death grip now. He hurt for Frannie, even poor Rick. God knew he recalled the shock and terror this speech evoked. That his father would repeat it now with his last two children, when the old man was the richest son of a bitch in Chicago, was infuriating. Surely the old man could spare *some* change for his offspring. Honey wouldn't be able to spend a fraction of it, even if she lived fifty lifetimes.

"George is here to amend the will tonight." Harrison picked up his coffee cup. "Thank you for the presents. You're all excused."

"Come to bed soon," Honey said in a sultry tone, kissing Harrison's withered cheek. As inappropriate as the thought was, Devon caught himself wondering how the old man hadn't died of a coronary already.

It took the others several seconds to rise, and once upright, they moved stiffly, like sleepwalkers, except for old George, who lugged his briefcase as if it held gold bricks. Devon stepped forward, the offer to carry it on his lips, mentally running through room options where they could go to sign over the trust.

"Stay behind. I need to speak to you in private," Harrison said, and for a moment Devon assumed it was directed at George. But no, his father looked right at him.

"I have to meet with George. I'll return when I'm through."

"You'll sit down." The old man cocked an eyebrow. Devon was prepared to ignore him and follow George out, except for the warning on the lawyer's face. He was not prepared to defy Harrison and work on Devon's rightful inheritance tonight after all.

At the door, a teary-eyed Frannie threw Devon a troubled look, and he winked. The decision on his eighteenth birthday to change his last name had been the catalyst for getting tossed out on his ear. No announcement could possibly apply to him, unless his father was about to extend the olive branch after all and put him *back* in the will.

How fast could he get out of here and make sure she was all right? She needed to buck up until they could figure out how to get her out from under Harrison's thumb. Her smile was tremulous, and then the door clicked shut. He sucked in a breath and spun around. "What's up?"

"I'm surprised you haven't heard." And that was how fast his father could switch from wrecking ball to cat-and-mouse.

Devon glanced at his watch. "I've wasted enough time watching you play these twisted mind games. Just blurt it out."

Harrison shrugged, smiling slyly. "You're right. It's late and there's too much to go over. Profit and loss statements, marketing forecasts... I'd like to get an early start tomorrow. Eight o'clock, my home office."

Devon frowned. "What?"

"Late this afternoon, the Wickham Corporation

tendered an offer to acquire Ashby Enterprises. At a surprisingly low cost—I didn't know your assets were so tied up until I looked into the situation."

Tendered an offer? Getting the privately held company's financial information? "Wait a minute." What an imbecile, letting his father get him all worked up like this. "Eric and I hold fifty-one percent—"

"*Held* fifty-one percent." As Harrison took a leisurely sip of coffee, Devon fought the impulse to snatch the delicate cup and hurl it into the fireplace. This was just a psych- out, and he wasn't going to take the bait.

"Meaning?"

Harrison gestured with his cup. "Did you even *think* to draw up a contract between the two of you?"

"We have a contract."

The hard stare was so familiar—part condescension, part questioning how his offspring could possibly be this stupid. "And you didn't stipulate an agreement giving each of you first rights to any liquidated shares?"

Moisture beaded Devon's lip. No. He hadn't. This was Eric Ashby, his cousin on his mother's side, his best friend...soon to be his best man. He was *family*, for Christ's sake! Surely Eric, the CFO, would have told him if he'd sold shares. "You're bluffing."

"Am I?" Nothing in those hardened features indicated so.

Devon kept tight control of his expression, aware that any shock or panic was an added bonus for the bastard. "Aren't you getting ahead of yourself, old man? My board and major shareholders are loyal friends. They'll never accept your offer."

"Wesley is expediting the deal and assures me your *friends* are quite unhappy with your leadership. I expect to own your company before my wedding. Thank you for the birthday gift; I'm sorry I have none in return."

Devon gripped the back of the loveseat as the icy reality of his failed night of triumph cut through him. All the blood, sweat, and toil that had gone into creating his company... Just to be snatched by Harrison, who had as many international irons in the fire as Donald Trump. Christ, there was no way Devon could return to Manhattan and face Nicole with this news. "Why are you doing this? To any of us?"

"How tediously dramatic. If you'll excuse me, I have a fiancée waiting."

Yes. This was how he could get his father to see reason. "I have three words for you: Anna Nicole Smith."

Harrison stiffened and set his cup down hard. "Honey's an heiress in her own right."

Scoffing would be too immature. If only Nicole were here, sporting "that look." No man could stand up to her frosty disbelief and derision. Devon spread his hands, willing his voice calm. "Then why disinherit Frannie and Rick? You didn't during your other engagements. Why is wife number four winning the lottery? And what if, a year down the road, this marriage ends in the dumpster like your last two? Please tell me you had her sign a prenup."

Harrison's lips quivered into a snarl. "How dare you speak to me like this." "How dare you force Frannie to live here."

"That's none of your goddamned business—"

"How dare you give Rick a week to find a job and a place to live—"

"You presume to come into *my* house and tell me how to run it?"

"And you presume to take over Ashby Enterprises?" Their volume had grown louder with each exchange. Devon clenched his jaw. This was beneath him. "You're not getting my company, old man," he said softly. "All you did was declare war."

Was it his imagination, or did his father's hand tremble ever so slightly? When he refocused on the gnarled fingers, Harrison clenched his fist, but the illusion of invincibility was broken. His father suddenly resembled exactly what he was: a seventy- year-old man, trying desperately to remain the fire-breathing dragon in a broken-down castle.

Devon spun on his heel, suddenly ill with shock or the lack of food followed by a ton of sugar. He had to get out of here while he could still stand.

He stalked the length of the room but hesitated when he reached the door. He swung around and met Harrison's glower. The question he'd ignored for so long resurfaced with the blinding intensity of a neon light. He didn't *care*; he just wanted to know—ever since he'd been a small boy. "What did I do to make you hate me this much?"

The glare turned to disdain rather than surprise or shock. "Let's start with you dropping your God-given name like you were ashamed of it. If you didn't want to be a Wickham, then you weren't getting a Wickham cent. And you damn sure weren't living under *my* roof."

"Frannie and Rick *want* to be Wickhams, yet they got the same treatment tonight, so I call bullshit." Devon groped blindly for the doorknob, blood boiling. "And you know exactly why I'm an Ashby. I'll *never* share a name with the man who murdered my mother."

Harrison huffed a breath. "I expected the histrionics when you were nine, but I didn't tolerate them twelve years ago, and I won't now. Your mother committed suicide. Grow up."

A haunting sense of powerlessness sagged Devon's shoulders. "You're lying." But the words were barely audible and steeped in resignation. Harrison had been powerful enough even back then to shut down the investigation and get a suicide ruling. Devon would go to his grave knowing his mother had loved her children too much to take her own life. But he'd never be able to prove it.

CHAPTER TWO

Devon slipped into his mother's old painting studio, which was now a drab sitting area, stuffed with more grandiose relics and artifacts. No lingering scent of oil paints or turpentine remained. He closed the door softly behind him and dug out his cell phone, his fingers shaking so hard it took several tries to scroll down and tap Eric's number.

"Tell me the good news, Renegade," his cousin greeted cheerfully, and the pop of a champagne cork followed.

"Did you sell shares?" Devon said through clenched teeth. The background sitcom laughter stopped abruptly, the ensuing silence a yawning pit of hell. He groped for the nearest marble statue as disbelief threatened to take him down.

"A few. Why?"

"And you didn't think to tell me? Or give me first offer?"

"This was totally temporary, Dev. I sold last week, and I'm about to purchase them back. What the hell's going on?"

Devon wiped the sweat from his upper lip. "We no longer hold the majority of shares, and somehow my father just launched a hostile takeover. We're officially at DEFCON 1."

"Wait...takeover? I'm the damn CFO. I haven't heard anything. Why? How?"

"I don't know." He paced to the window, the whole evening blitzing through his mind. Something wasn't right. The timing was too odd. Too convenient. "I know my old man, Eric. He'd have figured out a way to destroy me long ago, when we were a fledgling upstart. This isn't his idea. I want to know who's behind it and why." He started for the door. "Wake up a damn private investigator. Get as much information as you can on a Honey Hartlett and a Wesley O'Brien."

"Will do. Did you sign for the trust at least?"

"No." He stopped in his tracks. "Jesus fucking Christ. It's already pledged to secure the bank deal. What happens to my money if we're taken over?"

The abrupt silence on the other end was his answer. He'd just lost millions. He'd left twelve years ago, penniless and unemployed, and in the space of twelve minutes tonight his father had done it to him again. Devon's breath came in short bursts. His shirt clung to his back.

"I'll check with our lawyers," Eric finally answered. "Surely they can try to find a loophole to get some of it back." The words held hope, but the tone didn't. "What are you going to tell Nicole?"

Devon closed his eyes. *Shit.* She'd said she'd wait up by the phone, and he doubted it was with any semblance of patience. Nicole was the kind of woman who rewarded brilliant business acumen. They both had high expectations of each other and were well on their way to staggering influence. Or had been. What could he possibly say to her about tonight? She didn't suffer failure, and despised excuses. Until now, it'd never been a problem. He wasn't ready to watch his demise in her esteemed regard; there were too many unanswered questions.

"I'll text her that the birthday reunion is turning into a late one, and I'll call her in the morning."

His cousin's grunt held a distinct warning, which Devon ignored. He could handle Nicole; it wasn't any of Eric's business.

He ended the call and made his way upstairs and over to his sister's wing. Outside her door, he took a couple of deep breaths and refocused on her problems. Harrison rolled over others without mercy, and she'd never stood up to the old man like he had. She'd never hardened through their torturous childhood, so if tonight had been a shellshock for him, it must have been an atomic bomb for her.

He knocked softly, and Frannie answered in seconds, blotting her puffy eyes with a tissue.

"Hey." He drew her into a bear hug. "I came as soon as I could."

"What did he say to you?"

"Nothing important." He'd come to talk her into defying the old man's blackmail, not burden her with more horror. "You got a raw deal, Frannie—"

"At least she isn't homeless like me," Rick called, sinking onto the floral sofa in the suite's living room. He tilted his wine glass and finished the last drop.

Devon bit back a harsh reply at the pity party. Twelve years ago he'd left for New York that very night and never looked back. Granted, he'd smashed Hannah's heart in the process, and the guilt sometimes still rendered him sleepless... But he hadn't sat moping, even when he was dirt broke and sleeping on Eric's spring-less sofa. "Put the glass down and sober up," he said. "I'm here to help you guys figure something out."

"There's nothing to figure out, Dev. We're disinherited." Frannie teared up again. "But you sure made it look easier than this."

"Stop letting him win, Frannie. You don't have to stay." He winced at his outburst, but her waterworks meant surrender, which was abhorrent.

"Defying him means robbing my son of his trust fund."

"You know he wouldn't disinherit Todd. Call his bluff."

"I can't risk it." She sobbed, and although he gave her his shoulder, he stood too stiffly, patted her back too mechanically. Everything in his life was neat and clean and lacked messy emotions. There was something to be said for compartmentalizing. Crying wasn't problem-solving. It was a wasted reaction, something he couldn't deal with and hadn't since...jeez. Since Hannah. Funny how everything kept coming back to her tonight.

"What about me?" Rick interrupted. He spread his arm to encompass the living room. "At least she has a roof over her head. I have nothing."

Devon hesitated. "Isn't your mother still alive?"

"I'm not living in Phoenix!"

Devon frowned down at his sister. "It's not the weather," she whispered, sniffing. "Susanna is a surgical nurse."

So no middle-class living for Rick. New York would shake the entitled attitude right out of him. "You went to Northwestern, right?" Rick nodded.

"What was your major?"

"Econ."

Devon shrugged. "Come out to Manhattan. I have a lot of connections, and you can stay with me until you get on your feet." He checked himself. Even though he and Nicole didn't live together, she'd have a problem with a slacker brother underfoot indefinitely. "I mean, at least through the winter while you get your bearings."

Rick's lips twisted. "Maybe." His gaze went to the bottle, although he didn't reach for it.

Yeah, Nicole would have his hide for this impulsive invitation. She had little tolerance for anyone who wasn't grimly ambitious and rock steady in climbing to the top of the social scene. It was what they loved about each other. They knew what they wanted in life and had found the best partner to get there. Rick would be a serious speed bump along that road, but Devon wasn't going to take it back if his brother needed him. Eric had once offered him a leg up from homelessness, and Devon would pay it forward too.

"You're limiting your choices, Rick, and you're in no position to do so. Cut the pity party, man up, and both of you fight for what you want."

"I want to stay here." His brother crossed his arms.

"That's no longer an option. Rearrange the world until it's something else you want."

"Easy for you to say—getting a massive trust fund."

Devon opened his mouth to snarl an obscenity, but Frannie waved him off. "We only have each other. Let's not say anything we'll regret in the morning."

He scrubbed a palm over his jaw. They were going around in a circle, and he had his own problems to deal with. Besides, Frannie was right; they needed to band together. "How long has Harrison been dating Honey?"

"Six weeks, give or take," she said softly.

Stupefying. "How did they meet?"

"I think some charity auction. She moved into his adjoining suite within three weeks."

"I still can't believe this," Rick spat, his face flushed crimson. "Blonde hair, big boobs, and she gets all my money. I'm so mad I could fucking smash something."

Or set the house on fire? Devon frowned. "Either of you know anything about the fire?"

Rick shrugged and looked away.

"We all evacuated the house Tuesday just before midnight," Frannie said. "Firefighters put it out easily enough, but something makes them think it's arson."

Devon was quiet a moment. "Harrison didn't seem too concerned that someone had tried to torch his house."

"He's adamant it's something electrical."

Honey, the fire... When did his father get so old he was blind to the glaringly obvious? "Who discovered the fire?"

"Joseph."

Joseph? What was the old butler doing up that late and in that section of the mansion? And why withhold the detail tonight in the foyer? A sense of foreboding stiffened Devon's spine. "Anything else going on I should know about?"

His siblings looked at each other and shook their heads.

"I have a crucial meeting in the morning, and then need to reschedule George, but I'll bump my flight back a little and help you guys figure out what to do."

"Have breakfast with Todd and me," Frannie said. "I want you to meet my son."

They agreed on a time, and he hugged her once more. As he walked to the door, he purposely ignored her telltale sniff. He could solve problems until the sun came up, but was clueless when it came to emoting empathy or comforting tears—a negligible flaw once he'd surrounded himself with people who were the exact same way.

He unknotted his tie as he roamed toward the other end of the house. Industrial fans grew louder with every step. This wasn't anywhere close to his mother's old room, where he'd sleep, but he needed to know something he couldn't bring himself to ask his siblings. After crossing through the first editions library, which linked the east and west wings, he turned the corner and stopped. A haze lingered down the long hallway, even though the fans in the theater now sounded like turbo engines. Inside the gallery, a few sooty paintings still hung on the walls. He grinned and turned away.

Question answered: Hannah would be back tomorrow.

CHAPTER THREE

Hannah Moore gratefully took the mug of coffee Gretchen Allen handed her, and sat in one of the plastic orange chairs in Moore and Morrow Restoration's break room. Thankfully, no one else had arrived for work yet. She had no energy for the cheerful-boss mask, and with Gretch, she didn't have to. Once her personal trainer, Gretchen's energetic, positive outlook had catapulted her from a weekend Starbucks buddy, to best friend, and now Moore and Morrow's office manager.

"Let's see it," Gretch ordered, looking darling in a black spandex onesie with anatomically correct skeletal bones glued on. Halloween was her high holiday. No one else in the office would bother dressing up today. After all, Halloween wasn't until Tuesday.

Hannah reached into her purse and slid the red eviction notice across the Formica table. "Thirty days," she said, even though their hours-long phone call last night had covered that in the first sentence.

Her friend scanned the information and shook her head. Not a strand in her spiky blonde hair moved, although her skeleton earrings jingled as they danced.

"How can they tear down an entire block? We need to call the local news. Get some neighborhood protests started."

Hannah fingered her mug handle. She had no time to march with a sign when the project of a lifetime had just fallen in her lap. She didn't even have time to find another apartment. "I looked up some realty links after we talked. The majority of places I can afford are either in unsafe neighborhoods or too much of a commute."

"How'd your aunt take it?"

"She was up half the night. So agitated that even *with* the oxygen tank, she had one of her episodes. I don't think her health can take the stress of a move. I mean, she's eighty-seven. She's lived there since before I was born."

"It says here they're holding a meeting tonight." Gretch underlined the sentence with her finger as she read aloud. "'To assist with alternate housing possibilities and answer any tenant questions, as your welfare and transition to new living arrangements is our utmost concern.' What a bunch of bull." She glanced up, slitting her espresso-brown eyes. "We're going, and we're fighting this."

"I don't have time to make a fuss."

"No, you don't *want* to make a fuss. Embrace conflict! Take a stand." She jabbed the notice in Hannah's direction like a saber, the bones attached to her forearm making it look like two emphatic people. "Meet me at Bakers Square at five; we'll have dinner, and I'll go with you."

The potential in-your-face conflict made Hannah's stomach churn. "Why waste the energy? There won't be anything we can do; the sale and teardown are legal." She nodded to her open briefcase, where apartment leads were neatly paper-clipped together. "I have thirty days to find a place, pack for both of us, move, and still coordinate an expedited restoration of the Wickham art." She petered out and sipped some caffeine, fighting the cloud of doom.

"Breathe from your gut." Gretch morphed into her commanding personal-trainer mode. "You'll get through this. Give me some of those leads, and I'll call in between doing payroll and receivables."

"Thanks. I'll really owe you." Hannah handed over a third of the stack, but her relief was short-lived. Shoving any of her work onto someone else, even her best friend, was proof she was drowning. She'd been brought up to finish her chores, fix her own problems, and never complain. Period. "Any place that's wheelchair accessible and takes Boots." She should be ashamed that at the ripe old age of thirty, she was bunking with her maternal great-aunt and Aunt Milly's ancient tabby, but Moore and Morrow Restoration was still in its infancy. Every penny that didn't go toward Milly's meds and in-home care went straight back into the company. The Wickham project took precedence over protests and media interviews.

As if reading her mind, Gretch tossed the red notice back. "How did it go over at the Wickhams' yesterday?"

"I told you. We won't know the full extent of damages until we clean the soot off."

Gretch folded her impressively toned arms, quite a feat with the clunky bones. "I'll rephrase. How did *it* go?"

Damn the curse that made redheads blush this easily. It all came down to Devon and those ten months of soul-encompassing love soooo long ago. Why did that moment and that man still haunt her? "It was weird," she admitted. Simply walking into his house had brought back a tsunami of memories she'd buried long ago, and they'd kept her on edge all day. Even after eight hours of hauling art from the smoke-filled gallery down to a sitting room they'd used to pack and crate, the jumbled emotions had kept her tossing and turning last night as much as the eviction notice.

"Was there any sign of your guy?"

"Devon. And he's not my guy." For Pete's sake, it was eons ago and she was well, *well* over him. But her heart stuttered over the phrase *my guy* and she tapped her foot rapidly. "There's no trace of his existence in that mansion, which is no surprise." And was actually a relief. If she'd come upon a photograph or gone into the family gallery to see whether his portrait still hung there, she'd have been unable to function. And dealing with Harrison Wickham had required every professional brain cell.

"Did you run into anyone besides the father? *Someone* knows how Devon is and what he's doing."

"I honestly don't care, Gretch." Immediately her palms prickled, and Hannah pretended to fix her ponytail to rub them against her wide plastic barrette. No way was she going to admit she Google-stalked Devon regularly and knew he was a hotshot private equity CEO about to marry the heiress of Tucker's Fine Chocolates in seven months. And two days. And approximately nine hours, given the time difference.

Gretch stirred her coffee thoughtfully. "Do you think he came back for that party the servants were setting up?"

Hannah smiled at the thought. "He won't ever come back to Chicago. Not even if the house *had* burned down. Or if Harrison had died in the fire that burned the house down." She'd seen the last of Devon on that stormy night when he'd stood on her mom's porch steps, soaking wet and spewing hateful words about his father and the final argument that had gotten him kicked out.

Then he'd tugged her hand and insisted she go with

him on a Greyhound to New York. Knowing her mom had end-stage ovarian cancer. He'd refused to consider staying in Chicago, getting a job—even for a week or a month. Who gave that kind of ultimatum? "Let's talk about something else," she said sharply, desperate to dissolve the image of his stricken face when she'd chosen her mother. Of his sudden realization that he literally had no home, no family, no money, and no love of his life. "How did it go here yesterday?"

"Walter's on a tear about Bernice again. Told me to tell you she started the Matisse project using beeswax and resin as the backing."

Hannah swallowed her dread. "I'll handle it on my way out."

The skeleton earrings jingled again. "He's furious. He wants you to fire her." Hannah stood and rinsed her mug without answering. There was no way she was going to fire Bernice, and Gretch knew it. Even if Bernice had screwed up and used some 1970s restoration technique that was proven to tighten over a decade and cause the paint to crackle.

"I'll handle Walter," she murmured, returning to the table and her briefcase. "I have to get to the Wickham estate before the team arrives. Oh, and make sure Walter gets these." She slid yesterday's restoration summaries, art measurements, and crating supply needs across to Gretchen. "And I'll need releases faxed to Mr. Wickham before I can begin transporting his paintings."

"Got it."

She pointed to the tiny red shape Gretch had glued under her left breast. "The little paper heart is adorable, by the way."

"I'm going to use it again when I'm Grinch at the Christmas party."

Despite herself, Hannah laughed. "We don't dress up for Christmas parties, dummy."

Gretch quirked an eyebrow. "Have you checked the employee suggestion box lately?"

Still snickering, Hannah stopped by Bernice's lab, still dark and empty. Humor morphed into relief. *Thank God she's not here yet.* Hannah jotted a note ordering the Matisse backing to be stripped and redone using mulberry tissue. Then, not leaving anything to chance, she also recommended applying the tissue with a boar's-head brush. An elementary choice and probably insulting to Bernice, but Walter was the *Morrow* in Moore and Morrow Restoration, and Bernice was on wafer-thin ice. Maybe today would be one of her good days and the project would be a snap.

Anxiety ate at Hannah as she trudged out into the bright, chilly morning. Eventually she'd have to deal with Bernice. Using the Wickham project and her hunt for housing as authentic excuses would hopefully mollify Walter, for now.

Once on the El, crowded with jostling commuters, she held on to an overhead pole and texted him that the Bernice situation was under control. Walter was born for sales and schmoozing clients. No doubt he'd find a way to tell Bob Schmidt—probably over golf or cocktails—that his Matisse would not be restored by the original promised date.

Hannah pocketed her cell phone and focused on the day ahead. Not the custom crating of priceless art or dealing with Harrison Wickham. More like drumming up the courage to step back into that mansion and deal with those body jitters again.

She'd stupidly peeked into the smoke-filled theater after the fire chief had left. Even through the haze, those ruby-velvet seats had caused her heart to squeeze painfully. The years had vanished in an instant, and she'd half expected Devon to magically appear, striding out of the smoke with that crooked, suggestive grin. They'd spent so much time in this dark hideaway, groping each other with the urgency of dumb, young lovers. Oh, the many nights they missed "seeing" the movie.

It was a crying disgrace—a professional restorer in the midst of a project of a lifetime, frozen at the entrance of a theater like a lovesick teen. But then again, the last time she'd been in there, she *had* been a teen. And lovesick. The visceral memory of Devon's delicious mouth and the slinky feel of worn velvet on bare skin was as real as if it'd happened the day before.

But today would be different. The memories wouldn't be so stark, she'd avoid the theater at all costs, and, like she'd told Gretch, there was no speck of evidence Devon had ever lived in that mansion. He'd probably be relieved to hear it. She exited the train, smiling at Gretch's impossible suggestion that Devon would ever come home.